THE NAKED EYE

Other Nebraska Mysteries by
William J. Reynolds

THE NAKED EYE

A NEBRASKA MYSTERY

William J. Reynolds

G. P. PUTNAM'S SONS   NEW YORK

*My friend John Kerwin, Jr., an Omaha lawyer,
provided much valuable technical and legal information.
Any errors contained herein are mine, not his; and I will
hide behind the shield of creative license.*

G. P. Putnam's Sons
Publishers Since 1838
200 Madison Avenue
New York, NY 10016

Library of Congress Cataloging-in-Publication Data

Reynolds, Williams J., date.
The naked eye : a Nebraska mystery / William J. Reynolds.
p. cm.
ISBN 0-399-13526-X
I. Title.
PS3568.E93N35   1990   89-70077 CIP
813'.54—dc20

Printed in the United States of America
1 2 3 4 5 6 7 8 9 10

This book has been printed on acid-free paper.
∞

For Peg, of course

1

I spent two nights cruising Loring Park, checking out the boys, many of whom were too young to be doing what boys do in Loring Park, many of whom were too old to be considered "boys." The first night out, the boys kept their distance. They didn't know me or my car, an impressive- and expensive-looking number I had rented for the occasion. Second night out, I made tentative contact with two or three boys who were nervy enough—or hungry enough—to gamble that I wasn't a cop or a creep. Third night out, I got lucky.

"Yeah, I remember him," the kid said, studying the photos in the beam of the penlight I held for him. He was pale and thin, anorexic even, with long, limp, blond hair that fell into his eyes when he inclined his head to examine the pictures. It's true that as I continue to creep up on age forty, "kids" continue to get younger and younger. But I would have bet everything I owned, such as it was, that this kid *was* a kid—fifteen, sixteen at the outside.

"How old are you, Randy?"

He looked at me and sniffed. The waist-length jacket he wore was too thin for this Minnesota November night. I guessed that was half the reason he had agreed to get into the car.

"Eighteen," he lied. "I'm legal."

I smiled and nodded and took back the pictures. They consisted of a standard wallet-sized school portrait and four color snapshots of a seventeen-year-old boy named Eric Matthew Sperry.

"What'd he do?" Randy wanted to know.

I looked at the top picture. Eric Sperry had a mop of dark-blond hair, a short, turned-up nose, and a spray of faint freckles across his cheeks and the bridge of his nose. One morning not quite a week earlier, Eric left for school at Westside High in Omaha, Nebraska, and never showed up. His parents called the police, naturally, who investigated and found no reason to suspect that which we quaintly call foul play.

"Looks like he ran away from home," I told Randy. Based on conversations with some of Eric's friends, the cops concluded that this had been on Eric's mind for some weeks.

"Oh yeah?" the kid said. "How come?"

I put the photos on the dashboard. "He told his parents he was gay. They disagreed."

The kid sniffled and nodded his head. I noticed he hunkered down into his jacket and leaned toward the heat vents in the dashboard. I moved the fan lever up a notch. "Yeah," Randy said. "That can be rough."

He would know more about it than I would, I judged. It is partly the nature of the investigator's role to be removed from the difficulty or grief that generates his involvement. In this instance, as is frequently the case, I was brought into the matter by a lawyer: Mike Kennerly, an old friend who has sent many cases my way through the years. He was the Sperrys' lawyer. When they turned to him for advice, his advice was to hire me to look for their boy. I had met the parents for approximately fifteen minutes in Kennerly's office four days ago. I had formed no opinion of them. I had no way of knowing what life in their household had been like in the weeks between Eric's announcement and his disappearance. I didn't know whether the boy was better off now than he had been at home. All I knew was that I was expected to do a job. And so I was.

"You sure you're not a cop," the kid said.

"Private. My name is Nebraska. I'm working for the boy's parents. They want to find him. They want to talk with him, see what can be worked out. . . ."

"Like the state Nebraska?"

"Yes, like the state. How I came to have the same name as the thirty-seventh state of the Union wouldn't interest you. Let's just say I'm happy that when my family patriarch reached this continent, he didn't settle in Saskatoon."

The kid gave me a look. The look said, What the hell, the car's warm and he doesn't look too psychotic. Then he turned and looked out his window again, out toward the dark, cold park. "No one ever sent any private detective looking for me," he said quietly.

"Maybe they did and he couldn't find you," I said lamely. The reason it was lame is that everybody leaves a trail. Period. The only question is how easy or difficult the trail is to follow—and whether anyone tries. Eric Sperry, for instance, left a trail you could have followed at night, in a snowstorm, while blindfolded. I had had misgivings when Mike Kennerly first contacted me about the case. Several days had passed since Eric's disappearance, and the trail would have begun to cool noticeably. But I needn't have worried. If the Sperrys' had gotten off the dime sooner, if they had realized their son had not gone on vacation but had gone to take his chances on the street, if they had viewed his running away not as an insult or a stunt but as a plea for help—if, in short, they had put me on the case right away when the kid split—I could almost have been in the Twin Cities to meet him. That's how clear his trail was. That's how slow the Gray Dog is compared to the Friendly Skies.

As it was, I had done a whole lot less pavement-pounding than on some jobs, and the trail was still holding up.

I angled my chin at the pictures on the dashboard. "He was hanging around the park, then?"

Randy nodded, and sniffled, and shivered inside his flimsy jacket, despite the fact that the interior of the car was growing almost uncomfortably warm. "He showed up, I don't know, maybe a week ago. Hard to say. You don't have a lot of friends out here, y'know, and even your friends aren't, like, *friends.* Anyhow, he was pretty lame, this kid. He didn't know from nothin' about staying alive. A couple of us, y'know, sort of looked after him—we were like certain he'd pick up a cop and bring the heat down on all of us. So we took him with us to this . . . uh, place we stay, some of us, and kind'a like showed him, y'know, how to tell the heat from the creeps, how to spot the ones with wives and kids, the ones who feel so guilty they come across extra—that kinda stuff."

"So what happened to him? Why doesn't he hang around here anymore?"

Randy half-laughed and held his hands out to the dashboard heat vent. He had long, slender fingers, badly chapped from the cold wind. He had chewed his nails down to nothing.

"'Cause he got lucky, the little bitch." He sniffed. "He was only here a coupla nights before some rich dude up and tooked him home with him. Can you believe it?"

I could, and easily. I had spent a lot of time tracking down a lot of runaways. Several of them had been "rescued" from the streets by benevolent protectors. Most of them would have been better off taking their chances on the street.

"What makes you think this 'dude' was rich? You know him?"

"I seen him once or twice. I know a coupla guys been with him. He's rich. He's like so rich he doesn't hardly ever cruise—just for kicks, sometimes, I guess, or like when he's between, uh, friends."

I nodded to show I understood. "Has he got a name?"

Randy smiled slyly, and I did understand. Hardly anyone on the street has a name—at least not one that matches what their birth certificate says. "But his car does," the kid said. I looked at him. He was grinning, and the silly smile made him look all of twelve or thirteen years old. I felt the old impulse, the one that made me want to shove him in a hot tub, buy him a hot meal, and just keep him. Not for any illicit purpose. I'm just a soft touch for strays.

"His *car?*" I said. "Like what—Chevrolet?"

Randy's smile widened. "Like Jaguar." He pronounced it *JAGwire.* "Convertible. Real dark gray, like almost black. Real leather inside. And one of them whatchamacallit plates . . ."

"Personalized."

"Right. DIMAND. Not like, y'know, jewels—d–i–m–a–n–d. *Di-*mand." The way he said it let me know he approved, and mightily. I went into a pocket and came out with a twenty and handed it to him. It disappeared like it was never there, and he yanked back the door handle.

"Hey, Randy," I said softly, and he looked back at me, a ribbon of blond hair falling across his forehead. "See about getting cleaned up, huh? I guarantee, you'll get those vanity plates faster."

Then he was out the door and back on the street. I might as well have waited until he had gone before dispensing my ten-cent advice. It would have done as much good to offer it to the empty seat.

I sighed, and put the car into gear, and left the park.

2

Over the years, I've spent just enough time in the Twin Cities to know how to get really lost. On the St. Paul side, none of the streets seem to cut through; toward the river that more or less forms the boundary between St. Paul and Minneapolis, they start running at crazy angles, as if something in the water causes them to lose their senses. The situation in Minneapolis isn't a lot better. Just about when you think you're on the right track, you run into a goddamn lake and have to detour through Canada to get back on target. Homing pigeons have to stop at gas stations and get directions.

Generally, then, I stay in one of the fifty thousand hotels along the I-494 "strip" that runs just south of the airport and which features virtually every franchise and chain store known to man. The strip feeds easily into both cities as well as the southern suburbs. And what's true of most American cities is true of Minneapolis-St. Paul, too: The one landmark that is well lighted and well defined is the airport. No matter how lost I get, I can find my way back to the airport and from there back to 494.

I also know where the police stations are and how to find them, not only because I've ended up dealing with the PD on just about every visit I've ever made, but also because it's always a good idea to check in with the locals before you start doing business in their backyards. The times I haven't done that have usually resulted in some grief—for me. More about that later.

As soon as I left Randy, or he me, I found a public phone near the Walker Art Center–Guthrie Theater complex and called the Minneapolis police. I wanted to get moving as quickly as possible on the DIMAND license plate; too much time had passed already. I asked for a cop who knew me, one I had worked with a time or two, a detective named Delgado. He was currently on the day shift. So I ID'd myself to the officer on the other end of the wire, explained the nature of my business, and asked him to run the plate for me. One of the few benefits of shelling out for a PI license is that you can usually count on at least grudging cooperation from the authorities. And indeed the cop I was dealing with, whose name was Gamble, was just as nice and as pleasant and as friendly as could be. Unfortunately, Gamble didn't know me from Yassir Arafat, and I ended up having to come in and transact my business in person—a delay I had wanted to avoid, which is why I had hoped that Delgado would be working that evening. Still, I could hardly kick. Gamble was just going by the rules. We are all but cogs in the big machine called Bureaucracy.

Despite all us cogs, and all our computers, the machine works slowly. It was getting on toward midnight before I left police headquarters with the vital statistics about the owner of license plate DIMAND.

Dimand was the man's name—Steven Jeffrey Dimand. I might have been able to guess at least the last third of that ID, but you never know: There currently was someone driving around Greater Omaha in a Volkswagen Jetta with the license plate JETTA. Go figure.

As for Steven Dimand, he drove a 1989 Jaguar XJ-SC Cabriolet—that's "convertible," to the likes of you and me—he had no record nor any outstanding warrants against him, and he lived in a condominium building just south of the Nicollet Mall, downtown Minneapolis. A short drive from the police station. No lakes got in the way, just lots of one-way streets. It's hard to resist the urge to drive the wrong way up a one-way street when there's no other traffic.

The place looked like a ten- or twelve-year-old apartment building gone condo. Bronze-colored brick box with a security entrance; your standard buzzer-lock setup. There are plenty of imaginative ways to get into a security building without announcing yourself. Some of them work. Me, I tried the time-honored trick of pressing the little round button next to Dimand's name on the intercom console. Pretty sneaky, huh?

"What?" the tinny speaker blurted after a short interval.

"Mr. Dimand, my name is Nebraska. I'm a private investigator. I would like to talk with you about a young man named Eric Matthew Sperry."

"Do you know what time it is?"

"Yes, sir, I do, but thanks anyway."

Another short interval. Then the lockbox on the inner door farted and I went into the building.

Dimand lived on the seventh floor. The furnishings in the public areas were nice, but nothing to wet your pants about. The same was true of Dimand's apartment, as I saw when he opened the door in response to my knock. He, or his decorator, was still in the stark white-minimalist mode. Track lights threw illumination against the ceilings. Some of it bounced back.

Dimand was a little taller than six feet. He had a bony, chiseled face, features well defined but somehow indistinct, like the face on a department-store mannequin. Although I wouldn't have said he was any older than me, he was already quite bald. He wore his blond hair very short, giving his head an almost-shaven look. What hair he had looked almost white against his deep store-bought tan.

"I hope this is important," he said by way of greeting.

"I hope so too." I showed him my permit.

He looked at it closely. "How unique," he said after examining it. "Is that thing any good in this state?"

I folded it away. "Depends what you mean, Mr. Dimand. It does not permit me to set up shop in this state; however it does permit me to conduct my investigation here. Anyhow, the local police know all about me. They're the ones who gave me your name and address."

His heavy-lidded eyes widened the barest fraction. Score one for the home team. I didn't feel inclined to explain further. If he thought he was known to the cops, so be it. Keeps 'em honest.

"I see." Dimand turned and wandered into the living room, which stood at the back of the place, off of a short corridor from the front door. "And this investigation takes you all the way from Omaha to my doorstep at"—he consulted a brass clock ticking softly on the wall—"twelve-thirty at night. I guess it *must* be important." He stopped and turned to face me. "So talk. You said you wanted to talk."

I produced one of the wallet-size photos of Eric Sperry and

handed it over. "He ran away from home last week," I said. "I would like to talk to him."

He looked at the picture, looked at me. "Would you like a cup of coffee?" He made a vague gesture in what I supposed was the direction of the kitchen.

"I would rather talk to Eric," I said.

"Yes." He studied the photograph some more. "Do you need this back?"

"I have others."

He propped the picture on a marble-topped table beneath the brass clock. Then he folded his arms across his chest. It was a well-developed chest. He wore a close-fitting cable-stitch sweater that showed his broad shoulders to good advantage. He had pushed the sleeves back almost to the elbows, displaying the long ropes of muscles and the thick cords of veins in his forearms. Besides the sweater he wore faded denims and pair of unlaced Avias, no socks. "I think you should understand, Mr. Nebraska, that *if* Eric, or anybody else for that matter, is here, he's here of his own free will."

"Great. I'd like to hear that from Eric, if you don't mind."

"Yes," he repeated, but he made no move to do anything about it.

I said, "Mr. Dimand, I didn't stick a pin in the phone book and land on your name. I'm here because I traced Eric Sperry from the bus depot in Omaha to the bus depot in Minneapolis, and from there to Loring Park, and from there into a Jaguar with the license plate DIMAND. So there's no point asking me to dance—Eric Sperry *was* with you just a few days ago. From what I know of you, and from the way you're acting, he probably still is. All I want to do is talk to him and make sure he's okay and give him the chance to come back to Omaha with me if he wants."

Dimand snorted derisively.

I said, "As far as I'm concerned, seventeen is old enough to start making your own mistakes. If Eric is all right, and if he convinces me that he really wants to stay here, fine."

"Uh-huh. But you'll tell the police, of course, and as far as they're concerned Eric is a minor."

"The police aren't my client; Eric's parents are. I will tell them, and what they do after that is their business."

"I can imagine what they'll do."

"If I don't see the boy in about thirty seconds, you won't have to do any imagining. You will see with your own eyes the uniforms that descend on this place and you will hear and read the charges they slap on you. That for starters."

Dimand took in a deep breath and uncrossed his arms, shoving his fingers into the back pockets of his jeans. Then he let out about half the air he had inhaled. The effect was to pull his shoulders back, accentuating their broadness, and puff out his chest. I didn't know whether I was supposed to faint or just go *ooh,* so I did neither, and waited. Finally he said, in a low voice that I imagined was meant to sound dangerous, "I am not the sort of man you want to mess around with, Mr. Nebraska."

"I'm certain of that," I said. "The boy?"

Dimand kept his cold eyes on me a moment longer, then turned and moved quickly down a short corridor. He stopped at a closed door, knocked, and opened it. "Eric," he said. "Company." Then he moved back to his previous position.

The boy emerged, rumpled and drowsy looking, a few seconds later. His hair was a mess and his eyes were bleary and he wore a flannel robe that was about two sizes too large, but otherwise he looked okay. "What's goin' on?" he demanded sleepily.

Dimand drew the boy gently in front of him, facing me. He had one hand on the boy's shoulder, possessively, protectively, and with the other smoothed Eric's unruly hair.

"Eric," Dimand said gently, talking the way you might talk to a frightened pet, "this man is a detective. Your parents hired him to find you."

The boy frowned. "Really?"

"Really," I said. "They want to make sure you're all right. They miss you, and they're worried about you."

"I bet," Eric said sourly.

I shrugged. "They're paying me a lot of money to find you."

"So you found him," Dimand said. "So go back to Omaha and collect your money. You can see Eric's just fine. Tell them that. He's better off with me—*I* care about him."

"What do you say, Eric?"

He glanced up, over his shoulder, at Dimand, then back at me. "I don't want to go back," he said. "Why do you think I left?"

"There," Dimand said triumphantly.

I looked at him. "How about giving us a little space."

"Right," he said sarcastically. "I leave the room and you snatch Eric." His fingers tightened on the boy's shoulders.

I sighed. "If I was going to drag him back to his parents, why wouldn't I have showed up here with the cops?"

"How should I know?"

"Good point. Look, you stand there"—I took the boy by the arm and guided him away from his friend, toward the other end of the room—"and we'll stand down here. All right?"

It wasn't, but he was trying not to make a big deal of it. For the boy's sake, I figured. Hell, what did I know—maybe Eric was better off with this guy. He had money, that much was obvious. And he did seem to care about the boy, in a proprietary sort of way. The way you might care about an AKA-registered malamute. He glowered at us and flexed his muscles a bit more.

The room was long and narrow, terminating at a set of sliding doors that opened onto a small terrace. I took Eric over near the doors and said quietly, "You asked me why I think you left home. I think it was because you spent a lot of time and a lot of sleepless nights coming to some tough decisions. Not only about your sexuality, but also whether to be honest with your parents about it. Close?"

He said nothing, but looked away from me and out the sliding doors, over the darkened city.

There were trees in the near distance. We were above them. Bare of either leaves or snow, they waved gnarled black fingers against a sky that was navy and gray. The night was windy and cold, starless, empty the way a snowless wintry night can be. In the pale light from overhead, his hair uncombed, Eric reminded me of the boy from the park. Randy. Like Randy, maybe Eric was better off where he was now than where he had been. How could I tell? More important, how could I know whether what seemed best for Eric today would still be for the best tomorrow, next week, next year?

The short answer: I couldn't. And maybe it wasn't my problem. Eric was nearly an adult, and living with the consequences of your decisions is what adulthood is all about.

I had nothing against Dimand. Like a lot of these guys who build a little muscle, he confused the window dressing with the genuine goods. But that didn't mean anything. Maybe he really did care about the boy, and vice versa, and they would live happily ever after. But I'd've been happier about the deal if Eric didn't seem so alone, so off-balance. If I'd felt he had acted rather than reacted—first to his parents' response to his big news, second to the circumstances that put him on a street corner.

So I made a choice: I chose to take the boy's silence as a yes and plunge on. "Okay, so you came to terms with your sexuality, then you decided to do the stand-up thing and tell your folks. And they weren't real wowed by what you had to say. This was a shock?" He almost laughed. "Most parents figure their kids will follow a life-style pretty much along the lines of their own. You come at them with something like this, out of left field—which is where it came from, as far as they know—of course you're going to knock them for a loop. Can't you cut them a little slack? How long did it take for you to finally come to terms with being gay?"

"I don't know," he mumbled at the carpet. "Long time, I guess."

"I bet. Looks notwithstanding, I'm not *so* ancient that I can't remember what it was like being your age, what a bitch it was trying to get all this sex stuff figured out—and I only had to worry about *me,* not what my family and friends and society would think. So consider how long it took you to get a handle on everything and get your head screwed on right. Don't you think you should give your parents at least that long to get used to the idea?"

He took a long moment to think about it, staring first at the carpet, then at the dark sky beyond the window. I gave him his time. When he looked at me, his eyes were red. "Maybe," he said hoarsely.

"What I told your friend is true. If you say life's a bowl of cherries, then I leave. I will tell your parents where I found you and they may well decide to take action—you are still a minor—but I won't force you to come with me or do anything you don't want to do. On the other hand, if you want to give your folks another chance, we can be on a plane to the Big O in the morning. From what I see, you're adult enough to think for yourself. So what do you think?"

He glanced at Dimand, who had not moved but who reso-

lutely avoided looking at us. Then he examined the carpet
some more. It was nice carpet, but I didn't think it warranted
the attention it was getting. "The answers aren't printed
down there, son," I said.

Eric looked at me and squared his shoulders slightly; I
doubt he even knew he did it. "Steve's been real nice to me,"
he said. "He bought me a lot of great clothes . . ."

"Uh-huh."

"But . . ." Another glance, then back to me. "I feel bad about
. . . you know, about my folks. I . . . Well, they *are* my folks.
I don't know if we can fix things up, but I guess maybe I better
try."

I said, "In about eighteen months you'll be graduating.
You'll be an adult. Then no one can stop you doing what you
want. Including moving back here, if it's what you want."

He nodded. "I'll go with you. But . . . what do I tell Steve?"

"You want me to tell him?"

He did, but he said no and walked back across the room.

Dimand took the news about as well as Eric's parents had
probably taken the news he had given them. "You can't be
serious!" he said loudly, then he pushed Eric out of his way
and came across the room at me.

"Go pack your bag," I told the boy. He backed down the hall,
his eyes wide.

"You son of a bitch," Dimand breathed into my face. "What
did you tell him?"

"That he should make a decision. He did. If you care
about him, then you'll accept his decision and stand behind
him."

"You *bet* I care about him. That's why I'm not letting you
take him back to those people."

"I assume you mean his parents."

"That's what *you* call them. How can you, when they
turned their backs on him just because he was honest enough
to tell them who and what he is? That's not what I call parent-
ing."

"They didn't turn their backs on him, Dimand. My being
here proves that. Anyhow, there's nothing to discuss. Eric has
decided. He's going home."

"This is his home."

"Well, then leave a candle burning in the window."

I moved to get past him. He had other ideas. He planted his palm against my chest and pushed hard. I stumbled backward and nearly tripped over a small ottoman.

"Dimand, this is stupid."

"You got that right." He pushed me again. "This is the biggest mistake you ever made, cornhusker."

"I doubt that. Look, I don't want any trouble."

"Then leave. There's the door." He had backed me up to the glass doors. Behind me was the little terrace, then a seven-story drop to the cold pavement.

"Well?" Dimand said, grinning. He flexed the long muscles in his forearms a little, just for show.

I sighed. "You know, the problem with guys like you is you get used to doing battle with the Nautilus or the Soloflex, not machines that can strike back. Or first." Then I raised my right foot and brought the heel down hard on the instep of his right foot. I was wearing black dress shoes, leather with leather heels; he was wearing sneakers—expensive ones, but still sneakers. He yowled in surprise and pain as I mashed down on the small, delicate bones of his foot.

Then he yowled in surprise and pain as I drove the palm of my right hand up under his nose. Not hard. I wanted to calm him down, not kill him by driving bone and gristle up into his brain. But it's a move that doesn't have to have a hell of a lot of force behind it to be effective. I felt the cartilage give, and a second later blood rushed from his nostrils. His hands went up to his face and when they did I elbowed him in the gut. He doubled over and I pushed him. The ottoman was behind him now; he went over it and ended up in the easy chair on the other side of it, moaning, holding his hands over his face. Blood oozed out between his fingers and stained the chair's upholstery.

Eric emerged from the hallway, dressed and carrying an overstuffed vinyl duffel. "What's going on? What happened to Steve?"

"He tripped over the footstool," I said. "He'll be all right."

"Yeah, but not *you,* you bastard." I turned and looked back at Dimand. His face was a bloody mess, and blood still streamed from his nose, ruining his sweater. Tears of pain and rage and humiliation washed down his cheeks and disappeared into the hemorrhage. Oddly, though, his gray eyes were still cold, almost lifeless. "You are *dead,* asshole. You don't know who you're messing with."

I laughed. I didn't mean to. From my side it was nervous release but from Dimand's side it was a laugh, and one aimed at him. He colored.

"That's right, laugh it up, Nebraska." Dimand's voice was thick, partly from rage, partly from his inability to breathe properly. "Keep laughing. I'll fix you—"

"From the look of things, Dimand, you're the one who needs fixing. Call a doctor, for crying out loud."

3

We went back to my room at one of the Dillon Inns along 494, where I checked on flights to Omaha. The news wasn't too bad, especially if you like staying in hotels. We could get home without being routed through Bogotá if we sat tight until 9:50 the next morning, when there was a United direct flight scheduled to leave MSP and arrive OMA at 11:03. As if they operate with such precision.

I booked us on the flight, arranged a room for Eric, then drove us to a Tom Thumb and got him some overnight items he hadn't packed, as well as a supply of junk food. He uttered maybe a dozen words throughout, which brought the total number he had spoken since leaving Dimand's up to almost eighteen.

It was past two by the time we got back to the hotel, but neither of us was sleepy. We convened in my room to watch a movie neither of us was interested in. During all this Eric contributed maybe another ten monosyllabic words to what I generously call the conversation. Finally, during the end credits, I said, "You know, it's natural you'd be having second thoughts."

He looked a little surprised. "No. It's not that."

"Then what?"

He sighed, and pushed aside the visitor's magazine he had been leafing through, and rolled onto his back on the double bed. "People keep getting hurt," he said to the ceiling. "My mom and dad, Steve. . . . It's not what I wanted. It's not what I expected."

I peeled the tab back on one of the Cokes I had bought at Tom Thumb. "What did you expect? You would tell your folks your big news and they'd say, 'That's nice, dear, now go wash up for dinner'? Like I said, give them a little time."

"Yeah, I guess . . ."

I leaned forward in my chair, bringing the front legs down onto the floor. "Eric, when people care, people get hurt. It's too bad, but the alternative is worse."

"What's the alternative?"

"Death. Being a corpse that doesn't have the good taste to quit wandering around. You've seen them, you probably even known a couple—the people who don't give a great goddamn about anyone or anything but themselves. Corpses, walking corpses. If you're a corpse, you don't feel anything. If you're alive, if you care, sooner or later you get hurt."

"I feel bad about Steve."

"Sure," I said. "Me too. But, Eric, he brought it on himself. You were there. You told him you were leaving and he flipped. He tried to show me out via the back door."

Eric frowned. "There is no back door . . ."

"There is if you don't mind that seven-story first step." He thought about it a moment, then laughed. I tossed a Coke at him and he caught it. "Listen," I said. "Steve pushed me and I pushed back, only when I push back I push hard. It isn't the way I wanted to handle it, I'm not particularly proud of it, but I'm not particularly ashamed of it either. It's just how things worked out. You go on from there. Same as with you and your parents."

The boy nodded, then shook his head. "You really let Steve have it."

"He'll be all right. It looked worse than it was."

"When you told me to get packed, I almost didn't. I didn't think there was any point—I figured Steve would tear you apart. No offense, but Steve's a tough guy. I mean, he's bigger than you and—"

"Better built? That's true. So then why did you pack?"

Eric shrugged. "Steve was pretty mad. I thought maybe I'd rather be someplace else when he finished with you. I didn't know he wouldn't even get started. How did you, you know, take him?" He looked at his hands. They were slender and long-fingered—the hands of an artist—unblemished and un-callused. "I've never been very tough," he said apologetically.

I disagreed, and he looked at me in mild surprise. "Eric, being tough doesn't have anything to do with being able to lift your weight in Snickers bars. Toughness is a matter of attitude. It's a mental quality. It's setting your mind to something that you may not want to do but which must be done—and then following through. I'm certain your friend Steve can bench press more than I could, and do more crunches, and run farther, and jump higher, and all that neat stuff. Unfortunately, tonight he didn't stick to what he knew. He thought he was tougher because he's athletic. He was wrong. *I* was tougher because I knew what the situation called for and I wasn't afraid to follow through."

"Something you didn't want to do but which had to be done?"

"Something like that. But I'm not telling you anything you don't already know."

He gave me a half-surprised, half-confused look.

"Eric, don't you think leveling with your parents the way you did qualifies as tough? I do."

He looked away from me and fiddled with the tab on the pop can. "But then I ran away."

"Yeah, well, that was cowardly."

His head came around sharply and his eyes flashed. But as fast as he had taken offense he took my point, and nodded ashamedly. "You know it too," I said. "Good. Take responsibility for your weaknesses, but take credit for your strengths. For instance, your going back now to face the music. That's being strong. That's being tough—making the hard choices."

Eric sighed. "I wish they weren't all so hard. I wish there was an easier way."

"There is. Running away is easier."

He looked at me steadily. "No it isn't," he said.

4

A little better than twelve hours later, Eric was reunited with his parents. The event took place where the assignment, for me, had begun: the small but plush conference room just off of Mike Kennerly's large but plush office overlooking the Central Park Mall in scenic downtown Omaha. It was an awkward reunion, as such reunions generally are. Nobody knew what to say or what to do or where to look. Mrs. Sperry in particular seemed embarrassed by having had to turn to strangers to address a family problem.

I say "address" rather than "solve." There were no solutions here. If those were to come, they would have to come later, and only the Sperrys could concoct them.

They went back to their lives. I was set to do the same, but Kennerly stopped me with a look. He's a small, dapper, white-haired man who lives behind a pair of gold-rimmed glasses. One of these quiet types who communicate more with a gesture or a facial expression than most of us can get across in a whole series of lectures. It was with a look, a slight pursing of the lips, that he indicated he would like me to hang around after the Sperrys left.

"I've got news," Kennerly said when he returned from escorting the family to the elevators. "And it isn't good."

"Ah."

"Yes. The word I get is that when the decision comes down next week, it isn't going to be what we want to hear."

I smiled. At least, that was my intent. I felt a little numb. "And what is it that we want to hear?" My lips felt full of Novocain.

Kennerly made a lopsided grin. I figured it must have about mirrored my own. "I assumed we did not want to have your private-investigator's permit revoked. If I was mistaken, please tell me so I can stop feeling bad about letting you down."

"Don't be an ass. You didn't let me down. Look what you had to work with."

What Kennerly had had to work with these past few months was a private investigator who seemed to have gone out of his way to get his papers yanked. And believe me, it's a lot harder to lose a PI permit than it is to get one, at least in this state. Getting one, in the State of Nebraska, means going to the Secretary of State and getting the right form. That's pretty much it. You fill it out and send copies to the Secretary of State, the Nebraska State Patrol, and your local county attorney. The latter two entities check you out, which mainly involves making sure you don't have a felonious violent past. Then you cough up your dough and show proof of bonding, and the sheriff gives you your license and your weapon permit, and they stamp CW on your driver's license to show you're allowed to carry a concealed weapon.

To lose your license, on the other hand, takes effort. It's not like on TV, where the cops are always threatening to take away the square-jawed hero's license. In Nebraska you have to commit a felony. Or you have to get the cops or another city official so peeved that they're willing to file a formal complaint and go through an insanely protracted—and expensive—judicial process that inevitably ends up on appeal in District Court. You don't lose your PI permit because a local cop doesn't like your tie.

In my case, I had authorities in two cities in two states irked at me. It was all a misunderstanding—I hadn't understood how ticked off everyone would be if I left the scene of a murder or two without notifying the proper agencies.

The cops in Omaha had taken a dim view of my leaving the scene of a gangland execution here one morning almost three months back. A couple hundred miles north, the cops in Sioux Falls, South Dakota, had taken a similar view of my leaving a murder site there the night before. I explained that the scene of the first murder was supposed to have been the scene of my murder as well. I pointed out, as if anyone could miss it, the lump of bandage that still covered the spot where a bullet had grazed my thick skull and peeled away the tip of my ear as it trundled past. I mentioned that I had left the

scene not only in pursuit of my would-be killer but also in the
hope that I could prevent the second killing—vain hope, since
the subsequent investigation indicated that the "second" killing, the one in Omaha, occurred shortly before the one that
was supposed to have included me.

I might as well have saved my breath.

The cops were understanding enough. Not pleased, not
happy, but understanding enough. Typical. Cops, with a few
spectacular exceptions, are a reasonable lot. Practical. Goal-
oriented. They're more concerned with the ultimate outcome
than with every step, misstep, or cut corner that leads up to
it. Find out what happened and figure out a way to get it to
make sense on the report—that's the creed. Who needs to go
out of his way looking for trouble?

But bureaucrats are different. The lawyers, the politicos,
the Guys in Ties—the ones who feed on fine print, whose
continued existence depends on technical smokescreens and
legalistic mumbo-jumbo—were not to be appeased. They
were sympathetic, in that synthetic-sympathetic way of
theirs, but unmoved and unmoving. The proceedings were
over before they began, and for once I didn't carry the day.
But on the bright side, Kennerly pointed out, the Guys in Ties
declined to press criminal charges against me.

"Meaning they don't have a case," I said. After all the weeks
of questioning and re-questioning and explaining and re-ex-
plaining, I knew their ilk well enough to know that any reluc-
tance they felt was not due to all the milk of human kindness
sloshing around inside them.

Kennerly shrugged. "We'll appeal, of course."

"I can't afford the justice I've gotten so far."

"And I told you once we weren't going to worry about that.
Worse comes to worse, I'll put you on my payroll and garnish
your wages."

"My pal. You have rocks in your head if you come within
a hundred feet of me after this, Mike. Same with every
other lawyer in the state. And the cops, and everyone else.
You know the drill—a PI gets his papers yanked, he's about
as welcome among his former associates as a dog in
church." And that was the worst of it. Losing the bond, losing the supplemental insurance policies, losing the privi-
lege of carrying concealed weapons, even losing the right to

contract with clients—all of which comes with losing your license—was bad enough. But the biggest punishment of all is the one that isn't codified. It's becoming a pariah amongst the people that you work with and work for. We may like to think of ourselves as Philip Marlowes, as solitary knights on the mean streets, but the fact is that a PI who can't plug into the official power grid isn't worth much. And a PI who's had his papers yanked can't plug into the official power grid, period. Your old man can be Chief of Police, you're still out in the cold.

It was someplace I didn't want to be.

Kennerly said, "We're not dead yet. We're still a long ways from that. Until then, it's business as usual as far as you're concerned."

"If you say so. What happens if we lose the appeal?"

He frowned. "You can make application for a new permit after two or three years. It's strictly at the discretion of the Secretary of State."

"And it's tougher to re-obtain a permit than to obtain it the first time out, am I right?"

"They would scrutinize a candidate more rigorously the second time, yes." He paused. "Nebraska—how vigorously do you want to pursue this? I mean, for years now—I don't know how many years—you've talked about getting out of the investigations business and becoming a full-time freelance writer. Maybe this is a good time to do exactly that. Why spend the time and effort and money to protect a permit to perform a job you don't want to do?"

"Partly because no matter how much you dislike a job, you'd still rather quit than be fired," I said. "And partly because I'm not that sure I want to quit—it's been suggested to me that if I really did, I would have done it by now. And partly because I'm no fan of starvation. Last year I cleared about twelve grand from my literary career. Hard to keep myself in the style I'm accustomed to on less than, oh, thirteen thousand a year, Mike."

"Maybe if you had more time to write, you'd make more money."

"Maybe." I tried another smile. "It's a scary thought—going out there and working without a net. No reason it should be. I've been self-employed for, what, twelve years now. But as a

PI, a career I *know* I can make a living at, albeit a modest one."

"I suspect you could make a living at the other, too. You've done all right so far. Magazine articles, two books . . ."

"One and three-quarters. Four-fifths, maybe. I can see the light at the end of the tunnel, but I'm not quite there yet. That's part of what I mean. Detective work I know I can do. I just roll out of bed in the morning and do it. It's *real.* But writing, you have to make it up, from scratch, every damn day. You never get up in the morning and panic and think, 'My God, I don't remember how to run a credit check anymore. I never did know. I can't do this anymore.' But, oy, if I had a dime for every time I sat staring at a sheet of paper staring back at me and thought, 'I don't know how to do this. Who am I fooling?' " I sighed. "I think maybe that's why I don't want to let go of the other. It's my security blanket. Come what may, I *know* I can do investigations. If they'll let me."

"The fat lady hasn't sung yet," Kennerly reminded me.

"I think I hear her warming up in the wings." I moved toward the door.

"Nebraska." I stopped and faced him. "Just something to consider: I've done a little checking, and a lot of private investigators are licensed in other nearby states. For instance, a good many Omaha private detectives are licensed in Iowa. We could probably get you licensed across the river with no problem, and you could set up shop in Council Bluffs."

"Are you kidding?" I said. "The way I've criticized Iowa drivers?"

5

I went home and drank more cheap bourbon than I should have but less than I would have liked. That was no solution to anything, but what good is it being a grown-up if you can't sit around feeling sorry for yourself every once in a while?

That isn't all it's cracked up to be, though, and after only a few hours my mind turned involuntarily to more practical matters. Like how I was going to make a living if the state ultimately did prohibit me from leading the glamorous life of a professional keyhole-peeker. Mike Kennerly was right when he said I made an awful lot of noise about supporting myself as a writer, but the fact was that I had never really taken the plunge. I always knew that if the writing assignments, or the checks therefrom, didn't come fast enough I could scare up a sleuthing job to see me past rent day. And I had done exactly that on more than one occasion.

Now it looked like they were going to take away my crutch.

So now I would have to get real serious real fast about this writing business. That meant stepping up the number and frequency of query letters I had in front of various magazine editors. And it meant finally completing the not-quite-complete manuscript of The Next Book, my second detective novel, as yet untitled. (Actually, *The Next Book* wasn't such a bad title. But if I used it, what would I call the *next* one?) And it meant getting cracking on another book.

It meant, in a word, working—and working hard.

Either that or filling out an application at Domino's Pizza.

Which reminded me that I was hungry. I threw together a stir-fry of leftover chicken and some vegetables that wouldn't last much longer, and had about finished it, a bottle of Harp, and the six o'clock news when the boys from down the hall stopped by with my mail and newspapers from the past four days.

The boys, Jim Marineaux and Robert Olson, aren't really boys—they're both in their late twenties, early thirties—and they don't live down the hall, since our apartment building doesn't have a hall, at least not a central interior hallway: all the units open to the outdoors. But Jim and Robert share the apartment that is the mirror image of mine, at the other end of the little brick building on Decatur Street. In exchange for some small break on their rent, the boys handle minor chores for our absentee landlord—keeping the walks cleared, collecting rent checks, and so on. In the course of my inventing imaginative reasons for not paying the month's tribute in a timely fashion, we became pretty good friends. Good enough that Robert felt free to raid the fridge and Jim to flop on my sofa as I leafed through the collection of bills and other junk mail they had saved for me.

"I'm relieved you guys didn't go crazy and pay any of these for me," I said.

"None of them were marked past-due," said Robert. "We steamed them open, naturally." He handed me another Harp and threaded across the small room with one for Jim. Jim's a compact fellow, narrow hips, narrow shoulders, with sandy hair cut short in back and on the sides, full on top, and a thin sandy mustache. Robert is about my size, maybe ten or fifteen pounds lighter than me, with the spring-kneed gait of an athlete. Jim is a midlevel manager at a credit bureau; Robert is with a long-distance company.

"So how'd everything go up there?" Jim wondered, but only after a long pull on his beer.

"Not too bad. They gave us stale peanuts and bad coffee and they told us to extinguish all smoking materials."

"I think he means up there in Minneapolis," Robert said, flipping through an old *New Yorker.*

"Oh, up *there,*" I said. "Fine. The prodigal is returned to the bosom of his family. God is in his heaven, all is right with the world, and my check is in the mail."

"That explains the somersaults," Jim said.

I looked at Robert. "Overjoyed you're not," he said.

"Or at least you forgot to tell your face."

I took care of half an inch of beer. "Hell," I said gently, "is this gonna be one of those close, warm, buddy-buddy exchanges? If so, I'd like to throw up now, before I drink any more of this expensive imported beer."

Robert looked at Jim and grinned. "James, you forget the big, strong, half-boiled—"

"Hard-boiled."

"—private-eye just isn't into talking about his feelings and all that namby-pamby crap."

"At least," Jim added sagely, "not as much as those of us who are, you know, *that way.*"

"Hmm," Robert said. "Emotionally stunted. I've seen it before."

"Maybe some childhood trauma, resulting in an unwillingness or inability to get in touch with the more sensitive side of his personality."

"What some refer to as the 'feminine' side?"

"Although that is pretty sexist. What do you think, Nebraska?"

"I think," I said, trying to keep a straight face—never easy when those two went into their routine—"that the two of you, individually or collectively, should go take a flying fuck at a rolling doughnut."

They looked at each other for several seconds. Then Jim, frowning slightly, shook his head. "No. No, he still hasn't got it."

"If I could get it by hanging around you two, I would've gotten it long ago. Look, I appreciate you guys' concern. But I'm fine. I heard today that the decision's going to be against me on my licensing case, that's all. You know how it is—even when you *know* something's going to happen, it's still a shock to the system when it finally comes to pass."

"This case you just wrapped up should tell you that you've got what it takes, even without a license."

"Travis McGee never had a license," Jim pointed out. Jim is big on the McGee books. Ever since he found out I'm a private investigator, he's tried to put me and McGee into the same pigeonhole.

I made a face. "You think anyone'll believe I've gone into the deep-sea salvage trade? In a landlocked state?"

"We have a river," Robert said.

"I've heard that rumor, too," I said, and drank some beer. "It's funny, when all this crap first hit the blades, my attitude was, 'Screw 'em. I don't need a piece of paper to do this job.' I knew it'd be tougher without the official okey-dokey, and that there would be jobs I simply couldn't take on, but I figured, you know, no big deal. It's like if they take away your driver's license. It doesn't mean you *can't* drive, physically can't. It just means you're not supposed to. And you'd better not get caught doing it. But now that I'm staring down the barrel of a revocation, I don't know. I think I would feel . . . funny if I undertook an investigation without that little bit of paper that said it was jake with the guys in Lincoln."

"Funny?" Robert echoed.

"Conspicuous. Self-conscious. Naked."

"The naked eye," Jim said, snickering.

I had to smile. "Sounds like the title of one of those 'racy' paperback novels I used to read when I was a kid."

"Remember that TV show *Naked City*?" Jim said. "Used to be sponsored by an aspirin company. When I was a kid, I thought the announcer was saying, '*Naked City*—brought to you by Bare Aspirin.'"

Robert laughed, and choked on a mouthful of beer. I raised my voice to be heard over his coughs and splutters and said, "Guys, it doesn't get any better than this."

Despite my liberal applications of anesthetic, sleep was elusive. I felt a kind of cold, vague jitteriness—a more somber cousin of the nagging anxiety you feel when you're subliminally aware that you've forgotten an appointment. I wouldn't go so far as to call it a nameless dread, poetic though that may be, but a definite uneasiness perched itself on my shoulder, and I did not know its name.

I supposed it had to do with the news Kennerly had given me that afternoon. And why not? I had invested a goodly chunk of my life in the investigations racket—one way or another, for one employer or another—and the thought of having to abandon it did not go down easily. Then there was the little matter of making up the income, minuscule though it may have been, that PI work provided. And then too there was the simple matter—in and of itself, divorced from any resultant difficulties—of having my papers lifted. At the very least, it was a blow to my ego. The state was saying, quite literally, "You're not good enough to be in this profession." I never gave much of a rip whether the state approved of me or not, but when I thought of some of the sleazoids from hell who carried valid PI permits. . . .

That had to be it. The reason for my nerves.

My mind kept drifting back to the threats made by Steven Dimand, but I just as quickly dismissed them. I had been threatened before, by people a lot scarier than Dimand. And I had been threatened by people like Dimand, humiliated men with overinflated opinions of their own importance or competence, men who felt the need to have the last word, even if it was empty. Over the years I had come to discount threats and the people who make them. The ones who squawk the loudest are the most obnoxious but the least dangerous. It's the ones you cross but who emit not the slightest peep that you have to beware of.

So I told myself that it was the imminent loss of my license—and, potentially, my livelihood, or at least a significant slice of it—that had me on edge, not Steven Dimand and his empty threats. And then I set about putting both of them out of my mind.

I began to suspect I had made a mistake late the following night, or rather very early the day after that.

◇◇◇

The phone rang at 1:32 A.M. I know it for a fact. Like most people, I have a clock by the side of my bed; like most people, I assume that middle-of-the-night calls are trouble, which for some reason makes it important to lock in the time, important enough that it becomes automatic.

It was Jim Marineaux. He didn't identify himself, but I recognized his voice, rushed and breathless though it was. "It's Robert," he blurted. "He's in the hospital. I just got a call. Someone beat him up. He's in surgery—"

"Where are you?" I was wide awake.

"Home. They just called me."

"Give me five minutes."

I required less than that, although I wasn't going to be making any best-dressed lists tonight; it took only a few minutes more to arrive at the emergency entrance of St. Joe's, on the Creighton University campus. I stuck the car in an EMERGENCY PATIENTS ONLY stall. It was Jim's car, although I felt better with me behind the wheel than him, and he put up no argument. My car's whereabouts were unknown. I had loaned it to Robert, whose own car was in the shop. Since Robert worked when most of the rest of us sleep, his using my venerable Impala for a day or two caused me no trouble. Until now, that is. But I wouldn't worry about the machine until I found out about the man. I'm funny that way.

Jim was out of the car before I shut off the engine, and through the automatic doors to the emergency room a second after that. I hurried to catch up.

Jim identified himself to a young black woman at the information desk, who gestured toward a uniformed officer. Omaha cop. He was already stepping over toward us.

"Mr. Marineaux?" He mispronounced the name, but Jim let

it slide. "I'm officer Sawicky. I'm the one who called you a little bit ago."

"What's happened?"

The cop looked at me. "I'm a neighbor," I explained. I gave him my name.

"Oh yeah. . . ." Sawicky looked down at his clipboard. He was a short, square man, solid-looking, wearing a close-trimmed brown mustache shot with gray. He pawed through some papers under the clip. "Are you the owner of the car Mr. Olson was driving?"

"That's right. Can you tell us what happened? How's Robert?"

"He's in surgery right now," Sawicky said. "He has some head injuries that they're worried about. Some swelling. The doctors can fill you in on that. As far as what happened—well, we're not real sure. It looks like someone ran him off the road. Down here just off the North Freeway, by the Cunning Street exit. It looks like they ran him off the road and into a light post, then dragged him out of the car and beat him up good."

"Oh God," Jim said. His eyes were wet.

"Who?" I said.

"Two or three guys at least."

"Oh God," Jim repeated.

"Do you have any idea who would want to do something like this to your friend? Any enemies, someone he locked horns with, maybe at work or someplace. . . ."

"No, no," Jim was saying. "No one. Everyone likes Robert."

I said, "Was he robbed?"

The cop looked at me curiously. I went into my wallet and pulled out one of my cards. I figured I might as well use them up, seeing's how they wouldn't be of much use in the future. Too bad, too: I must have had four hundred of them left. Heavy, textured light-gray stock with the raised printing that surely no one mistakes for engraving anymore. My name, the word INVESTIGATIONS, my permit number, and my telephone number. Understated elegance—that's me all over.

"Oh," said the cop, who handed back my card. "No, we don't think he was robbed. He had a wallet containing credit cards and twenty-two dollars in cash, and he was wearing a gold watch and a diamond ring. I've got those things, and the other personal items he had on him," Sawicky added conspiratorially. "You don't want to have that kind of stuff lying around a hospital."

Jim snuffled, and blew his nose quietly.

I said, "I suppose Robert took the North Freeway to and from work." Jim acknowledged this with a nod. "Then he would get off at either Cuming or Hamilton. Do you suppose someone, another driver, got hacked off at him for some imagined or real reason—cutting him off, tailgating him, whatever—and decided to give him what-for?"

Sawicky shrugged. It was as much an attitude as a gesture. "You hear about that kind of thing happening in big cities—people going ape on the freeways, causing all kinds of grief. But we've never had anything like that around here, and I haven't heard any reports of that kind of stuff recently or anything. The traffic's just not that crazy around these parts, I guess. Now, this could be some creeps who thought it'd be fun beating up on some guy, and your friend was in the wrong place at the wrong time. But I doubt it. I've got to figure this was someone who had a real grudge against your friend and got some pals to help teach him a lesson. Or else . . ."

He let it hang. Jim said, "Go on."

The cop took a breath. "I have to ask, is your friend gay, Mr. Marineaux?"

"Yes, we are," Jim answered stonily. "Did they remember to put that on his hospital bracelet?"

Sawicky looked at me expressionlessly. "It's a problem we've had off and on over the years," he explained. "Now with AIDS and all, it's gotten bad again lately."

Like many cities, Omaha has had its problems with "gay bashing," of the physical and not just metaphorical variety. But all the incidents of which I had heard were cases in which someone who was identifiably gay—someone exiting a gay bar, for instance—had been pounced on by a band of "real men," the sort of Neanderthals who believe they have not just the option but the duty of stamping out anything they don't understand. Unfortunately for the rest of us in this so-called society, those blockheads don't understand much of anything.

I said, "Robert was coming home from work, not from an event or place that might call attention to his sexual inclination. He was just a guy in a car on a highway. He was anonymous."

Sawicky nodded. "Which brings us back to someone having a score to settle with him."

Him or somebody for whom he was mistaken, I thought.

At my best I'm slightly paranoid—it is both a side-effect and a side-benefit of the type of work I'd been doing so long—and I had not been at my best these past couple of days. Which knocked "slightly" out of that description and left a nice big gap for all sorts of nasty thoughts to slide through. Robert Olson was about my size, about my coloring. No one would confuse us if we stood side by side, but if you had only a general description, either of us would fit it.

A guy who looks something like me leaves the building where I live, gets into my car, and goes for a ride. A person wouldn't have to be much of an athlete to jump to the wrong conclusion.

I didn't share any of this suspicion with either of the men. Suspicion, after all, was all it was: I had absolutely nothing to hang it on, nothing except my own vague anxiety and well-documented paranoia. If I was wrong—I probably was—then better for Robert that I keep quiet. If someone did have it in for him, I wouldn't want to give Robert or the police reason to think he had merely been the victim of misidentification. Better, in that case, that everyone be on the alert.

On the other hand, if my paranoid delusion was right, then it was my neck on the line, not Robert's. Robert was safe.

As safe as anyone around me.

7

By seven-thirty that morning I was well on the way to believing that I wasn't paranoid, just prudent.

Seven-thirty was when I decided that someone had tampered with the lock on my apartment door.

I had spent the previous six hours with Jim at the hospital, parked on uncomfortable chairs under uncomfortable fluorescent lights, drinking machine coffee. There was a pot on in the e.r. waiting room, but it was decaffeinated coffee—no good in the pre-dawn hours.

Robert came through surgery well enough, and although his condition was graded critical, the doctors were guardedly optimistic. The beating had been severe, with more than one blow or kick to the head, but Robert's age and good physical condition were in his favor. I stayed with Jim until the hospital people thought it okay for him to look in on Robert; then I decided to stick around a while longer to see if Robert would regain consciousness. He did, very briefly, around six. He couldn't speak, and gave no indication that he knew where he was or why he was there, but he did open his eyes and see Jim there, by his bed, and he smiled weakly.

So Jim reported, after the nurse shooed him out of the room. I didn't make an effort to get into Robert's room, and I doubt the medicos would have let me if I tried. Rightly so, in all likelihood.

After his expulsion, I made Jim accompany me to the cafeteria, where I force-fed him some breakfast. Then he called his boss to tell him he wouldn't be in. He gave me the keys to his car and I drove back to Decatur Street.

Would I have noticed the shiny scratches on the metal doorknob, the small whitish gouges in the wood of the door and the jamb, if I wasn't already on edge, on the alert—if my paranoid glands hadn't already begun their secretions? Who knows? I like to think I'm as observant as the next fellow, maybe a bit more so, but who knows? The scratches were tiny. They might have been the product of my ordinary fumblings to get the key into the keyhole. Except they weren't. They were deeper, two or three bright, shiny marks against the darker copper color of the lockset, near the keyhole. They had been made with something sharp, not the blunt end of a standard housekey. Something sharp. A lockpick?

Then there were the gouges in the wood. Perhaps they had always been there. Who studies a doorknob, after all? Who would notice the pale indentations in the cheap, dark-stained wood? But there they were, and they were new, not weathered dark, and perhaps it was coincidence that they were on the door near the knob and on the frame near the dead-bolt strikeplate, and perhaps it wasn't.

Ordinarily I would have turned around at that point and gone back down the steel-and-concrete stairs at the front of the building, down to my car, and got out the .38 I keep in the glove compartment. I would have checked to see that it was loaded, although it always is, come back up the stairs, and entered my place slowly, cautiously, every fiber, nerve, and muscle on the alert.

But my car was in a towing company's lot, waiting for me to make arrangements for it, and the glovebox .38 was in the apartment, with its twin in the filing cabinet in my office. I had removed it from the car before I loaned it to Robert.

So all I could do was enter the apartment, with my fibers, nerves, and muscles in the condition already described.

The place was empty. It was in the state of daily disarray in which I had left it: too many books, too many magazines, too much furniture in too small a space. Be it ever so humble, and so on. The fridge hummed contentedly to see me, the bent second hand on the electric clock over the dining table scraped its plastic face as it passed the nine, and the building vibrated almost subliminally in response to the morning traffic on the Northwest Radial Highway out front.

I checked all the rooms. The place showed no sign of invasion. Certainly not by a band of fanatical housecleaners.

When I got to the bedroom, which doubles as my office, I popped open the filing cabinet and fished out the glovebox .38.

The apartment may have been secure, but I hadn't imagined the marks on and around the doorknob, nor had I imagined what had happened to Robert.

The gun and I went out to the kitchen, where I put up a pot of coffee.

◇◇◇

"If someone does have it in for you," Koosje said, "shouldn't you tell the police about it?"

We were back at her place by then, after a leisurely dinner at the Neon Goose, just around the corner from her office in the Old Market. Koosje Van der Beek—the name is Dutch, as is she, and works out fairly close to *KOHshuh VANderbeck*—is a psychologist. It was Koosje who helped me realize that the reason I hadn't dumped the private-eye racket was that, despite what I had been telling myself and anyone else who would listen, I liked it. Too bad I came to this realization at just about the same time it was becoming too late.

Which was not Koosje's fault. Neither was the fact that our relationship was not what it once had been. The blame for that belonged to me. She had trusted me, implicitly at least, and I had let her down. It was as simple as that. Not so simple was getting things back on track, largely because it was hard to define exactly where and how and how badly things were *off* track. We still saw each other, though with neither the frequency nor the ease, the effortlessness, of old. We still cared for each other, though she with a guardedness and I with a guilt that stopped the emotion just short of love. And we still made love, occasionally, though with a kind of sentimental fondness standing in for passion. It was not a satisfying relationship. It was somewhat like visiting a once-robust friend who is now a sick and pale shadow of his former self: equal parts sorrow and nostalgia.

But now, at least, we were together, in Koosje's living room, the only light being that which strayed in from the kitchen range and the soft green glow of the stereo receiver, which currently pumped the sounds of Liz Story's piano into the room. I sat on the carpet, my back against the sofa, and sipped coffee-and-brandy from the big mug Koosje had just handed me. After many months of my tutelage, she had mastered what the TV commercials call the secret of good coffee. It has nothing to do with what color can it comes in. It has to do with using very fresh coffee and very cold water, with letting the water come to a full boil but never boiling the coffee, and with not leaving the pot on the burner forever and a weekend.

"Good coffee," I said.

"Mm." She sipped from her cup. "That's high praise indeed, coming from you. That's also ducking the question."

"Not really; merely taking a side excursion. You know how I am about coffee."

"I know that you're Juan Valdez's best customer."

"And I'm on a first-name basis with Mrs. Olson."

"So I accept the compliment, and why not tell the police?"

"Because I've tried to tell the cops how to make coffee, and they're beyond hope. And to un-duck the question, what good would it do to tell them I'm getting paranoid in my old age? All I've got are maybes. Maybe the guys who beat up Robert thought he was me. Maybe someone tried to jimmy the door to my apartment. Trouble with maybes is, maybe-nots work just as well. Maybe Robert got someone good and pissed off at him. Maybe the marks on my door were made by a common burglar who got scared off when someone arrived or left the building."

Koosje raised her eyebrows. "In that neighborhood?"

She was right. The burglars in that district are not renowned for stealth. They wouldn't attempt to pick a lock, even if they knew whether or how such a thing could be done. They would stave in the door, grab the television and the stereo and whatever else was convenient, and split.

"Well. . . ." I said lamely. "Maybe the marks on the door have been there for months and I only just noticed them today."

"Maybe," she agreed lukewarmly. "What would it hurt to tell the police? At least tell your friend Kim Banner. Off the record, so to speak."

"What's the point? I mean, let's say someone has it in for me. Now what? OPD is going to put round-the-clock surveillance on me? Question everyone I may have torqued off in the course of my illustrious career?" I made a disparaging noise. "If I went to the cops, including Banner, they'd say, 'Gosh. Be careful, then.' And that's what I intend to do. It's no big thing." I drank some coffee.

"Uh-huh," Koosje said. Then she leaned across and flipped

back the side of my sport coat, revealing the .38 in the clip-on holster on my left hip. "No big thing."

"Like I said, I'm being careful. This is insurance is all." I rearranged the coat to cover the gun.

"You never used to go on dates armed," Koosje said disapprovingly.

"Oh?" I said virtuously. "And how would you know?"

She laughed wickedly. "You *know* how I would know." She slipped down to the floor next to me. "As I recall, I searched you for concealed weapons more than once."

"As I recall, you found one more than once."

Her lips tasted of sweet coffee.

"Anyhow," I said several minutes later, "I carried a gun all the time. And I've always got one in the car—even now, with the loaner."

Her fingers toyed with the hair that curled over the back of my shirt collar. I was overdue for my semiannual checkup at the barber. "Not *all* the time, Nebraska. On specific occasions, when you believed the circumstances called for it."

"Well . . ."

"So you must believe circumstances call for it now."

I gave it some thought, decided she was right, and said so. "But it's still no call to go crying to mommy. For the reasons I've already mentioned. When I have something specific—*if,* I should say, since I'm not entirely convinced this isn't just a case of coffee nerves—then's the time to call in the cavalry."

"If it's not too late by then."

"Why, Dr. Van der Beek," I said, sliding my hand along the smoothness of her left leg. "That almost sounds like you care."

Koosje looked at me over the top of her eyeglasses. "I almost do." Her hand slid around my belly, until her fingers encountered the holster under my arm. "Is that a gun in your pocket, or . . . oh, never mind." Then she leaned toward me again.

8

I stayed late at Koosje's. By the time I headed back toward Decatur Street it was getting on toward two. There was a time when I would have stayed what remained of the night, leaving for my place when she left for work. That time was not now, however. Now, by tacit agreement, we woke alone. Whatever pleasures and intimacies the evening may have held for us, when we woke, we woke alone.

My thoughts, such as they were at that hour and with the pitiful amount of sleep I had had, were on that unspoken agreement; the car followed the familiar and well-worn path from Koosje's door to mine on its own, although it was not my faithful Impala. That old brute was in dry dock at Rosen-Novak Chevrolet, awaiting a new fender and grille. I was lucky—and so, especially, was Robert—that he had been coming off the North Freeway, decelerating on the exit ramp, when his assailants forced him off the road and into the light post. Had he been traveling at freeway speed, the impact almost certainly would have taken care of both him and the car.

I had, on loan, a little red Nova. It was shiny and sporty and comfortable and new, and I couldn't wait to get my own wheels back under me.

The night was cold and cloudless, cracklingly crisp the way they can be out here late in the autumn, when winter is poised to strike. Dead quiet, or nearly so. There was the omnipresent murmur of traffic along the Radial, but after all these years of living on the highway I hear it, if at all, as simple white noise.

I was across the Radial from my place, drifting slowly down Decatur Street to the five-way intersection of Decatur, the Radial, and Happy Hollow Boulevard. The Radial at that point sits in the hollow, running north-south; Decatur runs eastward at a gentle slope down to the Radial, crosses it, and slopes upward again past my place. Happy Hollow angles down into the intersection from the southwest and doesn't emerge on the other side of the Radial. My vantage, then, was from an elevation across the highway; otherwise I don't know if I would have seen the flicker.

It was a brief yellow-orange glow behind the otherwise dark windshield of a gray Ford Tempo parked up ahead, on the opposite side of the street, alongside my building. The glow of a lighter. That identification came to me in a flicker as brief as the flicker of the flame itself, and the small hairs on the back of my neck came to attention.

The light changed, and I let the car idle through the intersection.

Although the building's address is Decatur Street, it faces the Radial. On the Decatur side, along the street, is a little six-car parking lot that my second-floor apartment overlooks. Whoever was parked in that Tempo had an ideal view of the lot and anyone who might come and go on that side of the building. Like me, for instance.

I glanced at the LED clock on my loaner's dashboard. One fifty-eight A.M. Strange hour of the night for people to be sitting in cars smoking cigarettes.

I had done enough sitting in cars at two in the morning to know a stakeout when I saw it.

I gave the gas pedal a nudge and pushed the car up the hill, past the Tempo, past the apartment building. The Tempo's interior was now completely dark again, and its tinted windows defeated the faint light from the streetlamps. I cruised up the hill and paused, my eyes on the rearview mirror. No sign of the Tempo pulling away from the curb to pursue me. The occupant or occupants hadn't recognized me, then, if they even got a decent look at my features in the dark.

I made a right at the top of the hill, onto Forty-fifth, then cut right again in the middle of the block, down the narrow, overgrown alley that bisects the block.

The alley runs along the south side of the apartment building, where there is another miniature parking lot. A little Buick, black or dark blue, was parked in the first slot, half up on the sidewalk fronting the building. The lettering on the nameplate on the back of the car, between the taillights, was cracked. It looked like BLICK. Because the car was parked with its nose toward the building, and because there's a floodlight on the building there, near the south stairs, I could clearly see the silhouettes of two heads above the front-seat headrests. I stole a glance at the rear license plate. Local. But there was a small metallic-looking decal on the bumper that might have been the kind rental agencies slap on their cars. I didn't have time to study it, though. The alley is rough and rutted, which gave me an excuse for traveling it slowly, but I didn't want to go so slowly that I would call attention to myself. I sure as hell didn't want to stop.

From the alley you can make only a right-hand turn onto the Radial. This I did, and headed on northward and then west as the Radial curved into the Benson district.

Though the night was cool, I realized I was sweating. I kicked down the car heater and cracked the window a couple of inches, and hoped the cool air would help me think.

There are eighteen apartments in the building, counting mine. Twenty-some people were living there at the time. Yet I didn't for an instant entertain the thought that the welcoming committee could have been for some other tenant.

Nor did I waste time trying to convince myself that the watchers were there for some benign purpose. What had happened to Robert Olson barely twenty-four hours earlier said quite the otherwise. His assailants must have realized their mistake not long after committing it. It wouldn't take a lot of expertise to find out they had hospitalized the wrong man. Hell, they may have just followed the ambulance—in which case they could have been lurking around the e.r. when I was there, therefore knew I wasn't home, therefore decided to break into my place and plan a surprise party for my return. Since the doors to those apartments are out in the wide open spaces, any of my neighbors coming or going would have scared off the would-be attackers. So they adopted Plan C—stake out the joint after dark and wait for me to come home if I was out, come out if I was home.

It fit. And except for the fact that I was on edge, more alert than usual, more on the lookout for little things I might otherwise not have noticed, it would have worked. I would have parked the car and strolled over to the building, as I had done probably thousands of times. It didn't matter which side of the building I parked on, or whether on the street or in one of the lots. The only way into the place if you're not Batman is up one of the two open stairways at the front of the building. And those two cars were perfectly positioned vis-à-vis the stairs: no one could possibly enter or leave the building without those cars' occupants seeing it.

Okay, so they were thorough. Who the hell *were* they?

The Radial curved westward away from my neighborhood; I followed it as far as Maple Street, then veered off onto Maple, due west. I was just driving. I didn't know where I was going. Not consciously, anyhow. Driving itself was the point of the exercise. There was little traffic; I could drift along these dark, narrow streets, these familiar streets of my home, on autopilot. In the darkness I was anonymous. Safe.

But the darkness would last only a few more hours, and I couldn't drive forever.

◇◇◇

Think, dammit. *Who?*

"He tripped over the footstool," I said. "He'll be all right."

"Yeah, but not you, *you bastard." I turned and looked back at Dimand. His face was a bloody mess, and blood still streamed from his nose, ruining his sweater. Tears of pain and rage and humiliation washed down his cheeks and disappeared into the hemorrhage. Oddly, though, his gray eyes were still cold, almost lifeless. "You are* dead, *asshole. You don't know who you're messing with."*

Steven Dimand had been right. I didn't know who I was messing with. A windbag, I figured, whose ego, not just muscles, got pumped up on the Nautilus. Had I underestimated the guy? It wouldn't be the first time I was wrong, and usually when I'm wrong I don't do it halfway.

Sure, there were plenty of people around who wouldn't have minded seeing me slip on a banana peel, but most of them either were in positions where they couldn't very well do anything about it or would have had ample opportunity to strike at me long before now if they had been so inclined. Dimand I had pissed off just this week. That made him the most likely candidate.

Okay, say these guys worked for Dimand. That told me who they were. Now who the aitch was *he?*

Whoever he was, he had connections. Not connections with a capital C, as in Cosa Nostra, but connections good enough to have or know how to get at least three bullyboys, and get them quickly. I was fairly confident that Dimand didn't have mob connections, at least not important ones. For one thing, the old stereotype is still valid: you have to be of Sicilian or at least Italian extraction to get into the club, and Dimand did not strike me as a Sicilian moniker. For another, *I* had a nodding acquaintance with the local outfit as well as the Chicago office, and I was pretty sure they wouldn't let out-of-towners come poaching on their preserve without some compelling reason. If they had that reason, I was pretty sure I would at least be tipped off in advance.

So I was pretty sure that Dimand was minor league at most. Pretty sure, pretty sure, pretty sure.

The flip side of that coin was that Dimand was so well connected, with a capital C, that he could not only go gunning for me in another gang's backyard, but also arrange it so that the local hoods, for whom I had done a couple of favors, wouldn't alert me to it.

Which brought me back around to the question I had started with: who the hell was Dimand?

One thing was certain, at least: I could not spend the night at home.

In fact, I didn't dare go near the place until I got some answers to some questions.

Who was Steven Dimand?

And what did I have to do to defuse him?

◇◇◇

I let Maple take me west as far as Highway 31; then I dropped back toward the south.

By now the car was no longer on autopilot: I was driving again. The trip out of town had cleared my head; the cool air whistling through the gap in the car window had crystallized my thoughts.

Decatur Street was out of bounds. So too were my friends. I had seen what they did to Robert, and that was accidental. What would they do if they decided to try to get at me through my friends? The best thing I could do for them right now—the only thing—was stay clear.

I had been working hard the last couple of days trying to

hold back my natural paranoia. Now I twisted the knob the other direction as far as it would go and invited the paranoia to flow freely. My delicate nerves had saved me from harm, or worse, back on Decatur Street. If I gave them half a chance, they just might keep me alive a little longer.

Highway 31 shot straight down into Millard, a southwestern suburb of Omaha. Near the Millard airport I swung off onto an unpaved road and, half a mile further on, off of that and into the dimly lighted yard of a self-storage center. The place was hardly convenient to my home, but it was open round-the-clock, and its remoteness was a plus. I signed the little slip that the pimply-faced kid in the gatehouse shoved under my nose, got back into the Nova, and drove among the barracks-like buildings until I came to mine, way back at the south end of the compound. It had a standard overhead garage door, same as all the rest in the joint. I unlocked the door, raised it, found the light switch, lowered the door, and locked it again from the inside.

There was a lot of junk in there under the unflattering illumination of the single bare light bulb. No particular order to it, either, or so it would seem to the casual observer. There were boxes of old files and papers and books and other stuff that didn't fit in my apartment or my life but which I didn't want to get rid of. Some old furniture. Some things that Jennifer, my sometimes-wife, had left behind. Some things that belonged to the uncle who raised me.

One of those things was a small, old-fashioned safe, black steel with gold-paint filigrees on the door. I kept it shoved clear to the back of the bay, where the light was no good owing to a makeshift shelf I had rigged up on the wall over it, and boxed it in with furniture and cartons. Now I cleared a path to it and worked the big, clunky dial, and the solid little door *ka-chunk*ed open and swung out as easily and silently as the day it had been made, three-quarters of a century ago.

Inside were some of my uncle's papers and memorabilia. Nothing too important. The important things I kept back at Decatur Street; the really important things I kept in the safe-deposit room at the Omaha National.

Except, that is, for a small brown envelope at the very bottom of the safe. It was an ancient, brittle bit of paper, the kind that has dime-sized paper disks on the back of the envelope and on the flap, and a bit of red floss to figure-eight around the disks by way of securing the contents. Nothing extraordinary or interesting about it. Which was the point.

I unwound the floss while I moved into better light. Then I shook out the envelope's contents onto the top of an old dresser that had been mine when I was a kid. The envelope contained four smaller and newer envelopes, standard manila variety, unsealed. Each of those envelopes, in turn, contained various papers and cards in the name of four different individuals.

My secret identities.

They were not forgeries. Each of them, every birth certificate, every Social Security card, every driver's license, passport, passbook, credit card—all of it—was strictly legit, inasmuch as it had been issued by the appropriate agency, department, or institution. It's just that they had been issued to dead men.

I had kept these secret identities as my hole cards since my early days in the private-investigation dodge. Not many of those days had had to pass before I realized that a guy in this line of work could get people pretty ticked off at him, and that someday it might be prudent to take a vacation and not leave an easily followed trail when you did.

Going about the task was easy. I had tumbled to the method by accident, when a matter I had been investigating suddenly required an immediate trip to Europe. Naturally, I didn't have a passport. I hopped a flight to Chicago, which was the nearest place I could get a passport on the spot, and only then discovered that the birth certificate which had served me in good stead for nearly three decades, which had gone to school with me and gone to war with me and gotten married with me and done all the typical stuff a birth certificate is supposed to do, had never been notarized. It was not, in the eyes of the passport office, sufficient proof of my having been born, and without that the passport was no go.

In a panic I called the Douglas County Courthouse to see what could be done quickly. That was easy: I show up downtown and give them some loot and they give me a valid certificate. But I'm out of town. No problem: mail us the loot. But I need it *right now.* So send a friend. All he needs is your name and date of birth. And the loot, of course.

Boing.

Shortly after I got back from Europe, I set about collecting the first identity. It was startlingly easy. I combed through obituaries in back issue of the *World-Herald* in search of guys about my age who were no longer residents of this mortal coil. Thanks to a little thing called the War in Vietnam, there were plenty to choose from. The only criteria were age and race and that they had been born in Douglas County.

Patrick Francis Kilpatrick. John David Goldman. Charles Michael D'Agosta. Roger Jeffrey Nelson. That's me. I chose these four for resurrection not only on the basis of the criteria mentioned, but also because of the commonness of the names. The world is full of Kilpatricks, Goldmans, D'Agostas, and Nelsons. If I ever got cornered I could simply say, Nah, you're thinking of some other Roger Nelson.

Once I was armed with the birth certificates—acquired over a period of a couple of years, lest I become a familiar face at the courthouse—everything else fell into place. Social Security number. Driver's license. I had to take the driving test five times, once for myself and once for each of my deceased friends, but that was all right. I got a higher score each time. With the IDs, I opened small bank accounts. Approximately fourteen minutes later, BankAmericard and Master-Charge—as Visa and MasterCard were known in those days—as well as eighty-eight department stores, gas stations, and other enterprises were after me, which is to say my alter egos, to sign up. Hell, in those happy-go-lucky days of easy credit, some places just sent the cards, uninvited. They were free.

Periodically, in a kind of informal rotation, I would use the cards and promptly pay the bills, which came to me circuitously, via a series of blind-alley mail drops I carefully established, using the appropriate checks. In that way I established real live credit histories for these really dead men.

The system was not perfect. There was no true employment history, for one thing, except for the fictions I invented for various application forms, no school records, medical histories, and so on. My mail drops gave me a certain degree of security, but I knew a dedicated investigator could conceivably trace the trail to me eventually. But I always figured that if the situation was such that I had to go to ground and truly adopt one or more of these identities, a bill collector was going to be the least of my worries.

I put everything back into the appropriate envelopes, stuffed them into the large envelope, and returned to the safe.

There were a dozen small red boxes in the back of the safe. I pulled them out and took them to the dresser. The boxes were the kind that check blanks come in, and they contained my canceled checks and deposit slips dating back to before you were born, almost before I was born. I lifted the lid on the first box, removed the stack within, slipped off the rubber band, and began to quickly shuffle through the old papers. Every so often I came across a bit of legal tender, folded and centered so as to be invisible to anyone who simply picked up the stack and riffled the edges.

Twenties and fifties. Nothing larger. Many of them going back quite a few treasury secretaries. By the time I finished with the last box I had quite a pile of bills on the dresser. By the time I got them unfolded and counted, I had about fourteen hundred dollars, cash.

I knew it had to have been a thousand or more by now, after my years of diligently squirreling away a nugget here and there against a cold winter to come. I had no idea exactly how much, though, because I had purposely kept no accounting of it, lest I be tempted to raid it to cover ordinary expenses. To stay away from that money, to fool myself into forgetting it was even there, had required a supreme effort of will at times, times when the wolf was at the door and had brought several of his friends. I knew, or sensed, that that was about the limit of my willpower—that if I started dipping into this emergency fund for nonemergencies, the balance would never be restored.

I closed up the safe and hid it again, pocketed the cash and the big brown envelope, and went back to the car after triple-checking the lock on the overhead door. Then I drove back to town, where Patrick Francis Kilpatrick rented a hotel room.

9

I lay awake and stared at the dark ceiling. I may have slept; if so, I was not aware of it; I did not dream. The ceiling had a rough texture to it, little nubs and knobs, and the pale, bluish light that slipped in between the heavy, plastic-lined drapes over the window made long, pointed shadows behind every bump and protrusion. Cold and blue-white, it looked like an alien landscape, like Hollywood's vision of other worlds in those ridiculous sci-fi flicks I used to sit through goggle-eyed when I was a kid. In my semiconscious state, it seemed to me that the bed was on the ceiling and I was looking down on this bleak terrain, as if I was in some kind of spacecraft, getting ready to set down, to boldly go where no man has gone before, as they say. Whether or not I wanted to.

Eventually I rolled onto one side and drew my knees toward my chest and tried to be as small as possible.

10

When I woke, if in fact I had slept at all, I was far from refreshed—although, curiously, not tired. A little weary, perhaps, a little worn, but not tired, if you appreciate the distinction. Chalk it up to adrenaline. Or fear.

Whichever, it infused in me a kind of resolve that crackled at its edges with nervous energy. It would be too much to say that I had a plan; I had nothing in mind that I could set to paper in good outline form. But a great many random thoughts and feelings, ignited by that small orange flame behind the windshield in front of my apartment, were beginning slowly to drift together, to collect and congeal, coalesce, into something that would eventually evolve into a plan, a course of action.

In the meantime I knew subconsciously, at least, what steps had to be taken. And which had to be avoided.

Step One was to shower and dress in yesterday's clothes. I had no razor or deodorant or salon-formula styling mousse. I would have to acquire such necessities, as well as some new duds, fairly quickly. I made do with what was available. Fortunately, the Ramada thoughtfully provided soap and Vidal Sassoon shampoo.

Step Two was to get on the phone. I called my friendly Chevy dealer and made arrangements to keep my car on ice, saying something vague about having to go out of town for a while. There were no strenuous objections on the other end— in fact, they were glad of the leeway, since they were having more trouble finding a prehistoric Impala fender than they had anticipated—though there was some understandable concern about the loaner. I assured him I'd get it back to him before the day was out.

It wasn't that I was all that concerned about my wheels; it

was just that I knew that when cars reach that vintage, they start becoming conspicuous. The last thing I needed or wanted at the moment, under the circumstances. Fixed or not, the car had to stay on blocks for a while at least.

Step Three was to call Pat Costello. It was nearly eight; he would be at the store—and he would be the only one at the store, which opened at nine. He answered on the third ring. "Tenth Street Pharmacy."

"Hi, I need a prescription refilled."

He paused for only a beat. Anyone eavesdropping wouldn't have caught it.

"Sure thing, sir. What's the number on it?"

I gave him the phone number of the hotel. "And my name is Patrick Kilpatrick." So he would know whose room to ask for when he called back.

"Okay, Mr. Kilpatrick, we'll take care of it."

"You always have," I said, and hung up.

Fifteen minutes later the phone rang. "Pat Kilpatrick," I said into the receiver.

"Where are you?" Costello said.

"The Ramada at Seventy-second and Grover. Where are you?"

"Grossenberg's." That was what the neighborhood people had always called a tiny medical-arts building three or four blocks from the drugstore Pat Costello runs. Old Doctor Grossenberg's two boys, both doctors and both well into their fifties, ran their practices from the building, and a dentist leased the basement level from them. I knew there was an old-fashioned wooden phone-booth outside the dentist's waiting-room door.

I said, "For an old guy, you catch on pretty quick."

Pat grunted into his receiver. "I figured it would look funny if I hung up the phone, ran out of the store, and used the pay phone across the street. This way, anyone who cares thinks I have a dentist appointment. *Does* anybody care?"

"I couldn't say. Tell you what—stay where you are; I'll pick you up in half an hour."

He sighed. "That means I got to let Tommy run the store." Tommy was one of Pat's innumerable kids. "I might as well call my lawyer, tell her to start the paperwork on my bankruptcy. Hey, Nebraska—you okay?"

I had to give it some thought.

"I haven't the vaguest idea," I finally said.

The clinic sits on a corner and is built into a shallow hill. You can enter upstairs, on the street level, where the Grossenberg boys have their offices, or you can come in on the lower level via the tiny parking lot behind the building. I swung the Nova up by this back door and waited. After a few minutes Pat Costello stuck his dark head out the glass door and looked tentatively toward the car. I had forgotten he wouldn't know what I was driving, and the Nova's windows were tinted enough to make it hard to see who was behind the wheel.

I popped the door and half-emerged, angling my head up above roof level. "Anybody here call a cab?"

Pat got in. "What's the story?"

I backed out and got to the street again and just drove through the familiar/strange neighborhood I had grown up in—a neighborhood of small houses, brick or stucco mostly, some in dire need of repair, some picture-perfect, all with trim, tidy little front yards; a neighborhood of small mom-and-pop groceries, corner drugstores, taverns with names like Bud's Place and The Tally-Ho; a neighborhood of narrow streets and narrower alleys and people who were born and raised here by parents who were born and raised here. The complexion of the neighborhood, literally and figuratively, may change; the names and the names' places of origin may change; the accents in the voices of the older residents may change; but the neighborhood itself remains the same, immutable.

Likewise the friendship between Pat and me. Time had no more influence on that than it did on the neighborhood. We had known each other all our lives—literally in my case, figuratively in Pat's, since he's five years older—and whether we see each other daily or annually, the friendship is just as solid as ever. We can almost pick up the conversation where it left off, no matter how much time has passed, as soon as we get together again. That kind of friendship has occurred in my life so infrequently that I still think it's downright phenomenal.

I filled Pat in, taking pains to distinguish between what I

knew—not much—and what I believed, felt, or inferred. It
didn't take long. Pat and I speak the same language.

"You think they're keeping an eye on your friends?"

"I have no way of knowing," I said. "That's how come all the
monkey business when I called you, just in case they had your
place scoped, just in case they had a wire on your phone. My
guess is that they don't, that they haven't reached that point
yet. After all, they pounced on Robert, thinking he was me—
I'm quite sure of that now—what, thirty-some hours ago is all.
They knew they had erred within a matter of hours, probably
started monitoring my place at sundown. Obviously they
know now that I didn't come home last night, which may or
may not make them think I'm wise to them. The prudent
course for them would be to assume I am and figure that I've
gone to ground—meanwhile keeping tabs on the apartment
in case I'm *not* wise to them."

"And move on to Plan B—keeping an eye on your friends,
places you frequent, and so on."

"It's about Plan D for them, by my count, but yeah, that's the
gist of it." We were stopped for a light in front of the old St.
Joe's hospital, the original brick behemoth on Dorcas Street,
not the slick new sand-colored model down by Creighton University. I looked at Pat. "And what it means is, despite my
precautions, I may have put you in danger by getting in touch
with you. If so, all I can do is apologize."

Pat shrugged it off. He's a tall, skinny fellow—though he'd
been developing a small potbelly the past couple of years—
with a long, olive-complected face and jet-black hair he
combs up and back the way Elvis used to. And may still, if the
accounts in the supermarket tabloids were accurate. If Elvis
was alive, why would he live in Kalamazoo? The question was
important to me, since it was obvious that I had to drop out
of sight too—though not for as long as Presley had, I hoped.

"Forget about it," Pat said easily. "You've taken what
precautions you could. Me too—calling you back from the
dentist's office and all. If they weren't good enough, well, hell,
we tried at least. The thing of it is, my friend, if these people—
or anyone—wanted to get at you through one of your friends,
there's not a hell of a lot any of us could do about it."

"That cheers me up no end, Pat. Too bad Typhoid Mary
didn't know you."

He shrugged again.

I looped through the streets of the neighborhood north of St. Joe's, the old Italian district, cutting a leisurely, indirect trail toward downtown. There was little traffic. Which is what I had hoped for, and why I was putting miles on the loaner on these residential streets. Tailing someone when there's almost no traffic is even harder than tailing someone in heavy traffic. I could think of no earthly way that Dimand's boys—which is how I was thinking of them by now—could possibly have picked up on me, but you never know. If they were quicker and more thorough than I hoped, they may have had wires on the phones of my close friends. It would have taken no detective work at all to learn those friends' names. When I called Pat, they may not have fallen for the Rx gag, followed him from the store, and been in the bushes somewhere when I picked him up.

It would require a hell of a lot of manpower—I don't have thousands of friends, but I have several good ones—and a hell of a lot of resources. Which made the scenario unlikely. Not impossible; just unlikely.

At any rate, we were in the clear at the moment.

"So what is it you need me to do," Pat was saying, "besides cheer you up? Want me to go by your place and pick up a few things for you?"

"Absolutely not. That address is off-limits for everybody, not just me. These guys'll keep the place under surveillance, you can bet the store on that. They see you go in and come out with a suitcase, they'll know they can get at me through you."

"Wouldn't be the first time I shook a tail," Pat sniffed.

"That wouldn't bother them. They'd drop by the house to chat with you. If you weren't in, they'd chat with your wife and kids until you got home. No, forget you ever even knew where I live, Pat."

He admitted defeat. "So what *can* I do?"

I slid a hand inside my sport coat and produced two envelopes. Hotel stationery. I handed them to Pat. "Mail those for me when you get a chance, will you? Sorry I don't have any stamps."

"You can owe me the fifty cents." He glanced at the addresses before cramming the envelopes into his shirt pocket.

"One's to my landlord, explaining that I've been called out of town unexpectedly. I've enclosed a couple months' rent."

"Christ, Nebraska—"

"Well, I *hope* to be reinstated long before then, but I have no idea. The other's a letter to Mike Kennerly. It explains briefly what's going on, and it contains a note for him to give to Kim Banner if I'm not back in a couple of months. That note outlines my suspicions, in case she decides to follow up on it."

"She's a homicide cop," Pat said needlessly.

"If I'm not back in a couple months, or at least back in touch, then it will be a homicide case."

Pat drew in a lungful of air and let it out slowly. "Look, pal, why don't you just tell Banner about this now and let her and her friends in the PD handle it?"

"Koosje asked me the same question . . . Jesus, was it just last night? Seems ages. Anyhow, at that time my answer was that I didn't know if there was anything to handle—anything beyond a case of nerves on my part, that is. The situation has changed completely since then. Now my answer is that bringing the law down on these guys' heads will do more harm than good."

"It will get them off your back."

I wagged my head. "Those guys aren't my problem. My immediate problem, sure, but not my *real* problem. See, these guys keeping tabs on me, they're pros."

Pat snorted.

"Yeah, they screwed up with Robert and they botched breaking into my place and they gave themselves away last night—but only the last of those was a real foul-up. The first was a natural mistake to make, the second was probably bad luck. Anyhow, my point is, Dimand didn't just round up a couple of thugs to come break my legs. He brought in some talent. That tells me two things. First, the cops can roust that talent and apply heat, but they won't sweat anything out of them—because they're pros. Second, Dimand has the resources, know-how, and determination to enlist that kind of talent—which means he'd be able to do it again if the first wave fails. You see? Take care of the surveillance team and all you've done is cut off a toe when the whole leg needs amputating."

Pat mulled it over a bit. Then he said, "Well, at least tell Banner what's going on and what you intend to do about it. If you're going underground, you need a lifeline back to the surface. She's better qualified than me. Or Kennerly."

"You're right. But I'm keeping her in the dark for her own sake. I don't exactly know yet what's going to happen—mainly because I don't know who Dimand is, how powerful or well connected he may be, so I don't know what I may have to do to shake loose of him. It may develop that Banner would be better off not knowing in advance."

I felt his dark, liquid eyes on me. "So what are you telling me, you're going to go to Minneapolis and kill this s.o.b.?"

"Oh, if only it were that simple." I glanced at him. "I'm joking. Halfways. If I thought slapping Dimand down would take care of the problem, that's what I would do. But I don't know that. Because, again, I don't know Dimand. If he's connected, then my riding in on a white stallion and whacking him is only going to make things worse for me. If he's not connected—if he's got connections but isn't *connected*—if he's just a bad sport with lots of dough who knows some of the wrong kind of guys, then I can probably take care of him without taking him out of the game. I don't know. That's the whole fucking problem—I don't know what I'm dealing with, who I'm dealing with." The anger and frustration that had been bottled inside me I don't know how long—at least since I realized that Robert Olson's assailants had thought they were beating up on me—spilled over into those last few words. I gripped the steering wheel tightly. Dark spots swam before my eyes. It passed quickly. I let out a breath. "So I guess I'll have to find out," I said.

I tried to make it sound light, offhand. Nobody in the car was fooled.

◇◇◇

As we wound through downtown Omaha, Pat sensed that my driving had become purposeful.

"Where are we headed?"

"Eppley."

"The airport? You're leaving already?"

"No, not quite yet. I have a couple of errands yet to do. You can help me with the first of them."

We drove out to the airport, where Roger Jeffrey Nelson rented a car for me. I chose Nelson because I had half a suspicion that my expenses were going to be stiff, stiff enough that I would have to bust out one of the identities—basically, take it for all it was worth, run up heavy credit-card charges, bounce some checks, and abandon it. I hoped it wouldn't come to that, not so much because it would leave the various card companies and banks holding the bag and was, in a word, felonious, but because if the sums involved were great enough, the injured parties might decide it was worth the effort to seriously investigate. I knew my blind wasn't perfect. The threads all led back to me, if someone wanted to spend the time and money to unravel them. And then I'd be in hot water up to my chinny-chin-chin.

Which is sort of where I was already.

Anyhow, I didn't know if I would have much choice, and Nelson was the candidate. With my coloring, I can pass for a Kilpatrick, a Goldman, or a D'Agosta with no problem. But a Nelson. . . . Not all Nelsons are blond, blue-eyed Scandihoovians, of course—just as not all Kilpatricks, Goldmans, and D'Agostas are *not* blue-eyed blonds—but enough of them are that I felt most comfortable sacrificing poor old Rog, if worse came to worst.

Rog, at least, took it well. He rented me a nice Chevy Celebrity sedan, dark gray. "Graphite," according to the papers, but it looked gray to me. It was a coin-toss between a Celebrity and a Taurus, because they're about the most popular cars on the road and therefore the most anonymous. I'm partial to Chevys. That the bad guys were driving a Ford entered into it too.

Pat drove the Nova and I tailed him to Rosen-Novak to return their property. Then I gave him a lift back to the neighborhood, dropping him off at Grossenberg's.

Just in case anyone *was* interested.

Before he got out of the car, Pat said, "Look, Nebraska, you gotta at least keep in touch with *me.*"

"Not a good idea, pal. What if I'm not just paranoid, but paranoid and *right?* Anyone doing five minutes' worth of homework knows you and I have a lot of history. They'll be expecting me to be in touch with you."

Pat scowled, and the fine lines around his eyes and mouth deepened. "Dammit, what if something goes wrong on this end? What if they decide to grab Koosje to lure you out of the woodwork? How're you gonna know? We have to have some way of keeping in contact, making sure things are copacetic on either end."

He was right, and I admitted as much. "Give me time to think," I said. "I'll be in touch."

Pat gave me a long look. "You damn well better be," he said, yanking up on the door handle.

11

I had many errands to run, many chores to perform. They were all the more exhausting for my performing them with one eye out for unwelcome company, all the more exhausting for knowing I had no home to return to when I was done. My home, effectively, had been stolen from me; my friends, too, since I feared that contact with me—even merely by telephone—would put them in danger. *More* danger: just knowing me could prove hazardous to them, as it had to Robert.

I ate alone that evening. I felt relatively secure in the anonymity of the hotel restaurant. If Dimand's men had been able to trace me there that quickly, then they were pretty damn good and they deserved to have me. Mostly, though, I felt cooped up, trapped—far too boxed in to face the prospect of dining in the even smaller box of my room.

After dinner I slipped into the bar next to the restaurant, where I nursed a cup of coffee for a quarter of an hour while making sure no one whom I had seen in the restaurant had followed me into the bar. I said I felt *relatively* secure.

At about seven-thirty I left the hotel. I was early for an appointment I had set up, but that was all right. The Celebrity had felt a little sluggish when I was running my errands around town, so I got it out of the lot now, took it to the Amoco across from the hotel, and shoved a bottle of Gumout into the gas tank. Then I drove south the block or so to the Interstate on-ramp and pointed the little sedan's nose westward.

Acceleration was slow, but I eventually ran the needle up to fifty-five and kicked in the cruise control. I told myself I was getting the feel of the car, seeing what it could do, and to an extent that was true. More than once my skin's been saved by my knowing exactly what the old Impala could do—and, more typically, what it could not. I had become pretty well acquainted with the Celebrity by way of jamming around in it all day, but that was stop-and-go city traffic nonsense. I wanted to see what it had under the hood.

And I wanted to think. I put a lot of miles on cars driving and thinking. It may not do much for the energy crisis—anyone remember that?—but it usually seems to help me. I don't know if it's the act of driving that diverts the mind and allows the subconscious to tackle whatever puzzles, problems, or concerns are uppermost, or, more simply, if it's the soothing motion of the automobile and the hum of the tires on the pavement, or, more simply still, if it's just getting the hell out and about—but it generally works.

Toward the west edge of town, Interstate 80 veers southward while I-680 peels off toward the north. I followed the latter route. I-29, I-80, and I-680 form something of a ring around the city; 680 runs more or less due north, from the direction I was traveling, to about Irvington, then veers eastward. You can follow it across the Missouri into Iowa, where it merges with Interstate 29, and then southward back to the Big O or northward through Iowa and the Dakotas and, eventually, to the Canadian border. A tempting thought: just keep on driving. I shrugged it off, with not a little difficulty. Just as I had done the other umpty-hundred times the notion popped to the surface today.

The car was warming up nicely now, running more smoothly as the coke and sludge that had clogged it up began to dissolve. I tapped the brake pedal briefly to disengage the cruise control, let gravity slow the car to about forty-five, then jammed the gas pedal to the floor. The car hesitated a moment, as if confused about my sudden change of mind, then it farted and shuddered and surged forward, easily accelerating to seventy miles an hour. By then we were to the Mormon Bridge and across the Missouri River and into Iowa. I eased back on the accelerator and let the needle drop to sixty-five, where I kicked in the cruise control again.

At the appropriate point I followed 680 north, where it flows into Interstate 29, and stayed with it as far as the first exit. There I again vanquished the impulse to just keep on going and instead doubled back around to follow the same route back to town.

Almost, at least. Just over the Mormon Bridge, I took the Thirtieth Street exit southward, into North Omaha.

It is a historic part of town, this area that used to be Florence, Nebraska. There is an ancient mill there, which I drove past now as I had hundreds of times before without really noticing it. It contains portions of the oldest existing structure in the Omaha area.

The mill was built by the Mormons. In 1846, during their migration from Illinois to the Salt Lake Valley, the Mormons built dozens of communities in Iowa and Nebraska. One of the largest stood about where I now drove. Winter Quarters, they called it. More than three thousand people lived there, coming in waves as their great westward trek continued. A tenth of them died there, from various diseases that swept the community.

I swung off onto State Street and found the Mormon Cemetery. I hadn't been there in eons, but they hadn't moved it.

I drove past the main entrance to the far side of the cemetery, the Thirty-fourth Street side, and found a parking place. There's a nice paved lot over to the other side, just south of the cute little visitors' center that the Mormons run, but I learned at a tender age that you don't want to park there. The Mormons as a whole are a grand bunch of people, I'm sure, but given half a chance one of their troops will zero in on you like a fly on a drop of honey, and stick about the same, and want to give you the grand tour, including the slide show, and will be just so effing nice and all that you can't bring yourself to tell 'em to go climb a rope. After about the first such experience, you learn to back-door it and hope no one across the street spots you.

I did; they didn't.

It was quite dark, except for the artificial illumination, and that was fine. A few blocks east, traffic rattled and grumbled on Thirtieth Street, but here all was peaceful.

I sat on a low bench in front of the bronze statue that is the memorial's centerpiece. It depicts a pioneer couple standing over their infant's prairie grave, a monument not only to those who died that terrible winter but also to the determination of those who didn't.

After a few minutes of serene contemplation, I got company. It came up the curved path from the main entrance and stopped near me and said, "Helluva place for a rendezvous."

"Local color," I said.

The other man looked around. "Too dark here to see any

colors," he said, and hunkered into his long black overcoat. "It's freezing."

"It's brisk. Take a pew." I patted the bench next to me.

Tom Carra looked around a bit and then sat, or perched, on the edge of the bench. He was uneasy, out in the open like that. I said, "Relax, Tom. This is high ground. You can see anybody coming from any direction, but sitting like this gives us a low profile, makes us lousy targets for anyone below."

He smiled crookedly. "You figure all the angles, huhn, Nebraska."

"My *New Yorker* subscription's paid up through next year, and I'd hate to see the money wasted."

"Huhn?"

Carra is muscle for the local outfit, and he carries much of that muscle around between his ears. But we had some history between us, Tom and I, and I felt more comfortable with him than with any of his colleagues. Which means I had my revolver in my coat pocket instead of in my lap.

"Skip it," I said. "How's business?"

He shrugged his massive shoulders. "Same old sixes and sevens. You could've asked me that over the phone."

"I'm not just being polite. Anything happening I should know about?"

He looked at me levelly.

"Look, Carra, where do we stand, you and me?"

He thought about it. "I got nothin' against you."

"And your boss?"

"Who, Tarantino? Him neither, far as I know. You did Baron Mike a big favor, Nebraska, and that makes Tarantino look good back in Chicago." Paul Tarantino was the local chief; Baron Mike was Mike Berenelli, one of the big bosses back in Illinois. I hadn't done him as big a favor as he thought, but I wasn't disabusing anybody of the notion. It never hurts to have markers to call in, and anyway that business was part of what was costing me my license—I should get something for my trouble, I figured.

"So you know anything about some buttons hanging around my front door lately?"

The big man shook his head slowly. "Not our guys," he said.

"I didn't reckon they were your guys. What I want to know

is, do you know anything about them? In other words, did Tarantino give them his blessing?"

Carra frowned. "Why would he do that for imported talent? If he wanted you whacked, we got guys here could do it."

"I know. I'm sitting next to one of them. Try to focus, Tom. Work on getting some of that hemoglobin up into the gray matter."

"Huhn?"

"Much better. The question is, has anyone from out of town put the finger on me, and if so did he do it with Tarantino's okay?"

The frown grew deeper; Carra's deep-set eyes all but disappeared beneath it. "I never heard nothin' about nothin' like that."

There it was. I always figured Carra was too stupid to lie well, if at all. So I was about ninety-nine and forty-four one-hundredths percent sure that I could buy what he was peddling. The problem was, Carra's employers, knowing that he and I had done some business now and then, and knowing Carra was no rocket scientist, might have kept him in the dark to prevent him from even accidentally tipping me.

A reasonably remote possibility, I told myself. The Omaha operation is an offshoot of the Chicago–Kansas City action. Though profitable, it isn't large—and it's tough to keep secrets in a small organization. My guess was that Carra would have heard *something,* and having heard it would be too slow-witted to do much of a job of keeping it from me.

Too bad it was only a guess.

Carra said, "Some wise guys giving you trouble, Nebraska? Maybe we can do something about that. . . ."

"That occurred to me," I said, and it was true. As I said, I had some goodwill stored up with Carra's bosses. It made me feel like the mouse in those old cartoons: if the cat got too obstreperous, I could always call on my friend the bulldog to cut him down to size.

But calling in the badguys had the same attendant problem as calling in the goodguys—namely, they could handle the guys watching my apartment, but what about the guy or guys behind them? And with the mob, I had one more problem— even after meeting with Carra, I could not be absolutely certain that these jokers weren't operating with the Omaha boss's okay.

"Let's see if I can't get out from under on my own first," I said vaguely.

Carra shrugged. "Your funeral."

"You have a lovely way of putting things. You ever heard of someone named Steven Dimand?"

He made a face. "Yeah—he sang that dumb 'Song Sung Blue' thing, didn't he?"

"Yeah, that's him, all right." Carra having not heard of Dimand didn't mean Dimand wasn't connected, just that he wasn't well known to those in the trade. It meant he wasn't a mobster; it didn't mean he wasn't cozy with one.

Carra made a noise and tried to fit more of himself into his overcoat. "Christ, it's freezin' out here. What'cha want to go meeting outside on a night like this? Don't you know any good bars or restaurants?"

"I like the outdoors," I said. "More exits."

He did the noise again. You might call it a *brrr,* but only if you'd call the noise an antitank gun makes a *bang.* It was a little like sitting next to a bomber as the pilot guns the engines. "Place gives me the creeps," Carra said. "What is this, some kinda cemetery or something?"

"You're kidding," I said. "You've never been here? Mormon Cemetery?"

"I been on the Mormon Bridge. . . ."

"Next best thing, I guess. . . ."

"Hey, are we done here? I want to go thaw out."

I studied his pleasantly ugly features for a few seconds. He had the perfect poker face. And I doubt he even knew it.

"Clear out, Tom," I said, and he did.

I lingered a bit longer, studying the statue. What I knew about the Mormons would fill a thimble—maybe—and most of it's probably wrong to boot. But I knew they had been here, near what is now Omaha, and I knew they left; what I never figured out was why. Why didn't they stay? They left Illinois in the face of persecution, but there was no persecution here— they were about the only pioneers on the block, except for the troops at Fort Omaha. They got along well with the Indian population. They built a temporary camp that was so well constructed and designed that no one but the Mormons believed it was temporary. So why didn't they just save themselves a lot of trouble and hang out along the Missouri?

Some people just don't know when to quit.

I was one of them. Kim Banner once told me I never really got going good on a case until I had been fired from it. Pigheaded, she called me. I like "resolute" better, but there was more than a little truth to it all the same.

I had spent the better part of the day talking myself out of pulling a permanent vanishing act. It would be easy. I had plenty of phony IDs, a little money . . . I could basically reinvent myself someplace else, as someone else. And this was not the first time that that impulse had come over me. After all, what did I have that was so swell that I couldn't bear to leave it behind? My rented digs on Decatur Street? My ancient rustbucket? My glorious career? Except for Koosje and maybe half a dozen friends worthy of the name and some distant relations I see about as often as we see a reduction in the National Debt, I had absolutely nothing that I couldn't have anywhere else on the planet. So why not let it go? Why not concede the match to Dimand? Why not permanently adopt one of those alternate identities in my pocket—any of whom was in better financial shape than I was—and just disappear? Why not?

I didn't have any good answers.

Except, maybe, that this was my home, and these were my friends, and this was my tattered little career as a detective and my fledgling little career as a writer. I didn't have so much that I couldn't afford to build again from scratch, but what I had was mine, and not to be lightly discarded.

Pigheaded. I could live with that. I wasn't at all sure I could live with myself any other way. When I suggested that running away was the easy out, Eric Sperry had disagreed. Now I knew what he must have meant.

I looked at the statues, at the parents' faces. Equal parts grief and determination. Say what you will about the Mormons, they were determined. They had fought and died to find a new home.

I was determined too, now. I would fight, and with luck not die, to keep my home. Even if I had to first abandon it to do so.

12

How long before the bulb went out? They always seem to pop when you turn the lamp on; if you never turn it off, and therefore never turn it on again, will the light bulb just burn forever?

Thoughts on a midnight stakeout.

The bulb in question was the one screwed into a table lamp in my living room. I had turned the lamp on last night, before I went out for the evening. It was still glowing behind the living-room drapes, still waiting for me to come home. I could see it from my hiding place, across the highway from the apartment building and partway up the curve of Happy Hollow Boulevard, not far from where I had first spotted the surveillance team nearly twenty-four hours ago. The gang was all here.

They had not been there during the daylight hours, when I had made a point of swinging by in the course of my errand-running. Not too surprising, that; it's hard enough to keep a place staked out, doubly so in a heavy-traffic residential neighborhood in broad daylight. I reasoned that they would wait until dark to set up again, and toyed with running upstairs and grabbing a few necessities. I quickly nixed the notion. Just because they weren't readily apparent on the street didn't mean they didn't have an eye on the place. My nemesis had gone to a lot of trouble and expense already; it was folly to assume he was covering only the obvious angles. It wasn't worth the risk, I decided, not even to rescue my Atra razor, my Gold Toe socks, and all the neat junk I've bought at Target over the years.

Now it was just shy of midnight, and I had been sitting in my graphite Chevrolet for not quite half an hour, waiting, watching the late-night traffic whisk by, thinking about the life-span of light bulbs.

I had given the old homestead a drive-by first, of course. The Tempo wasn't in position; that slot was filled by a yellow Volkswagen Rabbit that I knew belonged to one of the home-owners along the street. *They've gone away,* I thought gid-dily. *They know I'm onto them, so they've decided to forget about it!*

Episodes like that last about fourteen seconds, but they're nice while they last.

The BLICK was about where it had been parked last night. I got into position across the street and started peering around, looking for the Ford, wishing I had thought to have one of my four credit-card-loaded secret identities pick up a pair of binoculars for me. But I finally spotted the Tempo with my naked eyes. It sat not far from last night's location, on a little strip of pavement that runs perpendicular to Deca-tur, connecting the street and the parking lot of another apartment building half a block north of mine. The car was half-hidden by several old maples in the little rectangle of yard bounded by the Radial, Decatur, the parking lot, and the alley leading to the lot.

Whether the Tempo had moved for strategic reasons or just because someone else was parked in its previous location, the occupant or occupants had as good a vantage as they had had last night.

I gave the matter some thought, wishing I still smoked, wishing I could start the car and run the heater. Which I sure could, if I didn't mind my playmates seeing the exhaust from my car.

The short street or alley that runs from Decatur to the other apartment building doesn't go anywhere else; it has no access except from Decatur Street. Still, I could maybe park back in the neighborhood somewhere, thread through backyards on foot, and sneak up behind the Tempo, six-shooter in hand. And then what? Let's say I decommissioned the Tempo team. And let's say they weren't in walkie-talkie or cellular contact with the Buick team—which I wasn't set to bet much money, or my life on. I then could sneak around the south side of the building and repeat my glorious escapade. Then what? Call the cops and have these guys charged with loitering? That would show them I meant business, all right. Yessir, they'd think twice about messing with this hombre again.

Besides, just because I had spotted only those two cars

didn't mean there weren't more, or other hidden watchers just waiting to come out of the woodwork.

Anyhow, the whole scenario addressed the symptom and not the disease, as I had told Pat Costello. Nice fantasy, though.

The rental agency had thoughtfully given me two sets of keys to the Celebrity. Now I shoved the spare ignition key into the switch, turned it to the accessories position, and flipped on the radio, very low. The reason you do this with a spare key is so that, if something goes down and you leap from the car in pursuit of badguys, you don't come back to find you've locked your keys in the car.

I hunkered down in the seat. No heroics tonight. Tonight we kept our eyes open and learned what we could learn.

There are many similarities between the two career paths I have followed; one of the biggest is that the core of each consists of tedious, even boring work. People think that both jobs, investigator and writer, are exciting and glamorous. And they are—maybe one one-hundredth of the time. The rest of the time, it's just doing the job. Sitting at the type-writer, trying to get the thoughts that were so clear in your mind to gel properly on paper. Sitting behind the wheel of a parked car, listening to "vintage rock" and waiting for some-thing to happen.

I tried to think like the badguys. It used to alarm me how easy that is to do. Not anymore. The main difference between the badguys and the goodguys is that the badguys act on what the rest of us pretty much only daydream about. Criminolo-gists and others have all sorts of theories as to why this should be so. My theory is it's because they're badguys.

Darkness fell early these short autumn days. By five it was already dark enough that you would feel safe staking out a place. I might be inclined to wait until six or so, however, to give traffic time to thin out good. On the other end, then, while it would still be pretty dark at seven A.M., the work force would be hitting the pavement. You'd want to have wrapped it up by then. Figure a good twelve or thirteen hours of useful darkness, then, at this time of year. Too long to reasonably expect one team to stay on duty and alert.

I was betting on a shift change halfway through, sometime between midnight and one A.M.

The spooks didn't disappoint me. At 12:41 by my watch, a

light-colored Accord came up the Radial, northbound, turned onto Decatur, and pulled over to the curb. There's no parking on that side of the street at that point, so when the Accord's brake lights went off, I sat up in my seat. I watched while they waited—a brief wait, though it didn't seem so at the time—and then I noticed the Tempo's headlights flicker briefly on, then off.

The person or persons in the Accord noticed it too, for the brake lights immediately came on, then, momentarily, the backup lights as the driver shifted from Park through Reverse to Drive. He nudged the Accord away from the curb and into the mouth of the dead-end street where the Tempo was parked.

They were pretty good. If you weren't watching, weren't looking for it, you might not even have noticed. But I was watching, and I was looking for it.

The Accord paused in the middle of the road, even with the Tempo. As if they had rehearsed it—which maybe they had—the four men involved popped open their car doors and exchanged places. A well-organized Chinese fire-drill. In about three seconds flat the Tempo's occupants were in the Accord, the Accord's occupants were in the Tempo, and all the doors were softly closed. Saves a lot of parallel parking.

I had had no chance to get a good look at any of them; the changing of the guard was too swift, and it was dark, and the trees interfered with my view. The dome lights in the two cars had been disabled, of course. I would have been disappointed were it otherwise. I was barely out of sight of the rental agency that morning before I popped the bulb out of the Celebrity's courtesy light.

I could tell that the individuals involved were men, and that there were four of them. Beyond that, your guess would be as good as mine. I didn't worry about it, though. I was less interested in what they looked like than in where they were going now.

The new driver steered the Accord into the small lot at the end of the dead-end street, circled around, and headed out the way he had just come, which was his only choice.

Once he got to Decatur, though, he had several options. I had the Celebrity fired up and in gear, lights out, foot on the brake, waiting to see what he would choose.

He chose to go out the way the relief team had come in, south on the Radial.

I gave them a few seconds, then flipped on the headlights and rolled into the intersection, turning, just as the traffic light went yellow.

I kept half an eye out for the occupants of the Buick, in case they were being spelled now, too, and heading back to the barn along this same route in a car I would not recognize. But I wasn't too concerned. They didn't know this car, and I was confident that the windows were tinted darkly enough that no one could get a good look at my features.

The driver ahead of me was taking it easy; he was in no hurry. Why should he be? He was off-duty. And he wouldn't want to attract any official attention. He'd obey all the speed limits and watch for no-turn-on-red signs and use his turn indicator properly, and basically do it all they way the driver's-education manuals say.

I pulled in behind them, one lane over and a few car lengths back.

The Accord followed the Radial south, then east, then along the shallow curve onto Burt Street. From Burt they accessed the North Freeway.

Less than a block away, Robert Olson had had his brains beaten in the night before.

The Accord negotiated the spaghetti works near Creighton and ended up eastbound on 480. So did I. I-480 doesn't do a heck of a lot more than connect downtown Omaha to the rest of the network, and to Council Bluffs across the river.

These guys weren't going to CB, though. They followed 480 in the right direction, all right, but just this side of the river they exited, wound back under the freeway, and ended up driving northeastward on Highway 165. That was queer. There were only two good reasons for their following this route, and one of them was that I had been made. Under other circumstances I would have skipped the exit and found another route or doubled back at the first opportunity. But in this instance I would have to go clear the heck across the river before I could turn around again, and there was no other way across the river within miles of there.

It was a good way to shake a tail.

It was a good way to box a guy in, if you had pals in another car who radioed you that you were being tailed.

I swallowed hard and took the same exit the Accord had, snapping off my headlights as soon as I reckoned my tail-lights were below the level of the guard wall on the exit ramp. My eyes went to my rearview mirror repeatedly as I nego-tiated the deserted streets. No one appeared behind me. A good sign, I hoped.

Unless you live in Carter Lake, an Iowa town that somehow found itself on the Nebraska side of the river, there's only one good reason to be driving that route at that time of the night: it takes you straight to Eppley Airfield. There were lots better routes from my place, but they required a good working knowledge of back streets. Until the city got around to build-ing the proposed Storz Expressway to connect the North Free-way and Abbott Drive, which fronts the airport, someone who was unfamiliar with the town and relying on one of those rinky-dink maps the car-rental people give you might think this was the best route.

Indicating, as I had suspected, that these guys weren't local talent. I didn't know what that was worth, but in this racket you glom on to everything you can, just in case it proves useful later.

A couple of cars appeared in my rearview, but 165—which by now had become Abbott Drive—carries a certain amount of traffic even at that hour. Thinking like the badguys again, if I were going to hot-box me, I would have done it back by the off-ramp, where there was far less maneuvering room than out here in the wide open. I put on my headlights again and breathed a little easier. I also opened up the space be-tween me and the Accord, since there wasn't a great deal of traffic and the road was pretty much a straight shot. Not too much space, though; I doubted that the airport was their des-tination—not at that hour, not with the job barely started—figuring instead they were headed for some kip nearby, and I didn't want to lose them now.

I shouldn't have worried. The Accord—still signaling, still obeying the rules of the road—pulled off of Abbott and into the parking lot of one of the discount motels that cluster around airports like groupies around rock singers. The Sky-Liner Inn. I drove past it and doubled back a block farther on. You'd be surprised how different a car looks when it's coming from another direction. By the time I got to the scene the Accord was parked and its occupants were heading toward one of three long, low-roofed buildings that made up the Sky-Liner Inn.

I found a good spot, parked, and waited a quarter of an hour. I figured if one or both of them was going to come back to raid the ice machine or go grab something to eat, they'd do it within fifteen minutes or so. I also half anticipated a second carload of them to show up, but none did. Perhaps they were on some kind of staggered shift. Or maybe they had stopped off en route for a quick one.

The light in one of the guys' rooms went out after about ten minutes. The other's stayed on, and an occasional flicker against the curtains told me he was deep into the pleasures of late-night TV.

I checked the .38 in my pocket and ambled over to the Accord.

Like the Buick, the Accord had a metallic decal on the rear bumper. It was a rental car, all right. And locked. Not that there would be anything of especial interest inside—not interesting enough, at least, to break into the car and let them know they'd been made.

These guys take the AAA-approved route to a hotel near the airport in a car with a rental-agency sticker on the bumper. Could it be they're nonresidents?

I copied down the license-plate number and the numbers on the room doors. Then I drove around to the front of the place and went in and introduced myself to the night clerk. I showed her my soon-to-be-defunct license and my business card and my pearly whites, and asked her if she would mind looking up the registration cards of the fellow driving this car and renting one of these rooms.

She didn't mind.

I ended up with a name that didn't mean anything to me, but an address that did. Minneapolis, Minnesota.

It only confirmed what I knew in my gut, that Steven Dimand was behind recent events, but I was glad to have the confirmation. Now I could get down to serious work.

13

The drive from Omaha to Minneapolis-St. Paul is long, but at least it's boring. I drove the last two hours of it in a fine mist on icy highways. For reasons known only to them, Minnesotans have a kind of herd instinct that compels them to bunch their cars together when roads are slippery. My instinct in such situations is to give myself plenty of room, so I repeatedly dropped back, out of the herd. All that happened was that the next herd down the road caught up with me.

I made it to town nearly three hours later than I should have, but that was all right: the room was confirmed on one of my many credit cards. I went through the paperwork at the front desk and found my room with no undue trouble and collapsed on the bed. Some time later I rose and turned on the lamp on the little desk and, with a minor start, glimpsed myself in the mirror over the desk.

My own mother would have recognized me, if she were still around to do so, but someone who knew me only casually—someone who had seen me in person only once, for instance—would not. At least, that was the plan. I had had my hair cut very short, which had the effect of making it appear lighter in color, and combed it away from my face, which made my face appear longer and narrower. I had almost a week's worth of mustache, and a pair of horn-rimmed no-prescription glasses. For reasons I don't understand, some people think it's funky to wear glasses when they don't need to. I had been wearing these for the past two days, and they were a damn nuisance. But they added nicely to my altered appearance, and since they had glass in them, slightly grayed lenses, they appeared genuine.

Clark Kent fools everybody with a pair of specs. I needed to fool only one body: Steven Dimand.

◇◇◇

I had a late supper in a Denny's that shared a parking lot with the hotel, and scanned the classified ads in the *Minneapolis Star and Tribune* and the *St. Paul Pioneer Press-Dispatch.* Even with the help of my four generous friends, lodging and dining were going to bankrupt me fast if I had to spend any time in that town. Those towns. Whatever. The point was, I'd be dollars ahead renting a flat somewhere, even if I ended up breaking the lease and abandoning my deposit. With the aid of a street map, I determined that there were three suitable apartments within a couple miles of Dimand's condominium. It's always nice to live close to work. I also circled ads for a few places in St. Paul and suburbs, in case the Minneapolis ones didn't pan out.

By the time I had refueled myself, the mist had congealed into a light but wet snow. Good way to test the waterproofing of my new shoes. Everything I owned was new, bought on the cuff in the days before I left Omaha.

I climbed into the Celebrity and got it headed toward downtown Minneapolis. I got lost twice; that was all right: the point of the drive was to familiarize myself with the area around Dimand's condominium, and getting lost is as good a way as any to explore a neighborhood.

Ultimately I happened upon Dimand's building, and cruised around back.

I found a parking place along the curb, about ten feet from the ugly splotch on the pavement that I would have made if I had let Dimand escort me off of his balcony. I found that balcony by counting up from the street level and over from the north end of the building. A translucent drape was pulled across the balcony doors, but a faint yellowish light glowed on the other side of it. Maybe Dimand was home, maybe not.

I got out of the car and went for a stroll in the wet snow.

There were four ways out of the building, not counting the route Dimand had had in mind for me: front door, back door, and emergency exits at the north and south ends of the building. The back exit was a steel overhead door at the end of a short but steep ramp from the street down—an underground garage. Probably where Dimand kept the Jag. I tried the door but it was locked. I looked around. No control box visible, so I figured the tenants were issued radio transmitters for an automatic opener inside the garage.

They hadn't done away with the security foyer at the front

since my previous visit. The emergency exits opened only from the inside, and they were wired to set off an alarm if anyone opened them.

Effectively, then, there were two ways that Dimand could come and go, and no way that I could watch them both.

No problem. I'd try one for a while, and if it didn't pan out I'd try the other. I had lots of time. Nothing but, in fact.

I was on duty in front of Dimand's place bright and early next A.M. Early, at any rate. The snow had let up around midnight, having never really amounted to anything, and by seven, when I pulled up across the street from Dimand's building, was nothing more than crusted-over slush piled like coral reefs along the pavement. By eight, with the sun on it, it was already dropping from power wires and tree branches and eaves with fat, wet plops. By nine there wasn't even that much left.

And so ended the high point of my day.

Dimand never showed his face, at least not via the front door. I moved the car a few times, to avoid suspicion, and took a few quick walks down the block and back, to avoid catatonia, and visited a couple of public restrooms, to avoid embarrassing myself, but the front of the building was never out of my sight for more than a couple minutes at a time, and from seven A.M. until four P.M., Steven Dimand contributed exactly nothing to the wear and tear on the front door's hinges.

At four I left to look at a couple of apartments. But I was back in position by six forty-five, on the theory that someone going out for the evening would do so between seven and eight.

Not Dimand, of course.

Second verse, same as the first.

Only the second day out, I tried the back door. This was nowhere near as interesting as the front of the building. Once Dimand's neighbors had left for work, there was virtually no traffic, wheeled or pedestrian, on the back street.

While it was true that I had loads of time, I had greatly overestimated my supply of patience. In fact, I ran out of it entirely by nine A.M. the second day.

The main problem was I needed about twice as many of me.

For instance, I had spent yesterday watching Dimand's front door. But if he was taking his car, he'd've used the back exit. So now I was around back. But what if he ordinarily used public transportation and his taking the Jag yesterday had been an irregular occurrence? Then he might have exited the front door today while I was covering the garage entrance.

And if he worked at home, as I did—or had, in a life I led a century ago—then his comings and goings were probably erratic.

"The same goddamn problem," I told the steering wheel. "I don't know enough about this guy."

I got out of the car and walked around the building. It was a crisp, sunny morning. My breath formed a thin fog in front of me, and I felt a prickly sensation in my mustache as the fog condensed and then froze on the whiskers. My glasses whited-out entirely when I entered the overheated foyer at the front door. I slid them down to the end of my nose and peered over them as I thumbed the bone-colored stud next to Dimand's name on the intercom panel. After a long while a man's voice came down the line, sleepy and grumpy and perhaps several other of the Seven Dwarfs, but definitely Dimand's voice. "What?" he grumbled.

I lowered my voice a notch and put a bit of a drawl into it. "Sorry, man, wrong number."

"Idi—" was all that came over the wire before Dimand disconnected.

I went back outside. So Dimand wasn't a nine-to-fiver. What did that prove? That he worked at home? That he was independently wealthy? The kid in Loring Park that night a million years ago, Randy, had termed Dimand a "rich dude"—but "rich" is relative, and to a street kid almost anyone might appear rich. Did he work nights? I knew he occasionally cruised the parks at night, but I also knew, from Randy, that that was only occasionally.

There was a public library not far from Dimand's place; I had stumbled upon it while meandering, lost, through the area two nights ago. Now I found it purposely, found a city directory, and looked up Dimand. He wasn't in it. I looked him up in the phone book. It didn't tell me anything I didn't already know.

It's always so *easy* for the guys in the detective novels.

I wandered around the place a bit and mulled it over. I'm a sucker for libraries. I wasn't too worried about Dimand going out while I was away. For one thing, from the sound of his voice, I had buzzed him out of bed. Even if he decided he might as well now go out and greet the world, it would take him an hour at least, I guesstimated, to put himself together. For another, I was hoping to find during my absence some kind of handle, some tool, that would save me God knew how many hours hanging around his place waiting for something to happen.

It had occurred to me, as it probably has to you, that I could simply bully my way into Dimand's place and lean on him a little—harder than I had previously—and suggest he keep away from me. It's a technique I have used, and with some results. But I was in my current fix because I had leaned on Dimand once already, and I had no good reason to think that my putting the heat on him would do anything more than prompt him to turn up the heat on me. Plus I didn't want him to know yet that I was in his backyard. As long as he had his unsavories looking for me somewhere else, I was safe.

As long as he sat around his nice condo, he was safe—from me. The only way I could get a line on this guy, find out what he was and who he was, was to find out where he went and what he did and whom he associated with.

I scouted out a phone booth, invested some loose change, and dialed Dimand's number.

He answered on the second ring, sounding a good deal more alert than he had forty-five minutes ago. I didn't know if he would recognize my voice or not, after one conversation, if that's the word for it, more than a week ago, but I saw no reason to take chances. As I had when I spoke into his intercom, I lowered my voice slightly; this time, however, instead of an accent I opted for a soft, almost whispering tone. "Good morning," I murmured, "I'm calling for Mr. Steven Dimand."

"This is him."

Money can't buy good grammar, I thought. "Mr. Dimand, my name is Bob Kessler and I'm calling from Jaguar Cars. How are you today, sir?"

"Fine." It was the short, vaguely impatient tone you always use on telephone solicitors.

"Mr. Dimand, the reason I'm calling is that our records show you own a 1988 XJ-SC Cabriolet, is that correct?"

"Yes . . ." A little less impatience now, a little more concern, or at least interest.

"Mm-hmm, and you still own that car, is that right?"

"Yes . . ."

"All right. Mr. Dimand, we have had reports of some minor mechanical problems with that particular model—"

"I haven't had any problem."

"Well, that's good, sir, but you see, we've had reports of, ah, an unexpected decline in the efficiency of the braking system . . ."

"My brakes have been working fine."

"Well, that's just it, sir—it's an *unexpected* decline in the efficiency of the braking system."

"You mean the brakes just go, with no warning at all?"

"Well—yes. Did you receive a card from us in, oh, the past few days or so?"

"No." There was a certain note of alarm in Dimand's voice now. "I didn't get any card."

"Hmm. Well, frankly, I wouldn't wait, Mr. Dimand. My advice to you is to take your XJ-SC to your Jaguar dealer *immediately* and have the entire braking system checked. Now, let's see, you purchased your XJ-SC at—"

"Twin City Jaguar," Dimand supplied. I might have guessed at that one.

"That's right," I cooed. "Now what I will do, Mr. Dimand, since you haven't received your notice from us, is call Twin Cities Jaguar and tell the service manager you will be bringing in your XJ-SC. Naturally, you will not be charged for this. Now, let's see, do you think you'll be able to bring your XJ-SC in sometime today?"

"Yes," Dimand said quickly. "Right away."

"Good. I really wouldn't wait. Confidentially, your brakes could go at any moment, without the slightest warning, and, well . . . need I say more? Very good, then. You have a good day now, and I will call and make arrangements for you right away."

As soon as I put down the receiver I picked up the phone book. Twin Cities Jaguar Renault was listed on University Avenue West. I didn't call, of course; I just wanted to know where it was in case I didn't get back to Dimand's place in time to pick him up there.

I almost didn't, too, even though the library was just a few blocks away. I guess I put more of a scare into him than I had thought, because just as I was rounding the corner, he was coming up the ramp out of the garage under his building.

Coming *slowly* up the ramp, I should say, and driving *slowly* down the block, and *slowly* turning the corner, his brake lights on the whole time. I must have really rattled him.

I could about see me following this character across town at eleven miles per hour, so I let him find University Avenue for me and then abandoned him, going on to the car dealer solo and waiting fifteen minutes for Dimand to arrive. I heard him coming before he got there. More accurately, I heard the horns of annoyed drivers, followed by the angry roar of auto engines as they furiously passed him.

Then it was another twenty minutes I spent parked on the street out front while Dimand presumably had words with the service manager about this dreaded unexpected decline in the efficiency of the braking system of his pricey automobile. I felt bad about the trouble I had caused the dealer and possibly the manufacturer. Not real bad, you understand, but kinda bad.

Mostly, though, I wondered what Dimand would do when they threw him out of there. My hope was that, once flushed from his nest, he would go on about his business and thus provide me some clue as to what his business was and whether he was in fact a man not to be trifled with or just a rich s.o.b. with an attitude. If the latter, I figured I could solve his problem for him real fast and get the hell home.

It was just as possible, of course, that he would simply go home and draft a poison-pen letter to Jaguar Cars, Inc. That wouldn't be as good, from my perspective, but it would be all right. During the time I had spent parked in back of Dimand's building that morning, I calculated that the overhead door closed slowly enough that a reasonably nimble person could slip inside the garage after a car had exited or entered. I was reasonably nimble. If I got inside, I could probably figure out a way to get the overhead door open again and keep it open long enough to get my car inside, where I could resume the long, boring wait, but this time out of the sight of curious neighbors, passing patrol cars, and other potential troublemakers.

Meanwhile, I amused myself with the street map I bought

at a SuperAmerica gas station the night before, trying to acquaint myself with the lie of the land. It was like cramming for half an hour before taking the final exam: futile. There were a lot more streets here than in the Big O, and a lot more cars, and a lot greater likelihood of my losing the man even with his uncommon wheels and personalized license plate. Well, if that happened I'd just have to go back to his place and wait for him to come home.

Just about then Dimand stormed out of the dealership and got into his car and left some rubber behind getting it onto the street, where he was again greeted with a blast of horns, though this time for a different reason.

14

Dimand left the dealership like it was on fire, drove fairly recklessly through the light midmorning traffic—more recklessly that I would have, with a car like that—and eventually wound his way down to the Crosstown Freeway.

I followed easily, one eye peeled for street signs and landmarks, in case I needed to find my own way, the other eye alternating between my fellow motorists and the DIMAND plate on back of the Jaguar. Nearly all of the slush from yesterday was gone now, leaving the pavement wet in most places, worn dry in heavily trafficked areas. The sun was bright enough that I was glad of my phony glasses' slight tint, and Twin Citians seemed to be enjoying their near-miss with old man winter.

From previous excursions, I knew vaguely that the Crosstown links up with 35W in Richfield, just south of Minneapolis, and takes you northward right into the heart of Minneapolis. I wondered briefly if Dimand was merely heading home, having taken the long way around in order to cool off a little, but he quashed that notion by continuing east past the 35W interchange. He stuck with the Crosstown all the way into Edina, exiting finally onto Normandale Boulevard, heading north. Everything here is Somethingdale; the gag when Walter Mondale lost his bid for the presidency was that he was coming back to Minnesota to join Southdale, Ridgedale, and Rosedale as a shopping mall.

There was a lot of traffic out here. Ordinarily I'm glad of some traffic—protective coloring—but the fact was that Dimand was an embarrassingly easy tail. As near as I could tell, he hadn't looked in his rearview mirror more than half a dozen times since leaving the car dealer. I was still being fairly professional about the tail, following close, then dropping back; changing lanes frequently; driving in his blind spot when possible. But Dimand seemed not the least interested in or concerned about a possible shadow. He had certainly taken no evasive action, which would have indicated that he had made me, nor had he displayed any of the little tics that distinguish someone who has gotten used to watching his backside—frequent mirror checks, occasional slowdowns to see who passes and who matches speed, periodic departures from the road more traveled, and so on.

He drove like a man who hadn't a care in the world. That in turn made my day a little brighter. It supported my wishful thinking that Steven Dimand wasn't a man with connections beyond those that any healthy bank balance can buy. If he was a bad scout, he'd be watching his tail.

A little ways north of Edina Country Club, Dimand turned off of the well-traveled boulevard and its posh shops, offices, and restaurants; a few blocks further west he turned into a parking lot in front of a purplish brick-fronted building. Steel-gray letters on the façade read INTERLACHEN HEALTH AND RACQUETBALL CLUB.

That's all I caught on my drive-by. I went down a couple of blocks, turned around in the lot of a Mobil station—I didn't trust the town's windy, curvy, go-around-this-lake streets—and came from the other direction. I found a parking place down the block, and wandered back toward the club.

The front was two stories, but the building behind it was a curved-roof affair, the crest of which barely reached the same level as the top of the façade. Above the steel lettering and running the width of the building was a double-row of glass blocks. Except for that, and glass double-doors smoked almost black, the building was windowless.

There was a wooden sign, red lettering over yellow, near the entrance to the parking lot: PARKING FOR INTERLACHEN CLUB MEMBERS AND GUESTS ONLY. VIOLATORS TOWED AT OWNER'S EXPENSE. I thought that was extremely generous of whoever owned the place.

Outside of the Celebrity and its nice, cozy tinted windows, I felt exposed—naked again. If I entered the purple building, I ran the risk of encountering Dimand face-to-face and discovering that my brilliant disguise wasn't as brilliant as I had led myself to believe. But if I didn't go in there, then flushing

Dimand out of his lair and tailing him all the way out here had been for nothing. Sooner or later I had to risk facing the man if I was going to find out what I needed to know about him.

I went in.

The place was all glass and bright, cool lighting and neon accents—that and the heavy, musty smell of human sweat. There was a carpeted entryway, almost black after the brightness of the morning sun. Glass-block walls to eye level on either side, capped by wooden planters. Green neon tubes were hidden under the planters, giving the blocks a mint-green tinge. The motif, with or without planters, was repeated frequently throughout the place, sometimes with ice-blue neon.

It was funny: I was old enough to remember when both those glass blocks and neon were "in" the first time—and when they went hopelessly, irreclaimably out. I gave us another five years before we'd be wearing Nehru jackets and puka beads again.

There was a small unattended cloakroom to the right of the doorway, but I kept my cloak. I wasn't altogether sure I mightn't want to beat a hasty retreat and not stop to wrestle with wire hangers.

Three wide but shallow steps led from the entry down to a kind of lobby, also carpeted. I could see that the facility was partially subterranean. The half-dozen racquetball courts lining the opposite wall were mostly belowground; from here you looked down into them through heavy plate glass. Only two of the courts were in use. To my right was a glass cabinet containing T-shirts and sweatshirts and other overpriced junk bearing the club logo—the words INTERLACHEN HEALTH AND RACQUETBALL ringing the word CLUB, which was rendered in neonlike script. The space behind the cabinet had the look of some kind of reception area, although it was currently unpopulated.

The smell of steam and the occasional echoing clang of a metal locker door told me the locker rooms were dead ahead on the right past the glass cabinet. I'd been in locker rooms before, and even the nice ones were only marginally better than the not-nice ones, so I turned on my heel and trod the carpet down a wide corridor running parallel to the racquetball courts. At the end of the building the corridor doubled back on itself, opening into a spacious workout room. One wall was lined with mirrors, the floor was covered in a springy vinyl material, and a dozen or so women did their best to keep up with a young and exceedingly fit-looking blonde in aquamarine tights. The blonde was taking them through an aerobics routine that made me sweat just to watch. Or maybe it was that I still had my coat on. Or maybe it was the aquamarine tights.

I knew enough to keep my filthy street shoes off the vinyl surface and on the linoleum that ringed the room. I followed the linoleum around behind another glass-block wall. Here was the heavy equipment—the Air-Dyne bikes, the Cybex machines, the Nautiluses, and so on. More glass blocks were arranged so as to form semicubicles around the hardware, providing a semblance of privacy to the users.

At the moment there was only one user, a young redheaded fellow in a tight club T-shirt. He was giving the Nautilus a workout, but interrupted himself when he caught sight of me.

"Hi," he said brightly, reaching for a towel to wipe his face. The towel bore the club logo in blue stitching. "I'm Brad. Can I help you?"

"Yes," I said. "I'm thinking of joining."

"Great. Let's go out to the desk and I'll give you some brochures and things about the club."

We did. I listened with only one ear as the kid told me all about the place—most of which I had observed on my own. While we were standing around the glass cabinet near the entrance—the desk, as the kid called it—Steven Dimand emerged from the hallway leading to the locker rooms. He wore burgundy warm-up pants, a gray T-shirt that said JUST DO IT, and white Avias, and he had a club towel draped around the back of his neck. As he came out into the lobby area, he looked over at me and the kid.

"Hey, Brad," he said, "how's the boy?"

"I'm okay, Mr. Dimand, how 'bout yourself?"

"Not too bad."

Dimand gave me a look that said he thought he should know me but didn't. His nose was swollen, I noticed, and the area under his eyes was a little bluish. I had restrained myself that day, not wanting to break his nose or damage him too badly. Now, as I restrained myself again, I wished I hadn't. I held my breath against his recognizing me, but had to let it out when he mumbled a hi-how-are-ya and I said okay.

Then he kept on down the hall toward the exercise equipment without breaking stride.

When Dimand was out of earshot I said to the kid, "That guy looks kinda familiar. He come here often?"

"Who, Mr. Dimand? Yeah, I guess he comes here often. He owns the place."

15

The club was hideously expensive, but I joined it. That about signaled the end of the line for my Roger Nelson identity. Between purchases and cash advances, I had taxed his credit cards to their limits, and had pretty well wiped out his checking account to boot. It was what I had expected would have to be, yet I confess to a twinge of sentiment as I laid poor Rog to rest. Most of us die only once; old Rog had to go through it twice, once literally and once figuratively, when I divested my pockets and wallet of his various cards and papers.

This Patrick Francis Kilpatrick, whom I had become, was one sloppy-sentimental Irishman, all right.

What the Interlachen Health and Racquetball Club sold mostly was the Interlachen Health and Racquetball Club. It was one of those places where the wanna-bees and think-they-ares hang out in order to be seen by other wanna-bees and think-they-ares. Membership there offered, in addition to the use of the facility, the right to work oh-so-casual references to "the club" into conversations with the uninitiated.

As near as I could tell after a few days on the scene, the aerobics classes were well attended and a few dedicated die-hards kept the exercise equipment from seizing up with rust, but the joint's main attraction was the Health Bar, so called, and the tanning booths, both located on the lower level across from the racquetball courts. I toyed briefly with the idea of taking up the game, but I figured if I had to spend a lot of time around the joint, it would best be put to coaxing my creaky, paunchy body into a condition that might be said to resemble fit. If I managed that, maybe I wouldn't feel so silly running around like a lunatic inside a glass box chasing a little ball. Something to aspire to.

So, since there wasn't much of a line for the exercise equipment, I had Brad design a program for me. Partly that was my good Midwestern conservatism showing—I paid for it, I might as well get my money's worth. Partly it was my acknowledging that the older I got, the more difficult it was and would be to battle the bulge at my waistline, and that now was not only as good a time as any to do something about it, but also better than times to come. And partly it was that it would give me a good excuse for hanging around the club.

Notice how casually I worked "the club" into that sentence.

Unlike most of the members, I hung around not to be seen but to see. Steven Dimand spent a lot of time around the place. That would seem to be expected, since the club literature listed him as manager, but from what I could see Dimand did little of a managerial or administrative nature. Mostly he seemed to play with the exercise equipment, occupy a tanning booth, and hang around the Health Bar schmoozing with the clientele. It was Brad who ran the place, as near as I could tell.

Brad was mistaken when he called Dimand the owner of the place. I spent a little time prowling through Hennepin County public records, and quickly learned that Interlachen Health and Racquetball Club was owned by one Club Associates, Ltd. A little more prowling and I learned that Club Associates, Ltd., was a limited partnership of NorthLand Enterprises, Inc., and SJD Ventures. NorthLand Enterprises, Inc., had as its only shareholders Joshua Feinman, Sharon A. Fahy, and Steven J. Dimand. I could find no records pertaining to SJD Ventures. It was neither a corporation nor a partnership, then; I assumed from that and from the name of the company that it was Steven Jeffrey Dimand d.b.a. SJD Ventures.

That made Dimand at best *an* owner of the place. NorthLand Enterprises was the general partner in Club Associates, and Joshua Feinman was the president and majority shareholder of NorthLand Enterprises.

I had never heard of Joshua Feinman, but the world is full of people I never heard of.

"How come I never see Josh Feinman around here?" I said casually to Brad one afternoon. I had just finished half an hour on the Air-Dyne, he on the Nautilus, and we were heading for the showers.

"Mr. Feinman?" the kid said. "Oh, he doesn't come around very often, you know; it's really Mr. Dimand's place. You know Mr. Feinman?"

It was an innocent, conversational inquiry, the kind you can ignore without it seeming obvious, so I did. "I thought Dimand just managed the place for Feinman."

Brad, bent over the combination-lock dial on a blue steel door, shrugged. "As far as I know, Mr. Dimand owns the club—he's the boss, at least. I think maybe Mr. Feinman has some money invested in it, and I know he calls Mr. Dimand every so often and comes in from time to time and they hole up in the office. That's about all I know. You should ask Mr. Dimand, if you're interested."

"Just curious, that's all. A place like this would be a great investment, I bet."

"Oh, yeah." He skinned off his damp T-shirt and threw it into the locker. He had a torso that looked like it was molded of some kind of pink plastic, hard and shiny, hairless, supple. "It's not my place to say or anything, but I think the club is doing real well—better than anyone expected, even." And the conversation went down that road and off into how Brad would like to own a place like Interlachen someday, and what he would do differently if he did own such a place, and so on. Which had been my aim—to leave Brad thinking, if he thought about it at all, that we had had just an average, rambling, everything-under-the-sun exchange, not that I had been quizzing him about the ownership of the club.

My guess was that NorthLand Enterprises, which is to say Joshua Feinman, was the real force behind the club, with Steven Dimand, a minor partner in the venture, its nominal manager. Fascinating as all get-out, I'm sure, from an organizational-chart standpoint, but the real reason for my curiosity was that Dimand didn't seem to *do* anything. He would show up around the place midmorning—no earlier, sometimes later—play with the expensive toys, loll around the Health Bar, and disappear late in the afternoon, before the place filled up much as it did in the evenings. Sometimes, if he had come in during the morning, he would take long lunches starting around eleven-thirty. Sometimes he would return in the evening, but only to socialize. Sometimes he wouldn't show up at all for a day or two.

At no time did he seem to work, unless his job was to glad-hand and pass the time with the patrons. He had the knack of getting on fabulously with the female clientele—by far the majority—as well as with a certain well-defined group of the male population, and tolerably well with the rest of the men. It was, in all, a strange group, divisible into a number of fairly clear blocs. There were the Peroxide Women, the very middle-aged women with gimlet eyes and hard-set mouths and copious amounts of gold jewelry. Having gone to all the trouble to cram themselves into their ultrasheer tights and form-hugging leotards, they would be damned if they were going to get all sweaty. With few exceptions, they put in an appearance upstairs, perhaps deigning to participate in the cool-down stretches after an aerobics class, before repairing to the Health Bar for the duration of their stay.

Interestingly, the accent here was on "bar," not "health." In addition to juices plain and exotic and mineral waters plain and flavored, the health-minded patrons of Interlachen had a variety of wines and imported beers from which they could choose. Could, and did.

Besides the Peroxide Women there was a small but visible group of much younger women—girls, really—who participated in the exercise regimen but whose interests obviously lay, first, in showing off the latest of their electric-colored gymwear and, second, showing off for the male members. Members of the club, I mean. Call them Junior Misses.

And then there was a small but dedicated band, mostly women in their thirties, who seemed to be there to work out. The Sweat Set.

The Sweat Set also included a number of men—a number that I would say included me, for after a few days I found myself taking my regimen seriously, even if it was not my primary reason for being on hand. A few of these men were husbands of Sweat Set women. Several of them were gay, making no effort to hide it and none to flaunt it, either. And there were several gay men who were roughly analogous to the Peroxide Women in that they were there to be seen, and used the place as a social club rather than a health club.

My usual location was at the end of the short bar, right under the R in the hot-pink neon HEALTH BAR on the back wall.

It was the best vantage point in the place. There was nothing behind me except a pair of swinging doors into a back supply room. I could take in nearly the whole room without so much as turning my head; what my peripheral vision couldn't handle I could view by simply glancing at the dark mirrored tiles against the back wall, below the neon. The side wall, directly opposite where I habitually sat, was made of heavy but transparent glass, which was convenient for seeing who was coming or going. And if nothing of interest was happening in the Health Bar, I could at least check out the game in the first racquetball court, plainly visible through the glass wall of the bar and the glass wall of the court.

I signaled the bartender, Heather, for a refill. I was putting down a lot of caffeine-free herbal iced tea these days. Early into this adventure I decided it would be a good time for my semiannual caffeine cutback—my nerves were strung tight enough without chemical help—and to go easy on the booze besides, since clear thinking was called for. Then too I had begun to notice some results of my workout program and didn't want to derail it at this early stage with too many brown-bottled calorie bombs.

In the mysterious way of such things, however, exotic mineral waters, juices of unheard-of fruits, and herbal-tea blends, each more flowery than the last, cost more than a good old Harp. Go figure.

Heather supplied my refill and leaned against her side of the bar, a brass-and-oak affair. "We should see about getting your name engraved on that stool, Mr. Kilpatrick."

I smiled. "I'm a creature of habit, Heather. I usually park in about the same place in a parking lot, I usually use the same entrance to a building, and I usually occupy the same barstool. Of course, as usual, I could have any of them I wanted."

Generally I was the only one warming one of the eight low-backed stools; tonight was no exception.

Heather looked from the empty places to me. She was in her late twenties, probably, with light brown hair and matching eyes, a smooth, pale complexion, and a slight overbite that elongated her face. She said, "No one hardly ever sits at the bar. Easier to socialize over there, I guess." She angled her chin at the rest of the room, the tables and booths. The Health

Bar was about half full now, and starting to get noisy. She looked back at me. "So it's nice to have someone to talk to for a change. 'Hey, Heather, how 'bout a coupla Evians' isn't much conversation."

A fellow I had seen around the place, with whom I had a nodding acquaintance, stepped to the bar. "Hey, Heather, how 'bout a couple Mic darks?"

Heather looked at me.

"Variety, at least," I said.

She took care of the guy and drifted back over toward me. "So how come you don't socialize, Mr. Kilpatrick?" she said.

"I'm shy."

"Uh-huh."

"Besides, he does enough socializing for the both of us."

I nodded past her, over her shoulder. She turned to look. Steven Dimand was coming down the glass-walled corridor. He wore a powder-blue warm-up suit, the jacket unzipped to the sternum, displaying a white T-shirt stretched to the limit across his pectorals. He walked with the easy, rolling gait of an athlete, and he had it down to where it almost looked natural.

Heather looked back at me. "Mr. Dimand? Yeah, he's a people person, all right."

"You know him very well?"

"No, not too. I mean, you know, just from working around here the last five, six months. Why?"

"No reason. I'm just curious."

"And shy."

"And shy."

"Interesting combination."

"Isn't it, though? No, it's just that your Mr. Dimand seems to be one of these guys who knows everybody but whom nobody knows."

She looked at me.

"I mean, I see him around here, I see him glad-handing the clients, but I never see any real communication happening, you know? It's like the guy keeps a wall around himself, a fence, in spite of his socializing. Take you, for instance. What do you really know about the man?"

She gave it some thought. In the meantime, Dimand had entered the room and, after several stops and detours to greet his public, arrived at the bar. "Howya doin' there, Heath," he said. "Lemme have my usual, eh?" His "usual" was a Perrier over cracked ice with a lime twist. Heather set about building it and Dimand leaned against the bar, took in the room, nodded to a few well-wishers, and ultimately settled on me.

I was there to observe him, of course—to try to get some kind of handle on who he was, what made him tick, and, more important, what or who was behind him—and that almost of necessity meant he would occasionally observe me, too. The first few days, the prospect made me extremely jittery. I didn't want to blow my cover, so to speak. Even more, I didn't want to blow it and not know I had blown it—have Dimand make me but not let on, and arrange a reception for me at the little efficiency apartment I had taken in St. Paul. Now, however, the prospect of facing the man didn't unsettle me so much. I had watched him carefully on previous encounters, and I was certain beyond a reasonable doubt that there was no glimmer of recognition when his cold gray eyes landed on my smiling face. The don't-I-know-you flicker across his features had vanished after the first couple of times we met. By now, I figured, he thought he just knew me from around the club— part of the reason, too, I had been spending so much time there. After a while people forget where they know people from; they're just always around is all.

So now, when Dimand looked at me, I looked back.

"Hey," he said. "Howya doin' there . . . Pat, is it? Pat?"

"That's right," I said. "Pat Kilpatrick. I'm doing all right, Steven. Yourself?"

"Can't complain." He looked away, watching Heather fuss with the lime peel.

I observed him in profile. There was a small rise in the bridge of his nose, possibly the result of my attentions to it a couple of weeks earlier. Other than that, he looked none the worse for wear. He also didn't look like a crime lord or other kingpin, although I had no idea what one of those should look like, beyond Hollywood's versions.

However, I did have some idea of how they should—and did—act, and Steven Dimand didn't fit that either. Basically, there was no menace to the guy. It wasn't that he was gay. I've known some pretty menacing guys who preferred the company of men. And it wasn't that I was fooled by his loquaciousness, his quickness with a quip or a slightly off-color remark, his ability to make people like him. I've known some extraordinarily charming men who would cut your heart out just for the practice.

With them, though, as with any number of other rough customers I've encountered over the years, there was steel beneath the smooth surface. They may have presented themselves as good eggs, and successfully, but that was a façade, a pleasant, pliable mask. It was latex. Scratch it with your fingernail and it would peel back to reveal the hard, unyielding, even vicious countenance underneath.

Not so, I felt, with Steven Dimand. Having observed him closely for some little time now, I returned to my first impression of him—that he was a good talker. Oh, no doubt he would have knocked me around a little back at his place when I came for Eric. If I had let him. But that was bullying, not menacing. If you scratched Steven Dimand, you wouldn't find steel underneath. All you would do is let out the hot air.

But I hadn't dreamed Robert Olson into the hospital with a bashed-in head. I hadn't dreamed the attempted break-in at my apartment. I hadn't dreamed those hoods lying in wait for me back on Decatur Street. I hadn't dreamed the lead that connected them to this city.

So there was still no doubt in my mind that Dimand was behind my expatriation from the old homestead. I doubted now that Dimand possessed the kind of resources required to send a team of head-bashers after me. I doubted that he was connected, in any significant way, to any of the various organizations that collectively we call the mob.

The only remaining possibility, then, was that Dimand was tight with someone who did have such resources or connections. Very tight—in order to convince him to dispatch those head-bashers with such, uh, dispatch.

And after all these days of dogging Steven Dimand, I still had no clear fix on who that someone might be. Dimand appeared to have found a replacement for Eric Sperry, and consequently the club and his condominium were the places he spent most of his time. Of course, they do have telephones in Minnesota, and there was no telling how frequently Dimand made use of such instruments or who he used them to communicate with. All I knew was that there had to be a close relationship between Dimand and whoever had come down on me.

Close like a relative. Or close like a partner.

I had done a little poking around, trying to sniff out something interesting about Joshua Feinman, who essentially was NorthLand Enterprises, which essentially owned the club. I had not been astoundingly successful. The combination of my wanting to keep a low profile and not having any credentials to use even if I didn't want to keep a low profile severely limited my avenues of investigation. I dug through public records and found out that NorthLand Enterprises owned a great deal of real estate around town, either outright or in joint ventures. Lots of office buildings, some retail space, a few apartments. I went through indexes to local business journals, city magazines, and the daily papers, and came up with plenty of citations but nothing in the way of good, solid information about who the man *was.* The problem with business journals is they judge a man primarily on the basis of how much he has accumulated. City magazines go by who he associates with and what functions he attends. Newspapers go for a mix of those. None of them get at the heart of the matter, at what makes a guy tick.

However, those publications didn't totally waste my time. They let me know that Feinman was one wealthy cuss. And they let me know he attended the right functions and got photographed with the right people.

Money. Connections. And a relationship, maybe a tight one, with Dimand.

I needed a way to get close to Feinman. Dimand could provide that way, but to get close to him was to dramatically increase the risk that he would see through my modest disguise.

Showing up on Feinman's doorstep and introducing myself had a certain guileless charm about it, but I didn't seriously consider it.

Heather finished with the Perrier and lime and set it on the bar.

"Thanks, Heath," Dimand said, flashing a 200-watt grin at her an instant before aiming it at me. "Take it easy, now, Pat."

"I always do."

"You know," Heather said when Dimand had moved out of

earshot, "you're right. I've known the man for months now, but I don't really *know* him. Funny, isn't it?"

I was, like her, watching him work the room. Pause here. Trade a bawdy quip with one or two of the Peroxide Women. Pause there. Chat briefly with a table of young men, his free hand resting on the shoulder or arm of whichever happened to be nearest. Hello, Betty. Hiya, Donna, where you been hiding? Hey, Jim! Ultimately find someplace to light, but never for too long.

Tonight he settled with a dark-haired woman I had seen him with before. She was mid-thirties, I guessed, with shoulder-length hair showing a bit of gray. She had fine, almost delicate features, a sharp nose and a slightly pouting mouth. I had seen her leading aerobics sessions, as well as working out with the Nautilus. The tights she habitually wore left little of her figure to the imagination, and my imagination, for one, didn't mind in the least. Currently the view was obscured by the gray fleecewear pants and white-and-blue hooded sweatshirt she had pulled on over her exercise togs, which at least gave my imagination something to do.

As always, when she and Dimand sat together, they took one of the booths along the side wall and sat alone. They seemed to engage in true conversation rather than mere badinage, as was Dimand's habit with everyone else. In fact, except for the circumstances under which I had originally met Dimand, I might have concluded that they were romantically involved. And except for the fact that I had been around long enough to know that the gender issue isn't an either-or situation for everybody, I might have concluded that they couldn't be romantically involved.

I said to Heather, "That woman Dimand's with—I've seen her with him before. That isn't his girlfriend, is it?"

She gave me a look.

"Well, that's what I thought," I said, "but look at them. I mean, as far as they're concerned the rest of us aren't in the same building with them, let alone the same room."

"Yeah, you're right. . . . No, I'm certain Mr. Dimand is gay, period. I mean, this place is full of women, and women talk, you know? I'd've heard something—in the locker room, up in the gym, from one of the members or from one of the staff—if Mr. Dimand was ever, you know, *involved* with a woman, especially one of the women around here. Anyhow, I kind of know Sharon and I'm sure there's nothing, you know, between her and Mr. Dimand."

"Sharon? Do you know her last name?"

"Gee, I think so. Let's see . . . Feeny or something. . . ."

"Fahy?"

"That's it. Sharon Fahy."

Sharon A. Fahy, who with Dimand and Feinman owned NorthLand Enterprises.

16

I had no way of knowing whether Sharon Fahy could help me get close to Joshua Feinman. I had no way of knowing whether Feinman was worth getting close to. But I had invested a lot of time and energy—and especially money—in trying to get a line on Steven Dimand, without much luck. I couldn't see where trying the Fahy woman would hurt.

And besides, playing the silent watcher was getting old. There comes a time when you have to try something else just for the change, just to keep fresh and avoid doing something potentially stupid out of sheer frustration, and I could feel that time coming. I had the sometimes dizzying impulse to grab Dimand and crack him like a cashew. Ultimately I hoped to do just that, but it would be a far more satisfying experience if I didn't have to worry about whether he had important friends who would come crack *me* like a cashew.

Anyhow, from what I could see the prospect of getting close to Sharon Fahy was not unpleasant, even if nothing related to my mission came of it.

I hung around the Health Bar awhile, waiting to see if Inspiration showed up. After another iced tea, she did. And not a moment too soon—it was getting crowded and noisy in there.

One thing about it, though: no one smoked.

I wandered upstairs, taking my time, pausing to look down into the racquetball courts, generally acting like someone who didn't have much of anything on his mind. I needn't have bothered. Although the place was beginning to get busy with the evening trade, no one was paying any particular attention to me. Still, I played it out, studying the logo-emblazoned items in the lighted glass case near the front entrance, carefully working my way around the cabinet, behind the cabinet.

Brad had a small desk back there, and on the desk a Macintosh SE computer.

Computer literate I'm not, but from what I knew about the subject this was an automatic-drive kind of computer, something a halfway clever gibbon could blunder his way through. The machine was on, which was a blessing—in my limited experience, powering these things up is the trickiest part of the operation. The blue-gray screen displayed a big box or window in which were aligned a number of little pictures of file folders. The file folders all had names under them. One of them was named *Members.*

I had no idea what to do next.

A couple came in the front door and down the stairs. I grabbed the receiver of the telephone on Brad's desk, said a few words to the dial tone, and smiled and nodded at the couple as they passed.

On a vinyl pad next to the computer keyboard was a small box about the size of a cigarette pack, attached to the back of the machine by a thin cable. A mouse—I'm not completely computer *il*literate, either, and unlike Mr. Scott in whichever *Star Trek* movie it was, I knew the mouse wasn't a microphone. I ran it tentatively over the vinyl pad. A small black arrow appeared on the screen and danced in imitation of my movements of the mouse on the pad.

It was a little like trying to maneuver the grabber in one of those coin-op toy machines, but I eventually got the arrow onto the *Members* folder and depressed the little button on the mouse.

Nothing happened. The folder changed from white to black, but other than that nothing happened.

I did the logical thing then: I started hitting keys. All I managed to do was change the name of the folder from *Members* to *sahdguyu.* I moved the arrow to another folder, clicked on it, then moved back to *sahdguyu* and got the name put right again. Then I fiddled with the mouse again. Evidently the key to the task was to depress the button on the mouse twice rapidly. When I did, a new box sort of jumped out of the folder, and I saw what must have been the folder's contents: a bunch of little pictures that looked like tiny pages with writing on them, and a couple more that looked like decks of playing cards.

Each of the little pictures had a name under it, as had the folders. One of the decks of cards said *Alpha.* I clicked on it twice fast. My arrow turned into a little wristwatch and a little light on the front of the computer winked at me. Then everything vanished and I figured I had busted the stupid thing. Finally, though, the word *HyperCard* appeared at the top of the screen, followed by a picture that looked like an index card. The card was for a Marjorie Adamson. It listed, in addition to her name, her address, telephone number, place of employment, car make, model, and license-plate number, and whom to contact in case of emergency.

Some more people came in and I played with the telephone again, trying hard to look like I belonged there. I didn't know where Brad was, but I hoped he would stay there until I figured out how to get this thing to give up Sharon Fahy. And I hoped he would keep the rest of the staff there with him.

At the bottom of the screen, under the index card, was a rectangular box in which was the word *find* and a pair of quotation marks with a short vertical line between them. The line blinked on and off patiently, almost lethargically. I shrugged mentally and addressed myself to the keyboard and in an instant *fahy* had appeared between the quotation marks. Nothing happened, so I hit the Return key.

An index card identical to Marjorie Adamson's appeared, but this one bore Sharon Fahy's vital statistics.

The name and number after *In Case of Emergency Contact* belonged to Joshua Feinman.

I found a scrap of paper and wrote everything down. Sometimes old technology is still useful.

I screwed around a little while longer but couldn't figure out how to put the machine back the way I had found it. I had been in employees-only territory a good five minutes by now, and my palms were starting to get a little sweaty. So finally I went back to the keyboard, backspaced *fahy* into oblivion, typed *kilpatrick,* and got my own card on the screen. If a suspicious type was the next to sit down in front of the computer, at least he wouldn't have reason to suspect anyone had been interested in Sharon Fahy's card.

I got the hell out of there.

Thanks to the information I had copied down inside, finding Sharon Fahy's car in the parking lot required very little heavy detective work. It was a dull-gold BMW, one of those ugly little ones that looks like it was involved in a head-on collision while simultaneously being rear-ended. There was a fair amount of traffic in the lot at the moment, thanks to the arrival of after-fivers, but the evening was already quite dark, which worked to my favor. Also bloody damn cold, which made me wish I had grabbed my coat or at least my gloves.

I waited for a momentary break in traffic, then hunkered down between the BMW and the Chrysler parked next to it. I had my keys in hand and, with the smallest of them, carefully opened the valve in the BMW's front right tire. Then I stood, and straightened my clothes, and wandered nonchalantly around to the other side of the car, where I repeated the vandalism on the left rear tire. Then I moved my rented car nearer the BMW. Then I gratefully went back inside, where the central heating immediately frosted the lenses of my fake glasses. This despite the "antifrost" lens cleaner I had bought after getting tired of wiping the damn things down every time I came indoors.

Two iced teas and one hour later, by my Timex, the Fahy woman stood and, with a couple last words for Dimand, left the Health Bar. So did I, at a discreet distance. She headed in the direction of the locker rooms. I took a chance, took my coat from the coatroom, and took myself outside.

The chance I was taking was that she was heading for the lockers not in preparation for leaving the place but merely to retrieve something from her locker. As chances go, though, it wasn't too risky. I popped the hood on my Celebrity and stood around for a while—not quite twenty minutes, in fact. She had changed into street clothes and a long coat, and her shoulder-length hair, which she wore pulled back in the gym, was loose now around her neck and face. For a brief, unsettling instant, I thought she was Koosje.

I had had no communication with Koosje since that last night at her place. No *direct* communication, that is: I had asked Pat Costello to call her for me and simply tell her I had had to leave town unexpectedly. She would worry, and for that I felt bad. But of all my acquaintances, Koosje was in the greatest danger if the men watching my apartment decided to try to flush me out of hiding by threatening one of my friends. It would require no great amount of investigation to find out who my pals were. Koosje's name would be right at the top of any such list. But if the badguys had no reason to believe she knew where I was, I hoped, they would leave her alone.

I knew there was another way to look at the matter—namely, that knowledge of my whereabouts could prove a valuable trading chip if things got hot for Koosje, or any of my friends. The bottom line was, I couldn't do anything to completely protect the people who knew me, not in a situation where the simple fact of their knowing me could endanger them. I could only give it my best shot. On the whole, I figured ignorance was their best shield.

In case I was wrong—it happens—Pat and I had worked out a communication system. He had been right, of course: I needed a lifeline back to home base, and the lifeline stretched two directions. Every day at around noon Pat called and left some kind of nonsense message on my answering machine on Decatur Street. The machine was of the "beeperless remote" variety; I called home every day after noon, retrieved my messages, and reset the machine. If there was trouble, Pat was to so indicate. If Pat was in trouble, I would know by the absence of the nonsense message. If I was in trouble, Pat would know because he knew the code to remote-retrieve messages from my machine; if I hadn't cleared the previous day's nonsense message, it was time for him to call the Marines.

All of which made me feel only a little better. I was virtually certain that, by now, the badguys must have realized I was wise to them and given up as futile the continued observation of my place. Odds were they never had my friends under scrutiny at all. When you wait for the hammer to fall and time passes and the hammer doesn't fall, you begin to think that it won't fall—that it can't fall. Dangerous thinking. As dangerous as the thoughts I had been flirting with the past few days, thoughts of picking up the phone and calling Koosje. Just to hear her voice. What were the chances that her phones, her home, her office were bugged? Slim. At best.

But "slim" does not equal "zero," and "virtually certain" does not mean "absolutely certain," and as much as I ached for Koosje and wanted to hear her voice, I wanted to keep her safe as well. Having given up on Decatur Street, the badguys may have packed and gone home—or they may have elected to keep an eye on my friends, figuring that sooner or later I'd get homesick and call one of them. Just to hear her voice.

So I shoved the thought out of my head, repeatedly, and when Sharon Fahy strode out of the racquet club looking very much like Koosje Van der Beek, I swallowed hard and ducked my head under the hood of my car and told myself I couldn't afford to get comfortable.

I had managed to maneuver the Chevy into a spot directly ahead and two down from her BMW. She went right past me to get to her car. I greeted her—we had seen each other around the club, of course, so we weren't absolute strangers—and she said, "Dead battery?"

"Just a loose cable." I pretended to do something, then closed the hood.

By then she was in front of her car. I said, "If that's your Beemer, you've got a bigger problem than a loose battery cable." I pointed to the back tire.

"Oh, no. . . . Well, that's what I've got a spare for." She went around to the driver's side, unlocked the car, and threw her purse into the front seat. Then she reached inside the car, and an instant later the trunk lid popped open.

I had come around the front of her car by then. "Can I give you a hand?"

"Thanks." She moved back to the trunk. "But I've done this a dozen times."

"Okay, but I hope you have two spares back there."

She looked around the trunk lid at me, and I nodded down at the flat front tire.

"I don't *believe* this!" she fumed. "These tires are practically brand-new, and they weren't blue-light specials, either." I crouched down and pretended to examine the tire. "How can two of them go flat at the same time?"

I stood and went around the back of the car. "Oh, you know, the cold weather—and I'm not a hundred percent sure these tubeless tires are all they're cracked up to be either." I bent down and "inspected" the rear tire. "They look okay, anyhow, from what I can see. Probably just a bead leak."

"Two bead leaks," she corrected crossly. "Well, could be worse. I guess I'll call Triple-A."

"A cold night like this, they're going to be jump-starting cars all over town—you'll be waiting here till midnight.

There's a Mobil station a couple blocks down the street. Let's throw one of the tires into my car, get it fixed, bring it back, and take the other one in."

"Well . . . that's a lot of bother for you. . . ."

"No, it isn't. If it was, I wouldn't have volunteered." I smiled. "By the way, I'm Pat Kilpatrick."

"Hi." Her smile was a little awkward. She extended a gloved hand. "I'm Sharon Fahy."

"Hi, Sharon. I've seen you around the club, leading classes and what-all."

"Three afternoons a week," she said, "sometimes four, if one of the other girls is out. Let me do that."

I had begun extricating the spare and the jack from the trunk. Now I stepped back, jack handle in hand. "I'll get the hubcaps and loosen the nuts, at least." She assembled the jack efficiently, and in short order we had the back tire off and the miniature spare loosely affixed to the axle; it was safer than leaving the car jacked up. I threw the flat into the trunk of the Celebrity, and we drove to the service station. It gave us time for some chitchat, which had been the whole point of my malicious mischief. I learned she taught history at the College of St. Catherine in St. Paul and that she lived near campus. She learned that I was new to the Cities and had taken a tiny apartment not far from her house, and not much else.

We had just returned from our second run to the filling station and were beginning to put the front tire back into place when a white Saab 9000 Turbo pulled up behind Sharon's car and the driver stuck his head out the window. "Trouble?" he said.

Sharon had pulled off the spare while I wheeled the fixed tire into place. Now she stood, and brushed her hair out of her eyes, and said to the driver, "How do you always manage to show up just when the job's finished?"

The driver smiled. "Just lucky, I guess." He had a full, fleshy face, clean-shaven, framed by a halo of curly black-gray hair. When he smiled he showed a lot of teeth. I was eyeing him peripherally as I got the tire positioned. He was looking at me; then he looked significantly at Sharon.

"Oh, I'm sorry," she said. "This is Pat Kilpatrick. He volunteered to give me a hand when this wonderful car of mine came up with two flat tires." I stepped forward, extending my right hand. Sharon went on: "Pat, this is my brother, Josh Feinman."

You could have flattened me with a feather, but that would have been overkill. A mote or two of dust would have been sufficient. Still, I moved in and put 'er there and smiled and said I was glad to meet him. The stage lost a true artist when I opted for the glamour life of a private eye.

It wasn't all an act, though. I *was* glad to meet him.

"Thanks for helping out my kid sister, Pat," Feinman was saying.

I said, "She did most of the work; I just chauffeured."

"Yeah. She doesn't need much looking after, but you know how it is with big brothers. I appreciate it. You a club member?"

I confessed.

"Well, you're going to find your money's no good next time you go into the Health Bar."

I tried to tell him that wasn't necessary, but he wouldn't hear of it. "What do you do, Pat?" In smaller communities, people ask where you work; in larger cities, they ask what you do.

Since I hadn't expected to meet Feinman so quickly, I hadn't had time to work on what I would say to him when I did. I knew it had to be something that would give me an excuse to get close enough to him to find out whether he was the man Dimand had turned to to put the heat on me and, if so, how best to get him to turn off the heat, but I was a little shy in the detail department. So it was something of a surprise when I heard myself say, "This and that, Josh. I'm something of a consultant—people need something done, they consult me." I smiled. "You know."

He smiled too, and his look became more evaluative, even speculative. "Yeah, I know. You pretty well booked up at the moment?"

"As a matter of fact, I only just got to town and I'm free as a bird."

"Oh yeah? Someone tell you Minnesota was a good place to winter?"

I joined in his laughter. "It was shaping up to be a hot winter where I was before."

"Which was . . . ?"

I looked him square in the eye. "Somewhere else."

He nodded, as if privately confirming a suspicion. "If I need a consultant sometime, Pat, how do I get hold of you?"

I angled my head toward the building. "Here's as good a place as any."

"All right," he said, still nodding to himself. "You may hear from me."

Sharon had addressed herself to the tire during my exchange with her brother, tightening down the nuts and palm-hammering the hubcap back into place. Now she ambled back over to the Saab. "No, that's okay," she was saying, "I can get it. You guys just talk."

Feinman laughed. "I told you, Pat, she doesn't need much looking after." To Sharon he said, "Steve in?"

She nodded.

"I gotta have another do-better talk with him. The way he's sucking money out of this place, we'll be out of business before I can get inside. Good to meet you, Pat."

"Talk to you later."

"Count on it. See ya, Sis."

Sharon waited for the Saab to wheel away toward the building, then said, "You two seemed to hit it off."

"Yeah. Your brother seems like a nice guy."

"I sort of like him. What were you two conspiring?"

"I was asking him what he thought the best way would be to convince you to have dinner with me tonight."

"Oh yeah? What'd he say?"

"He figured I should just come out and ask you, and let my devastating charm take care of any obstacles."

"He did, eh?"

I nodded. "Nice guy. Good judge of character, too."

She shook her head. "Did he recommend a restaurant?"

17

Throughout dinner, I tried reminding myself that she was not Koosje.

They could have passed as sisters. Sharon was probably a couple of years younger. They had similar coloring, similar builds, similar ways of holding their heads at a slight angle as they listened to you. Koosje had a faint Dutch accent that grew stronger in times of stress or emotion; Sharon, naturally, did not. Still, there was plenty there to remind me of Koosje— plenty enough to cause a certain tightness in my chest and throat.

Between salads and entrées at Ciatti's in St. Paul, among the renovated brick buildings that constituted the Victoria Crossing shopping center, Sharon said, "You know, you still haven't told me what you do."

"As I told your brother, this and that. I'm a kind of freelance consultant. Business consultant. You have a business problem, I come in and try to help solve it."

"Sounds . . . vague."

"It is vague. The vaguer the better—keeps you from being pigeonholed. Anyhow, it beats working for a living. More wine?"

The restaurant was spacious, the main dining room at the front, a bar with additional tables at the rear. We were seated near big plate-glass windows looking out onto Grand Avenue, one of St. Paul's major east-west thoroughfares. It was Victoria Street crossing Grand that gave Victoria Crossing its name. Grand Avenue, at least in this Crocus Hill neighborhood, was a bizarre yet charming mix of retail centers and restaurants, stately old apartment buildings, fine old two-story homes—many of which now housed retail stores or restaurants or offices or even, occasionally, families. Evidently the city fathers had never heard of a little something called zoning.

As I refilled her glass, Sharon said, "Are you going to be doing some of this consulting of yours for Josh?"

"I don't know. Maybe—he said he might be in touch. What sort of work is he in?"

"Oh, my, all kinds of things. He's as bad as you are in that regard—no one thing. Sometimes I can't keep track of all his ventures. He started in real estate, years ago, and just kept going from there. He got into buying up property in crummy neighborhoods here about ten years ago. You could get things for nothing then, beautiful old houses—mansions, really— that were in neighborhoods no one wanted to live in. He just hung on to them, and then when the so-called urban gentry started moving in, he sold them at huge profits. I mean but huge—I know, because he steered me into a few of them, and even my piddly little investments quadrupled, quintupled. It was unbelievable!"

She took a swallow of wine—a big swallow, a gulp, as if caught up in the excitement of it again.

"Then he took the money he made from that and bought some more property—some office buildings, some retail space. He bought a couple of nightclubs over in Minneapolis. He's been a partner or an investor in all kinds of things—car dealerships, construction companies, movie-theater complexes, you name it. Sometimes people ask him what business he's in and he says, 'Making money.' I guess that's the shortest, quickest answer."

"Must be a bright guy."

She nodded enthusiastically. "He is, very bright. You may not think so to talk to him. He doesn't sound like an educated man. He is, though: he's a graduate of the U, and he's very well read. I think the way he talks is a put-on, a way of disarming people, maybe."

"It seldom hurts to let people underestimate you."

Sharon looked at me. "That's just exactly what Josh says. 'I don't care who thinks I'm a dumb s.o.b.—they'll find out differently if they have to do business with me.' Only Josh says, *they'll find out different,* and he doesn't abbreviate s.o.b." She laughed.

I said, "I take it Josh owns the club."

The waiter cleared our salad plates. That through, Sharon said, "For all intents, yes. It's all corporations owning companies in partnerships—for a whole litany of tax reasons that Josh has explained but which go *voosh!*" She ran a hand over the top of her head. "But the gist of it is, Josh owns about eighty-five percent and Steve—Steve Dimand—owns about ten percent and I own the rest." She looked at me over the rim of her wineglass. "I'd just as soon that not be common knowledge at the club. Most of the people there think I'm just a friend of Steve's, and that's how I like it. They find out I'm part owner—even if my part does come down to half a dozen bricks and a few tiles from the shower walls—and they start treating me differently. I like it the way it is, me just another aerobics instructor."

"Fine by me," I said. "So Dimand's just a minority stockholder and the club's manager, eh?"

"Mm-hmm." Our entrées were up. I asked the waiter to bring us another bottle of wine. "Are you trying to get me drunk so you can pump me for business secrets?" Sharon teased coyly.

I winced inwardly. Rather close to the truth, that, and it was the kind of undertaking I never feel like bragging about. "Damn," I said, "you guessed. I'm hoping to open a string of combination racquetball clubs and coin-op laundries all across the Midwest. Court-O-Mats. Like it?"

"*Very* catchy." She sampled her veal. "Anyhow, you may laugh, but Josh says the club has fantastic potential. He thinks health and physical fitness is going to be one of *the* growth industries on through the turn of the century. Isn't that crazy—'turn of the century.' In my line of work, that was way back then. Funny to realize there's another one on the horizon, less than a decade away."

"People probably said the same thing a hundred years ago. How's your dinner?"

"Delicious. How's the fish?"

"Very nice. It sounds to me like health and physical fitness will be a growth industry *if* your brother can get Steve Dimand straightened out."

Sharon smiled and shook her head fondly. "Steve is . . . well, Steve is Steve. He's always been the same, since we were kids. He's our cousin, you know."

"I didn't know." Things were beginning to focus.

She nodded. "And, as I say, he's always been the same. He's always been—what's the word? A dilettante? A dabbler, I guess you would say. He likes to play at this and that, but he doesn't like to work very much at anything. Steve should have been born wealthy, so he could be one of the idle rich. As it is, he's just idle."

I laughed. "I've seen that car of his in the parking lot."

"Case in point. He can't afford that. I mean, I can't afford my car, but Steve *really* can't afford the Jag. Or his condominium. Or the wardrobe that makes him look like he bought out Saks. But Steve likes the grand gesture. He likes to pretend money means nothing to him. In fact, it's the opposite. Money means everything to him. He's just unwilling to work very hard to earn any."

"I'll have to try laying off the work for a while, see if I can't afford a Jaguar."

"It's easy, as long as you have Josh with a net waiting to catch you when you fall off the high wire. My brother is a very generous man, Pat, and I'll be the first to admit I've benefited from his generosity. He's made me partners in companies without my having to put up much if any money, he's loaned me money so I could participate in good projects with him. There's no question that I would be nowhere as comfortable as I am today except for my brother. But I've never taken advantage of him—or at least I hope I haven't. When Josh lends me money, I see to it that it is a loan, one that gets paid back. When he makes me an officer in a company, I make sure I attend board meetings."

"Not so your cousin?"

She made a disparaging sound. "Josh has set Steve up in so many jobs over the years—jobs where he doesn't have to really *do* much except be on hand. This is the first one that Steve bothers to show up for regularly, and that's just so he can kibitz with the dye jobs in the Health Bar."

"Maybe it's time for Steve to try the act without a net," I said.

"Adversity is a great teacher," Sharon said in agreement.

"It's taught me I don't like adversity," I said.

She laughed. "The problem is, you can't not like Steve. He's just a big kid, basically, and he doesn't mean any harm." I had considerable reason to dispute that statement, but I didn't. "You know that if not for Josh looking after him, bailing him out, taking care of him, Steve would get hurt, and probably badly. Josh couldn't stand that. And neither could I, frankly. I get so mad at Steve that I could shake him, because of the way he takes advantage of Josh. But he's family, and I love him, and I would hate to see him hurt."

I said nothing.

Hours earlier, the deceptive, unreliable light from the fire would have made it easy for me to dupe myself into thinking she was Koosje. Not so easy now. Over a long dinner, over leisurely drinks afterward, through a lazy conversation that wound this way and that and seemed aimless (but which, more than once, had been carefully steered by me toward or away from particular matters), Sharon Fahy had crystallized in my mind as an individual, a unique person, not a stand-in for my lost love.

That was not altogether a good thing.

On the whole, I prefer to see and treat people as people. Though no more immune to stereotyping or prejudicing than anyone else, I suppose—and aware that there must be *some* reason a given stereotype got to be a stereotype—I do make the effort to deal with *people* rather than races, religions, sexes, political parties, hair colors, or zodiacal signs. This puts me in good stead with the ACLU, but it can complicate life.

Take Sharon Fahy, for example. When she was nothing more than a name on a piece of paper, nothing more than a way to get close to Joshua Feinman, I felt no compunction about doing whatever had to be done to exploit the possibility. Now that I was beginning to know her as an individual, how-ever, I felt a minor twinge of remorse at the way I had staged our chance meeting. Worse, I already felt my conscience being gnawed by the vague concern that, in extricating my-self from my difficulties with her cousin and, probably, her brother, I couldn't help but hurt Sharon as well. And I didn't want to. Because I was beginning to know her as a person, not just a name on a computer screen. And I liked her.

Now, in the living room of her narrow little two-story house, as Sharon sat before the fire sipping lemon tea, as I slouched on the sofa drinking coffee, as we talked about nothing in particular in the near-darkness of the room, I tried to put aside gloomy thoughts. I knew little enough of what *had* happened, let alone knowing what would or might happen subsequently. I couldn't predict it. I could only prepare for it as best as possible, and hope for the best. Whatever that may be.

Sharon's house was on Grand, several blocks west of the restaurant, near Cleveland Avenue. It put her just a few blocks north of the College of St. Catherine and a couple south of the College of St. Thomas. It was an older place, pre–World War II, no doubt, with hardwood floors and lots of unpainted woodwork. When I complimented her on the place, she said, "Grand Avenue—the next best thing to Summit."

I rewarded her with a blank look.

"Summit Avenue," she said. "It's the next block north of here."

"Oh."

"*Very* nice address. Much money on Summit Avenue. The governor's mansion is on Summit. So's the house that F. Scott Fitzgerald used to live in. Well, when he was a kid."

I had made that pilgrimage, though I didn't admit to it now. I also didn't share with her—couldn't share with her—my bit of literary trivia, namely that Raymond Chandler, as a child, lived briefly in Omaha, not far from my own Decatur Street haunts. As far as I was concerned, these days Decatur Street was just an address, Omaha just a town. Of course, Chandler was still Chandler.

Except for the occasional snap from behind the fireplace grille, the room was silent. It was the kind of silence that, on rare occasion, two people can allow to exist between them without feeling threatened. When Sharon broke the silence, then, it was not with the restrained desperation that people sometimes reveal when they think they must keep the conversational ball in the air at all costs, but rather with a kind of gentle curiosity.

She said, "Do I look very much like her?"

My gaze had been on the hearth; now I shifted it to her. I felt my mouth twist into a sheepish grin. "That obvious, is it?"

"No, not really . . . it's taken me all evening to figure it out. There's a kind of, I don't know—an aura, if you like. All night long I've had the feeling that you've suffered some kind of loss. The way you look at me, it's like you recognize me and yet you don't. I guessed that meant I reminded you of someone."

"Yes," I admitted. "I have lost . . . a great deal. Among it, someone I care for very much. You do remind me of her. In fact, when I've caught glimpses of you from the corner of my eye, I've almost done double-takes, thinking you were she. But it's one of those things—the more I get to know you, spending time as we have tonight, the more slight the resemblance becomes."

Sharon smiled faintly. In the gloom, I sensed as much as saw it. "Is she . . . still alive?"

"Yes. We— Well, things have not been the greatest between us lately. They were improving, I thought, but then I had to leave rather suddenly."

"Why?"

I hesitated a moment. "Some business reasons."

Several moments passed, broken only by the spitting and snapping of the wood in the fireplace. "Have you talked with her?"

"It seemed like a good idea not to."

More silence. I would have liked to tell her everything. I would have liked for her to know my name, and who I was, and what I was or what I hoped to be. It would have been easy. I trusted Sharon—provisionally, at least, the way you trust someone whom you do not yet know well; say, rather, that I felt she was worthy of trust. But I did not trust myself. The strain of this secret, guarded life I had wrapped myself in, the strain of being cut off from my friends, my home—myself, in the most basic sense—was telling. I could feel it. The way I had to keep talking myself out of calling Koosje. The way I had to keep convincing myself that it was *not* safe to assume the danger had passed and I could just go home and resume my life. The way I had to divert myself from blurting all, or at least too much, to Sharon Fahy. This must be the way a gambler feels when he's trying to steer clear of the table, or a drunk from a bar. It was almost a physical sensation, a clawing at my guts and brain, an almost compulsive desire to tell someone *who I was.*

Sharon Fahy would be a good someone, a very good someone. She was intelligent and understanding, lovely and very, very near.

And she had a brother who likely was the ultimate reason I now found myself in these straits. As much as I felt Sharon was trustworthy, I could hardly expect her to side with me over her family. She had expressed great love and loyalty for her brother and cousin. What would I say to her? "I'm really here because I think your cousin convinced your brother to hire some thugs to break my legs, and now I'm looking for some kind of lever to pry them off my back—but don't tell them." Charmingly honest, but hardly practical. I thought I knew what choice Sharon would make, forced into that corner. I knew what choice I would make. Was there really a choice at all?

Nor did I trust myself to reveal only a little, only a harmless snippet of the truth. Once started, I wasn't the least bit certain I could stop myself from telling all.

And so I didn't start, but rather said, "And how about me? Do I remind you of him?"

She looked at me a long while. With the fire more or less behind her, it was difficult for me to see her features. Finally she said, in a voice that was low and quiet and yet nonetheless firm with certainty, "Not in the least."

I waited. Waiting was easy, time had no relation to time as it ordinarily occurs. The silence was as natural as the conversation, and so the silent intervals did not drag on. I was reminded of an old song, I couldn't think of the name or the artist, that had as its opening line, "Sometimes late, when things are real. . . ." This was that. Things were real.

From somewhere in the gloom a cat appeared, dark gray and therefore almost invisible until it had moved near the fire.

"Company," I said.

Sharon moved fluidly from her half-reclining position on the rug into a cross-legged seated position. She rested her mug in the space between her knees and stroked the cat, which rubbed its chin against her knee. "Hi, buddy," she said to the animal. "I was wondering whether you guys were going to show yourselves. They're not big on strangers," she explained to me.

I put a hand down toward the floor and the cat, reassured by its owner, took a roundabout route over to me.

"Her sister'll be along any minute, now that Seek is out," Sharon said.

"Sikh?" I said, as the cat sniffed my fingers and repeated the chin-rubbing exercise with them. "That's an unusual name. What's it mean?"

"There she is," Sharon said as another feline shape emerged from under the sofa I was sitting on. It came out on the far end and circled wide and ended up behind Sharon, rubbing against her back as it passed. Sharon scooped it up and balanced it on her thigh, roughing up its fur. "This is Destroy."

"Seek and Destroy," I said. "Clever."

"They started out as Lucy and Ethel, but it turned out that Seek and Destroy were more accurate."

Seek jumped up into my lap with an easy spring and began kneading my leg with her front paws.

"I see she has her claws," I said.

"You mean you hadn't noticed the furniture?" I unhooked the cat from my pants leg and set it down on the cushion next to me, whereupon she began to groom herself where I had touched her. "Everyone said I should have them declawed, but it seemed cruel. If you can't have an animal in the house without mutilating it, then you shouldn't have it in the house. Besides, I've heard about declawed cats becoming biters, and I'd rather have to get the furniture recovered than have one of these jokers take a chunk out of somebody's hand."

Suddenly the cat in her lap got a wild hair and went racing across the floor, and the one next to me flew after her. The hardwood floors cost them some traction, but they picked up speed on the big rug behind the sofa and went rocketing up the stairs, sounding more like a dozen cats than two.

When I turned back toward Sharon, she was looking into the fire. "Brian Fahy was a big, blustery kind of guy," she said after a long while. "He was—I don't know . . . not imma-ture, not exactly. Unfinished, maybe." She sipped her tea, her eyes still on the fire in which she found some point in the past to focus on. "He came on like gangbusters, with his long, curly red hair and his bushy red beard and enough blarney to last till next St. Patrick's Day, and I liked that. He was fun. And he was gentle . . . at first. . . ." She let it hang there a long time before she added, softly, "And I was crazy about him."

She turned away from the fireplace. I could not see her eyes, but I knew they were on me.

"I was crazy about him through the drinking and the fighting and the three A.M. calls from jail. I was crazy about him through the jobs he couldn't hold on to and the women he couldn't stay away from and the days on end I wouldn't hear from him. I was crazy about him right up until the morning he walked out the door at eight o'clock and never came back . . . and for a long time after that, too."

"What happened to him?"

She shrugged, and sighed. "My guess is he met somebody, or had somebody, who had more to offer. I never heard a word from him again—it's been almost three years now. Someday he may show up again. Or not."

"What will you do if he does?"

"Throw the bum out. I divorced him after the first year—he probably doesn't even know it. I loved Fahy, and in a way I suppose I still do, but I must have had rocks in my head to put up with as much as I did as long as I did. I never realized it, though, until after the s.o.b. had dumped me—*long* after." Her laugh was low and bitter in the darkness. "Love is blind."

"Stupid, too, sometimes."

"He was a user. He used me—I *let* him use me. He used my brother—or maybe I did, wheedling him to give Fahy a job when no one else would give him the time of day. . . ."

For a while the room was quiet except for the occasional spitting of the fire. One of the cats, I assume the one who had investigated me earlier, suddenly appeared in my lap and began massaging my thigh with little pinpricks of her front claws.

Sharon said quietly, "I'm better off without the bastard."

In the unreliable light from the fire behind her, I couldn't see her features. All I could see was the glistening of moisture on her face, the only external sign of a broken heart.

18

I was midway across the Mississippi River, looking down on the locks that can be seen from the Ford Parkway bridge, when the weather started. Rain mixed with snow. Delightful. It had been a cold, dark, heavy day, and as the afternoon ground down into evening and evening into night, we could count on a drop in temperature—"temps," as the TV weather people all say now—that would leave the streets with a fresh new layer of ice. With luck, the snow would continue on top of that, polishing the ice nicely. It was very Omaha-like weather, and I was reminded of the words of wisdom I had heard years before, on one of my first trips to the Cities: Without the Vikings, the Twin Cities is just a cold Omaha.

It had the cold part down pat, that was for sure. An icy north wind whipped the rain into little razors as I steered the Chevy over the imaginary line that runs down the middle of the river and separates south Minneapolis from St. Paul's Highland Village. It was a pleasant neighborhood, Highland. The Parkway, which sliced east-west from the river to Snelling Avenue, a major north-south thoroughfare, was wide and tree-lined. On this end of it, once you got past the Ford Motor plant that gave the Parkway its name, shops and restaurants lined the street; further east, they gave way to apartment buildings and houses.

A person could do just about all his mundane errands in Highland, hardly ever having to venture out to the big suburban malls. A supermarket, a couple of drugstores, two bookstores—one of which also was a tobacco and gift shop—a few opticians, three or four restaurants, a couple of barbers, bars, dry cleaners, and banks, as well as a cut-rate movie theater and a bunch of other stuff were all clustered around the busy Ford Parkway–Cleveland Avenue intersection.

I took advantage of the situation. I stopped for groceries at the Lund's supermarket, picked up some necessities at Highland Drug, checked the inventory at the miniature B. Dalton—they had The Book, my first and so far only completed detective epic, in its paperback edition, so I rewarded them by buying the current *Newsweek*—and returned some books to the public library branch just up the Parkway.

By then I was tired of being followed.

The guy had picked up my tail shortly after I left the club upon finishing my day's sweating. I had had no trouble spotting him: I had been driving with one eye on the rearview mirror so long—ever since that night on Decatur Street—that I was practically cross-eyed. After you've been looking over your shoulder that long, it's almost pleasant to finally find someone back there.

Almost. And the sensation wears off real quick.

The object in my rearview mirror was a green Delta Eighty-Eight. It had stayed with me as I meandered aimlessly through Minneapolis, "cleaning" myself, convincing myself that I was being followed without letting my shadow know I had noticed him. The driver was a thickset fellow about my height but with considerably more bulk and considerably less hair. He was wearing a navy trenchcoat over a gray suit. I had watched him climb out of the Eighty-Eight and follow me into the supermarket. Then I had seen him in the drugstore. Then I had pretended not to notice him behind the wheel of his car when I came out of the bookstore. By the time I had covered the half-block between the mall and the library—on foot, no less, physical-fitness buff that I had become—the Eighty-Eight was pulling into the library's semiunderground parking lot.

Now he was busying himself at the card catalog. The card catalog didn't seem to get much of a workout, since the newer additions to the library were all indexed on microfiche, but it was a good place for the shadow to put himself, since the catalog files were shoved up against the north wall, right next to the exit.

The Highland Park branch library was not large. I dumped my books at the circulation desk and swung through the nonfiction stacks, effectively circling the room. I sidled up to the blue raincoat and murmured, "I have to stop by the post office on West Seventh, then I'll be heading to my place on Randolph near Edgecumbe Road."

"You've got the wrong guy, mister," he said into the card catalog.

"My mistake," I said, and left the building.

I went downstairs and ducked into the parking area. The library was built into the side of the hill, with parking tucked under the western half of the building. It opened onto Ford Parkway, and that was the only way in or out.

About ten feet back from the entrance, the east wall cut in about four feet. That's where I was standing, alongside a Subaru, when the blue raincoat came hustling toward his car, maybe forty-five seconds after I had left the building. As soon as he passed me, I stepped out of my hiding place and moved right up behind him. I crooked my left arm across his throat. At the same time I brought my right arm around, pinning his right arm to his side and shoving the revolver in my right hand into his belly. I hadn't been in the habit of carrying a weapon on me, if only because Pat Kilpatrick didn't have a permit to do so, but keeping a .38 in my car had seemed prudent. Now especially.

The blue raincoat emitted a gasp that turned to a gurgle when I bent my elbow a bit to put some pressure against his windpipe.

"Shut up," I recommended.

I spun him around and into the back of the Subaru. He groaned, then remembered my suggestion and stifled it. With the barrel of my gun still in his gut, I patted him down with my left hand.

"You carrying?"

He shook his head.

It looked like the truth. "Let's see some ID—left hand, Horatio, and like *real* slow, okay? I'm a little high-strung these days."

He did as instructed. I had noticed upstairs that he wore a wristwatch on his left wrist, a good though not foolproof sign he was right-handed. Had he worn it on his right wrist, I would have insisted he use that hand.

As it was, he was right-handed; I judged that by the way he fumbled getting a cheap imitation cowhide wallet out of his back pocket and thumbing open the brass snap on it. Inside it had one of the plastic-window ID holders. He offered it to me and I took it from him.

His name was George A. Bonacci. He was a private investigator.

It was to laugh, but I figured I'd do that later. For now, I removed the pistol from the roll of fat to the left of Bonacci's navel and threw the wallet back at him.

"So you have a license," I said. "Goodie for you. What's the big idea?"

"Nothing," he said sullenly. His voice was a little raspy from the choke hold I had used on him. He straightened his clothes and tried looking indignant. It was a so-so effort; I gave him a C-plus, maybe a B-minus. "I told you upstairs, you got me confused with someone else."

"Yeah, I got you confused with the guy in the green Delta Eight-Eight, Minnesota plate FAV 204, who picked up my tail at the Interlachen Health and Racquetball Club, stuck with me while I wasted rubber all over the City of Lakes, and practically rode in the kiddie seat of my shopping cart in Lund's. I move the previous question, George: What's the big idea? Who's financing your sightseeing tour?"

"Look, mister, the town is only so big, you run into people all the time—"

I was pretty much done listening to him. He wasn't going to give up his client's name without my applying more inducement than I felt inclined to provide in a public parking lot. I would have been just as stubborn, in his shoes. Anyhow, I had a good idea who was footing the bill for George A. Bonacci's time and expenses.

"What's the deal?" I said. "Feinman having trouble vetting me, so he wants you to see what sort of lowlifes I associate with, what sort of dives I frequent, and like that?"

"Who's Feinman?" Bonacci said, but he had to think about the response just a fraction of a second too long.

Now seemed a good time to laugh, so I did. The sound echoed against the low ceiling, multiplying geometrically and prompting me to laugh all the more. Bonacci, massaging his throat, regarded me as if I had lost my marbles.

Which, in a way, I had. My howls of laughter weren't entirely justified by the amusing irony that Feinman would dispatch a private investigator to keep an eye on me. I realized, even as I worked to regain some composure, that a lot of nervous energy, bottled up for too long now, had just come uncorked.

Finally, though, it worked its way through my system, leaving me limp. I leaned against a nearby Volvo and said, "Sorry, George. Nothing personal. It'd take too long to explain, and you still wouldn't appreciate it." I hiccupped down some tardy giggles. "Look, I don't want to take bread out of your mouth, but why don't you tell Feinman if he wants to know something, he should just ask. He won't necessarily get an answer, but he'll save money in the long run."

"Who's this Feinman?" Bonacci said with some dignity. "Who says I've got a client named Feinman? Who says I'm even interested in you at all? Sure, I'm a private investigator, but I have a library card, you know, and this is a public place."

"As were the supermarket, the drugstore, and the bookstore. Fine, George, you stick with that. Anyway, your energy will best be directed toward figuring out what you're going to tell Feinman."

I floated toward the exit, stopped, and turned back. "One thing you can tell him. He's trying to figure me out, find out who I am and what I am and whether I'm on the level. Remind him for me that I don't know the answers to the same questions about him."

I went out into the rain.

The Elway Station post-office branch was in a long, low building that, despite every decorative effort, still looked like a former supermarket. I went in and collected mail from four lockboxes in the lobby. Mostly bills, some junk mail. None of it was addressed to me; it all belonged to my alter egos Kilpatrick, Goldman, D'Agosta, and Nelson. I had arranged for it to be forwarded from my lockboxes in Omaha, formerly the last stop along tortuous routes planned to maximize the difficulty of tracing the mail from its starting point to its final destination: me.

My own mail, the stuff delivered to Decatur Street, was being diverted to a box in the C Station on Vinton Street in Omaha. Pat Costello or one of his countless kids went up there a couple of times a week, emptied the box, went to the counter, bought a padded envelope, shoved everything into it, addressed it to a lockbox at the main post office in St. Paul, and mailed it on the spot. They entered with nothing that could be linked to me, they exited with nothing that could be linked to me—if anyone was interested. I had chosen the C Station partly because it was convenient for Pat, so his making use of it would cause no suspicion, and partly because it was small. Easy to tell at a glance if someone was waiting for more than a first-class stamp. In which case Pat and his brood had standing orders to immediately about-face and never return.

If, despite the precautions, some sharp-eyed someone was hanging around the station, the most he could possibly get a load of would be a PO box number in St. Paul. And when it came to collecting the mail on this end, I was my usual paranoid self—varying the day and the time of day I went downtown, taking a different circuitous route each time, waiting in the lobby until the lockbox room was either deserted or very crowded.

God bless George A. Bonacci. Until he showed up on my tail, I was feeling foolish about all the cloak-and-dagger. It's a short step from that to deciding that all the precautions are unnecessary. Bonacci, unknowingly, had prevented me from taking that short and potentially lethal step.

There was no sign of my new friend on my way over to Elway; nor did I catch sight of him or his Eighty-Eight when I came out of the post office and got back into my car. He may have called in replacements, though, so I did my usual aimless tooling homeward and circled the block once before parking down the street from the apartment building I was living in. If George had traded off to a partner, the partner was a better hand at shadowing than George had been. But I was pretty sure that, his day spoiled, George had done as I suggested and gone back to Minneapolis to make his report.

I put away the groceries and took care of the mail. Most of it was junk, and a lot of the rest of it was bills that, frankly, Goldman, Nelson, and D'Agosta had no intention of paying. I wrote out checks for the stuff that absolutely positively had to be paid—mostly Kilpatrick's debts; since I was using that as my working identity, I had to keep current on his bills—and got them ready to mail. The rest of it I loaded into a plastic garbage bag that I would smuggle out of the building in a briefcase the next time I went out. I would dispose of the garbage off-premises, and likewise post any non-Kilpatrick mail at a pickup box, so nothing would be lying around that had any name on it but Patrick Francis Kilpatrick.

Then I fixed a late lunch and waited for the phone to ring.

19

The phone didn't ring very often, since I—which is to say Kilpatrick—didn't know many people in town. Mostly I got sales pitches, wrong numbers, and important messages from Bob the Talking Computer. Half the time I let the answering machine field them. But I was pretty sure I would be hearing from Joshua Feinman, so when it rang now I grabbed it on the third ring, before the machine kicked in.

"Mr. Kilpatrick? Can you hold for Mr. Feinman?"

"Can, but won't," I said. "If he wants to talk to me, he can call me himself."

I hung up. The world is full of malletheads who think they're too important to place their own telephone calls. Me, I think *I'm* too important to sit around on hold while the malletheads twiddle their thumbs and try to gauge how long to keep me waiting so as to impress me with how *terribly* busy they are.

The phone rang again three minutes later, and I answered.

Feinman said, "I hear you two kids had a nice time last night."

"Don't try to change the subject," I said. "What's the big idea bird-dogging me?"

"Yeah . . . Bonacci called me."

"At least you're not playing innocent," I said. "Wise choice. Your PI didn't do a very good job of it."

"Bonacci's okay, he's done a lot of good work for me. And he's good at forgetting who hired him. As for me, Pat, I have too much respect for you to insult your intelligence by playing dumb."

"Oh yeah? When did that start?"

"When you made Bonacci," Feinman said truthfully. "Also, I had lunch with my sister today. She couldn't shut up about you. How come you didn't tell me you were Superman, Sir Lancelot, and Albert Einstein all rolled into one?"

"I figured you'd find that out for yourself when you checked up on me," I said.

"Yeah," he said. "That and your phone number are about all I did find out about you."

I said nothing.

After a short interval he said, "So what do we do from here, Pat? You want to tell me to go to hell? Or you want to sit down, talk face-to-face, maybe see if we can't do each other a little good?"

The cards were being dealt, and the hand had to be played just so. I didn't want to appear too eager; that would make him suspicious. On the other hand, I didn't want to come off so cool that I blew the chance to get close to Feinman, because that was my best way of finding out, first, whether he was in fact the man Dimand got to put the squeeze on me and, second, how I could undo the squeeze.

Actually, I was 99 percent sure on the first question. What Sharon Fahy had told me about her cousin affirmed my suspicion that Dimand lacked the know-how or the money to do much more than complain about me—although he had someone good to complain to, someone who did not lack those items that Dimand lacked. His cousin Feinman, I was willing to bet. Feinman obviously had the money. If he was just half as clever as his sister thought—even allowing for sisterly exaggeration—then he would know how to use the money to make things happen. And the way he had responded knowingly to my vague job description led me to suspect that the things he made happen were not always strictly legal.

Also, his evident readiness to talk to me, to "maybe see if we can't do each other a little good," and the way he had moved quickly to check up on me suggested that something was up. Whatever that something might be, it bore a striking resemblance to my ticket in.

"What the hey," I said into the phone. "I guess I can tell you to go to hell just as easily in person."

◇◇◇

Any doubt I may have had about whether Feinman had the wherewithal to hire the kind of talent that shoved me out of my home evaporated as soon as I got off the elevator. According to the directory in the lobby, NorthLand Enterprises had the top two floors of the building in downtown Minneapolis. Prime real estate. Whether Feinman owned the building or was merely a tenant, maintaining that address took loot. The lobby was all red granite and gold leaf; the top floor was all thick carpet—hunter green, with burgundy accents that complemented the flocking on the wallpaper—oak paneling, and antique brass fittings.

There was no immediate evidence that anyone but me was on the floor. The lush reception area behind the tinted glass doors that said NorthLand Enterprises in gold lettering was deserted. Maybe everyone had left early because of the weather. The place was silent, in that vague, almost subliminally humming way that that constitutes silence in office buildings.

No, not quite. As I paused in the middle of the dark-green carpet, I heard the dull thrum of a muffled voice. I went toward it, toward the unmarked door from which it seemed to emanate.

Feinman's office was behind the door, and so was Feinman. He stood behind his desk, talking on the phone.

"Tell him he's crazy," Feinman said into a telephone that had more buttons than you see inside the cockpit of a jetliner. He glanced up as I opened the door, and motioned me into the room. "No, *you* look," he told the phone. "You tell the guy that now is not the time to hondle. No, he's got a legitimate offer in front of him right now. Tomorrow that offer goes down fifteen grand, and fifteen every day after that until—*poof!*—it's gone. No, you just tell him." He put down the phone and looked at me. "Pat," he exclaimed as if my visit was unexpected. "You found the place okay, huh? Come on in."

Feinman's office was big; it could have stood a couple of rest areas between the door and his desk. The desk was a half-moon of mahogany polished to a painful brilliance and balanced atop a cube of the same red granite as was in the lobby. Unspoiled by any sign of paperwork, it sat in front of a bank of windows which framed almost perfectly the IDS tower, a great blue phallic symbol on the skyline.

At the moment the view was spoiled. The top of the tower was lost in a swirling fog of snow. In the past hour the wind had gone from nippy to outright biting, the rain had given up the ghost and let the snow have its way, and the roads were clogging fast—not just with snow but also with the afternoon commuters, who were no doubt finding the drive home a little longer than usual.

"Sorry I didn't meet you by the elevators," Feinman was saying. He had come out from behind the desk to shake my hand and usher me in. "I got trapped on the phone."

"So I gathered. Trouble?"

He rolled his eyes. "Stupidity. We're all set to close on this little strip mall in West St. Paul, all of a sudden this jerk decides it's time to dicker—come up ten grand and I'll throw in the doorknobs. Who needs it, right? I don't mind hammering out an agreement—that's the game, right?—but you do that *first,* not last. Lunkhead's gonna end up *losing* money, he thought he was so smart—you watch and see."

I remembered what Sharon Fahy had said about her brother hiding his shrewdness behind a mask of unlearnedness, and reminded myself to be on guard.

"People are their own worst enemies," Feinman said. He shook a Benson & Hedges out of a pack on the desk and lit it with a spark from a lighter in a granite cube identical to the one that formed the base of the desk. Except for size, that is.

I said, "Not always."

He gave me a look and waved at a couch and a couple of chairs arranged around a low coffee table against the far wall. I went and took a chair. Feinman went over to a built-in wall unit near the furniture setup and pulled open a pair of foldback doors that revealed a small but complete-looking wet bar. He took a couple of glasses from a narrow shelf.

"What're you drinking?" he said.

"Just a Coke or something, thanks. With those streets the way they are. . . ."

"I hear you," he said, but I noticed he poured himself a neat Scotch.

He handed me my cola and sprawled on the couch. "Salut," he said, hoisting his glass.

"Hail Moscow."

Feinman took a pull on his cigarette and set it in a stone ashtray on the table. He squinted at me through smoke. "Patrick Kilpatrick," he said speculatively.

"Joshua Feinman," I said.

"Well, where do you want to start? You want me to say I'm sorry I sent a private detective to check up on you?"

"Wouldn't it be more truthful to say you're sorry I made him?"

He considered it. "A fine distinction," he said, "but a legitimate one. Okay, Pat—I asked around about you some. Would you expect me to do anything different?"

I let the question pass and said, "Learn anything fascinating?"

"Sort of." He took a drink, then reached for the cigarette, then fixed me with a steady gaze. "I didn't learn a goddamn thing about you, Pat. That's the fascinating part."

I shrugged. "Maybe you didn't ask any of the right people."

"Oh, I did, Pat." He smiled. "Believe me, I did." He stood, and wandered over to the window, and looked out upon the scenery. "It's like Patrick Kilpatrick just floated down out of the sky, full-grown, one afternoon." He waggled his fingers in the air, presumably indicating my descent from the heavens. Then he turned toward me. "Don't you think that's kind of strange?"

"What do you want, bank references? You want to run a credit check?" I slid a hand inside my camel's-hair jacket, came out with my wallet, and began extracting credit cards and other vital documents.

"That's all bullshit," Feinman said, waving it away. His tone throughout had been casual, conversational. It remained so. "What I want to know is, don't you think it's kind of strange that no one—but *no* one—knows you? That no one can tell me a thing about you? That no one even heard of you until I told them your name? Don't you think that's strange?"

"Not really," I said truthfully. "It would have been stranger if they had heard of me."

He took the cigarette out of his face and looked at me.

I made a little show of taking a handkerchief from my breast pocket, taking off my phony glasses, and polishing the lenses. Feinman had never met me except as Kilpatrick, so I didn't have to worry about him recognizing me without my Official Secret Agent GL-7 Disguise. "Josh, let's make sure you and I are on the same wavelength. The other night I thought we were speaking the same language; maybe I was wrong. Let's see, how to phrase this politely. . . . You made some calls, talked to some people, right?"

He nodded.

"The people you called . . . were they the sort of people an average guy might call for references on another average guy?"

He smiled. Me too. "All right, then. Josh, the line of work I'm in, the kinds of jobs I've done and the kinds of people I've done them for—none of it mixes very well with publicity. I'm not a butler or a governess or something, traveling with an impressive list of references and letters of recommendation. My value is my discretion, and my anonymity." I held my glasses to the light from the window. The grime on the lenses was smeared to a nice uniform consistency. I put them back on. "You ask around about me, you turn up nothing. That means you turn up nothing about my clients. And if we do some work together, the next guy who checks up on me will turn up nothing about Joshua Feinman, too."

"Uh-huh." He had at the cigarette again. The smoke drifted aimlessly a bit, then was sucked up into the room's ventilation system. "That's great. But how do I know you are who you say you are?"

"Same way I know you are."

He spread his arms. "I'm an open book. My office, my business, my holdings—hell, I had my picture on the cover of *Corporate Report* and everything. I belong to the Chamber of Commerce, the Rotary, all that happy crap. You can find out all about me. What do you want to know?"

"Are you connected?"

His eyes widened. Just a little, and not for long, but they did widen. "How do you mean, connected? There's something you want me to get you wholesale?"

I smiled indulgently. "I've done some work with the pizzatwirlers," I said offhandedly. "I wasn't wild about it."

He grinned at me, stuck a thumb at himself. "Joshua Aaron Feinman," he said, laughing a little. "Sound Eye-tie to you, Pat? Sure, I've done business with them now and then—same as you. Hell, they're everywhere, you can't do any business without tripping over them. But I run my own business and I call my own shots. Why—you in some kind of Family trouble?"

I kept my expression as it was and shrugged serenely.

"Oh, yeah, I get it. I lay everything on the line, but I ask you a question and you put on that Mona Lisa smile. I gotta tell you, Pat, you don't do this job-interview thing real good. You won't tell me squat, I don't know anything about you, you expect me to hire you?"

"Hey, Josh, I never asked you for a job."

"I'm trying to do you a favor, pal, 'cause you helped out my sister. Also I was thinking maybe you're the kind of guy I could use to handle a little business situation I got. But you gotta meet me halfway, Pat."

"What do you call halfway?"

He looked at me hard. "You a cop?"

I laughed. The laugh was genuine. "No," I said. "I'm not a cop."

"The rubes think you ask a cop point-blank if he's a cop and the cop lies, you're off the hook for anything the cop sticks you for." He smiled. "You got some kind of proof?"

"Proof that I'm not a cop? Like what, Josh? Cops carry badges to show they're cops; the rest of us don't get anything to show we're not. It's not the sort of thing you usually have to prove."

"Then give me the name of someone—someone dependable, someone I know is dependable—who can vouch for you."

I stood up. "We're getting nowhere, Josh."

"You gotta give me something to base a decision on, man."

"The people I deal with, business people like yourself, are used to making decisions based on instinct. Gut feelings. Yeah, it's risky, but we live in a risky world, Josh, you know? You want to win big, you have to gamble big. I thought that was your philosophy, too, but I guess we just read each other wrong. That's cool. No problem, no hard feelings. See you around."

I moved toward the door.

He was supposed to say, "Wait a minute" and call me back and smooth everything over, then offer me a job of some sort so I could get a bird's-eye peek at him and his setup and figure out where my lever was. He must have forgotten to read the script, though, because he flubbed his line. I got through the door and into the elevator and out the lobby and down the street and into the parking ramp and into my car, and he still hadn't called me back.

◇◇◇

Maybe I overplayed my hand—but how else could I have played it? Patrick Francis Kilpatrick didn't exist except on paper, and there only superficially. To have invented an impressive *vita* would have been easy enough, but ultimately fatal. My phony résumé would check out for Feinman just as well as my phony name had.

Besides, I didn't know what kind of "consulting" work Feinman was interested in, so I couldn't very well concoct a suitable track record to guarantee snagging the assignment.

I had the distinct impression, however, that whatever Feinman had in mind was not squarely on the up-and-up. No doubt a good many legitimate consultants are hired via contact made on the premises of health clubs and other such pricey playgrounds, but even with my low opinion of the business world I can hardly believe such hirings are handled so casually and yet so cautiously.

Of course, no hiring had occurred in this case. I may have blown the gig, or I may not have. Maybe the gig was blown before I ever showed up. In any event, I had a better-than-pretty-good idea that Josh Feinman was up to something at least slightly shady. That could prove to be the lever I needed to pry him and his cousin off my back.

The afternoon had not been a total loss.

20

We had talked about dinner out and a movie, but with the weather as dour as it was, we opted instead for dinner in, at her place. Sharon hadn't planned on company, so we rummaged through the fridge to see what looked edible.

"I could work up a couple of my world-famous peanut-butter omelettes," I offered.

She gave me a look.

"People always give me that look," I complained. "It's a perfectly ordinary omelette, only you throw in a couple spoonsful of peanut butter just before you fold it over."

"And then you eat it?"

"Of course you eat it. What else would you do with it?"

"I could think of a thing or two," she said, turning back toward the interior of the refrigerator.

"It's really delicious," I said defensively. "If you like peanut butter, that is. . . ."

"I like peanut butter on apples."

"Yick."

"What do you mean, 'yick'? Peanut butter on apples is good. Peanut butter in an omelette is disgusting. Anyhow, I've already had two eggs this week, and that's enough for me." She eyed me speculatively. "You too, probably."

"Hey, I've lost five pounds since I started working out at that club of yours." I patted my stomach. "I'd like to think I'm showing some results."

She extracted a number of Tupperware containers from the icebox and carried them to the counter near the sink. "You are," she said easily, opening the containers and inspecting the contents. "But if you really want to see results, you should sign up for my aerobics class."

"Here it comes," I said. "The sales pitch."

Sharon laughed. "I get paid by the hour, not the head. But

I'm serious. Twenty to thirty minutes of aerobic exercise kicks your metabolism into high gear, and it stays there for hours after you finish the workout, burning calories at a higher-than-usual rate. Geez," she said to one of the plastic containers, "what did *you* used to be?" She put the lid back on it and shoved it aside. "Then, too, you should be giving some thought to cardiovascular fitness. Your weight machines and whatnot are fine, but they don't do much for your heart. Neither do peanut-butter omelettes."

"Peanut butter contains no cholesterol," I said virtuously. "Of course, the name-brands throw in sugar and hydrogenated oils and all kinds of other nasties, but if you scout out pure peanut butter, with no additives, or make your own in a food processor, you're safe. You see, I'm not completely ignorant on the subject."

"Congratulations," she said. "You should still take up some kind of aerobic activity. Okay, I've got a couple of leftover chicken breasts sautéed in lemon and some wild rice. We can reheat it in the microwave, and I'll make a big salad to go with it."

"You could use Egg Beaters in the omelette," I suggested helpfully.

"Skin these carrots, will you?"

I did, and twenty minutes later we were eating.

"Did Joshua talk to you today?" Sharon asked conversationally.

"Yes, he did. As a matter of fact, I had a meeting with him this afternoon."

She smiled. "He said he was going to get in touch with you. He had to call me this morning to see how things went last night."

I put on a perplexed look. "Things?" I said. "Last night?"

She threw her napkin at me. "Thanks a lot, Pat."

I retrieved it and tossed it back. "So how did things go last night?"

"No complaints here. You?"

"Ditto."

"You sweet-talker, you," she said.

A few minutes' worth of dining ensued, after which she said, "So will you be working together? You and Josh, I mean."

"It doesn't look like it. We couldn't quite agree on terms."

"That's too bad." She sounded genuinely disappointed. "Josh said he had some sort of project or something he wanted to talk to you about. I was hoping it would work out."

"Me too," I said, and it was the truth. "But so it goes. We didn't even get around to discussing the project. Do you have any idea what it was?"

She shook her dark head. We were in her dining room, illuminated only by a cluster of candles in the center of the table. She had a CD on the stereo, something light and soft but kind of jazzy, and the light caught the highlights in her hair when she moved her head.

"It could be anything," Sharon said. "Josh is into so many different things. . . ."

"He does sound like one eclectic fellow."

"I don't even know half of what he's involved in," she said, confirming my belief—and hope—that she was ignorant of any unsavory activities her brother might be involved in. That meant she wouldn't be much help providing the lever I needed to pry Feinman, and Dimand, off of me, but it also meant that when I finally did find it, she wouldn't have to suffer for it.

Which fell under the category of me fooling me. It was hard to conceive of any way of shaking Feinman loose without doing him some injury, and that automatically meant injuring Sharon, too.

It was like I had told the Sperry kid, a million years ago: when people care, people get hurt.

Sharon cared about her brother, and I was probably going to have to hurt him. Which in turn would hurt her. Which in turn would hurt me. Ripples on the surface of a pond. None of us is isolated.

"Should I put on a pot of coffee?" Sharon said.

"That sounds good," I said halfheartedly.

I helped carry débris into the kitchen and scraped plates into the wastebasket while she fiddled with her Krups coffeemaker. "I still hope you and Josh can work together," she was saying. "He's such a great guy. And so are you." She looked at me and smiled.

"Garshk," I said.

"I don't know what I would have done if not for Josh. When Fahy took off, I mean. I was devastated—absolutely knocked flat. Josh pulled me through. You might say, 'Well, he's your brother, he's supposed to be there when you need him.' But it was more than that. He was my big brother, but he was also my confessor, my shrink, my security blanket, and, when I needed it, my drill sergeant. He was my friend, in other words—and nowhere does it say someone's your friend just because you happen to have the same parents."

I felt like three-day-old sewage.

The doorbell rang. Sharon glanced automatically at the digital clock on the microwave oven and said, "Who could that be? The coffee'll be ready in a second; help yourself. The cups are right there. I'll be back in a minute. . . ."

She headed for the front door. Her cats, which had been invisible since shortly after my arrival, now materialized and likewise went to see who had come calling.

The coffeemaker heaved a sigh at having completed its job, and I poured out two cups. When I recognized the voice from the front room, I made it three.

"Hello, Josh," I said when he and his sister entered the kitchen.

"Pat. I told Sharon, I tried calling your place a couple of times. I thought maybe you'd be here. . . . I hope I'm not interrupting anything."

"Don't be silly, Josh," Sharon said angelically. "A man and a woman having dinner alone, by candlelight, while winter rages outside . . . what could you possibly be interrupting?"

Feinman looked a little flustered.

"Oh, I'm giving you a hard time." Sharon laughed. "Here, have a cup of coffee, get warm. What on earth are you doing out on a night like this anyway?"

"Thanks." He sipped gingerly from the cup I handed him. "Actually, I needed to talk to Pat."

Sharon glanced at me, smiled, and winked.

"Here I am," I said.

"This looks like a good moment for me to visit the little history-teachers' room," Sharon said. "I'll be right back. Go into the living room, make yourselves comfortable."

We didn't, though. We stayed where we were in the cramped kitchen. Feinman peeled off his overcoat and slung it over a kitchen stool. He was dressed casually in a blue plaid shirt under a thick cable-stitch sweater, sleeves pushed back.

A fat wristwatch, studded with diamonds set in crusty-looking gold around the face, nestled in the thick dark hair on his left arm. A ring, a big clot of the same style of rough-surfaced gold, encircled the third finger of his right hand. My guess was he was wearing a good ten or fifteen thousand dollars. Not counting the sweater, which probably added another two-fifty to the total.

I said, "This is a surprise, Josh. I thought we wrapped up our conversation three hours ago."

"You walked out."

"You wanted something I wasn't prepared to give."

"I don't suppose that's changed?"

"You don't suppose correctly. As I said before, Josh, imagine yourself as a former client of mine. You'll appreciate my evasiveness more that way."

"Yeah. . . ." He looked into his coffee cup, as if something to ease his doubts about me might be floating around in there.

Sharon, as good as her word, returned. "You two guys getting everything worked out?"

I shrugged and looked at Feinman. He glanced at his sister, smiled briefly, and said, "Okay, Pat, tell you what. I've got this little situation, you might call it, down at the company. It's an area we've never been involved in before, and I was thinking maybe you'd had to deal with something like it at some point in your . . . mysterious past."

"As I told you, I've done a lot of different things for a lot of different people." As far as it went, it was the truth. When lying—even when living a lie—try to stick as close to the gospel as possible. Less to come back and bite you later.

"He is the mystery man, isn't he?" Sharon said, smiling, over the top of her coffee cup. She didn't see the long look her brother gave her.

Feinman continued his internal debate a few seconds longer, buying time by dawdling over a sip of coffee. Then, as if reaching a hard decision, he said, "Well, all right, then. Let's give it a whack, see how we like working with each other, right?" His voice lacked the enthusiasm of his words, but Sharon didn't seem to notice. Her delicate features split into a wide grin, and she set down her cup so as to have both arms free to put around us, one to a customer.

"This is great," she said enthusiastically. "You guys are

going to work together great. This is the perfect partnership. You're both so much alike."

Feinman and I caught each other's eye over the top of Sharon's head.

Sharon let us go and beamed up at each of us in turn. "So what is it you need Pat's help with?" she said to her brother.

"Yes, I'm dying to find out," I said innocently.

Feinman gave me an I'll-get-you-for-this smile, glanced at his sister, and said, "Kind of a personnel matter, is all. Probably not that interesting for someone of Pat's background"— he flashed me a smile—"but, like I said, we've never had a situation like this before. I figure Pat's input will be valuable."

"Great," Sharon said again. "This is great. Tell you guys what—you go on into the living room and get comfortable, Mother Hubbard here will check the cupboard and see what she's got in the way of a celebration dessert."

"Sounds okay to me."

"Me too," Feinman said, "but the thing is, this situation of ours—the personnel matter—it's been going on for a few days now and I really need to get it resolved ASAP. I was sort of hoping Pat could come back to the office with me right now."

"Now?" Sharon protested. "Josh, it's nearly eight o'clock. Plus there's the weather. Can't this wait till morning?"

"Not really." He was looking at me, though speaking to her. "Tomorrow's Friday already. I really don't think we can let things go over the weekend, so the sooner we get started the better. What do you say, Pat?"

I looked at Sharon. "Weren't you the one just telling me how much you wanted this?"

"Possibly. But that isn't all I wanted." She sighed, and smoothed the lapels of my sport coat. "All right. Will you at least drive carefully in this mess? And call me when you get to the office, so I'll know you guys made it okay?" She looked at Feinman. "Are you sure this isn't something you two can discuss here?"

"No, we need some papers and things back at the office. And we will drive carefully in this mess. And, yes, we will call when we get there. And I promise to make sure he buttons his coat and eats lots of green vegetables." He grinned at me.

"Patrick Francis Kilpatrick," he said, "I bet you never had a Jewish momma before."

Sharon hit him playfully. "I was right—you two are alike. You both have rocks in your head."

We drove across separately, and Feinman met me in the lobby of his building.

His sister must have been right about us: you had to have rocks in your head to be out in weather like that. Our only defense might have been that plenty of other people were out in it too. According to the radio in my car there already were four inches of wet, heavy snow on the ground—although everywhere I looked seemed more like eight—with another three inches possible by morning. On the plus side, the wind was supposed to die down by midnight.

"I already signed us in," Feinman said. "Let's go on up. Thanks, Howard," he said to the uniformed man who sat behind a small desk near the elevators.

In the elevator car, he said, "What's the big idea putting me on the spot in front of my sister like that?"

"Good clean fun," I said. "Don't you feel cleaner? Anyhow, you must be used to, shall we say, skirting issues with her by now."

A grin jetted across his big ugly-handsome features. "I suppose that's right," he said around a chuckle. "I hate fibbing to Sharon . . . only I usually don't fib—I usually just don't say much of anything."

"Hard to get into much trouble that way."

"Got that right. Sharon's a good kid. Too good, maybe. She wouldn't understand that . . . well, you know, that to get ahead in business, guys like us have to cut a corner here and there, right?"

"Right," I said, meaning I didn't think Sharon would understand, not the kind of corner-cutting I suspected Feinman was involved in.

"Right. Anyhow, she's sure glad you and me are working

together, huh?" He grinned at me. "She likes you, Patrick, me bucko," he said in a thick brogue.

"I know—Superman, Lancelot, and Einstein, all in one good-looking package."

He laughed, then quit suddenly and looked at me, his hand on my arm. "Be nice to her, huh, Pat? She hasn't had it easy. She deserves better than what she got. . . ."

"She told me about her husband."

"The goddamn mick bastard. No offense, Pat."

"No problem. He sounds like a real prince, the way he just up and disappeared one fine day without so much as a fare-thee-well."

"Yeah. . . . Did she mention he beat her up?"

I looked at him. His face was like stone. "No," I said.

"Just once—as far as I know. But that was once too often." Feinman went silent for a minute, then the emotion seething in him boiled over. "The son of a bitch," he growled. His face darkened and he ground his teeth, and for a long moment I wasn't there, as far as he was concerned. Then he seemed to remember me and, with some effort, dragged himself back from his hate-filled reverie. He tried a self-conscious laugh. It came out closer to a gasp. "Lucky for Fahy he did take a powder, right? I'd like to tear the bastard's heart out."

"I'd hold your coat. I don't care how crappy things are, you don't hit—period. And you don't just walk away. If you have to get out, then get out. But have balls enough to say that's what you're doing."

"The only family I have in the whole world is my sister and my cousin, who I love like a brother," Feinman said. "I'd sooner die than see them hurt. I'd sooner kill than let someone hurt them."

There didn't seem to be much to say to that.

We went up to Feinman's office. He led the way; he knew where the light switches were. Inside, he threw his coat and gloves into one of the armchairs. I did likewise. He went over to the cupboard that concealed the miniature bar and busied himself with glasses. "You drinking the same?"

"Yeah," I said. "Coke or something."

He made it happen. We took our positions from earlier that day and he lit a Benson & Hedges. The windows by night were mirrors, reflecting the office back on itself. Us too. I was almost used to the "new" me—the glasses, mustache, and close-cropped hair. Not that I wouldn't be glad to go back to being the old me.

Feinman leaned forward, elbows on knees.

"Here's the story, Pat. I don't think much of your mystery-man bullshit. But I'm in a bind, and I do get the feeling you can help me. Plus, Sharon's keen on you, and that counts for something with me. She's usually a good judge of character."

"Except with Brian Fahy."

"Yeah, well, that's why I say 'usually'—and why I'm not that wild about flying blind on you. Like you said this afternoon, guys like us, we gotta takes risks. Risks I can handle. You can manage risks. You can't manage gambling, though, and gambling is what I'm doing with you, Pat."

"You want me to have the secretary read it into the minutes? For cryin' out loud, Josh, I think I've already figured out your feelings on the subject. And I already told you there's nothing I can do about that. All that's left is whether you want me to try to help you or not. If you want me to, great. If you don't . . . great. Doesn't matter to me either way." I could almost have convinced myself.

"I wouldn't have come looking for you if I hadn't already made up my mind," he said heatedly. "I'm just not real happy about it, that's all."

"So noted."

"Okay. . . ." He let out some smoke. "You any good at finding people, Pat?"

"You mean specific people?" I smiled at the irony of it. If I hadn't been any good at finding people, if I hadn't found Eric Sperry, I wouldn't be there now pretending to be somebody else. "Yeah, I guess I've tracked down one or two in my time."

He nodded. "I had a feeling. I have a guy who's worked for me five, six years now. One of my managers. Good guy, real straight-arrow, a trusted employee—or so I thought. Monday afternoon sometime he burned me real good, then up and disappeared. Man, you think you know someone. . . ."

"You called the police, of course."

He fixed me with a look. "Oh, of *course.*" He crushed the cigarette in the granite ashtray on the coffee table. "I don't want him arrested, Pat, I want him back. Him and the brief-case."

"Briefcase."

Feinman drained his glass at a gulp and moved to replenish the supply. "You know how it is," he said over his shoulder. "Sometimes we need to have large sums of cash on hand. Special payments, contributions, things like that. . . ."

"Money is the grease of the bureaucratic machinery."

"Exactly. So anyway, these briefcases come through now and then, you don't want to leave them lying around. There's a safe in Dave's office—Dave Nordquist, the guy we're talking about—and so I usually give the briefcases to Dave to park for a few hours, maybe overnight, until they can get to where they're going. Are you with me?"

"Arm in arm. Monday you gave Nordquist a briefcase to put on ice but instead he took it for a walk with him."

Feinman sighed heavily. "That's sure how it looks. Monday afternoon around quitting time I called downstairs to have Dave bring the briefcase up here. He wasn't in his office. They got to checking around, turns out no one had seen him since before noon. I got a guy in here, got the safe opened. . . ." He ended it with a shrug.

"You have been sheared, my friend—in case you hadn't noticed."

Feinman shook his head in mild disbelief, "Man, the guy's been working right beside me all this time. You think you know someone. . . ."

"How come the safe's in this Nordquist's office and not yours?"

"I've got one," Feinman said. "But it's kind of full. Anyhow, like I said, Dave and me's done this lots of times and there's never been a problem, never even a suspicion of a problem."

"I guess he was just waiting for his opportunity."

"I don't think so." Feinman and his refilled glass moved back to the low couch. "Dave's had plenty of opportunity to rip me off—literally dozens of chances. Plus, he was in a good position to embezzle from the company all these years, if money was what he was after. I've had guys combing through the books since Tuesday, and everything looks kosher so far. So either Dave's been real cagey all this time, stealing from the company and burying the evidence so deep that six expensive accountants can't find it, then capping it off with a big score on Monday—or something happened."

"Like what something?"

"Like I don't know what. Something snapped inside him, maybe. Maybe he's got a drug problem, maybe he's a gambler, maybe he's into the shylocks for a bundle, maybe someone's got the goods on him. I figure it's gotta be something like that, Pat. 'Cause I figure I know the guy, and he's no thief."

"Sounds like he did pretty good for his first time out. How much did he boost?"

Feinman ignited another cigarette and exhaled a cloud of smoke. "Plenty."

I let it go at that; if he had wanted to tell me, he would have told me. "And he disappeared, presto!, into thin air."

"I had a couple of guys go through Dave's office, his house, everything. They didn't find anything that indicated he planned to disappear. I mean, the guy made an appointment to have his car worked on next week—you wouldn't do that if you didn't plan to be around next week, right?"

"A person leaves a lot of loose threads when he has to go to ground unexpectedly," I said. I felt a certain degree of expertise on the subject.

"Which only makes me more convinced that something happened to Dave, something sudden, to make him do this thing. That's why I don't want the cops involved—I want to get him back here and sit down face-to-face with him and ask him what the hell's going on with him."

I said nothing.

"So what do you think, Pat, can you give me a hand with this? The guys I've got working for me—my security team, I call 'em, whatever the hell that means—they're okay, but something like this is way over their heads. They can't get a single lead on the guy. They've come up empty."

"Which may mean there isn't a single lead to be got, in which case I'll come up empty, too. But if you want me to go over the ground again and see if I can spot something your boys missed. . . ."

"That's all I ask, Pat. Thanks."

"Save your thanks," I said, for more than one reason. "I haven't done anything yet."

"Thanks anyway," he said.

"I guess I might as well start with his office, as long as I'm here."

"Yeah, I figured that was as good a place as any—the scene

of the crime, like they say in the movies." There was a telephone on the coffee table, a smaller relation of the one on
Feinman's desk. He reached for it, slid it near him, lifted the
receiver, and tapped out two digits. "I was going over everything with my head of security," he told me. "That's when I
decided I'd better come looking for you. I told him to hang
around in case I could get you to look into— Yeah, Terry, it's
me. The man I told you about is here with me. We'll meet you
in Dave's office in a minute."

He put down the phone.

"Terry Thoreson," he said to me. "I should tell you, Pat, the
guy's not too thrilled about my calling you in like this. He
figures it's a slam against him. Maybe it is, I don't know. I
don't mean it that way. Terry and his guys, they tried their
best I'm sure, but they're out of their league. No shame in
that; there's always someone else who's better than you,
right?"

"Not me personally," I protested.

Feinman laughed. "I apologize." He took a last pull on his
cigarette and stabbed it out in the ashtray. "Dave's office is on
the floor below this one," he said, standing.

22

Dave Nordquist's office was in fact directly below Feinman's, but was nowhere near its size. It was in most respects a modest office, a midlevel executive's office, nicer than many but not as nice as some. Nordquist's windows gave him the same Minneapolitan view as Feinman's, albeit one story lower. A maple credenza sat beneath the windows, a matching desk sat in front of the credenza, and between them sat I, in a plush burgundy executive chair whose high back made me feel like I was six years old and sitting in a grown-up's place.

I slid shut the file drawer in Nordquist's desk, leaned back in his swivel chair, and studied the wildlife reproductions on his office wall.

How wealthy would I be if someone gave me a dime, even a nickel, for every time I've sorted through some absent someone's desk, dresser, closet, life? How many times have I sorted? Dozens? Sure—dozens my first week on the job. Scores. Hundreds. Perhaps thousands. If I had ever thought to keep track—and I have thought to, particularly with the dawning realization that the total must be staggering; I've just never bothered to—I certainly would have lost count long before now, and probably just as well.

I moved my eyes from the wildlife pictures to the north wall, which featured a year-at-a-glance planning calendar in a hardwood frame. Nothing noteworthy jotted in wipe-away ink in the little square cells. A full contingent of appointments, deadlines, and other important events occupied the cells prior to and following Nordquist's disappearance. Perhaps that lent credence to Feinman's theory that Nordquist hadn't acted so much as reacted—saw a chance and, for some as yet unknown reason, took it. Perhaps not. If Nordquist was clever, and had merely been waiting for the chance to score big at Feinman's expense, he may well have conducted business as if nothing was out of the ordinary, making plans and appointments he knew full well he would not keep.

"I told you, Kilpatrick, we been through everything twice already and there's just nothing here." My eyes went to the speaker, sitting in one of the two straight-backed visitor's chairs in front of the desk. Terry Thoreson was a husky red-haired man with deepset blue eyes, almost invisible reddish-blond eyebrows and eyelashes, and a jaw like Dick Tracy's. He wasn't shy about sharing his opinion that going back over terrain already covered was a colossal waste of time, especially his.

His boss wasn't shy about telling him to keep a lid on it. "Shut up, Terry," Feinman said without rancor. He was filling the other visitor's chair. "I already told you, this is how we're doing it. You can be a part of it or you can go home and watch *Knots Landing;* it makes me no never-mind."

Feinman was more easygoing with his employees than I would have been. I'd have fired Thoreson's ass out of there so fast he'd have thought he was shot from a cannon, and I would have sicced the cops, the FBI, and the Man from U.N.C.L.E. on Nordquist about forty-five seconds after I'd found out what he'd pulled. I suppose such open-mindedness toward one's employees is a trait that should be admired— and one that more than a few employers would do well to cultivate—but, with regard to Nordquist, at least, I couldn't help but feel it was a little off-center. Giving a fellow the benefit of the doubt is one thing . . . but how much doubt could Feinman have had about Nordquist? The way I read it, it was a pretty clear story. Which made me wonder if maybe I hadn't gotten an abridged version.

I looked at Thoreson. "Run it down for me."

He sighed, rolled his eyes toward the ceiling, and left them there. "Okay. Monday afternoon Mr. Feinman buzzes me and says no one can find Dave Nordquist. I ask around on the floor and no one can remember seeing him since before lunch. I check with the receptionist; Nordquist didn't ever sign out. I check at the desk downstairs, though, and the guard says he thought he saw Nordquist leaving around noon or so. He didn't pay any attention to it, which why should he, but he says there were lots of people coming and going, so he figures it was during the lunch hour at least."

"And Nordquist had the briefcase," Feinman prompted.

"Yeah. The guard says Nordquist was carrying a stainless-steel attaché—that's the kind that was supposed to be in the safe."

"Okay. Then what?"

"What do you think? We get the safe open, no attaché. I send one of my men out to Nordquist's house, but of course he isn't there. Nobody's home. My guy kind of let himself in."

"Nordquist lives alone?" I asked.

"Yeah," Feinman said. "He's divorced—five, six years now, I think."

"Girlfriend?"

"Not that anyone around here knows about," Thoreson said. He had the broad, somewhat lazy inflection of a northern Minnesotan—just this side of the McKenzie Brothers' exaggerated Canadian accents.

Feinman said, "Dave's a real closed book. Keeps to himself, minds his own business, doesn't really open up much to anybody. A good stoic Scandihoovian, right, Terry?"

Thoreson smiled indulgently, then turned to me. "He's got an old lady in a nursing home down in Worthington, and that looks like it for relatives, except maybe for second and third cousins he's never met—everybody's got them."

"You went through Nordquist's house?"

"Of course. It didn't look like he had planned to take a trip—I mean, there was mail in the box and the morning paper was still in the bushes out front. It looked like maybe he had thrown some things into a suitcase—there were some hangers lying around on his bed, and no toothbrush or razor or stuff like that in the can—but I figure he did it in a hurry and got out of there."

"Do you have an eye on the house?" My interest in the answer to that one went beyond the Nordquist matter.

Thoreson nodded. "Not an easy trick in these quiet, residential neighborhoods where an unfamiliar car stands out like a dog in church, but we got hold of a cable-TV van. Ought to do us a few days at least, we move it up and down the block a little."

"You took care of the phone, too, right?" Feinman said.

Thoreson glanced at me, then nodded, more slowly than before. "Yeah. . . . His phone rings, an extension on our end rings too. His phone gets picked up, a tape machine starts recording."

The room was not cold, but suddenly I was. I made a mental note to never again feel embarrassed about being paranoid, and said, "What about his friends? He may try calling them from . . . wherever he is." Once again, my intention went beyond the Nordquist case.

Feinman answered. "That's a lot tougher," he said. "You have to get into everybody's home, get the electronics installed . . . and then, of course, you really increase your chances of getting caught with your hand in the jar, right? We don't dig up Dave in a few more days, we'll probably have to consider it, but it's definitely in the last-resort category."

I nodded distractedly. I was wondering how I could get word to Pat Costello to beware of telephone repairmen, or other similar service people, if his lines were already tapped. Singing telegram, maybe. I shook off the thought—there wasn't anything I could do about it at the moment anyhow, and it was important that I give the Nordquist matter my immediate attention. I said, "What about his car? Has it turned up anywhere?"

"No sign of it," Thoreson said. "We have the license number on file, on account of Nordquist had an employee parking space, and I sent a guy over to the airport to check around in the lots and the ramp. No luck."

"Must only be fifty million cars out there," Feinman grumbled.

"I sent Jack D'Angelo, Mr. Feinman," Thoreson said in a different tone of voice than he was using with me. "He's very thorough."

Feinman lazily flashed his palms in a "whatever" gesture.

"Losing a car's no trick," I said. "You shove it in a public ramp, call a cab, and forget about it. Let's go back to the house. Did you find any kind of appointment diary, calendar. . . ."

"There was a wall calendar stuck to the fridge with magnets. Like the one here, it had appointments and stuff clear through the end of the month. We went through a ton of his papers and junk, too; no personal letters except from his mom and three college friends he kept up with."

I said, "Did someone check on these college friends?"

"You think we just got off the bus?" he sniffed. "Course we checked. He isn't with any of them, and none of them's heard from him for at least a month."

"How'd you check?"

His little eyes narrowed. With their invisible lashes, they became just dark slits in his face. "What's the goddamn difference?"

"You just called them up on the telephone, didn't you? I don't believe it."

"Well, what's wrong with that?"

I looked at Feinman. "Well, what *is* wrong with that?" he said.

"Nothing," I said. "Nothing in the world. Oh, unless you want to *find* the guy, in which case letting your fingers do the walking maybe isn't the best idea. Let's say Nordquist's a pal of mine and shows up on my doorstep. He wants to lie low for a couple of days—he might give me any of a dozen good reasons—and would I tell anyone who might ask that I haven't seen or heard from him since the Kennedy-Nixon debates. I'm a buddy; I go along with it. Then you call up and ask if I've seen ol' Nordquist lately and I say nope and you say thanks and go back to the crossword puzzle. See any gaps there, guys, any room for improvement?"

Feinman closed his eyes and rubbed his forehead. Thoreson said nothing while he exercised his Adam's apple a couple of times.

I sighed, and stood up behind the desk. "We're going to need somebody or -bodies to visit these friends in person. Say it's an insurance check, a credit check, an employment check—doesn't matter. Just get inside and talk with these people and see what can be seen. Probably better figure on keeping an eye on their homes for a day or two afterward, too, in case Nordquist is with one of them and decides to rabbit after the 'interviewers' show up. You know the setup here, Thoreson; you want to do whatever has to be done to make it happen?"

Not really, he didn't. He looked at Feinman, who canted his head toward the door.

Thoreson got up and left the room.

Feinman said, "You know your stuff, Pat; I had a feeling. I'm impressed."

"Yeah, I watch all the detective shows on TV." It relieved

me to learn that Feinman's organization wasn't all clock-work-like precision and efficiency. From what I had learned tonight, it was reasonable to conclude that they had instituted a similar eavesdropping arrangement on my Decatur Street phone. They were recording Pat's gibberish messages, then, and all the other stray gems my answering machine collected. For once I was glad of all the inane junk-mail-like calls that frequently interrupted my working day. Most of Pat's messages fit right in with them, which I reckoned afforded him a little protective coloring.

But maybe not enough. Could they trace an incoming call? Tracing a call is a trick that is at once easier and more difficult than it appears in the movies. Electronic switching makes it easier, since, if a trace is in place, you don't have to keep the caller on the line forever, a development that has got to be a bummer for scriptwriters. It also makes it harder, though, because the equipment necessary to trace these electronically controlled calls is extraordinarily sophisticated. Unfortunately, that kind of sophistication is a transient thing, and for all I knew, a halfway clever high-school kid could get everything he needed to build a better phone-tap at Radio Shack for fourteen bucks.

I would have to let Pat know that he should be using a variety of public phones for his daily calls. He may have been already—paranoia is contagious, and he had caught it from me more than once in the past—but it wouldn't hurt to den-mother him a little.

Meanwhile, what about me? I was sinking quarters into a different pay phone every day, but if my calls to Decatur Street could be traced, then they'd all be traced back to the Twin Cities and environs. That realization produced a tight feeling in my intestines, but there wasn't a hell of a lot I could do about it. I had to keep making those calls.

On the positive side, the fact that I was sitting there with Feinman was probably a good sign that my cover hadn't been blown.

At least, I didn't *think* it had been blown. . . .

Feinman startled me by rapping sharply on the desk. "Hello?" he said loudly. "Anybody home?"

I smiled sheepishly. "Just thinking." And I was. I was thinking that about three weeks had passed since I had slipped into the woodwork. That may have been time enough for Feinman to decide to risk escalating the search for me—by bugging my friends' phones, or worse—or it may have been enough time for him to decide that keeping up the vigil was more trouble, and expense, than it was worth. After all, it wasn't like I had heisted a briefcase full of bread from him. I'd just bopped his cousin in the bazoo and bruised his pride a little. Didn't seem like much comparison to me. But it all hinged on the relationship between Feinman and Dimand. Sharon Fahy had indicated to me that all three of them were as close as could be. Did that mean Dimand's injuries became Feinman's, his vendettas his cousin's also? I needed to know more. However, now did not seem a good time to ask.

Instead I said, "Ordinarily I would suggest pulling both this office and Nordquist's house apart stick by stick to find something—anything—that would hint at his getaway plans. A scrap of paper with an airline flight number on it. A travel agent's number circled in the telephone book. A brochure about sunny Rio. Anything."

"But . . ." Feinman said.

"But, like you, I can only conclude that Nordquist's action was totally unplanned. A spur-of-the-moment decision. Therefore he would have made no escape-route plans, therefore there would be no evidence of same to find, therefore demolishing his home and office would be a pointless waste of time."

"And we've had enough of that already."

"What about the mother?"

"What about her?"

"Have we checked with her?"

"First thing," Feinman said. "I did it myself. She knows me slightly. I couldn't talk to her, though—they had just put her in the hospital. Wasn't doing too well, either, by the sound of it. Well, she's an old lady. Anyhow, I talked to her doctor at the home and a nurse at the hospital, and nobody'd seen or heard from Dave. In fact, they had been trying to reach him all day."

"When was this?"

"Monday—like I said, first thing when we realized what had gone down."

"Anyone followed up on it?"

He frowned quizzically for a second, then it sank in. "Shit," he breathed harshly. He got up and reached for the phone on Nordquist's desk, then stopped himself. "I got all the numbers I need upstairs," he said.

"Go, my son, and sin no more."

He did the first part of it, at least.

I did a little more thinking. Let's say I'm David Nordquist and, on a whim, I decide to boost this briefcase. Why would I do it? There's the obvious reason—I like money—but according to Feinman, Nordquist had plenty of earlier opportunities to lift some loot. What made Monday special? His mother had been hospitalized Monday morning. Hospitals cost money. But the nursing home hadn't reached him with the news.

Still, put that one on hold till Feinman's checked it out. Move on.

Why else would you need a lot of money in a hurry? Feinman had called it: someone has an armlock on you. Gambling, drugs, blackmail, loan-sharking—there are as many possible reasons as there are people on the planet. So Nordquist's under the gun, but he doesn't let anybody in on it. A good stoic Scandihoovian, Feinman called him. Then Monday rolls around and the answer to his difficulty almost literally falls into his lap. He does one of two things: he either pays off his debt and disappears, or he keeps the loot and disappears. It all depends on who his creditor is—how big, and how likely to come looking for Nordquist if he skipped.

"Which tells me everything I need to know except where he would've skipped to," I said to my reflection in the window behind the desk.

I stood up and wandered over to the south wall. It was upholstered in cork, those dark-brown, adhesive-backed squares you can buy anywhere. A mahogany-veneer counter ran the width of the wall, at about hip level. Under the counter, on either end, was a mahogany-fronted cabinet. Between the cabinets was a built-in bookcase, two shelves, filled mainly with fat black three-ring binders with *Procedures and Practices* and *Building Code* and other such scintillating labels on the spines. The counter itself supported a few little knickknacks, some business and management books of the *In Search of Excellence* variety, and not a lot else. David Nordquist was not a man to clutter up his workspace.

Case in point, his cork wall. Nordquist hadn't taken full

advantage of the wall; most of the space was empty. I let myself be momentarily distracted from the cabinets and the bookcase by the few items pinned to the cork. Important- and unimportant-looking notes, out-of-date memoranda, a lapel button that said DON'T PANIC, three or four cartoons clipped from magazines. These things were all clustered in the center of the wall. Above them, slightly above eye level, was a set of eight-by-ten color photographs, carefully push-pinned at regular intervals the width of the cork wall. They appeared to have been taken near lakes—or *a* lake; hard to tell—during late spring or summer. Blue sky, blue water, green trees. There was no one in any of the shots, just water and sky and vegetation, from a variety of angles and distances. Lake homes could be seen in some of them, but they were merely part of the background, never the focus of the picture. I carefully pulled down the pictures, one by one, and examined them.

If you suddenly inherited a bag of gold, under circumstances that made you want to become scarce, you might just pop out to the airport and look at the TV sets and buy a ticket to wherever the next departing flight was headed. You might, but I wouldn't. I'm far too insecure or compulsive or something. I know people who think nothing of getting on a plane, flying to Europe, getting off the plane, and starting to look for a place to stay. I could never do that. Hell, I have to have reservations confirmed and reconfirmed weeks in advance if I'm just planning to drive across the bridge into Council Bluffs.

I had the feeling Dave Nordquist was the same. Reserved, methodical, steady—except for that one big upset Monday.

Maybe that upset threw his equilibrium off enough to effect a personality change. After all, he had turned thief; maybe he had also turned devil-may-care, and did simply hop the first available plane.

Or maybe he had fled to a particular—and familiar—place.

That's what I would do, I figured. Especially if I were the close-lipped type—the type of guy who might not share with his co-workers the location or even the existence of such a place.

It was a starting point for me, at any rate. If he had gone the mystery-tour route, my chances of finding him were slim. It would require hours of work at the airport—and who's to say he didn't drive to a nearby city with a sizable airport and catch a flight from there? Working from the assumption that he went to some specific place he knew of, I could at least start hunting for the needle in a definite haystack instead of every haystack in the field.

I wondered where these pictures were taken. I turned them over, and learned nothing except that the paper was made by Kodak. I put the photos back where they had come from.

Then I hunkered down to have a close look at the bookcase and cabinets. That put me at eye level to the counter, eye level to a little black triangle peeking up from between the back edge of the counter and the wall. Against the dark-brown cork, the black triangle was almost invisible.

I reached up and plucked a free push-pin from the cork and used it to pierce the triangle. It was a heavy, cardboardy paper. Using the push-pin as a lever, I eased the triangle out. The triangle was a corner of a standard picture postcard. The Parthenon at night. It must have once been stuck to the cork, but worked itself loose and slid down the wall to catch behind the bookcase.

I turned the card over and, automatically, read the handwriting on back.

Dave—

Athens in July, what could be better? Hotter than hell. Smog makes L.A. look like the "sky-blue waters" in the beer commercial. Greeks ga-ga over Bren's blonde hair. *This* is the cradle of democracy??

Kevin (and Brenda)

Thoreson came back into the office. I half-turned and said, "Did you see this?"

He came over and looked at the address on the card. "Where the hell is Battle Lake, Minnesota?"

"Do I know? See if you can scare up a map or an atlas or something, will you?"

Thoreson looked like he was forming a response to my request, but he kept to himself and left again. When he had, I turned back to the cabinets.

I tried the one on the left first. It opened to reveal a standard gray two-drawer filing cabinet. I pulled open the top drawer and sifted quickly through the pastel-colored file folders swinging in their ugly-green Pendaflex hanging folders. Correspondence, mostly, and that mostly pertaining to the buying, selling, trading, leasing, and general dinking around with various properties. Various legal and quasi-legal documents, photocopies of deeds and assessments, legal descriptions of properties, inventories of land improvements, options, purchase offers, and so on. A lot of money changing hands, at least on paper. It made my eyes water.

The bottom drawer held more of the same. One folder, however, contained only one item, a single sheet of paper bearing a typewritten list.

NORTHLAND ENTERPRISES, INC.
  NL PROPERTIES
    NL Property Management
    ParkCo, Ltd.
  NL LEASING CO.
  JAY-EF ENTERTAINMENT CO.
    EntertainmenTime, Ltd.
    Sven & Ole Co.
  CLUB ASSOCIATES, LTD. [SJD Ventures]
  PLAZA PARTNERS [Western Realty]
  NORLAN DISTRIBUTING CO.
    CeramiCo
    NorLan Appliance Co.

By and large, the list was gibberish to me. A list of companies, business entities of some sort, no doubt, and all related; evidently all ventures in which NorthLand Enterprises was involved. Feinman's fingers were in more pies than I had realized. And these were just the ones he was willing to brag about.

I folded the list, shoved it in my jacket pocket, and replaced the now-empty folder in its rightful location.

The other cabinet concealed a blue-green safe, the kind that works by key or combination. My safecracking was a little rusty, and I had plumb forgotten to pack the nitro.

Thoreson returned with a battered road atlas.

"Okay," he said. "Battle Lake is over by Fergus Falls."

"Thanks for clearing that up for me."

He produced a smile that might have been a smirk, and opened the book on Nordquist's desk. I went and looked. Minnesota on the left-hand page, Missouri on the right—no wonder most Americans don't know from geography. On the map, Minnesota looked like a tall rectangle someone had taken a bite out of. Just inside the bite, on the extreme east end of the state, a little below center, was a purplish glob. It looked like a grape-jelly smear. "Here's us," Thoreson said, stabbing a long finger at the grape-jelly smear. "And here's Fergus Falls." He traced along a fat green line that stretched in a rough diagonal from the grape-jelly smear upward, toward the left side of the page. The green line was I-94, and Fergus Falls was a little white dot just off of the green line. West-central Minnesota, twenty or thirty miles in from the North Dakota state line, by the look of it. Fergus Falls was large enough to get its name rendered in boldface caps; Battle Lake, southeast of it, was not.

Feinman blew back into the office. "We fucked up," he said tightly. "We should've sent someone down to Worthington instead of just using the telephone."

"Nordquist did go to see his mother," I said.

"Sort of." Feinman shook a cigarette from his pack, shoved it between his lips, and ignited it. Anger pulsed just beneath the surface. He drew deeply and exhaled in a sigh. "The hospital got in touch with Dave Monday morning, shortly after the old lady was admitted. Ordinarily the nursing home would've taken care of that, but the old lady was in lousy shape and the hospital people figured they'd better not wait. Good thing, too. The nursing home spent half the day calling Dave's home number—real bright, right, call a guy's home on a workday?—and didn't have the light go on for them until Monday afternoon."

"By which time Nordquist had already flown the coop."

"Right. That's why the jerks at the nursing home told me they hadn't been able to reach Dave to tell him his mother was in the hospital."

"If Nordquist knew his mother was in the hospital and in a bad way Monday morning," I said, "that might explain why he grabbed the loot."

"Hospitals aren't cheap," Feinman said sourly.

"Nursing homes either," Thoreson contributed. He looked at his boss. "No telling what sort of bills he's been running up with his mom in a home. Anyhow, we need to get someone down there right away, keep an eye on the old lady—Nordquist'll show up sooner or later."

"Absolutely right," I said, and Thoreson looked at me in some surprise.

"Yeah, you guys are right," Feinman said. "Too bad Nordquist showed up sooner—Monday night. He got there about half an hour before his mother died. This is according to her doctor. They've been trying to get in touch with him since then, you know, to make arrangements, but he hasn't returned the messages they've been leaving at his motel. I checked with the motel, too—he's checked in, all right, but he hasn't been picking up his messages or anything."

I said, "Here's how it went: Monday morning, Nordquist gets a call that his mother's very sick, possibly dying. Maybe she needs surgery or some kind of treatments. He doesn't have the money—it's costing him a fortune to keep her in the nursing home in the first place. Then you wander in with a briefcase you want him to lock up for a few hours. Bingo—here's the answer to his problem."

"Only he doesn't know what's in the case," Feinman said. "I never told him what was in the cases, just to lock them up until I needed them. And they always had combination locks that only I knew the combination to. It was the same with this case on Monday."

"Doesn't matter. Nordquist wouldn't have to be much of a genius to figure out the cases probably contained payoff money of one sort or another. And as for the combination locks—well, locks only keep out honest people. Given time and some privacy, he could get the case open easily enough. But his first thought is to get out of town. He boosts the briefcase, runs by his place to throw a few things together, and goes to see about his mother."

I was glancing over the open atlas on the desk, looking for Worthington. It was down in the lower left-hand corner of the map, not far north of the Iowa state line, not far east of the South Dakota line.

I looked up from the book. "But when he gets there, he finds

he's too late. His mother's at death's door and there's no bringing her back. He realizes that by now his crime's been discovered—there's no sneaking the briefcase back where it belongs
and hoping for the best. He's a thief and a fugitive. He leaves
the hospital and disappears."

"We blew it," Feinman said in disgust. "We could've had
him Monday night already . . . instead he's had, what, three
whole days to disappear good."

"Disappearing good isn't all that easy," I said knowledge-
ably. "Especially when you've never thought about having to
disappear, when you've never made plans for just that contin-
gency." I handed Feinman the postcard I had retrieved from
behind the cabinetry.

He looked at it. "So?"

"Catch the address," I said. He looked, and looked back at
me with a kind of flicker in his eyes. "Did Nordquist ever say
anything to you about having a lake cabin or something near
. . ." I looked at Thoreson.

"Battle Lake, Minnesota."

Feinman was shaking his head. "But like I said, Dave always kept to himself pretty much. It'd be just like him to *not*
say anything about it—sort of keep it a private retreat. Where
is this place?"

"By Fergus Falls," Thoreson said.

"Looks like, what, a three-hour drive, give or take?" I
handed the atlas to Feinman.

"I suppose," Feinman said, barely glancing at the book. "If
you drive it. Me, I'm taking my plane."

He got up and left the room.

Thoreson and I traded looks. "Shitty night for flying," he
said.

"We could stay here and watch *Knots Landing.*"

He snorted a humorless laugh and we went out after Feinman.

23

Thoreson had summarized it correctly: it was a shitty night for flying. I half expected, and half hoped, that everything would be grounded, but once again I underestimated Minnesotans' almost reckless attitude toward the weather. The little airport south of Minneapolis was open, the little Piper plane was gassed up and ready to go, and the pilot was waiting for us.

We went into the unfriendly skies.

I took my mind off the buffeting the ridiculously small plane was receiving by thinking of the corner I had painted myself into.

Because of my superior detective skills, there existed the possibility that we might actually find David Nordquist. That was both good and bad—good because finding Nordquist would put me in solid with Feinman, and that's where I needed to be to get something concrete to use against him; bad because I had no idea what would befall Nordquist when we did locate him. Feinman's demeanor certainly suggested a forgiving, even benevolent attitude toward his errant friend, but that could have been for my benefit. Who knew what Feinman really would do once he got his hands on Nordquist and the briefcase? If I led Feinman to Nordquist, was I signing Nordquist's death warrant? That would certainly give me the ammunition I needed to take care of Feinman, but at too high a price.

I flexed my left biceps and felt the reassuringly solid bulge of the holster strapped under my arm.

Clearly, I was obliged to try to save Nordquist if Feinman had some kind of nastiness planned for him. I hoped it wouldn't involve gunplay—nothing sours a relationship faster than putting a bullet into someone, and I still had no reason to believe my problems would magically disappear by taking Feinman out of the game—but if it did, it did. I wasn't prepared to be the Judas goat that led David Nordquist to the slaughter. Or the slaughterers to him.

◇◇◇

The sheriff's deputy was very helpful. Feinman explained that we worked with David Nordquist and that we needed to find him and relay some bad news. All we had was a post-office box number in Battle Lake; we needed to translate that into a location. The deputy asked a few natural questions— did we try telephoning Nordquist, what sort of bad news was it that we flew up in person rather than just telephone the sheriff's office. And he was satisfied with Feinman's an-swers—the phone was disconnected, and we had to tell Nord-quist his mother had died. The deputy got on the horn and got the local postmaster out of bed and had the location inside of ten minutes.

"I know where this is," the deputy said, evidently to him-self. "Out by Lake Clitherall. This is just a summer place, you say?"

"That's what we think," I said. "Probably why the phone's out. No sense paying to have it hang there until Memorial Day."

The deputy nodded, again to himself. Then he stood. He was a beefy, balding fellow in his early forties. Lazy manner-isms, quick eyes. He had a gap between his eye teeth that added a soft whistle to his esses. He took a fleece-lined jacket from an aluminum coat tree near the door to the office and a pointed hat from the edge of his desk and said, "Come on, you can follow me out there."

Thoreson and I exchanged glances.

"We've put you to enough trouble already," Feinman said. "Just let us have the directions; Gary here can find it okay, right, Gare?" Gary was the dour, husky, gray-bearded fellow who had met us at the little airport in Fergus Falls and driven us down to Battle Lake in a drafty, wheezing old Ford Bronco that sat sixteen or eighteen feet above the road.

The deputy looked at Gary. "You from Fergus Falls?" He made it sound like one word. *Fergusfalls.*

Gary nodded.

"Yeah, you better follow me, it being dark and all." He went out the door. We followed.

It was dark and all. Guys like me who don't get away from the lights of a city that often can easily forget just how black a night can be. In town, nights never really get to be more than a dark gray by comparison. Out there, the starless night was *black*. I didn't see much beyond the road ahead of us, illuminated in the Bronco's headlights, and, beyond the reach of the lights, the red taillights of the deputy's Dodge sedan. There was a lot of snow, but all of it was on the ground. What the Twin Cities were getting tonight these folks had gotten yesterday, and were by now pretty well dug out from under. An occasional snowflake, a big, fat, cotton-wool kind of flake, jumped into the beam of the headlights and flickered there a moment, iridescently, hypnotically, before vanishing back into the surrounding blackness.

Despite the darkness and my total lack of familiarity with the landscape, I gradually became aware that the narrow two-lane highway we were following had begun to bow, to curve, as if tracing the contour of some as yet unseen lake. Occasionally I thought I glimpsed, through the vegetation at roadside, a wavery yellow glow that may have been the reflection of lights on water. Or just a trick of the night and the snow.

We had not gone far when suddenly, for reasons known only to himself, the deputy ahead of us decided to fire up the bank of lights on the roof of the Dodge, and we went the next mile or mile and a half accompanied by the flashing of red and white lights.

"Terrific," Thoreson mumbled, and I couldn't think of anything to add to it.

Eventually the deputy pulled off the highway, lights still going, and we followed him down a sloping, rutted road that was little more than a glorified trail. The foliage on either side of us was so overgrown that it occasionally scraped the side panels of the Bronco, yet it had lost enough leaves this autumn that I knew the deputy's flashing lights would be at least occasionally visible to anyone with eyes.

Other, even narrower, paths veered off to the left and right, but the deputy stuck to the main route and we to him. Soon this road curved until we seemed to be heading almost perpendicular to our previous bearing. The vegetation to our left thinned and then vanished, replaced by a series of shapes that appeared hunched and squatting in the darkness. Most

of them were black; a few held pale yellow lights in whose
weak glows snowflakes danced like moths. Lake cabins. And
behind them, softly reflecting what scant light there was, was
the lake itself, blacker than the sky.

I know that some people use the word "cabin" with a kind
of false modesty, to casually deride what they should probably, by rights, call their lake *home*. I know the opposite is true,
too—that owners of modest lakeside shacks sometimes refer
to them as lake *homes* in the hope that the uninformed will
mentally picture something grand. From what I could see of
the structures peering at us from the darkness, "cabin"
seemed an accurate description. None of them looked particularly large, though none of them appeared to be a lean-to,
either. If I were to guess, I'd say they all looked comparable
to one- or two-bedroom houses. I'd also guess that no one was
spending the winter months in any of them.

Five or six cabins from the end, the deputy pulled off the
road and down onto the gentle incline leading to one of the
unilluminated houses. Gary steered the Bronco alongside the
official car, and everyone got out and stood around in the
snow. Somewhere in the night, off to my right, which I think
was east, water whispered lazily against a shore.

"Doesn't look like anybody's home," the deputy noted
sagely.

"You want to try the door?" I suggested to Feinman. He
nodded and went, while I tramped over to what looked like a
one-car garage, detached, to the side of the house. The *wish-
wish* of the lake was louder here. Using a flashlight borrowed
from the deputy, I peered through a dirty little window in the
garage wall and determined that the contents consisted of
little beyond a small boat of some sort. Not a shocker, that,
since the overhead door was located in the "back" of the garage, the side away from the road but on the lake. There was
no place around there to have hidden a car. I used the flashlight to scan the ground in front of the house, but it was
useless: any tire tracks in the graveled "yard" would have
been wiped out by the combination of snow and our eight
tires pulling in there.

Feinman knocked on the door and called Nordquist's name
a couple of times. Thoreson drifted over to the front windows,
as if trying to see inside the house, but it seemed to me, as I

came back toward the two cars, that he was seeing how much of a barrier they really were. Feinman came over just as I was handing the flashlight back to the cop.

"Buttoned up tight," he said needlessly.

"Windows too," Thoreson added, tramping back toward the rest of us.

"Closed for the season," the deputy said. "These little cabins down to this end of the lake, they're not built for the cold months, you know. Not like those places up to the other end"—he swung a dark-clothed arm—"where some of the folks live year-round or pret' near. May through September, October, that's about the best you can hope for with these little guys. You get a few folks come back down here for ice fishing, but acourse you won't see any of that till probably after the first of the year. Hell, lake's not even frozen over good yet." He looked out in that direction, though if he could see anything he was a damn sight sharper-eyed than me, even with my fake glasses. "I think you're going to have to look someplace else for your friend. Come on, I'll guide you back to town."

He climbed back into his car. The police radio on his dashboard began to kick up a fuss.

In my left ear, Thoreson said, "We've gotta have a look inside this dump."

"No foolin'. Think we should wait until we lose the law, or ask him to help?"

The deputy rolled down his window and stuck his head out into the snowfall. "Hey, you guys think you can find your way back okay? Some damn fool slid off the highway west of here and took a couple other cars with him. That's clear the hell the other direction. . . ."

"No problem," Feinman said quickly. "Gary'll get us back okay, right, Gary?"

Gary, not one to waste words, nodded.

"All right. Well, hope you find your friend."

"Thanks again, deputy," I said, but I said it to departing taillights. The car wasn't yet out of sight before he kicked on the siren.

"Damn fool, him and his flashing lights," Feinman grumbled. "If Nordquist was here, those lights would've scared him off for sure. He'd've scooted on out that way"—nodding in the direction the deputy had just gone—"so's not to pass us on our way in."

"*If* Nordquist was here," I said. "Let's see if we can find out, huh?"

Feinman looked at Thoreson and nodded.

Thoreson went over to Gary, who had been standing slightly apart from us, and the two went around the back of the Bronco, opened the gate and rummaged around in a tool box that had been rattling and clattering back there all night.

It occurred to me that this would be a grand place for homicide. A bleak, deserted landscape, no pesky neighbors to hear or see anything unfortunate, lots of good places to hide a body where it wouldn't be found until spring . . . if then.

After a few minutes Thoreson reappeared carrying a couple of screwdrivers and a short, flat pry bar with a curved, clawed end. He went to work on one of three small, narrow windows at the front of the place, first removing the outside combination window, then jimmying the single-hung sash beyond it. In short order he had the window open and climbed through it. A light went on inside, then the front door opened and Thoreson stepped out onto the concrete slab at the threshold. "Help me get that window put back together in case our cop friend comes back this way."

Putting the window together again took longer than taking it apart, but not by much. Soon we were all four inside, scoping the place out. There wasn't a lot to scope. The front door opened to a largish room that ran the width of the house. Kitchen sink and counter at the near end, old console television at the far, with inexpensive furniture in between. Dining table and chairs, sofa, reclining chair, coffee table and end tables—the stuff had the look of secondhand furniture, serviceable but not beautiful. A bricks-and-boards bookcase bearing paperback novels, mostly science fiction, old magazines, a small collection of classical tapes, and a portable stereo completed the picture. The floor was linoleum with faded, dusty-looking rugs at strategic locations. The walls were done up in cheap wood-grain paneling.

I gravitated toward the kitchen area. The floor of the stainless-steel sink was dotted with small puddles of water. On the counter alongside the sink stood a glass with a tiny pool of water left in the bottom.

"Somebody's been here recently, at least," I said.

Feinman grunted. "Yeah, until he saw flashing red lights," he said sourly. "Damn fool cop."

I said, "You're disappointed because you've been thinking all the way up here that this is it, we just walk in and say howdy to Nordquist. That would be nice, but usually the way it works is you find one piece that takes you to the next piece, and so on. It's a process, not an event."

He grunted again, but this time there was half a laugh on the end of it. "What is this, a philosophy lesson?"

"Philosophical is what you have to be," I said.

Thoreson, meanwhile, had disappeared through a doorway. I followed; Feinman followed me. The door took us into a narrow hall off of which were two bedrooms, both tiny, and a bathroom only slightly larger than the john on a Greyhound bus. We met Thoreson at the far end.

"Sheets and blankets on the bed in there," he said, nodding toward the first bedroom. "This one's stripped."

"Closets?"

"Haven't found one. Looks like this filled in." He jerked a thumb at the darkened doorway from which he had just come. I reached past him into the room and flipped on the light. There was a twin bed, stripped, as Thoreson had reported, a narrow pine dresser, and a free-standing metal clothesrack, chrome tubing on casters. The clothesrack was holding up a lot of wire hangers, some of which in turn were holding up clothes.

"No telling how long those clothes've been hanging there," Thoreson said.

I told him about the water in the sink and the glass.

"So he was here. Damn that idiot deputy! We should'a ditched him back in hicksville."

"We don't know how long Nordquist's been gone—he may have skipped when he saw the flashing lights coming down the road, he may have left a few hours ago, he may have left yesterday or the day before. I don't know how long the sink and the glass would stay wet. Anyhow, for whatever reason he left, he may be gone permanently or only temporarily. Let's case the joint in any case, just for drill. You guys want to handle these rooms, I'll take the front room? Don't forget the pockets in those clothes."

"Gee, thanks," Thoreson said icily, "this is the first time I ever tossed a joint."

"Shut up," Feinman said lightly, which saved me the trouble.

I went into the front room.

I thought of it as the "front" room even though it was at the back of the house, with the bedrooms at the front. Or maybe *that* was the back; maybe this side, since it opened out onto the lake, was considered the front. My experience with lake homes was nil.

Not, however, my experience sorting through someone's possessions while that someone wasn't around to help. Under the watchful eyes of Gary, who had made himself at home on the sofa and turned on the TV, I went to work. Such as it was. The living area required little effort. The paperbacks contained nothing beyond scraps of paper—gum wrappers, old receipts, torn bits of newspaper—used as bookmarks. Nothing was hidden under the rugs, the sofa, or the recliner. Nothing behind the television set.

"Was that plugged in already?" I asked Gary, who nodded. I peered behind the makeshift bookcase. The stereo was plugged in. Obviously the electricity was on—we had lights, Gary had TV. Would you disconnect the juice for the season? I decided not. You would want to have some heat in the place, if only to keep the waterlines from bursting, and the metal runners along the baseboards were electric central-heat units. If you were leaving for a period of months, then, and the power was still hooked up, you'd unplug your various appliances, wouldn't you? Most people would—most of us are pretty superstitious when it comes to electricity.

So not only had David Nordquist been there, and recently; he also either planned to return soon or had left hurriedly. Or both.

The contents of the kitchen cabinets and fridge confirmed what I had deduced thus far. They contained more food items than I figured most people would leave behind for a number of months, and the wrong kinds of things, too. Perishables. And there was half a pot of coffee left on the stove. Even the world's biggest slob would have at least dumped out the remaining coffee if he planned on being away awhile.

It occurred to me that half a pot of coffee had been turning into a science-fair project in my Decatur Street kitchen the last couple of weeks. Had Nordquist felt forced into pulling a vanishing act, the way I had? If so, I hoped he hadn't disappeared as thoroughly as I had, or we'd never find him.

The wastebasket under the sink contained a coffee filter and damp grounds, two empty Campbell soup cans, a brown paper bag, an empty box that had contained "super strength" wastebasket liner bags, and a paper wrapper that had belonged to a fifty-foot length of "extra heavy-duty" nylon rope. The bag contained a receipt for the rope, the wastebasket liners, an unspecified magazine, and a pack of chewing gum. It was time-stamped at 10:32 A.M. Wednesday—yesterday.

According to Feinman, Nordquist pulled the disappearing act sometime Monday. That was the day his mother died, too. My guess had been that as soon as he got the news, he made tracks for this place. His head would be pretty messed up. Not only did he have to deal with his mother's death, but with the fact that he had become a criminal for nothing. So far I had seen nothing to refute that guess.

Probably his first order of business was provisions. There was no residue of that purchase in the wastebasket, no receipts or empty bags, but that didn't mean anything; obviously he had emptied the trash between then and his Wednesday purchases.

I looked again at the receipt. Nylon rope, plastic liners, magazine, gum. Odd, the business with the wastebasket liners. I looked at the empty box again. Ten super-strength liners, it said—"super-strength" in quotes, so I guess they didn't really mean it. But the wastebasket I was sorting through wasn't lined. Where had the bags gone?

Feinman emerged from the back—or front—rooms. "Yeah, he's been here, all right, and recently. There's an electric shaver, one of those rechargeable ones, in the bathroom. Plugged in. Also toothbrush, deodorant, stuff like that. I figure maybe a guy would leave that kind of stuff behind, but not a nice cordless shaver, right?"

"Not plugged in, at any rate."

Thoreson came in. "Not much," he said in answer to the unspoken question. "I found some dirty clothes in a hamper in the bedroom he slept in, and a suitcase with some clean clothes and things under the bed."

"Any sign of the loot?"

"Oh, yeah, like I'd forget to mention that." He rolled his eyes, then pointed with his chin. "What's out there?"

"Out there" was an enclosed porch on what I've decided to call the front of the house, the lake side. It ran the width of the house and was perhaps seven feet deep. The three outside walls bore combination windows giving a panoramic view of the lake. At the moment, the view wasn't much. Inside, a picture window in the living area looked out onto the porch; a Dutch door made the connection between it and the house. I flipped the light switch next to the door and the porch was bathed in yellow bug-repelling light. There was a double bed supporting a naked mattress on one side of the door leading outside, a few sticks of outdoor furniture on the other. I dutifully went out and looked under the bed. "Nothing," I reported to the others when I came back in and closed the connecting door.

Feinman looked around the room. "No closets or anything," he muttered. "Basement?"

"No," I said. "Not this close to the water."

"Hell," he said. Gary watched David Letterman.

I said, "There's a chance he might come back."

"He's outta here," Thoreson countered with certainty.

"What makes you think he'll come back?" Feinman said.

"I don't think he *will,* just that he might. If I were Nordquist, I'd want to be ready to scram out of here at a moment's notice—or less. I'd keep as much stuff as possible—change of clothes, food, stuff like that—in the car. I wouldn't keep the loot inside. I'd either keep it in the car, or near it, ready to roll with me, or I'd bury it real deep someplace I could come back for it later."

Thoreson considered it, then said slowly, "You'd bury it. That way if you split and got caught, you'd have something to bargain with."

"See, you're already beginning to benefit from tagging along with me." He rolled his eyes but said nothing. I said, "I think I'd stash the car someplace else, too. Down the road, maybe. Then I'd keep an eye and an ear on the road"—I nodded in that general direction—"and if it looked like I was getting unexpected company, I'd slip out through the porch and cut along the beach to where I'd hidden the car. That'd buy me a few extra minutes."

"The deputy said most of these cabins are empty over the winter," Feinman said slowly. "Didn't he say the year-round places are on the other side of the lake somewhere? Then there wouldn't be a helluva lot of traffic on the road out front, right? Pretty safe bet that anyone who comes along might be looking for him."

"Might," I repeated. "Might. Would you run away and join the Foreign Legion because someone *might* be looking for you? Me, I'd get the hell away from this house, lie low for a few hours, then see if it was safe to sneak back. You know, figuring it's safe to hide in a place that's already been searched."

"These empty cabins, there're lots of places to hide."

"Yeah, maybe even places with a good view of *this* place. You told me Nordquist's not stupid. He did a stupid thing, but he'd not a stupid man. All right, we should figure he's thought of most of the angles, if not all of them."

"So what're you saying here, Pat—we stake out the place?"

"It might come to that, but let's see if we can't save a little time and effort first." I looked at my watch. Eleven-fifty. I said, "You guys leave. Make some noise going out, in case Nordquist's within earshot. Drive out the way we drove in. I'll hang around, quiet-like, and see if Nordquist comes back."

"You don't think he'll notice we came with four and left with three?" Thoreson said sardonically.

"We came with five," I reminded him, "and between the coming and going and the blackness of the night, I'm gambling that Nordquist, if he was watching, couldn't get a fix on exactly how many of us there were. Anyhow, what's to lose? You guys toddle along, Gary takes you to a hotel somewhere, you get a good night's sleep while I sit here in the dark, you swing back in the morning and pick me up, with or without Nordquist."

Feinman looked at Thoreson. "What do you think?"

"Sounds okay . . ." he said slowly. "But I should be the one who stays here."

I had seen that one coming from about a mile off; it was just a question of who would suggest it, Thoreson or his boss. I shrugged in what was meant to be a nonchalant fashion and said, "Far be it from me to interfere with your fun, but what's the difference?"

Thoreson looked at Feinman, who looked back. "Well, what *is* the difference, Terry?"

Thoreson looked a little exasperated. "The difference is we don't know the first thing about him."

"That's fair," I said, "I don't know the first thing about you."

Feinman laughed. "Touché," he said.

"Give the guy attaboys, Josh: he's looking out for your interests. See, what he's being too polite to say is that since you know from nothing about me, it could be that I'm working myself into a situation where I wait for Nordquist to show up, make him fork over the loot, then disappear in his car." The fact was, I was trying to work myself into a situation where I could exercise some control over Nordquist's fate if he did turn up. But I couldn't very well say as much.

"So it's occurred to you," Thoreson said tonelessly.

"Things occur to me all over the place; I have that kind of mind. For instance...." I whipped back my overcoat and sport coat, both of which were unbuttoned, and got the .38 into my hand in about as long as it takes to tell it. They were neatly arranged, with Feinman and Thoreson in front of me, Gary off to the side a little but still well within my peripheral vision. Thoreson started a little and Feinman's eyes widened fractionally; Gary, on the sofa, showed no reaction whatsoever. "It occurred to me a little while ago that I could pop you three right here, wait around for Nordquist, pop him, and disappear with however much he soaked you for, Josh. It occurred to me even earlier that I could keep quiet about finding the postcard in Nordquist's office, follow the trail here on my own, take care of Nordquist, and get the loot without going to the trouble of disappearing. You see, there are any number of ways I could turn this thing to my advantage if I wanted to. Point being, if I haven't pulled anything yet, I'm not going to."

I put the gun away.

Thoreson immediately grabbed for his piece—which verified my sneaking suspicion that he was carrying. Feinman placed a hand on his arm, stopping him. "Cool it, Terry." He looked at me for a long moment, expressionlessly. I did likewise. Then his face developed a small grin and he said, somewhat shakily, "I think maybe you're a couple bottles short a case, Pat."

"It's been suggested."

"What my old man would've called meshuggeh. I take your point, but you gotta keep in mind, Dave Nordquist was an honest man, at least by my lights, right up until the minute he ripped me off."

"I get your drift."

"So here's how we play it." He turned to Thoreson, whose face looked very hot. "Terry, you and Gare make yourself scarce. Do like the man says—go out of here making some noise, try to sound like maybe four, five guys, right? Go crash somewheres, come back for us in the A.M. Sometime after it gets light out." He looked back at me. "Sound copacetic to you, wild man?"

"It would be better to have more people leave, just in case Nordquist is keeping an eye on the place. But, yeah, sounds copacetic."

Thoreson, naturally, disagreed. He didn't want me to be on the scene at all, but if I was going to be around he wanted to ride shotgun with me. Feinman nixed that, though, and in the next breath declined Thoreson's offer of a gun. "No one's going to shoot anyone," he said decisively. Either he was showing me how trustworthy he was, or he was already armed.

In the end, Thoreson and Gary left, making a small racket of it as instructed. They put out all the lights as they went, leaving Feinman and me alone in the darkened little house. The place had not been warm to begin with, and with the lights doused it suddenly seemed even colder. I nestled into my overcoat.

"Now what?" Feinman said. In the stillness, his voice sounded very loud.

"Now we wait," I said quietly.

He stretched out on the couch. I pulled the reclining chair close to the makeshift bookcase, where I turned on the radio receiver, very low, and found a Minnesota Public Radio station. They were playing some of that quasi classical, quasi–New Age music that public radio stations put on late at night. I rested my revolver on the wide arm of the chair, near my right hand.

"You think you're gonna need that?" Feinman whispered.

"I'd rather have it handy and not need it than the other way around," I said.

24

With the house blackened, the sky outside the window became dark-blue, indigo, an almost purplish shade of black. Toward one o'clock, there was a little snow. The snowfall was thick and heavy, but brief; by one-ten it was all over. Even after it quit, though, the sky stayed thick and moonless.

Except for the occasional rustle of bare branches when the wind decided to flex its muscles, except for a noise in the brush that I decided was a foraging deer, except for the groans and pops that are the normal sounds of a house at night, all was quiet. I stood up a couple of times to stretch cold muscles, but for the most part I stayed put, motionless and soundless. The output from the radio was so soft as to be inaudible more than a few inches from the speakers. Nordquist's nerves were already strung to their maximum tension. I knew the feeling. I wanted nothing to alert him or spook him in case he was coming back to the cabin tonight.

Feinman seemed to instinctively pick up on this. Or maybe he just dozed off. In any event, he too was silent, and still, until almost two o'clock.

"What time is it?" he asked softly.

I told him.

"You think Dave's really going to come back?"

"He might—like I said before. He might not. At the moment, though, this is my best idea. My only one, in fact."

He gave a monosyllabic laugh.

The wind came up a little just then. It rattled the porch windows and the branches beyond them, and we fell silent and froze and listened expectantly for some sound other than the dull buzz of glass that was loose in its frame. None came, and the wind died down again.

Some time later Feinman said, "You don't have to worry about Nordquist, Pat."

"Was I worried about him?"

"I think so. That's why you wanted to hang around here, right? Instead of letting Thoreson, I mean. You thought maybe my idea was we'd find Nordquist, get the briefcase back, then whack him. You thought maybe me and Thoreson already cooked this up. So the only way to save Nordquist from big bad me was to make sure you were the one waiting to greet him if he shows up again. Right?"

"You're the one doing the talking," I said. "Too much of it, too, by the way."

"Nordquist isn't Superman, he can't hear a whisper from fifty yards away on a windy night. So why do you think I agreed to let you stay here, Pat? I mean, if I had it in for Nordquist, I could have gone along with Thoreson, let him be the welcoming committee. Why'd I go along with you?"

"You didn't. That's why you're here."

"Maybe I'm just here to keep you company."

"Remind me to thank you for that."

"Sure thing." He paused. "I wish I could have a cigarette."

"Lousy idea, Josh."

"I know that. Why do you think I'm wishing instead of lighting up." He sighed, but quietly. What he had said was true: Nordquist, or anyone else, would have to have ears like Rin Tin Tin to have overheard our conversation from outside. "The goddamn tobacco companies try to pretend nicotine isn't addictive. Like hell. This country really cared about public health, we'd ban smoking entirely. Period. No exceptions, no excuses."

"All you need is enough politicians eager to commit political hari-kari."

"It's the same with everything. Tax reform. AIDS. The war on drugs. Education. What a comedy."

"So when are you going to declare your candidacy, Joshua? I'll vote for you."

"Yeah, thanks, but I've got too much self-respect to run for public office. Anyhow, it's not the guy in front of the cameras who makes things happen. It's the guys behind him. I could see being behind the scenes, you know, getting something accomplished other than getting my face on TV. Maybe I will someday, I find the right front man."

"Why not your cousin?"

"Steve? That's a peculiar idea. Where'd that one come from?"

I wasn't sure myself; I took a moment to consider it. "I guess what you just described sounded a lot like the sort of job your cousin has at the club."

"Steve earns his keep," Feinman said, automatically and without much enthusiasm.

I said nothing.

"Most of the time," Feinman amended after a minute or so. He chuckled softly. "Some of the time. Who am I tryin' to fool, right? You and Sharon, you probably already talked about it. Well, what can I tell you that she didn't? Steve's a good sort, I love him like a brother, I really do, but, boy, there are times I could take and throw him off a building, you know? Mainly, his problem is he doesn't know what he wants to be when he grows up. Thirty-nine years old, the guy is. He's unfocused. He knows what he wants to *have*, but he doesn't know what he wants to *be*. Always been that way. When we were kids, I was forever pulling his bacon out of the fire. Steve was always good at getting in over his head. Then he'd come cryin' to me for help when he got his nose bloodied."

My mind flashed to Dimand sprawled in the easy chair in his living room, trying ineffectively to stanch the flow of blood streaming from his nose, ruining the upholstery. . . .

"Same kind of thing now he's grown up," Feinman whispered. "The guy's had some great jobs, you know—he's great with people, a real social-type guy—but he's always lousing them up. Decides he doesn't really feel like showing up today, or tomorrow, or maybe the next day too. . . . Then he's on the phone to me, wanting me to smooth things over for him, 'cause I know people around town."

I said, rather hopefully, "Maybe it's time to let him learn to fight his own battles."

"Maybe it's like thirty, thirty-five years *past* that time," Feinman agreed. "But, you know, what're you going to do? He's family, Pat. I couldn't just stand around and let him take his lumps. Not after all this time. We've always been there for each other. And maybe it's right that I'm responsible for Steve. I mean, he's the way he is at least partly because I've always been there to fight his battles. I made him the way he is, or I had a big hand in it. What am I supposed to do now, turn my back on him?"

And that answered that question. Dimand's battles were Feinman's battles. As long as Dimand said keep punching, Feinman would.

Lamely, I murmured, "I guess not."

"No. Hell, I even got to the point where I ended up hiring the guy. I mean, I was spending half my time lining up jobs for him and the other half trying to smooth his way back into them when he screwed up. Finally decided to eliminate the middleman."

"I thought Dimand owned a piece of the club."

A lot of silence went past before Feinman whispered, "You're certainly well informed, Pat."

I kept my voice casual. "I try. Just as you tried to check me out before you signed me on, I checked you out a little before I let myself be signed. And as you said, your life's an open book—comparatively. Most of what I know about you is the sort of stuff anyone could find out after a few hours in the public library and the hall of records. The club is owned by Club Associates, Ltd., which is a limited partnership of NorthLand Enterprises, Inc., and SJD Ventures. NorthLand Enterprises, basically, is you. I took a wild guess that SJD Ventures is Steven J. Dimand."

"A regular private detective, aren't you?"

I said nothing.

After another interval Feinman said, "Yeah, Steve owns a little chunk of the club, but most of the money behind the thing is mine, so the way I look at it is Steve works for me. I used to have him managing this little nightclub I own in St. Paul, but that was no good—he handed out too many free drinks. There's not too much trouble Steve can get into at the club, though. Not a lot of temptation, you know what I mean, with members having to sign for drinks. And this way I can keep an eye on him better."

"Was that the deal with Fahy, too?" I whispered. "Sharon told me you hired him on. . . ."

"That was altogether different. What I do for my cousin, I do for my cousin. Out of love, right? What I did for Fahy, I did for my sister. Also out of love. Fahy was a bum. Yeah, I gave him a job—I put him in charge of this appliance distributorship I own. But only because the s.o.b. had been fired from half the businesses in town, and I didn't want my kid sister to starve. If it was up to me, I wouldn't've given the bastard a swift kick in the balls, much less a cushy job he hardly bothered to show up for."

"Why do you suppose he took off?"

"Who gives a damn?"

"Your sister, for one."

He sighed. "Yeah, she loved the bastard—Christ knows why. I don't know why Fahy took a powder, and to be honest I don't give a great goddamn. I'm just damn glad he did. I suppose he must've got his claws into someone else he could sponge off of."

"That doesn't make sense—it sounds like he had a pretty cushy gig with you."

"Yeah. . . . Well, truth is, I canned his ass a couple days before he took off. The guy was a total screw-off, right? Anyhow, maybe when he found out he wasn't cutting any mustard with me, maybe that's when he decided to move on. Like I said, who cares? Anyway, I think you're right—I think maybe we shouldn't be yakking so much."

The room went silent once more. There was just enough light from the window in the near wall that a pale, bluish beam fell across my left hand. I moved it from the arm of the chair into my lap, into the darkness.

After a long while Feinman said quietly, "Pat. I never told my sister about my canning Fahy. Okay?"

"After all this time," I said, "maybe it doesn't matter anymore."

25

And so we waited in the darkness and the silence. It would have been easy for me to nod off—as I suspect Feinman might have—but I did not. Nordquist, for all we knew, may have been armed. Feinman, too, as I had already considered. And everybody was a little on edge. I wanted all my wits about me to make sure nobody got hurt. Especially me.

Especially—not exclusively. There was still something off-center about this whole Nordquist business. I was having a tough time buying into the assertion that Feinman only wanted to get his money back and have a long heart-to-heart with Nordquist, after which everybody would live happily ever after. Maybe that's what Feinman had in mind. Maybe Nordquist was a valued employee and friend, valued enough that Feinman would simply box his ears and slap his butt and put him back to work. Cynic that I was, though, I had a hard time believing it. I only had to think of my friend Robert Olson warming a hospital bed that should have been mine, or of the men in parked cars watching my apartment—or, for that matter, of the fact that we were here in the darkness, lying in wait for David Nordquist—to remember that Joshua Feinman, for all his talk and sentiments and genuine affability, could be one ruthless s.o.b.

And there was now no question but that Feinman was the man to beat. My conversations with Feinman over the past several hours had eliminated any doubt in my mind completely. They had convinced me, further, that Feinman would keep the heat on as long as Dimand wanted. And that I had little hope of convincing Dimand to cease hostilities against me as long as he had his cousin to fight his battles for him, since by his own admission Feinman wasn't about to stop now.

Therefore Feinman had to go. Somehow. I would have to be every bit as ruthless as him if I expected to ever be rid of him.

And yet I sat there in the gloom with a loaded revolver at my side, ready to use it in defense of David Nordquist, if the necessity arose. Which only proved I was still far from ruthless. I had enough ruths, whatever they may be, to know I could not sit by and allow Feinman to injure Nordquist, if that was what he had in his heart—even though doing just that would provide the tool I needed to take care of Feinman for good.

In the last analysis, there has to be something more than a couple of letters to distinguish the goodguys from the badguys. There has to be a line you won't cross, no matter how noble the ends. For me, in this case, the line was the sacrifice of an innocent bystander.

Beyond that, though . . . well, I would have to play it by ear. I couldn't guarantee Nordquist's safety indefinitely if Feinman had it in for him. And it wasn't my bright idea for him to rip off Feinman in the first place.

But it was all academic until and unless Nordquist showed his face.

◇◇◇

Near dawn, when the world takes on that cold, unearthly cast and time itself seems frozen, Nordquist returned.

My eyes were closed and my mind was floating in space, several planes above the one on which we dwell, but I was not asleep. I heard the soft tramp of a footstep on the concrete pad at the front door, the faint squeak of snow underfoot. I reached a hand behind me and snapped off the radio. Then I palmed my .38.

Feinman started, and moved up onto his elbows. I motioned for silence, and indicated that he should follow me. We moved quickly but quietly to the hallway across the room.

There was the scrape of a key in the front-door lock, then the *whoosh* of cold pre-dawn air. A long pause; in my mind's eye I saw Nordquist peering into the room, waiting and listening. He would notice the relocated chair—there was enough light for that—but how would he react? I was ready to chase after him if he retreated back into the cold.

But he did not. I heard him step heavily into the room, stamping snow from his feet onto the rough mat inside the front door, then the door shut solidly behind him. I heard him shoot the dead bolt.

Behind me, I heard a soft, wet click as Feinman opened his mouth to speak. I raised a hand in a halting gesture.

Nordquist came into my field of vision shedding a hooded parka, peeling gloves from his hands, crossing the room toward the Dutch doors in the opposite wall. He peered through the little window, looking out onto the porch, perhaps, or beyond it toward the lake. I stepped out of the hallway.

"Don't move," I said softly.

He moved. He jumped and spun around and flung himself, or fell, against the porch door. His eyes were wide and his mouth was open, and in the funny light his face was an unhealthy gray.

"Who are you?" he whispered hoarsely as soon as he could.

I felt, rather than heard Feinman move in behind me. Suddenly I wished he was in my sight, too. I waited for the thud of a sap or the roar of a gun, but nothing came, nothing except Feinman's gentle, relaxed voice: "This is Pat Kilpatrick, Dave," he said. "He found you for us."

Nordquist let out a small groan and sagged against the door. All I had ever seen of him was a standard personnel-department mug shot Feinman had showed me the previous night, one of those bland, badly lighted, stand-there-look-here snaps. In person Nordquist was a bigger man, although he still had a bookish, introverted look to him that I had seen in the mug shot. He had small brown eyes behind round gold-rimmed glasses; small, regular features in a smooth, clean-shaven face; and a mop of dark-blond hair now mostly hidden beneath a festively decorated stocking cap. He was a little taller than me, maybe a shade over six feet, and heftier—I had lost twelve pounds since going underground, not a weight-loss program I would recommend—but he was not a fighter, and even if he had been there was no fight in him now.

I moved away from Feinman and stepped over to the light switches near the front door and found the one that worked the ceiling lamp over the dining table. This was better: I had Feinman in my peripheral vision—although he appeared utterly nonthreatening, standing in the doorway to the hall with his hands in his coat pockets, calmly regarding Nordquist. Who, for his part, looked more than a little ill.

"Move over there," I said to Nordquist, indicating the dining table, "and put your hands on the back of that chair." He did as instructed and I patted him down. He was light. I let him straighten up again.

"I thought you guys had given up," he said, his voice shaking.

"That's what you were supposed to think. You had another hideout."

He nodded. "Some friends of mine, they have a cabin down the road," he blurted. "I've been parking my car down there, just in case. I have a key—we sort of look after each other's place, you know—and when I heard the cars and saw the lights last night, I ran out the porch here and spent the night over there. I thought by now you'd have given up and gone back to the Cities. I was going to get my things and be on the road before dawn."

"Where were you headed?"

He pulled out the chair in front of him and sat down heavily. "I don't know. Away. That's the whole problem here—I never thought anything through."

I looked at Feinman. He hadn't moved. He had a peculiar look on his face; I couldn't quite make it. "Talk to me, Dave," he said after a long time.

Nordquist looked at him for a very long time, then hung his head and began to speak in a low monotone. The story held no surprises. Nordquist was being buried alive under bills for his mother's care, then news came that she had been hospitalized. He was at the end of his rope when Opportunity presented itself, all dolled up in frilly clothes with a bow in its hair. "The briefcase was there, and I was there, and suddenly all I could think of was money. It's funny, Josh—" He looked at the man. "I must've had a hundred chances, a thousand, to steal from you over the years. I never even thought of it, not seriously. I'm a coward, basically. But Monday . . . I don't know, something just happened—it was like it wasn't even me, like I was standing apart watching this guy. The guy went over to the safe and he opened the safe and he took out the briefcase and he walked away with it, and the guy was me." He shivered. "And then I found out my mother was—"

"We know, Dave," Feinman said softly. "I'm real sorry about that."

Nordquist, his head down again, nodded and sniffled wetly. "So what did I need money for then? Huh? Only by then it was too late." He raised his head and looked at Feinman again. His eyes were wet. "Too late, Josh," he said.

Feinman looked very tired. And why not—neither of us had had a restful night. He said, "It isn't too late if we don't let it be too late. Do you hear me, Dave?"

He gave no indication that he had, but he looked away from Feinman and fixed his gaze on the space between Feinman and me. I glanced at Feinman, but his eyes stayed locked on his employee. There was something going on here, some kind of communication between them in a language that was meaningless to me.

"You know," Nordquist said to no one in particular, "after I found out . . . about Mom . . . I thought maybe I would just wrap the briefcase up, you know, pack it in a box and Fed Ex it back to the office. I thought maybe if you had it back you would leave me alone, let me just disappear somewhere. Nice dream, huh?" He glanced at me.

He wasn't simply sharing a dream; he was proposing an arrangement. An arrangement with me. I became aware of the weight of the gun in my hand, as I realized what Nordquist was getting at. Take care of Feinman and you can have the briefcase. Just leave me alone. If it occurred to him that I could take care of both of them and have the briefcase, he didn't let on.

"Don't be stupid, Dave," Feinman said. There was a hard edge to his voice now, a timbre that had not been there a moment ago.

"I've already been stupid," Nordquist said. He was looking at me directly now.

"Don't be more stupid, then. Nothing's happened yet that can't be undone. There's nothing here we can't all walk away from and forget about. Let's keep it that way, right?"

I had been looking at Nordquist too long. Now I looked quickly at Feinman. He was slowly pulling his right hand out of his overcoat pocket.

I moved the gun slightly. "You're making me nervous, Joshua," I said.

He stopped, fixed me with a long look, then slowly grinned. "This is not good, what you're thinking."

"What am I thinking?"

"Maybe about how far away you can get before Thoreson shows up."

"You'll never find the briefcase without me," Nordquist said quickly, a little shrilly.

"That old thing? I already know where it is." My eyes were still on Feinman. His eyes narrowed as I spoke.

"Pat . . ." he said.

"I think I'd like it a lot better if you took your hands out of your pockets, Josh, very slowly, and put them behind your back, fingers intertwined."

"Pat, this is very dumb . . ." But he was doing as I suggested.

"You may be right." I stepped forward and lightened his overcoat by the weight of a flat 9-millimeter automatic. "Or I may be right." I pocketed the piece and patted him down to see if he had brought any other playthings with him.

"What, you really think I planned to whack Dave? With you here as a witness? How dumb do you think I am, Pat?"

"I suppose either I wouldn't be a witness or I wouldn't stay one for very long."

He shook his head. "It isn't like that at all, Pat," he said calmly. "That's not how I handle things. Tell him, Dave."

Nordquist said nothing. I thought about Robert Olson in the hospital with a broken head. I wondered what Nordquist was thinking about. He had known Feinman a lot longer than I had.

"Thoreson gave me that piece last night," Feinman went on. "For self-protection. Looks like he was right—looks like I needed it." He eyed the gun in my fist.

"And it looks like I need this to save Nordquist's neck—and mine."

Feinman shook his head. "It isn't like that," he repeated.

I said, "The problem here is everybody's trying to guess what everybody else is thinking, and act or react accordingly. The only place that's liable to get any of us is the morgue."

"I'll tell you where the briefcase is," Nordquist said. "You just let me walk out of here, get to my car, and leave." Now that I clearly had the upper hand, he didn't feel obliged to be coy anymore.

"I already told you, that's old news. In fact, let's go retrieve it now. I want a look at this famous attaché."

Nordquist didn't budge.

"Look here, Dave, didn't anyone ever tell you that the guy with the gun gets to call the tune? Guess not. Well, who can blame you? I might be bluffing, after all, and from where you sit that briefcase must look like your only bargaining chip." I turned to Feinman. "Looks like it's up to us, Josh."

He shrugged his shoulders. "Up to you, you mean."

It was almost light by now. I said, "Let's go outside and watch the sunrise."

26

I steered the two men outside via the porch, out the lake side of the house. The air was biting. The world had that dull bluish gray cast it takes on just before sunup. It was very quiet.

There was a tiny patch of scruffy lawn on this side of the house, quickly giving way to sand now spottily coated with snow. The wind drew patterns in the light new snow, occasionally kicking up blinding clouds of the stuff. The ground sloped down to the lake, whose waters ate at the snow on the shore. The lake had a slushy, chunky look to it; in this light it looked like a wide crater filled with molten metal.

Straight down from the porch door there was a short, wide dock. Most of the snow had blown off of it. I directed Feinman and Nordquist out onto the dock. Nordquist appeared apprehensive. Feinman appeared completely emotionless.

The dock, though clear, was slippery, as Feinman proved to himself. "Watch your step, Josh," I said, "unless you're a member of the Polar Bear Club."

He gave me a look. "Do you think you'll get away with this, Pat?"

"Hard to say, since I don't know what I'm doing yet." I took my eyes off him long enough to peer over the edge of the dock. "Let's keep moving, men—right out to the end there. Now we know what they mean by a long walk on a short pier."

Feinman said, "I was so wrong about you, Pat."

Nordquist said, "I've got a little money saved up, in the bank. . . ."

I said, "Everybody shut up." I glanced over the side of the dock—no more than that, since I didn't feel like having an early-morning dip any more than Feinman did, and I didn't want to give my companions the idea that that might be just the thing for me. "No good," I mumbled. I couldn't see a thing except lead-gray water.

I looked at Nordquist. "You want to do the honors?" He looked awfully pale, but in that light so did the rest of us, and everything around us. He tried to pretend he hadn't heard me. I turned to Feinman. "Sorry, Joshua, your friend declines. So I'll need you to lie facedown on the dock, your head over the end."

"What the hell do you—"

"Just do it, all right? That's good. No, you'll have to scoot up to the edge more. . . . Dave, hold his legs." That had the added benefit of keeping Nordquist occupied, and where I could keep an eye on him.

Feinman swore colorfully but quietly. "Would you mind telling me just what the *fuck* I'm doing this for?"

"Because I asked nicely. Now look around, Josh. What do you see?"

"Water, you son of a—"

"Look around the underside of the dock and tell me what you see."

"Wood." His voice, coming from beneath the dock, sounded distant and small, all but drowned out by the sloshing and chopping of the lake. "Wet, slimy wood. Now can I get up, you goddam— Wait a minute. There's— Get me up!"

"Get him up, Dave." I assisted, one-handedly. Once we got him pulled up, Feinman didn't really stand but instead scrabbled across the dock, about three feet back from the end, where he flattened himself again and leaned out over the water. I gestured Nordquist to take Feinman's legs and counterbalance his weight, and he responded glumly.

"I couldn't reach it from down there," Feinman was saying. "It's clear back behind. . . . Gotcha!"

Nordquist looked at me dolefully. "How did you know?"

"Nylon rope and plastic trash bags—I found the wrapper and empty box in the kitchen wastebasket. And spent half the night wondering what you had used a whole box of plastic liners for, when there wasn't a single one to be found in the house. I finally figured you wrapped everything up nice and waterproof, then sank it in the lake on the end of a nylon rope that wouldn't deteriorate over the winter. Once the lake froze over, it'd be safe till spring. The dock was the most likely bet."

"Pull me up!" Feinman hollered.

We did. He rolled back into a sitting position and started hauling up a yellow nylon rope, hand over hand. "The end was tied to a crossbeam, practically in the middle of the dock. You must be half-monkey, Dave, to have tied it there." He glanced at Nordquist, who sat silently on the wet wood of the dock.

Eventually Feinman ran out of slack in the rope and began having to really put his back into the task. There seemed to be a lot more than fifty feet of rope there, but eventually Feinman reached the end and landed a bulky parcel wrapped in white plastic. Icy water streamed from it as Feinman, groaning, dumped it on the dock and got stiffly to his feet.

"What'd you weight it with—concrete?"

I jabbed the package with the barrel of my gun, piercing a couple layers of plastic. Clumps of frozen sand mixed with snow fell out. "You're half right," I said to Feinman. He turned away from Nordquist and looked. Nordquist apparently had wrapped the case in plastic, then partially filled two bags with dirty sand scraped up from the beach. He knotted the bags together and slung them over the top of the case, like saddlebags over the back of a horse. Then he wrapped it all in plastic once more and lashed the package together with a length of the nylon rope. He attached that to the longer length of rope, which he must have first anchored to the underside of the dock, and let it sink.

"Nice gift-wrapping," Feinman said.

"Especially for something as comparatively waterproof as currency," I noted.

Feinman looked at me long and hard, then bent and began to claw at the big knots connecting the long rope to the rope securing the package. But only for a minute. Even as I was watching him work, his left hand suddenly darted for the small pile of sand that had built up next to the case and, in the same movement, flung about a cupful at my face. I saw it coming, but couldn't seem to react fast enough. Most of the sand caught me in the face, and I turned my head to try to avoid it. It was damp, half-frozen, and it hurt when it hit. My fake glasses protected me less than I would have guessed. I staggered backward a couple of steps, fighting to keep my footing on the slippery dock, trying to see the edge of the dock and at the same time trying to keep an eye out for Feinman, all the while temporarily blinded by the grit.

I shouldn't have worried about Feinman: he found me. He plowed headfirst into my breadbasket with a force that was more than a little reckless, considering the narrowness of the dock. It wouldn't have taken much to send us both plunging into the frigid gray lake. So when he hit me, I tried to go straight down, not backward and down, and pretty much succeeded. I bumped my head on the wood when I went, which sent my glasses flying and maybe knocked some of the sand from my eyes. At any rate, I could see Feinman clearly enough. He was sitting on top of me, more or less straddling my chest—my going down the way I did must have caught him off-guard, and he seemed to be struggling to get his balance and get his hand on the gun in my right fist.

I had his automatic in my left-hand coat pocket, but when I fell back my coat got scrunched up under my back. I could feel the butt of the automatic digging into my spine. Completely inaccessible, what with approximately two hundred pounds of Joshua Feinman sitting on me.

I brought my left fist up and jabbed him in the ribs. His heavy overcoat padded the blow, so I tried it again a couple of times, finally eliciting a low groan.

He had both hands on my right arm now, one of them trying to keep it pinned to the dock while the other groped for the weapon.

I reached higher with my left hand, clawing at his face. He turned his head away. I was trying to get a handful of his curly locks, to see if I could pull him back away from my right hand, but I couldn't reach any higher than his neck. For fun, I raked my nails down the side of his neck, and he cursed.

He took his right hand away long enough to cock and aim a punch at my head, but I was expecting that. I turned my head and bent my neck and brought up my left shoulder, and took most of the blow on my collarbone. I don't know that it hurt any less than it would have if he'd hit my head, but at least it didn't put me under.

I grabbed at his right hand, the one he had punched me with. He tried to yank it away, but I caught the useless little tab near the end of his coat sleeve, which was wet and grimy from his lying prostrate on the dock, and I managed to work my fingers around his wrist, locking them tightly.

We stayed frozen like that for a long moment—me on my back, Feinman pinning my gun hand to the dock while I kept his right arm away from his body, and me. Sooner or later one of us would have to let go.

Probably me. Feinman was a hefty guy—what they used to call husky. Heavy, but not fat. Solid. His weight on my chest was making breathing a little dicey; I still hadn't managed to get back all the wind he knocked out of me when he butted me. The odds were, if we stayed locked like that, I would buckle first.

That was to be avoided.

I swung my legs up behind Feinman's back. The exercise regimen I had been forcing myself to endure at the club had paid off. I sort of had in mind grabbing Feinman's head between my ankles and pulling him off me—I saw it once on *All-Star Wrestling*—but Feinman was less cooperative than the victim on TV. He was leaning too far forward; I would have had to be Plastic Man to have bent my legs that direction, exercise regimen or no.

So I settled for the next best thing: bringing my legs up into the air as far as I could, then bringing them down again, fast, tightening my abdominal muscles and using the momentum of my legs to bring my torso up.

Feinman fell backward as his balance went. He loosened his grip on my right arm. I jerked it away and at the same time let go of his right wrist and pushed him, hard, with my left hand to his chest. He fell back further, almost off of me, almost off of the dock, and I rolled away from him and scrambled to my feet, gulping in cold air, blinking my streaming eyes, and bringing the gun up to where it could do some good.

I looked around for Nordquist. I had wondered for a sliver of an instant if he would come to my assistance, seeing as how he felt—with some justification—that he had to beware of Feinman. Or would he side with Feinman, trying to get back into his employer's good graces? It had not occurred to me, in that brief interval, that Nordquist might do what he had in fact done: split. The plastic-shrouded briefcase was where Feinman had left it, still connected to the yellow rope. Feinman was crouched near it, breathing heavily, rubbing his bleeding neck, and eyeing me murderously. And I was there, blinking grit from my eyes. But of David Nordquist there was no sign.

"Well," Feinman gasped, "now you don't have to worry about me killing him."

I looked at him a long time. Then I slid the revolver into its holster. Feinman's eyes widened just a little. "And now," I said, "you don't have to worry about me killing you." I closed the short distance between us. "Which I never had in mind." I stuck out my hand.

Feinman studied it as if it was the first of its kind, then he put his hand in it and let me help him up. He groaned, and stretched his back muscles. "I'm too old and fat for this kind of crap."

"I wish you'd thought of that before you started it."

"Hey, can you blame me? All I could think of was me and Nordquist down there where the briefcase used to be, with the carp nibbling on our toes, while you were living it up in Rio or wherever."

"Aruba, I think. Come on, let's go in and find a knife so we can cut the goddamn thing loose."

27

There was new snow, and the hour was early enough that the snow would be fairly undisturbed. I suggested to Feinman that we might be able to pick up Nordquist's trail. He shrugged it off.

"We got what we came for," he said, patting the parcel now sitting, dripping, in Nordquist's kitchen sink. Feinman had a serrated steak knife, the best thing we could find for freeing the package from its yellow lifeline, and was using it now to take care of the rope wrapped around the briefcase and the various layers of plastic wrapping.

"I thought we came to bring Nordquist back into the fold," I said.

"That too. But it didn't look like he wanted to be brought, right?"

Right enough. In fact, Nordquist looked downright horrified the moment he caught sight of Feinman. No poker-face, Nordquist—and his expression, I thought, was not merely that of an employee caught with his hand in the corporate cookie jar.

Nordquist had done a good job wrapping up the briefcase. The only moisture on its metal surface was that which had dribbled onto it as Feinman, cursing under his breath, shredded away the layers of plastic. Feinman took a handkerchief from his back pocket and wiped down the chrome surface. He glanced at me.

"Go ahead and open it," I said. "You're dying to see if it's all there, and I already know it's not Yankee dollars, from the way you and Nordquist have been acting. What does that leave? Jewels? Stamps? Bearer bonds, baseball cards, a Gutenberg bible? Call me pedestrian, but I'm thinking more along the lines of your standard mood-enhancing pharmaceuticals. In fact, the only thing I'm really curious about is whether you smoke it, snort it, or shoot it."

Feinman had a sort of half-grin on his face, a what-the-hell grin than matched what he said, which was "What the hell," as he hefted the case out of the sink.

Nordquist had had to break the combination-lock tabs on the case, though, so when Feinman lifted it up by the handle and the weight shifted, the case opened and the contents spilled out onto the linoleum. A dozen tightly wrapped bundles, each somewhat smaller than a standard brick, carefully sealed in transparent plastic.

"That's a lot of baking soda," I said.

Feinman knelt and began carefully picking up the bundles and replacing them in the attaché.

You couldn't blame Nordquist for having been jumpy. Bad enough to steal from your employer—but to steal what you thought was a briefcase full of money and find out it was in fact a briefcase full of cocaine. . . . Nordquist would have to know that that amount of coke indicated Feinman was a major player in the drug game. It was way too much to be his recreational stash, probably too much even to be for noncash bribes. People don't realize how picayune most bribes are: fifty to this inspector, a hundred to that contractor. If all that coke was for payoffs, then Feinman either was buying some pretty heavy-duty guys, or all the small fry in the upper Midwest. Dealing or not, he had to have some solid connections in order to come up with a score like that. That made him a major player, all right. And anyone who reads a newspaper knows that such people are not to be trifled with.

Was that the basis of Nordquist's fear? Or did it run deeper? Did he know, or suspect, something about his former employer, something that would have filled Nordquist with dread even if the briefcase had turned out to be loaded with chocolate chips?

Maybe I was projecting. I needed something heavy to lay on Feinman, heavy enough to balance the weight he had put on me. Drug trafficking was pretty damn heavy. But I was light on evidence. So maybe I was hoping that Dave Nordquist knew about other closets containing other skeletons and, not wanting to become a skeleton himself, had tried to bribe a total stranger—me—rather than take his chances with a man he had known and worked with for years. Better the devil you know, they say—but if the devil you know is really bad news, then maybe you'd figure yourself better off taking your chances with the devil you don't know.

What it all came down to was, I wanted to be able to ask Nordquist. What was he scared of? Obviously Feinman wasn't about to turn him over to the law—and maybe that's what scared him. Did he think Feinman would mete out his own justice? Did he have *reason* to think that, or was he just scared by his discovery of Feinman's drug activity? Without Nordquist I had nothing more than I had had all along: the certainty that Joshua Feinman was a wrong guy, but nothing solid to use as a weapon against him. Of course, I may have ended up with exactly that even with Nordquist—but I would have liked to have found out for sure.

I said, "Don't you think it was a little reckless parking this with Nordquist? I mean, I understand he was a trusted employee and all that good stuff, but still. . . ."

Feinman had the goods back in place and carried the open case over to the dining table. He was smiling at me. "What," he said, "you think I'm stupid?"

A light bulb appeared over my head. "I apologize, Josh—the junk was in Nordquist's safe, not yours . . . and that was the point."

"In case anyone got curious and dropped by unannounced-like. Geez, Dave, you sure did a nice number on these locks," he said in disgust. "Thing's shot. You know how much a case like this costs?"

The guy had a load of cocaine worth more than the economies of some nations, and he was complaining about having to buy a new briefcase. I had to laugh.

"Lash it up with that piece of rope," I said. "It'll get you where you're going."

He laughed. "Yeah, we'll look like a bunch of immigrants, but what the fuck." He went to work on it.

I said, "So that's it for Nordquist? We let him drift?"

"Like the new-fallen snow," Feinman said poetically. "What's he going to do, right? Call a cop, say he stole something from a guy and the guy came and took it back?" He spat a half-laugh.

"If he told the cop what he stole, it could mean some embarrassing questions for you, Josh."

"I don't embarrass easy," Feinman said carelessly. He finished with the briefcase and looked at his wristwatch. "Where the hell's Thoreson? I wanna get back to town, move this stuff before I get old."

"Is that for selling, or just for spreading around?"

He looked at me laconically and said nothing.

I shrugged, putting on my drowsy, languid, who-gives-a-damn face. Young Robert Mitchum. "You ever looking for some outlets, give me a jingle." It was bullshit, of course, but I didn't want to come off looking like a guy who was just too curious.

Feinman nodded, and looked at his watch again.

We got back to the Twin Cities around ten-thirty. Feinman wanted to take Thoreson and me to some diner in Minneapolis for what he called "a big, greasy, cholesterol-loaded All-American breakfast," but I begged off. I said I had an appointment later on to start work on a root canal, and there were a couple of things I needed to do first. The dental beg-off is one of the best. Except for a few truly disturbed individuals, no one enjoys talking about dentistry. Endodontia is the worst—worse than extraction even. Tell someone you have to run off for a root-canal job, that's the end of the discussion.

The morning was cold and clear; the sun was blinding, reflecting off the snow that had fallen last night. The roads were fairly clear by this hour, but traffic was moving slowly. Smaller cars were getting bogged down on those side streets where snowplows or traffic hadn't yet blazed a trail.

Feinman's idea of a tasty, untrendy, and undoubtedly unhealthy breakfast sounded appetizing, so I swung through the drive-up at the McDonald's on West Seventh Street in St. Paul, just off 494, grabbed a bag containing some unidentifiable yellow substance between two leathery English muffins, and took it back to my efficiency apartment. There I threw together a pot of coffee and took care of the little sandwich in about two bites. Then I pulled out the list I had swiped from Dave Nordquist's office the night before and flattened it on the rickety dining table.

NORTHLAND ENTERPRISES, INC.
NL PROPERTIES
NL Property Management

ParkCo, Ltd.
NL LEASING CO.
JAY-EF ENTERTAINMENT CO.
  EntertainmenTime, Ltd.
  Sven & Ole Co.
CLUB ASSOCIATES, LTD. [SJD Ventures]
PLAZA PARTNERS [Western Realty]
NORLAN DISTRIBUTING CO.
  CeramiCo
  NorLan Appliance Co.

The list didn't mean a heck of a lot more to me now than it had last night. Club Associates, of course, owned the racquetball club. SJD Ventures was one of the partners in Club Associates, so I could assume that the other bracketed name, Western Realty, was one of the Plaza Partners. Perhaps they were involved in the strip-mall deal Feinman had mentioned to me. NorLan Appliance had to be the no-show job Feinman had given his brother-in-law.

I got out the St. Paul and Minneapolis phone books. There was a so-called comedy club in Minneapolis called Sven & Ole's; maybe Feinman owned that via Sven & Ole Co. ParkCo appeared to be one of those parking-lot-management operations; logical enough. Similarly, I found CeramiCo in the Yellow Pages under Ceramics—Equipment & Supplies. Also logical. EntertainmenTime handled vending machines "of all types & lines," according to the little ad.

I got out a felt-tipped pen and drew some dollar signs next to some of the names: ParkCo, EntertainmenTime, and, after a moment's thought, Sven & Ole Co. Those seemed most likely to be generators of sizable quantities of lovely anonymous cash. Then I drew arrows next to both of the NorLan Distributing companies, CeramiCo and NorLan Appliance Co. You didn't have to use up a lot of brainpower figuring out that they were set up for distribution. After another moment's thought, I penned an arrow next to EntertainmenTime. With big coin-op machines to lug around, they'd have trucks and loading docks and all the rest of the distribution trappings.

Cash comes in over here, product—drugs, maybe?—goes out over there.

And what better way to distribute an illegal product than

through a legitimate distribution setup? No one would give a second thought to trucks coming and going, people hanging around, rough-and-tumble types drifting in and out. Why should they? And if some of those trucks carried something besides iceboxes and jukeboxes, who was to know?

I turned back to the phone catalogues and looked up some addresses.

I grabbed a pencil and started to write them down on a piece of scratch paper. Then I stopped, and tore up the paper, and went and flushed it down the toilet. It was no good, writing things down these days—and for a guy who's spent half his working life as a writer and the other half as an investigator keeping track of things for eventual reports, breaking the habit was tough. But I couldn't afford to have anything suspicious on me in case I was braced, and I couldn't have much around the apartment in case Feinman decided to have someone toss it. I had had to risk it last night with Nordquist's list, of course, since I'm not blessed with a photographic memory. For that reason, too, I couldn't now destroy that list as well. I looked around the dinky apartment for a good hiding place.

I settled on the dining table. It was an ancient, wobbly thing constructed of some mysterious yellowy wood. It showed many years of abuse, which is the fate of furnished-apartments' furnishings. Once upon a time it had had a leaf or two to go with it, but there was no sign of one around the place today. I pulled the two halves of the table apart a couple of inches, refolded Nordquist's list twice the long way, and Scotch-taped it to the inside edge of one of the halves of the tabletop. Then I shoved the halves together again. The list, hidden in the eighth-inch-wide groove down the middle of the table, was virtually invisible. When I repositioned the doily and cheap vase of plastic daisies—also part of the furnishings—it was completely invisible.

I went downstairs and got into my car.

It was late morning—it almost wasn't morning anymore—and the streets were clogged with people who skipped out of the office early to grab some lunch or run their noontime errands. I drove out West Seventh, a.k.a. Fort Road, to where it melds into I-494. The airport was just a couple miles farther west.

On the ground level of the main terminal, not far from the

transportation cops' office, was a bank of telephone booths. Not the silly, copper-plated, open-air cubicles you found upstairs, but real honest-to-God telephone booths, with folding doors and dim lights that came on when you closed the door and little ventilation fans that did no damn good as far as anyone could tell. There was never much traffic on this end of the terminal: the baggage carousels were up on the other end. I slid into the booth on the far end and dropped some change.

Three or four hundred miles away, in the Cornhusker State, Pat Costello answered the phone in his pharmacy.

This time I gave as my prescription number the number on the strip on the front of the pay phone. I gave him a false name, too—I mean a different false name than the one I had been using all this time.

We were in luck: the pay phone was one of the old-fashioned ones that will take an incoming call. I answered it on the first ring, three minutes after I had hung up.

"Is everything okay?" were Pat's first words.

"Relatively," I said. "I'm alive, which is usually a good sign. And I've managed to get close to Feinman."

"Feinman? I thought you said his name was Dimand?"

"Sorry—I confused our indirect communication with the genuine article. Dimand is the mouth; Joshua Feinman, his cousin, is the muscle. Likable guy, in a lot of ways, but definitely a wrong number. Dimand gets himself in over his head and Feinman yanks him out of the soup. I guess it's been like that since they were kids. Feinman's dirty—well, he'd just about have to be, in order to pull the kind of practical joke he pulled on me—and I'm hoping that by sticking to him, winning his confidence, and keeping eyes and ears open, I can get something to barter with."

"Blackmail, you mean."

"Ugly connotations, but an otherwise accurate word. Listen, the reason I'm calling is that I found out for a fact that Feinman's people have the know-how and the wherewithal to tap into a phone line. They did it with an employee of Feinman's who went missing: whenever the guy's home phone rings, a phone that belongs to Feinman rings also. I don't know if that means they can trace. Let's assume they can, and let's definitely assume they've rigged a similar deal to my phone, okay?"

Pat pretended to be offended. "You think I just stepped off the banana boat, bub? I've been calling your answering machine from pay phones the whole time, and I've been varying the pay phones, too."

"Good. Just for fun, try not to use the same phone twice. By the way, where are you calling from now?"

"I'm in Danny Greca's office," Pat said. Greca ran a little Texaco station down the street from Pat's store. "I figured it'd beat slamming dimes down a slot, and anyway I've got one of the cars in for an oil-change this morning, so it won't look funny, my coming up here. In case anyone's interested."

"I'm glad to see some of my paranoia's rubbing off on you."

"I'm glad to see your paranoia has paid off," Pat said. "Or maybe I'm not, on second thought."

I knew what he meant. You get into a jam, and you spend half your time trying to convince yourself you're overreacting. I still found myself having to shut up the little voice in my head that kept insisting everything was all right, things aren't—can't be—as bad as they seem. If you're really in a jam, listening to that little voice can be bad news. The worst, even.

"How's life in the big city?"

"Pretty fair," Pat said. "I haven't smelled any trouble. Yet. There was a car hanging around the block three-four days ago, over by the liquor store, but I haven't seen it the last couple days." It was the sort of neighborhood that saw mostly "regulars"; an unfamiliar car would stand out.

"Ford Tempo? Buick SkyHawk?" I said, remembering the two rental cars staking out Decatur Street that fateful—and potentially fatal—night.

"No, one of those little Toyota sportscar thingies. Corona, Corolla, who knows? I copied down the plate number, but like I said, it hasn't been around again. Probably casing the liquor store; Sid hasn't been held up in almost a year now."

"You're probably right," I said. Or maybe the badguys traded in their rentals. "All the same, be careful."

"Like always. Christ, it's good to talk to you. When I call up your machine and see you've erased my message from the day before, I figure you're alive and more or less well. But it ain't the same as hearing your voice and *knowing* you're still okay."

"Believe me, I know exactly what you mean. How's Koosje doing? You been keeping an eye on her for me?"

Pat cleared his throat. "Yeah . . . well, the way it is, I kind of ignored your instructions and clued her in to what was going on with you. As much I knew, that is, which wasn't much."

"Hey, you knew as much as I knew."

"Right. Anyhow, Koosje's too smart to fall for that business about your being suddenly called out of town, all that crap. She'd wonder why you never got in touch with her. She'd figure out that the reason must be you're in trouble. And she'd worry. Plus, if there's a chance these jokers might try to flush you out through one of you're friends . . ."

"You're right: she'd be top of the list. Better she should know to keep her eyes open. Anyhow, I had already told her my suspicions after Robert was ambushed, so she knew that much of it at least. Once again you're thinking more clearly than I was, Costello."

"Yeah—it's lucky I use my powers for good," he drawled. "I've been in touch with Koosje every two or three days. She's fine. Hasn't noticed anything unusual or suspicious or anything. She's a little nervous, naturally—for you as well as herself—but she's okay. Very levelheaded, Kosh is."

He was right. It made the back of my throat ache just to think about her.

It hurt, too, to realize how much I had missed having someone to talk to these past weeks—someone with whom I could be myself and to whom I could talk about what was really on my mind. As Pat Kilpatrick, I was always on guard. I had to stay in character. I had to watch my voice, keep to the timbre and pattern and cadence I had affected—not just when I was around Steven Dimand, but all the time, at the supermarket, at the gas station, at the post office, lest I get lazy and slip up when it was important not to slip up. I had to watch what I said, make sure I gave away nothing that might link me to my real life, nothing that might start someone thinking along lines I would rather he not think along. Even with Sharon Fahy I could not relax. I felt I could trust her—at least to a point—but I didn't dare let something drop that she might pick up and comment on, in all innocence, to her brother or her cousin. I had to keep everything inside, all the time. To a great extent I'm a solitary man, but no one is that solitary. At least I hope not. For his sake.

I said pretty much all this to Pat.

"I hear you," he said. "It's bad enough not being able to tell Angela or the kids or anyone else what's going on with you— they know something's up, from the way I've been acting— but for me, it's just having to keep a secret. For you, it's having to live a secret. It's gotta be hell."

"You're a great little cheerer-upper," I said.

"I aim to please. Look, something else just occurred to me. You gave me letters to give to Mike Kennerly and Sergeant Banner in case I didn't hear from you. But it sounds like a lot of stuff has changed in the last couple of weeks. If something did happen to you, God forbid—"

"I agree."

"—the cops would have to start from square one trying to find out what. I could tell them some of what you've told me now, but I'm thinking maybe you should be writing this stuff down or something, keeping everything current."

It was a good idea, and I said so. The problem was, how to do it? It wasn't something I would want to have lying around my St. Paul digs, or in my car, or on my person. I could stash it in the safe-deposit box I had rented at First Bank Grand, on Grand Avenue, where I kept nearly everything that had my right name on it, but then there was the hassle with keys and signatures and whatnot for anyone else who might need to get at it. I could mail it to Costello, either directly or through one of the post-office boxes he was already checking for me, but it wouldn't be healthy for Pat to have the notes in his possession if Feinman's unsavories put the arm on him.

Finally we decided that I would mail reports, as events warranted, to myself via one of my lockboxes. Pat, or one of his kids, would collect it and handle it the way they handled the rest of my mail, except that instead of forwarding it to my St. Paul box, they would immediately send it on to a pharmacy-school friend of Pat's who had a store in Norfolk, Nebraska. Pat would instruct his friend to put the envelopes, unopened, in the pharmacy safe and leave them there until Pat told him what to do with them. Convoluted, I know—that was the point. Nothing to trace back to me, nothing to implicate Pat, and no reason for anybody to ever pester Pat's friend.

I could have decided to send my reports straight to Mike Kennerly. He would have honored my instructions not to open them unless Pat or I gave him the go-ahead. But as my friend, my sometimes-lawyer, and my sometimes-employer, he was automatically at risk. It wouldn't do for him to have my notes lying around in his office safe. I also briefly considered sending them to Kim Banner at OPD. She was at risk, too, as were all my friends, but she was a cop: she was used to living with risk, and she was good at it. But since she was a cop, she was also a snoop, and she would open them and probably send for the cavalry. I couldn't afford that—not until I had all my ducks in a row.

So we decided on the indirect route. If Pat felt he could trust his friend, that was good enough for me.

It would be good, too, to organize my thoughts on paper. After all, I'm a writer; to me, nothing is real until it is rendered in black and white. Besides, occasionally an investigation has had facets, angles, patterns that didn't show themselves to me until I began to assemble my case notes preparatory to writing a report for the client. That could be the case here. If I had thought about it, I might have toyed with writing up ongoing reports to myself, then immediately destroying them. Sometimes the marking down is what's important, whether you ever refer back to it or not.

I told Pat to watch his backside, he suggested I do the same, and we ended the call.

I sank more loose change into the telephone's greedy little mouth, and eventually learned I could use a small room and a manual typewriter in the library at the College of St. Thomas. I would have to supply my own paper, which was fine by me. Along with the paper I would also bring a large envelope and enough postage to get it where it was going. Then I would mail it on campus as soon as I was finished with it. Minimal exposure.

28

Saturday I somehow let myself be talked into spending much of the day at City Centre. The way it happened was, Sharon called up and said did I want to, and I said yes. A very tricky woman, she.

My aversion to shopping malls is legendary. City Centre, being in downtown Minneapolis, sprawled upward rather than outward, but despite this novelty—out in this part of the world, we tend to go for filling up land rather than sky—it was still a mall. And this was a Saturday. And that meant this upright mall was swarming with a staggering number of people.

Sharon didn't seem to mind. She thought it was fun.

Actually, I didn't mind much, either, once I became acclimated. There were one or two decent bookstores, a couple of places that sell nifty gadgets and all kinds of useless devices to people who have too much money, and a good record store that didn't sell records, only casettes and compact discs. I had already let one of my aliases invest some of his rapidly dwindling funds in a boom box with radio, tape, and CD functions—it had been on sale at Target—so now I picked up a few CDs to play on it, if only to see what all the hoopla was about. *Suite for Flute and Jazz Piano* by Claude Bolling and Jean-Pierre Rampal, *Rossini Overtures* by the Orpheus Chamber Orchestra, and *The Memphis Record* by Elvis Presley. I try to be eclectic.

Sharon picked up a few things for her house from one of the nifty-gadget stores, a Mannheim Steamroller cassette—on my recommendation, although I couldn't tell her that half of the reason I recommend Mannheim Steamroller to people is because of the Omaha connection—and a software package for her personal computer. We grabbed a little lunch at the

Cecil's delicatessen there, agreed that it wasn't as good at the original Cecil's in Highland, and were threading our way back through the skyway maze to our parking ramp when a voice cut through the buzz of the Saturday-afternoon population:

"Nebraska!"

My brain said to ignore it, but my body, acting on its own fatheaded impulse, turned toward the voice. It belonged to Joe Delgado, the Minneapolis cop I had worked with once or twice in the past. He was a fellow of average height, with thinning curly hair, a scraggly mustache, and aviator-style glasses. He was with a plump blond woman and a couple of kids who currently were bored and showing all the signs of becoming truly horrid in just a few minutes.

"Nebraska," he repeated. "I almost didn't recognize you."

I was aware of Sharon's eyes on me. I smiled—at least that was my intent, though my facial muscles seemed to have turned to wood—and said, "Sorry, friend, you have me confused with someone else."

Delgado was a pro. If he hadn't been, he wouldn't have recognized me in the first place, cuss him. But it worked in my favor, too, because now, without missing a beat—almost on top of my own words—he said, "Oh, I'm sorry—for a minute there you looked like someone I knew. Sorry." His eyes didn't once stray toward Sharon, not even for an instant.

"No harm done," I said hopefully. I looked at his kids, then back at him. "Enjoy."

He rolled his eyes. "Riiight."

The Delgados disappeared into the crowd and Sharon and I stepped onto the elevator we had been waiting for.

My heart was pounding so loudly, I thought someone in the elevator car would comment on it, or at least turn around to see who was playing the bongos. No one did. There are over a million people living in the Twin Cities metropolitan area. Of that million, maybe two dozen had ever done any business with me in my true identity. Of them, perhaps six actually knew me. Maybe two would penetrate the clever disguise I had effected—glasses, mustache, much shorter hair, and now almost fifteen pounds lighter than I had been in many a year. Naturally one of those two people would run into me when it was least convenient.

This is why I never cheated on my wife while we were still together.

Sharon did not seem unduly curious or suspicious about the incident. It's the sort of thing that happens so frequently that it hardly deserves a second thought. I hoped.

In her car, winding her way out of the parking ramp, she said, "Strange."

"Anything in particular, or life in general?"

"That man back by the elevators."

"He thought I was someone else, that's all. It happens all the time. I must have that kind of face."

"What was it he called you? Nebraska? Weird."

"Yeah, real weird. Must be a nickname—you know, like Tex or something. Probably went to college with some guy from Nebraska, thought I looked like him. Did you notice his wife?"

"No, not really . . ."

Good. "She looked like she was going to die of embarrassment. The guy's probably one of these bozos who's always going around to people saying, 'Don't I know you?' Well, takes all kinds." I was talking too much, so I clamped it shut. The damage, if any, was done. The thing to do now was shut up about it and hope it would disappear along with all the other insignificant things that happen to us every day. It wasn't Sharon I was worried about, exactly. The danger was, she was a very open, uncomplicated, honest person—and she was very close to her brother. If Sharon should happen to mention it, just in passing, just as an odd, kind of funny occurrence. . . .

Well, what was I going to do? Take Sharon down to the river and bump her off? There were risks—there are always risks—and all I could do was accept them.

After all, it was a risky game I was playing.

She broiled two marinated, skinned chicken breasts and put together a spinach salad. I supervised the boiling of frozen vegetables and the opening of the wine. She had the Mannheim Steamroller tape on the stereo in the other room. It was a pleasant, casual, relaxing evening—or rather it would have been if I had been able to allow myself to relax. The chance run-in with Joe Delgado had reminded me—as if I needed reminding—that I was walking a tight-rope.

"You seem a little distracted," she said after dinner. We had stacked the dishes and cutlery in the dishwasher and taken coffee upstairs, to the spare bedroom she had turned into a TV room. We left the lights out and sprawled on the floor in a tangle of afghans and comforters, and didn't pay much attention to a movie on cable television.

"Do I? I'm sorry." I smiled. "No reflection on the company."

"Is anything wrong?"

"No. I guess I just have some things on my mind, that's all."

"Anything I can help with?" She was very close to me, and suddenly, somehow, her lips were on mine.

"I like your idea of help," I said a little while later.

She sat back and regarded me. Her eyes were dark crescent slits. Colored light from the television played on her face. "There's more where that came from, sailor. If you're interested."

"Oh, I'm interested. . . ."

"But . . ."

"But my . . . circumstances are such that I don't know how long I'll be around. I didn't plan to come here in the first place, and I don't have a set departure date, either. The way things go for me, I just don't know."

"And there is someone else," Sharon said.

"Yes, there is, but as I told you before, I don't really know where that stands. What's really on my mind, Sharon, is you: I don't want to hurt you." It wasn't really what was on my mind at the moment, but it had been there, off and on, and it was a good stand-in for what *was* occupying me—a subject I couldn't discuss with her. "I wouldn't want to hurt you in any event, because you're a wonderful woman and I've grown very fond of you in a very short time. But I especially wouldn't want to knowing how badly you've already been hurt."

She reached up and stroked my mustache with the tips of her fingers. There was a slight, sad smile on her lips. "That was a long time ago, Pat. Time heals. I know I've said it before, but his walking out on me is the biggest favor he ever did for me, or could have."

"Your brother told me he beat you up."

She smiled tolerantly. "I've told Joshua a million times not to exaggerate." Then she paused, introspectively. "Fahy hit me. He shouldn't have, but he did. It wasn't my fault—for a long time I thought it was, but I know better now. We were arguing. Toward the end there, that's all we did was argue. About his drinking, his running around. About money. Usually about money. I was making about eleven cents a week as a TA, and we had my college expenses and everything, but we were living in a two-room apartment in Dinkytown and Fahy was making pretty good money at the warehouse, but somehow there was never any money."

Sharon was looking at the flickering image on the television screen without really looking at it. "Anyhow, checks were coming back and people were calling, and we were fighting—you wouldn't believe the yelling and screaming we used to do—and all of a sudden Fahy turned around and clouted me. Right here." She took my hand and put it against her left cheek. Her skin was smooth and warm. "He didn't do any real damage. Nothing was broken. It didn't even really hurt that much—I was surprised more than anything. But it swelled up to the size of a baseball and turned all sorts of pretty colors, and my left eye went black. It looked a lot worse than it was.

"Unfortunately, Joshua came over to see Fahy the next day. And, well, you know how bruises are—they always look worse later than they did when you first got them. Josh took one look at me and went off like a bottle rocket. He was so mad, I think he would have killed Fahy if he'd been around. But luckily Fahy had taken off right after belting me, and he hadn't come back yet. That gave me time to get Josh calmed down—and believe me, that *took* some time."

"I can believe it," I said. "Josh seems very passionate when it comes to family."

"He's always been that way. And even more so since Lisa—his wife—and their little girl were killed six years ago."

"I didn't know about that. I didn't know Josh had ever been married."

Sharon nodded. "It was a terrible car wreck. Amanda was only four. . . . Anyhow, Joshua was set to tear Fahy limb from limb. I talked to him for hours, praying Fahy wouldn't come back while he was there. Finally I got him to calm down. I begged him not to take it out on Fahy—partly for Fahy's sake, partly for my own: he had been fired from more jobs than you could count, and if Josh kicked him out I didn't know who would ever hire him or what would become of us."

"Josh would never have let you starve."

"No, but I couldn't have taken handouts from him. I know that Fahy's job at the warehouse was a handout, but we all agreed on this little fiction that he was earning his pay, and I could manage to live with that. But I was terrified that Fahy would screw up so badly that Josh couldn't overlook it anymore. And it turned out I had a right to be scared: Josh had come over that day because Fahy hadn't even bothered to show up at the warehouse for nearly a week. I had no idea. I knew Fahy was lax in his work habits, but I thought he was at least going through the motions on this job. But it had got to the point where the other men were beginning to complain—why should they have to work for a living when the manager doesn't even show up, much less do anything when he's there? Josh said he was willing to keep Fahy on the payroll—for my sake, though he didn't say so in so many words—but Fahy had to meet him halfway and at least pretend to be working. I promised to talk to him. I promised things would change."

"But Fahy never came back?"

"Oh, no—he came home late that night. Drunk, of course. He had been in a fight, and someone had really beat the stuffing out of him. If you can believe it, I blamed myself for that, too. I thought if I hadn't made him so mad that he hit me, he wouldn't have gone out and gotten drunk and picked a fight. He was making enough noise to wake the dead, so I got out of bed and helped him get cleaned up and everything. I told him what Joshua had said, about the job. I told him he had to straighten up, straighten out, and get his act together."

"What did he say?"

"Not a damn word. He got into bed, turned his back to me, and went to sleep. He stayed home the next day—he was a wreck, between the hangover and the beating. I was in and out all day. We didn't say two words to each other. I think he was really upset by what he had done. Hitting me, I mean. I know he was as surprised as me when it happened, I could see that in his face. And he ran out as soon as he had done it, and got stinking drunk and probably started a fight with someone, and I think maybe it was because as lousy as he had been sometimes, he had never hit me." She took a deep breath. "And the next morning he got up early—seven o'clock, which was early for him—and got dressed to go out. I asked him if he was going to work. He said yes. He left, and that's the last I saw of him. Why are you frowning?"

"I don't think much of guys who hit women," I said. A slight fib. I *don't* think much of such guys, but that wasn't why I was frowning.

I drank a little coffee. It was vanilla nut. Sharon had bought it just that afternoon, on our excursion, and it was fresh and nutty and only a little sweet. "I don't understand why he left like that, without a word of warning. I mean, he knew he pretty much just had to show up at work fairly regularly to collect his pay, and he knew Josh wasn't about to let his kid sister starve—who in his right mind would walk away from setup like that?"

"Well, for one thing, Fahy was *never* in his right mind," she said laughingly. "But really—I think it was his way of apologizing to me."

"For hitting you."

"For hitting me, for cheating on me, for all the jobs he couldn't or wouldn't hold on to, for the drinking and the lying . . . for the way things had worked out. Or hadn't worked out. Fahy never said anything—he wouldn't have—he never apologized for swatting me, but I know he felt bad about it. When he came off that last bender, I think he concluded that the best thing he could do for me was to get the hell out of my life."

She was still holding my hand against her face. Now she moved it to the base of her throat, just inside the open neck of the flannel shirt she was wearing.

"That's all ancient history," she said quietly. "I cram ancient history into bored students' heads all week long. I'm not interested in history tonight. I'm not interested in the future tonight. I'm only interested in right now."

I can't for the life of me remember the name of the movie on the tube.

29

Sunday afternoon I called Joe Delgado at home.

"Who do I know who'd be calling me in the middle of the Vikings game," he said when he came to the phone.

"Vikings," I said. I could hear the sound of the televised football game coming over the wire. "Vikings. . . . Baseball, right?"

He groaned into the telephone.

"Anyhow," I went on, "you don't know me. You mistook me for someone else yesterday, remember? Downtown."

It took a moment or two for him to say, "Oh . . . yeah. The woman you were with, she doesn't know about your wife and two kids back in Cowtown?"

"Two wives, one kid."

"Sorry. Seriously, I hope I didn't mess anything up for you."

"Me too. I'm involved in kind of a low-profile thing right now. Thanks for playing dumb."

"It's one of my best things."

"Listen, I was planning to call you anyhow. You working tomorrow?"

"Yeah, I'm nine-to-fiving it these days, weekends off. So I can catch the games."

"I'll be brief," I said. "I need anything you have on a man named Joshua Feinman."

"F-i-n-e?"

"F-e-i-n."

"Right letters, wrong order. What am I looking for?"

"Anything at all," I said. "I just want to know if he's got a sheet and, if so, what's on it." There was no point telling Delgado any more than that, since I had nothing concrete to share with him.

"I think we can manage that," Delgado said in the distracted way people have when they're talking and writing at the same time. "Where can I reach you?"

"You probably can't: I'll be in and out most of the day tomorrow." It was true, although it wasn't my main reason for not giving Delgado my number. My main reason was that I was reluctant to have the number at my apartment linked to the name Nebraska, even if just by one person and him a cop. For that reason I was calling him from a pay phone at the College of St. Thomas. "How's about I give you a call around lunchtime or so?"

"Sounds good."

A muted cheer went up in the background on Delgado's end of the line.

"Sounds like a great game," I said cheerfully. "Shouldn't you be getting back to it?"

He hung up and I hung up, and I went to search out the typing room so I could start work on my dissertation.

30

The address in the phone book translated into a tatty-looking concrete-block building in a South St. Paul industrial park. The black letters bleeding rust down the front of the building spelled out NorLan Appliance. Actually, they spelled out NorLan Appli nce, but in my line of work you get used to having to fill in the blanks.

My breath disappeared into the frigid, gray morning air as I climbed out of the car, and the snow creaked and crunched under my feet as I walked over to the place. It sat back from the street a distance, and there was enough pavement to allow a semi-trailer to get turned around and back up to two of three loading doors in the front of the building. The third loading door had a kind of concrete ramp up to it designed to bring a pickup-truck bed up to loading height. I knew that not so much because of the worldly kind of guy I am but because there was a pickup sitting there at the moment, a huge steel-banded cardboard carton sitting in the bed.

Next to the pickup, at the top of a handful of snow-packed concrete stairs, there was a steel service door. I went up the stairs and through the doors.

It wasn't a lot warmer inside.

Nor did the place deliver more than the exterior had promised. It was just a big, drafty, badly lighted barn. Cartons and crates were stacked everywhere, in rough wood racks, from the concrete floor clear up to the steel beams in the ceiling two stories up. Stoves, washers and dryers, air conditioners, refrigerators, and other "durable goods," by the sizes of cartons and the markings thereon. A forklift operator was positioning one of the crates while a co-worker acted as ground crew.

Thirty or thirty-five feet back from the loading area there

was a thrown-together glass-and-drywall "office." Near it, a heavy black man in beige workshirt and pants was transacting some business with a tall, rangy fellow in denims, Western-cut fleece-lined jacket, and cowboy boots. The black man was having the cowboy sign some forms on a clipboard. I guessed the cowboy belonged to the pickup and the forms belonged to whatever he was getting ready to cart away.

There wasn't much else going on, by the look of things.

I wandered into the aura of a space heater on the bare floor, not far from the office. The heater was fighting a losing battle in that space. I took off my gloves and warmed my hands. There was an odor in the air back here—a thin but sharp chemical smell. I looked further back into the warehouse, but there was nothing to see except rows of the wooden racks and the cartons and crates they held and, in the far wall, at the end of a kind of throughway between the racks, a windowless steel door that may or may not have led outside.

I didn't recognize the odor. The thought crossed my mind that not all the cocaine that came Feinman's way had to stay in powdered form. It didn't take much in the way of laboratory or know-how to convert it to crack or crank, value-added derivatives of coke. It would have been nice to think that the peculiar, acrid odor was emanating from a drug lab in the back of the building—the more dirt I had to throw at Feinman, the greater likelihood that something would stick—but I had to admit to myself that the odor could have belonged to anything: cleaning solvent, paint thinner, anything at all.

Anyhow, my chances of getting a peek at any such illicit operation were slim to nil, and I would need more than a funny smell to get the cops interested in taking a look. I was there mainly out of curiosity. That and the old tried-and-true practice of stirring up the pot to see what floats to the top.

The heavy man and the cowboy wrapped up their transaction. The cowboy mosied off, and the black man ambled over to me. "What can I do for you, buddy?"

"I'm here to see Mr. Brian Fahy," I said.

The black man chuckled. He had broad, friendly features behind steel-rimmed glasses. "You're too late, buddy. Mr. Fahy hasn't been with us for, oh, almost three years now."

I frowned, and opened the leather portfolio case I was carrying, and consulted some forms therein. They were forms for discount magazine subscriptions and a Bush Foundation Fellowship and some other stuff I had picked up at the college yesterday, but I didn't share that information with my new friend. "Then we have a problem," I said.

He chuckled again. "What do you mean 'we,' Kemo Sabe?"

I looked up at him and chuckled too. "You're right ... *you're* the one with the problem—that is, if you're the manager of this business, Mr.—"

They say laughter's contagious, but the black man stopped almost as soon as I started. "Glass. Bob Glass. What sort of problem? Who are you anyway? If you have some sort of beef with Fahy—"

I reached into my pocket and pulled out my credentials. My *real* credentials, with my right name on them and everything. Most of that kind of stuff was safely locked away at the bank, but I had kept these near to hand, hidden above the headliner in my car, just in case I needed to get at them in a hurry. It was funny to be using them again, funny to be representing myself as myself, not in the guise of some poor sod who died fifteen or twenty years ago. After so long using false identification, using the real stuff again *felt* like using false ID. Of course, by now the State of Nebraska probably had revoked my permit, so in a way I *was* using false credentials . . . and that felt odd, too.

"I'm a private investigator," I said for the first time in weeks. "I'm employed by Consolidated Insurers National Corporation. This is a spot-check investigation." I like to use the word "investigation": it has such a nice authoritative, authoritarian ring to it. "Now, according to CINC records, the manager of this business is a Brian Fahy. You're telling me that that hasn't been so for three years. Let me ask you, Mr. Glass, have you had to file any insurance claims in those three years?"

"No, huh-uhn, we're very safety-conscious here—"

"And very lucky."

"Now wait a minute, Mr.—whatever. I never heard of any Consolidated Insurance—"

"Consolidated Insurers National Corporation. CINC."

"Yeah. I never heard of any CINC. Our insurance company is—"

"No, you don't understand, Mr. Glass. I'm not working for

your insurance company. Your insurance company doesn't have anything to do with this. I'm working for CINC, which is a *network* of insurance carriers. It's sort of like a credit-reporting bureau; all we handle is information. Your insurance company must buy information from CINC, else I wouldn't be here, but this is strictly CINC business—a spot check, as I said. And it's a good thing for you I came along before your company here had to file a claim."

"But if you're not the insurance company . . ." He was confused. That was the idea. When in doubt, confuse them. The best way to do that is to start talking insurance. Nobody understands insurance.

"You ever hear of a 'loophole,' Mr. Glass?" I said. "Just between us kids, we both know these insurance companies have guys lying awake nights trying to figure out how *not* to pay claims. This one here would be a beaut. Someone takes a half-gainer off your loading dock there, files a liability suit against you guys, and your insurance company says, 'Wait a minute—our papers say Fahy is manager, but you say he's been gone for three years. Guess what, guys? You haven't had any insurance for three years.' Never mind you've been paying premiums the whole time. That means NorLan Appliance is on the hook for, oh, maybe a mil."

"A *mil!*"

"If you're lucky. Let me ask you, Mr. Glass: your boss, is he a philosophical man?"

Glass swallowed noisily. "Well, shouldn't the insurance people have taken care of—"

"Probably. But that's what lawsuits are made of, Mr. Glass." I smiled beatifically. "But as I said, you're lucky—lucky I came along before an accident did. If I can get all the information I need from you, then I can put this on the wire and feed it back to your insurance company. Any problem, you're covered from both ends."

Glass swallowed again. "Step into my office, won't you?"

We went into the cramped cubicle and Glass shut the door. There was a desk, a desk chair, and an armless straight-backed chair, and that about took care of all the available space. At Glass's insistence I sat at the dented-up old steel desk while he took the visitor's chair. The desk was buried under a staggering array of invoices, manifests, receipts, and other paperwork. There was a coffee-stained Norelco Dial-a-Brew on the edge of the desk nearest the wall. Glass shook Styrofoam cups out of a plastic wrapper and poured out two coffees.

"Thanks," I said. "Now let's see. . . ." I riffled through the junk in my portfolio case. "Well, of course they didn't give me the right forms back at the office." I smiled at Bob Glass and shook my head. He managed a lopsided smile in return. Whatever happened to that happy-go-lucky soul I used to know? "But I guess these spot checks usually turn up exactly zilch. Anyhow, it's all pretty standard stuff." I tucked my forms behind the pale-green pad in the portfolio and took out a ball-point pen. "I know everything I'll need to update the record, and if I forget something here, I'll just call you later from the office. Let's see. . . . Name of business, NorLan Appliance." I wrote it down. "Business address. . . ." I wrote that down. I wrote down the number of employees, the square footage, type of heat, primary insurance carrier, HMOs, taxpayer ID number—all the mind-numbing trivia I could think of that seemed remotely like the kind of mind-numbing trivia that insurance companies seem to think important. While I worked on a list of all the manufacturers whose products NorLan distributed, I asked Glass casually, conversationally—the way a person might—where his predecessor had gone.

"I don't really know what became of him," Glass said, glad to talk about anything besides insurance minutiae. "You see, Mr. Fahy wasn't always real . . . reliable, you might say. I mean, maybe he'd show up for work, maybe he wouldn't; maybe you'd hear from him, maybe not. Well, one morning Mr. Feinman came in here first thing, said Mr. Fahy wouldn't be coming in anymore, and made me manager on the spot. I'd sort of been running the place anyhow, you know," he added with more than a little pride. Justifiable pride, from what I knew of Fahy.

"Mr. Feinman?" I asked.

"Mr. Joshua Feinman. He owns the company, you know."

"I didn't know." I laughed, and wrote the name down at the top of the first page. "Gee, I'd better write that one down."

Glass laughed too. He'd finally come to believe I wasn't there to close the place down on him. I was glad. He seemed like a decent sort, and I didn't want to spoil his whole day.

"Okay, then. . . ." I turned back to the page I had been working on. "Westinghouse, Whirlpool, White. I guess that's that. Now, how much do you have around in inventory, on average, every month? Just roughly."

"I've got that here—" Glass reached over to a wallful of clipboards hanging from nails. He selected one and started whipping through the attached sheets.

I said, "You say this Feinstein—"

"Feinman," Glass said distractedly.

"—you say he came in here one day. He doesn't work on the premises, then?"

"No, he's got a big office in downtown Minneapolis some-where. He owns a lot of businesses, you know."

"I'd better note that, too. . . . Pretty big deal, having the big boss come down to promote you in person, huh? I mean, he could have just called. . . ."

Glass looked up from his clipboard and beamed. "Yeah, that was nice of him. Mr. Feinman's a great guy. He said my promotion was long past due, he knew I had really been run-ning the place, and so he wanted to come in and give me the good news himself, in person."

I could just imagine the scene—old Josh turning up the burner under the charm, telling Glass he'd been aware of his fine work for X years now, what a pleasure it was to finally reward Glass's efforts and loyalty in a suitable way, et cetera, et cetera. No question about it, Joshua Feinman could lay it on thick and smooth when the occasion called for it. Dale Carnegie had nothing on him.

Glass found the number I had asked for. I had no idea anybody would keep track of such a thing. But, good sport that I am, I wrote it down. "That's great," I said, writing. "About your boss, I mean. And he showed up first thing, huh? You open, what, six, six-thirty?"

"Six."

"Wow. And Feinstein was here that early, huh? I'm im-pressed. Most of these fat-cat types, they'd hardly bother—and certainly not at six in the A.M., right? Nice to know there are at least a few left who aren't afraid to put in a good working day."

"I don't think Mr. Feinman's allergic to hard work," Glass said loyally. "That's how he got to be where he is today."

And exactly where is that? I wondered. "Seems kind of

funny he didn't give you any idea where Fahy was going or anything, though, doesn't it?"

"Yeah, I thought so too. I even asked, you know—just making conversation, like. Mr. Feinman just said it wasn't working out for Mr. Fahy here, and that was that. Fahy never even came back for his stuff."

"Stuff?"

"You know, from the office here." Glass nodded at the desk at which I sat. "There wasn't a helluva lot, but you'd think a guy would come get what was his, wouldn't you? There was a picture of a woman—his wife, I suppose—a windbreaker, a Thermos that was about three-quarters full of Scotch—junk like that. I still have it all in the back somewhere. Thought maybe he'd turn up for it in a couple days, you know. . . ."

"Mind if I have a look at it?"

Glass frowned. "What for? What's that got to do with insurance?"

Good question.

"You know how insurance companies are," I said, vamping like mad. "No matter how much documentation you give them, they want more. I have this feeling I'm going to get back to the home office and file my report and some overpaid pencil-pushing geek's gonna say, 'Yeah, but what about Fahy? We need to know where he went so we can fill out a form eleven-seventy-two' or whatever."

Glass's chuckle came back. "Yeah, I hear you. . . ."

"So maybe there's something in Fahy's stuff that will give me an idea where he went. You mentioned an appointment book; maybe it shows a date for a job interview, something like that."

The black man shrugged. "Could be; I never looked real close. Anyhow, since he never came back for his stuff, there must not be anything too important in it—so what's the harm of letting you look at it?"

I sure couldn't think of any.

Glass led me back to a large steel cage bolted to the back wall, near the steel door. Even back here I couldn't tell whether the door led to the great outdoors or a back room. There was no exit sign on or over the door, if that meant anything. I couldn't think of a plausible reason to ask Glass about it or try the door myself, so I let it go.

The cage contained tool chests, some boxes, some miscellaneous equipment. Glass wore one of those retractable keyrings on his belt. He went through a dozen keys and selected one that fit the huge padlock on the cage door. "This is where we keep the stuff that's likely to go for a walk if it isn't under lock and key," he explained. I nodded knowingly.

He had to hunt for the box; it was buried under three years' accumulated stuff. While he hunted, I looked around—trying to be inconspicuous and nonchalant while simultaneously attentive and observant. A medium-sized cardboard carton caught my eye. Its markings indicated that it held, or originally held, laboratory glassware. What would an appliance warehouse need with laboratory glassware? Of course, cardboard boxes are notoriously perambulatory, and there was no telling where this one might have come from. Still, I would have liked a peek inside—and I might have risked a peek if it hadn't been tightly sealed with plastic tape.

Next to the carton stood a tall red tool cabinet, the kind you sometimes see in automotive garages—heavy steel, drawers in the top half, cupboard in the bottom half, locking wheels. A padlock dangled from the door latch, but whoever was last in the cabinet neglected to close the padlock completely. Wrapping my hand around the lock to muffle the sound of metal against metal, I opened the lock. The cupboard hinges were well greased, and the door opened silently.

"Hey, what're you doing there?"

I willed myself not to jump, flinch, or wet my pants. Instead I remained there crouched, running my hand over the cabinet appraisingly, as if that's what I had been doing all along. "My uncle was a mechanic," I said reminiscently. "He used to have a chest just like this one."

"Yeah?" Glass worked at taking some of the sharpness out of his voice. "Well, that cabinet doesn't belong to your uncle. What you're interested in is over here."

Reluctantly, I straightened and went over to him. I didn't have a chance to get even a glimpse at the cupboard's contents. Not that I knew what I expected to find there, or had any reason to expect that what I expected to find would be there, but it was making me crazy to just *think* that Feinman could be running drug traffic through that building and I couldn't get a lock on it.

Glass had retrieved a carton slightly smaller than the glass-ware box, and balanced it on top of a tool cabinet similar to the other one. The carton said BOOKS on the side, which proba-bly meant it was a hand-me-down, which probably meant the glassware box was secondhand, too. Maybe. Glass was using a pocket knife to slice open the plastic tape that had held the carton closed. Then he bent back the flaps and began extract-ing the contents. A green nylon windbreaker. A stainless-steel vacuum bottle, which I uncorked and which did, as Glass had said, contain cheap liquor. A five-by-seven photograph of Sharon Fahy in a chintzy, discolored frame. A dime-store magnifying glass. A credit-card-sized calculator. A handful of plastic pens. A cheap LCD clock, not currently working. A gray vinyl-covered pocket appointment book, two years old.

I fanned through the book. "When did you say you got your promotion?"

"January fifteenth," came the prompt reply.

I turned to that week. Nothing. I flipped back a few pages. There were some entries, not many. Fahy hadn't relied on this book to keep track of his activities. That was not much of a surprise, considering how unreliable and basically un-stable the man was. Maybe he thought that using the book would keep him on course, but he never developed the habit. Then, too, if he kept the book at his office but was himself seldom there, that would put a crimp in things.

I spied a couple of notations that looked like betting infor-mation. No wonder he and Sharon never had any money. There were some women's names—first names only—and tel-ephone numbers. There were names without numbers, names with times, and numbers without names.

I turned to the week after January fifteenth. Fahy had noted a luncheon appointment with someone from Hotpoint on the twenty-third. I went forward a few more pages. He had writ-ten down a dental appointment for February eleventh.

It reminded me of the calendars in David Nordquist's home and office: they proved whatever you wanted them to prove. Did you want Nordquist to be a clever thief? Then he made appointments he never intended to keep, just to throw people off the trail. Did you want him to have yielded to sudden temptation? Then the appointments proved he had had no plans to disappear. You could play the same game with

Fahy's appointment book, and in much the same way. He either planned to take a powder or he didn't; take your pick.

I put the calendar book back into the box. There was a slender green box there, somewhat smaller than the kind check blanks come in. I lifted it out.

"Oh, yeah," Glass said. "I forgot about that."

I popped the lid. Inside, wrapped in some tissues, was a gold pocket watch on a gold chain. Heavy gold—the rich eighteen-carat gold that used to be common, not the lighter, more yellow sixteen- or fourteen-carat gold we're used to seeing. The watch was not the kind that had a pop-open cover; it just had a heavy glass crystal protecting a cream-colored face with big black roman numerals. "A railroad conductor's watch," I said.

"No foolin'? I can't believe he never came back for that. It's a nice watch. Still runs, too—or it did when I packed it up, at least."

I gave the stem a few cranks, and the second hand, which was located on a separate miniature face at the main face's six o'clock position, dutifully began to move. The watch emitted a loud, steady tick. I turned it over. There was engraving on the back:

FOR A G F
FROM V H
23 SEPTEMBER 1911

"Some kind of family heirloom, don't you think?" Glass was saying. "That's why I was sure he'd want to come back for it, even if the watch isn't valuable."

"Oh, it's valuable, all right," I said, repacking the timepiece. "But if A.G.F. was a Fahy, you'd think it would have sentimental value, too."

"That's what I figured—that's why I wrapped it up like that and put it under lock and key. Guess Fahy isn't the sentimental kind."

"Guess not," I agreed. I began to put everything back into the carton. "Well, nothing here that's much help to me," I told Glass. "Thanks all the same, though."

"No problem." Glass had a roll of transparent plastic tape on a heavy dispensing gun. He resealed the carton, then hauled it back where he had gotten it. I glanced longingly at the tool cabinet, but it took Glass far less time to replace Fahy's carton than to find it in the first place. I barely had time to slide the cabinet's padlock back where it belonged. Then Glass was escorting me out of the cage and buttoning it up again.

"You know," he said helpfully on the way back to the front of the warehouse, "the person who'd probably know about Fahy is Mr. Feinman. Maybe you ought to go talk to him."

"I'm sure you're right," I said.

◇◇◇

I let the car warm up and did some thinking. What if NorLan Appliance was Feinman's depot, maybe even a lab? What was I going to do about it? The neighborhood was not especially conducive to staking out the place—too many open spaces, too many flat-walled buildings—but I might be able to manage it. What was I going to see, though? Trucks coming and going. From a heavy-appliance distributor's warehouse. Very suspicious.

Sneaking in for a private tour was pretty well out of the question. I noted the steel doors and the iron bars over most of the accessible windows, and I had learned, on behalf of CINC, that the place was equipped with a burglar-and-fire-alarm system.

If Feinman had a distribution center, this place was perfect for it. Hell, it already was a distribution center! If he wasn't that heavily involved in the trade, this would still be a good place to receive the stuff. Freight it in in a microwave oven crate and store it in the back until Feinman, or whoever, called for it. Perfect. I would have bet my last dollar—an item that was coming into view, since all I had to balance my expenses these days were more expenses—that Feinman operated a drug depot and possibly a laboratory, and that they were housed in this crappy-looking building.

And there wasn't a thing I could do about it.

31

EntertainmenTime, Josh Feinman's vending-machine operation, occupied a beige block building that must have once been a gas station. It sat on a corner of Emerson Avenue in Minneapolis, on the fringe of the Uptown district. The neighborhood was residential, mainly apartment buildings that were constructed during some long-forgotten age when they tried to make apartment houses look like houses, not dormitories or barracks. Most of these had big open porches, columns, and all kinds of gingerbread. Most of them, too, were in ill repair.

I drove past EntertainmenTime twice before I decided it must be the place. There was no signage on the building, no street number either.

Even after I found it, I sat out in the car for a couple of minutes and tried to think how to play it. My snooping around NorLan Appliance worked as well as it did—however well that was—because I had a hook, an angle: Fahy. Obviously, that angle would not work here. And I had no other angle coming readily to mind. I could try the CINC nonsense again, omitting Fahy, but if word dribbled back to Feinman that several of his business were being sniffed around by an investigator, he would get suspicious. He would check, and he would find that CINC existed only in my fevered imagination.

I got out of the car and went in.

Beyond bricking up most of the front windows, removing the hydraulic lifts from the bays, and patching the wounded floor with concrete that was a lighter color than the rest of the floor, no one had bothered to try to disguise the filling-station décor. The place had three work bays, two on the Emerson Avenue side, the other facing the cross-street. Together they formed a fairly large open area, part of which was taken up by machines of various type, age, and state of disrepair. There was a tiny office in the front corner of the place, a storage room in the back corner, and a tall, angular, grimy kid on the floor, cursing a jukebox he labored on with a soft, steady cadence.

I walked over to him. "Morning."

He didn't look out of the back end of the machine. "How'ya doin'."

"I'm okay. Are you Norm?"

He pulled his head out of the machine's innards and dragged a sleeve across his forehead, leaving a dark, greasy smudge. He was in his early twenties, with sharp, bony features, dark-blond hair, and deep-set eyes. When he spoke I could see his teeth; they, in turn, had not seen a dentist recently. "No," he said. "Who're you?"

I wandered casually, glanced over the machinery piled against the far wall and on the long workbench along the back wall. Jukeboxes; pinball machines; coffee, cocoa, and hot soup dispensers; those old Pong-type videogame tables you used to see everywhere; old-fashioned gum machines; cigarette machines; and lots of unidentified cannibalized parts for the above, lying around everywhere.

The kid threw a pair of slip-joint pliers into a battered steel toolbox on the floor next to him and got to his feet. He wiped his hands on a red rag he produced from his back pocket. "Can I help you with something, mister?"

I set down a peculiar-looking tool I had been pretending to examine, putting it back on the workbench where it had come from. "Only if you're Norm," I said pleasantly.

"I already told you I'm not. There's no Norm works here."

I was wandering the length of the workbench, dragging my fingertips along its smooth but grimy sheet-metal surface.

My wandering led me to the end of the bench, near the kid, who stood where he had stood all along, eyeing me. I smiled at him. "I don't know who works here and who doesn't," I said reasonably. "All I know is I'm supposed to meet Norm here at"—I consulted my wristwatch—"eleven-thirty."

"Well, your friend isn't here. I'm the only one here. So maybe you sh— Hey!"

The storage room was behind the wall that served as the backstop for the workbench. You went up two concrete steps and through a battered wooden door—which is exactly what I did now. I moved quickly but not hurriedly, opened the door, which was not locked, and peered in. The storage room was long and narrow. There was a half-sized desk and a chair shoved against the outside wall just inside the door. The rest of it looked like more tools, parts, and supplies. I got no more than a glance before the kid was next to me. But a glance was all I needed. There was barely room for a family of mice back here, let alone a drug depot, let alone a drug lab.

I looked down at the kid and smiled again. "Nope, no Norm back here." I rechecked my watch. "Well, then, the hell with him, huhn, kid?" I pulled out a fin and shoved it into his shirt pocket. "Thanks for the use of the hall."

I went back outside.

CeramiCo was a bit easier. It was housed in a low-roofed stucco affair on a lower middle-class block not far from the Schmidt brewery in St. Paul. The place looked closed—it had that dusty, disused, slightly careworn appearance—but the red-and-black dimestore sign in the door said, YES! WE ARE OPEN. A flyspecked sign in the front window touted POTTERS' SUPPLIES—CERAMICS—KILNS—WHOLESALE & RETAIL. That's what made it easier. Unlike NorLan and EntertainmenTime, CeramiCo was open to the general public, of which I'm a card-carrying member.

The place didn't look all that promising, but, making a mental note to have a word with Feinman about all his businesses with capital letters in the the middle of their names, I got out of the car and went in.

They hadn't wasted any money on décor. The door opened to a big, brightly lighted, dusty room filled with long, free-standing shelves laden with little ceramic figures, utensils, and gewgaws. Greenware, or whatever they call it—all I knew about the subject was that you painted these prefab items in some fashion, threw them into a kiln and fired them for X amount of time, then gave them to somebody. I've always had a mental picture of all these artsy-craftsy types spending countless hours making things to give to each other—an endless loop. Pretty soon, I kept thinking, they'll all have so much stuff lying around that they'll have to stop making new stuff and start recycling the existing supply. The inventory on hand at CeramiCo, however, indicated that they thought that day was not near at hand.

There was an odor in the air here, too—a warm, heavy, kind of earthy aroma, not quite the same as that of a greenhouse.

A short, stocky, pleasant-looking old woman came out of a room in the back of the place. She wore a soiled laboratory apron over a sleeveless smock and polyester pants. "C'neye hepyoo," she growled, teaching us once again that looks can deceive.

"Just looking around," I said cordially. "My aunt is thinking of taking up a hobby. Do you give classes here?" It seemed to me the sort of thing you'd want to take a class in.

"Toosdain Thursday," she snarled. She had a smooth, pink face, snow-white hair pulled into a bun, gray eyes that twinkled behind her glasses, and a voice as soft and grandmotherly as Raymond Burr's. "Sixty dollars fate weeks."

"Uh-huh." I glanced around. "I don't see any kilns. . . ."

She turned and went back into the room from which she had emerged. I followed her. There were more shelves back here, bearing mostly work that was cooling or setting or curing or whatever it did, and some that looked like it was waiting to be fired. There was a single window and a steel door, both wide open to the twenty-eight-degree outdoors. Despite that, the room was smotheringly hot—the doing of four round stainless-steel contraptions against the back wall. The kilns. They gave the room the look of a college-dorm laundry room.

"I see," I said. I also saw, at the far end, a door marked EMPLOYEES ONLY. I tried to judge the size of the space behind the door, given the size of the main room and the size of the firing room. Six or eight square feet, say. Big enough for a lab? Maybe. Big enough for a depot? Sure. Big enough for an office, though, more likely. This was a quiet residential block; you couldn't have deliveries coming in here at all hours, and you couldn't have big deliveries, period. The alley outside the back door wouldn't accommodate them. Not that I was envisioning Mack trucks bulging with contraband; on the contrary, I was imagining small illicit bundles hidden in big shipments of completely innocent cargo—in fact, the bigger the shipment, the better. Sort of a twist on the needle-and-haystack gag. Nor would every truck be hauling junk; some would be one-hundred-percent legit. It would be safer that way, limiting the number of people involved as well as reducing the risk of accidental discovery.

The CeramiCo setup ruled out little parcels in big trucks. Of course, little parcels fit in little trucks, too—as well as cars, dune buggies, and bicycle baskets—but a halfway sizable operation meant lots of junk coming in, being processed, and going out again. I was betting that Feinman's was a halfway sizable operation—sizable enough that CeramiCo couldn't play a significant part in it. With NorLan or EntertainmenTime, you could have lots of activity—trucks, people, shipments coming and going—without raising suspicion. But that sort of hubbub would attract attention in the neighborhood around CeramiCo. An occasional visit from the UPS truck, an occasional run with whatever deliveries CeramiCo might need to make around town—that would be closer to the mark. Hard to move very much junk that way.

I smiled down at the woman. "This looks very nice," I said. "I'll tell my aunt."

◇◇◇

Mitch's was a dark, cozy bar along West Seventh Street, or Fort Road, in St. Paul. They had had a pretty good luncheon menu there on one of my business trips a few years back, and it wasn't far from CeramiCo, so I pulled in there. They had added a kind of dining room to the north end of the bar since my last visit, but otherwise it was much as I remembered it: dark red carpet, dim lighting, black-upholstered booths, chairs, and barstools. There was a free booth along the south wall, so I grabbed it.

I took out a scrap of paper and doodled on it. Like a smoker who's trying to quit and chews gum to keep his mouth occupied, I doodled to keep my hands occupied at a time when I would ordinarily be making notes to myself. Alone, at my place, I could jot things down for the sake of jotting, then destroy the evidence. Here, though, there was too much risk. If someone who knew me as Pat Kilpatrick should materialize, it might strike him as odd that I suddenly wadded up and ate the paper I was writing on. So I doodled.

I drew a little map of the United States while I thought about the morning. It was not a total loss; not at all. There's a tendency to think that if you haven't got something to show for your efforts, some product, then your efforts have been wasted. In this line, though, not coming up with a product is often just as good. For instance, I had ruled out CeramiCo—to my own satisfaction, at least, and mine was the only one I was concerned with—as a likely candidate for any depot, laboratory, or way station Josh Feinman might have had in his drug dealings. That was something.

Similarly, I had all but ruled out EntertainmenTime. I could see junk moving in and out all right, but not sticking around. No room to store anything. Certainly no room to cook anything. There was a certain limited amount of storage inside some of the machines lying around the place, but the quantity of coke that David Nordquist had lifted from Feinman convinced me that Feinman was a major player. That meant major facilities.

And that left NorLan Appliance, by far my best bet. Industrial setting—no one to gripe about the truck traffic. Legitimate distributorship—nothing suspicious about trucks coming and going all the time. Big warehouse. Good security.

I started drawing in states on my little map, starting at the center: Nebraska. South Dakota, North Dakota, Wyoming, Colorado . . . these big square states were easy. The Northeast was tough. The states never wanted to fit.

So NorLan stayed in first place on my imaginary list. And that, too, was something. However, it was a considerable distance from my suspicions, however neat and logical they were, and having something to hang on Feinman. Or hang Feinman on.

My lunch came over, followed closely by a waitress. Turkey on dark bread with bean sprouts, pickle spear, a handful of chips, light beer. A balanced meal—the not-so-good stuff balanced the good stuff.

NorLan hadn't been a complete waste, either, though. The Fahy angle interested me. I thought about Nordquist's disappearance and Fahy's disappearance. I thought about the way Nordquist had looked and acted when we caught up with him. I thought about the items Fahy had left behind in his desk, his cushy job. I thought about his wife. I thought about her brother. I thought about things each of them had said.

I finished the sandwich, left half the chips and all of the pickle, and took the beer with me up to the phone on the wall by the door.

Joe Delgado was in.

"Your Feinman looks like a citizen," he said. "He was picked up five years ago on a DWI, bargained down to reckless. Suspended. That was before they started getting so tough with these guys. One moving violation two years ago, a fender-bender where he failed to yield the right-of-way. Other than that, guy's as clean as a hound's tooth."

"Have you ever really looked at a hound's tooth?"

"But here's something, for whatever it's worth: Feinman has a permit to carry a concealed weapon. Reason given is that he owns several cash business and sometimes carries large sums of money."

Interesting, but useless. "Thanks," I said. "You have another favor in you?"

"Let's hear the favor first."

I asked him to check the records for anything about Fahy's disappearance. "Three years ago this coming January. The m.p. report was probably filed by his wife, Sharon."

"Got it. This may take an hour or two. You'll call me?"

"I'll call you." I hung up.

32

My eyes were burning, my throat felt like it was lined with parchment, and my arms and legs were cooked spaghetti. That's how I knew it was time to quit.

I climbed off the Air-Dyne and wandered around the room, letting my heartbeat come back down into the normal range. I had the place to myself except for two young men on the Cybex machines. They must have reached the same conclusion I had: late in the afternoon, before the nine-to-five crowd is liberated, the club was a *private* club in almost the exact sense of the word. Except for us, and half a dozen women on the aerobics floor, the place was deserted.

I did some leg stretches, pampering the muscles that had been worked the hardest for the past twenty minutes. Then I did some arm stretches, since the bike gave them a workout, too, and since I had preceded my ride to nowhere with half an hour of weights. I was learning. I was learning that deep, rhythmic breathing was better than the gasping in-out-in-out breathe-to-the-beat favored, in my time, by gym teachers and drill sergeants. The former puts oxygen in your bloodstream; the latter only makes you out-of-breath. I was learning that warming up and cooling down and carefully stretching the muscles that had been imposed upon were not "extras" but essential components of the workout. When I took the time to do things right, I didn't have sore muscles the next day, no matter how hard I had worked them. And I was learning that a sensible exercise program, in tandem with a moderate, halfway intelligent diet, paid off. I was losing some excess weight, I was toning muscles that had been on the inactive list for ten years, I was sleeping better and waking up better and, in general, feeling better. This despite the stress-filled life I had been living for nearly a month now.

I hated to admit it, but it looked like there was something to this diet-and-exercise crap after all.

On my way to the showers, I paused and looked in on the aerobics group. Which is to say I looked at Sharon, who was leading the session. She was done up in hot-pink tights with black shorts pulled over them, a black T-shirt, and a pink bandana rolled and tied across her forehead. The headband was darkened with sweat, as was a small triangle between her breasts. I looked at her thinly populated class. They were mostly college-age girls, and they had spent a lot of money on their wardrobes. Their hair was pulled back just so, and they wore plenty of makeup, and earrings and gold bracelets and slender gold watches, and they didn't sweat. They sort of hopped and bopped to the beat—mainly, I think, to let the light catch their jewelry just right—but they didn't seem to work. All of them were slender. None of them looked healthy.

Sharon was giving me these come-hither looks. I had added the Air-Dyne to my workout with the weights largely in response to Sharon's arguments about the importance of aerobic exercise to the cardiovascular system, but I wasn't ready for anything that required coordination. And sure as hell not with a bunch of girls half my age.

I was in the wide hallway leading to the locker rooms when I was accosted by Feinman and Dimand. I hadn't seen Feinman all weekend, not since we got back from David Nordquist's lake home. I hadn't seen Dimand around the club since early the previous week. He too had one of those show-up-if-you-feel-like-it jobs that Feinman seemed to be in the habit of giving out. I wondered if I could land one—and just as fast put the thought out of my mind. That isn't what I was here for. It was important to keep the real goal in mind.

"There you are," Feinman said unnecessarily. "I've been trying to reach you all day. Don't you ever stay home?"

"I'm a man on the go," I said, pushing on into the men's locker room. "What's up?"

"First things first. Steve?"

Dimand nodded, and ambled around the little room, checking the aisles formed by the short rows of steel lockers and the wooden benches in front of them. Then he ambled back and nodded again.

"Good." Feinman handed me the briefcase he was carrying,

a metal job that looked identical to the one we brought up from the bottom of the lake Saturday morning. "For you," he said.

I looked at him inquisitively, but he just stood there with a Cheshire cat grin on his face. I shrugged, and set the case on the bench in front of my locker, and popped the latches.

It was loaded with cash. All in my favorite shade of green.

No wonder Feinman had a concealed-weapon permit.

I looked at the man. I suppose there was something on my face, some kind of ridiculous look. From my side I couldn't tell, I felt a little numb, a little disembodied, detached from the scene.

Feinman burst out laughing. "Best of all," he managed to gasp, "you get to keep the briefcase too!"

◇◇◇

I met them in the Health Bar—I was almost to the point where I could say the name with a straight face—where I was to meet Sharon when she was done. The briefcase, with its still-uncounted contents, was under padlock-and-key in the men's locker room. I still felt a little dazed, and something told me I wouldn't feel any less so when I got through tallying it up.

The Health Bar was empty except for Heather behind the bar and the two cousins tête-à-tête in a booth against the wall. It was unusual, seeing them together like that. I don't think I had seen Feinman in this part of the club at all since I had begun spending time there.

I slid into the booth next to Dimand. Things were at the point now where I hardly gave a thought to him recognizing me. If he was going to, I reasoned, he would have by now. He had never given the slightest glimmer, though. And if he had recognized me, why would he keep it to himself? I tried not to be overconfident, however. As I said before, I had to stay in character twenty-four hours a day.

I gave Heather the high sign, indicating she could go ahead and pour me my usual iced herbal tea. Then I looked at my companions.

"Got any more good surprises?" I asked Feinman.

"What surprise?" he said innocently. "You didn't think I was going to pay you for the work you did the other day?"

"I guess I never gave it a lot of thought," I said truthfully.

"Huh," Dimand said. "Must be nice."

I got up and collected my drink from the bar. When I got back to the booth and sat down, Dimand said, "We were just talking about your clothes, Patrick." He had a funny glint in his eye.

I looked down to see if my fly was open. It wasn't. I was wearing gray cords and a heavy wool sweater, charcoal gray with a small pattern of green diamonds, made in Ireland. Like virtually all the clothes I owned, it was new by only a few weeks.

"I was saying to Josh maybe you could give him some pointers," Dimand went on. I looked at him. The funny glint had been joined by a little half-grin, and I knew I was being set up.

"What's wrong with the way I dress?" Feinman protested.

I hadn't especially noticed the way either of them was dressed. I did now. Feinman was in a three-piece pin-striped navy blue suit, white shirt with French cuffs, red silk tie. *Fortune* magazine. Dimand was wearing rough, nubbly pleated pants, gray with a small windowpane pattern, a narrow-collared white pencil-stripe dress shirt buttoned to the neck, and a black silk cardigan with dolman sleeves.

"Nothing," Dimand sniffed. "Except red silk ties are out. And vests are *completely* out."

"Out?" Feinman said dramatically, feigning ignorance. "Out where?"

Dimand looked at me and grinned. They had had this conversation before. "Out of style, Joshua," he said patiently.

Feinman shook his head. "Impossible." He looked at me. "I have tried educating this boy, Pat, but it doesn't stick. See, he has *style* confused with *fashion*. That's why he says stupid things like vests are out of style. Style either is or isn't. Fashion is what goes in and out. Fashion is artificial—it's something fashion designers keep changing so's to stay in business." He sat back and shot his cuffs. "I could have worn this suit in any boardroom in America ten years ago and fit right in, and I can wear it in any boardroom ten years from now and fit right in."

"No doubt," Dimand said dryly, "but it's *today* I'm talking about."

Feinman turned to me in mock exasperation. "You're a man of the world, Pat; what do you think?"

"I think you look like Frank Furillo on *Hill Street Blues.*"

Dimand was in midswallow and nearly choked. He erupted in a combination of laughing and coughing. I was grinning broadly.

Feinman looked from one of us to the other. "Well, then fuck you," he said. Then he started laughing. "Fuck you both."

After things died down a little, Feinman said, "Look, Pat, we didn't ask you to join us just to be social."

"Okay."

"Steve's got a little business venture lined up."

"An acquaintance and I are expecting to receive a shipment of merchandise," Dimand said oh-so-casually. "In a day or two."

"What sort of merchandise?"

Dimand looked at his cousin, who nodded.

"Watches," Dimand said. "Ladies' watches. Nice, but not too fancy. The kind you'd buy at Dayton's or another department store for, say, two or three hundred dollars."

"Branching out a little, are we?" I knew from the way Dimand was acting, the way he was trying to play it cool, that this was not an everyday occurrence.

"Hey, this has nothing to do with me," Feinman said magnanimously. "This is all Steve's baby—I didn't even know about it till this afternoon. He only talked to me because he's looking for buyers for when the shipment comes in. I thought maybe you'd be interested."

Just what I needed: a load of hot watches. Women's, no less.

By way of stalling, I said, "You have somebody inside?"

Dimand nodded. "Warren—my partner—knows a driver. He slipped him a few bills. Then sometime in next day or two, while he's making his deliveries, he gets 'held up.' Nobody gets hurt, nobody gets hassled. It's easy. It's all insured, anyway."

God Bless Our Escalating Premiums.

"How much does 'a few bills' buy these days?" I asked.

"We had to come up with twelve."

"Ouch."

Feinman made a noise. Dimand gave him a look. "I already told you, Josh," he said patiently, "there's nothing to worry about. Warren is a little cash-poor right now, that's all. This enterprise will take care of that, and I get my twelve back right off the top, before the split. Anyway, it's my money, not yours."

Feinman looked at me and winked. "Another first," he said.

Dimand ignored him and turned his attention to me. "We're expecting no fewer than five hundred watches, and maybe as many as a thousand. Now, these things retail for two or three hundred, which means they wholesale for one hundred to one-fifty or so. Warren knows where he can place five hundred for one-fifty, cash, no questions. It's a retail jeweler, small but very well known, very well established. They'll sell the watches for a hundred dollars more than what you'd pay at a department store, and the old ladies in the fur coats will scoop them up, thinking that if they're more expensive they must be better." He allowed himself a small, almost soundless chuckle. "The man can only take five hundred, though. We need to find someone who can handle the rest."

"Why don't you just boost the five hundred," I said, "since you know you've got a market for them."

"Because it doesn't cost any more to steal a thousand than five hundred," Feinman supplied. "I've made some calls, and I think I can get rid of a hundred, maybe two, but only for a yard apiece. So I was telling Steve, maybe Pat knows some people." He gave me a knowing grin. "You've been around, right?"

I grinned back, but my smile didn't go any deeper than my facial muscles. I had not deluded myself into thinking that Feinman had fallen for me one hundred percent. That business Saturday morning at the lake illustrated graphically that we didn't trust each other to any great extent. A briefcase full of money didn't change that for me; I was certain it didn't change it for Feinman. Each of us, for different reasons, were in situations where we didn't dare trust each other—or very many other people, for that matter—completely.

So when Feinman made his remark and grinned his grin, the first thing that popped into my head was, Is this a test?

"Let me make some calls," I said slowly. I was stalling. "I won't promise anything—middling is outside my usual line. But I may know some people who may may be interested. When did you say the balloon goes up?"

"Tomorrow or the next day," Dimand said. "It has to be before Thanksgiving." Thanksgiving was Thursday already.

Christ—another year shot in the head. It would be nice to be home for Christmas. . . . "We don't have to unload right away, of course," Dimand went on, "but the sooner the better."

"Okay." That would give me a little time to figure how to play things. I didn't especially want to be involved, but if I had to pretend to be middling for someone else and use some of Feinman's money to buy a few watches in order to protect myself, then that's what I would do.

Feinman was looking over my head and to the left a little, and I automatically turned to see what had caught his attention. It was his sister. She came over to the booth and slid in next to Feinman. She had showered and dressed and was looking good and smelling wonderful. "You three look like you're up to no good," she observed solemnly.

"You know us too well," Feinman said lightly. He glanced at me, then back to Sharon. "You two off to do the town?"

"We're off to do the Uptown. They're showing *Casablanca* and *Play It Again, Sam.*"

"In that order, I hope," Dimand said. "I saw them the other way around there a few years ago, and whenever there was a scene in *Casablanca* that had been in *Play It Again, Sam,* everyone in the audience would laugh, remembering what Woody Allen had done to the scene in his movie."

"That's the only explanation," I said. "On its own, *Casablanca* isn't exactly a guffaw-fest."

◇◇◇

We saw the flicks in the right order, so the only audience reaction during *Casablanca* was some rather strenuous hissing and booing when Ilsa tells Rick he'll have to do the thinking for both of them. Who says feminism is passé? Afterward we stopped for a drink at the bar at Figlio's—"Yuppie Central," Sharon called it, and I could see why. She took in the young and not so young people, all painfully trendy, all looking somehow like cookie-cutter duplicates of one another, and sighed. "Don't they get tired?"

"Of what?"

"Of *trying* so damn hard. Of keeping up, keeping in, staying with it. Do they ever reach a point where they say, 'The heck with it, now I'm going to start having a *real* life'? Or have they spent so much time and energy—and money!—on the façade that they think it *is* real? Or don't they think about it?"

"There are plenty of them here," I said. "Want to ask one?"

"I've tried asking Steve," she said. "It's pointless. I think they must regard us the same way we regard them; they think we're putting on our life-styles just as we think they're putting on theirs. And just as we sort of shake our heads and feel moderately sorry for them for leading such superficial, shallow lives, they probably pity us because we miss what is to them the whole point."

"Yeah, yeah," I said. "Now tell me how you like your BMW."

She smiled sheepishly. "Well, I never said they don't have good taste."

And so on. The conversation drifted and looped and detoured the way conversation will between two people who have found themselves on the same wavelength and who have no agenda to stick to.

In fact, though, only one of us had no agenda. After my visit to NorLan Appliance that morning, I was interested in finding out a little more about Sharon's ex-husband. With a little effort, I steered us in that general direction—very little effort, since our conversation of Saturday night and the closeness we had enjoyed then and on into the small hours Sunday morning were still with us. Actually, it was Sharon who opened the door, by saying—for perhaps the sixth time—how glad she was that we had had that long talk and everything that followed it. It had brought us much closer that much quicker, she thought. And she was right.

I said, "Do you ever think about him coming back?"

"Fahy?" She smiled. "For a long time I did. At first it was hoping—praying, even—that he would, and everything would be right this time. Then later it was sort of idly hoping he'd show up again so I could break a hockey stick over his head. Now . . . hardly ever. And even when I do, it's all sort of . . . cool. Detached. Clinical, you might say. I would be curious, I think, to see him and hear what he had to say for himself. I'd be interested in my response, too. But I don't wish he would come back or wish he wouldn't, or expect he will or won't, or even give it a lot of thought. Not anymore. Why do you ask?"

Why did I? To bring the conversation around to Fahy, yes—but why that particular question and not any of a dozen others that would have served the purpose just as well? Maybe it was that I recognized parallels between Sharon and her ex and me and my . . . well, I thought of Jennifer as my ex, although technically, and for reasons that probably had more to do with sentiment than good sense, we were still lawfully wedded. I hadn't seen Jen in almost a year. Every twelve or eighteen months she breezed into my life for a few days, then blew out again. When the wound had just about healed, it seemed, she showed up and opened it again. Would it have been better if she had simply left all those years ago and never let me hear from her again? It was impossible to say.

"No reason," I said. It wasn't a lie; it was an admission that I just didn't know the reason. "I was just sort of wondering about, you know, not knowing. I mean, if he had said, 'That's it, I'm outta here,' that would be one thing. But to just walk out the door one morning and never come back, never get in touch for . . . how long did you say?"

The waitress, exasperated by the slow pace of our drinking, stopped by for the third time to see if we were, as they say, "okay." Sharon, being kindhearted, ordered another Seven and Seven. I had treated myself to a Harp, but now switched to club soda.

"Three years," Sharon said when the girl had gone. "Three years this coming January fifteenth."

That jibed with the date Bob Glass, Fahy's replacement at NorLan Appliance, had given me—the date Feinman promoted him to manager, saying Fahy wouldn't be coming in anymore.

Sharon's eyes had gone kind of unfocused and dreamy. "Three years doesn't seem like such a long time when you say it, but when I think back to then, and think about how much has changed . . . how much I've changed. . . ." She looked at me. "I think the quick, clean cut is best. It hurt like the devil at the time, and for a long time afterward. But I think it would have hurt a lot worse if he hadn't just . . . left." She smiled slightly. And fondly. "Fahy was a bastard, but give him some credit. Leaving was the best thing he could do, and he did that right."

"But didn't you report him missing?"

"Not exactly. . . ."

Raised-eyebrow time. I was a little surprised, but not flabbergasted, speechless, or stunned. Bob Glass had said nothing about the police calling or coming by NorLan—as they almost certainly would have if they were looking into Fahy's disappearance, and which Glass almost certainly would have remembered and mentioned to me. So I had been pretty sure no such investigation had taken place. But I had to wonder why, and thus the eyebrow.

Sharon gave a half-smile of slight embarrassment and said, "You have to understand, it wasn't all that unusual for Fahy to stay out all night. He would go on these benders . . . well, I already told you he had been out all night and all the next day after he belted me. So when he didn't come home that night, I wasn't very concerned. Disappointed, yes, but not concerned. When I didn't see or hear from him the next day, though, I did get a little worried. I didn't call the warehouse. I was afraid of what I might find out. I certainly didn't call my brother. But I knew some of the places Fahy used to hang out at, some of the people he used to see. None of them had seen him, and he hadn't been in any of his usual places. That's when I got panicky."

The waitress, with that incredible timing they have, returned with our drinks. Sharon paused. I could never be a waiter; I'm too paranoid. I would start to think everyone in the place must be talking about me, the way they clam up whenever I came near.

"I waited until the next morning. When he hadn't showed up by then, I called Josh," Sharon said, laughing a little. "Once a baby sister, always a baby sister, I guess. He said he'd check into it. I about wore out the phone lines calling him; he would say there had been no news yet, I should relax, I should be patient. And a few days later he admitted that, though he called the police and highway patrol to see if there had been an accident or something, he never reported Fahy missing."

She paused, and pursed her lips, and regarded the glass in front of her. "I know what you're thinking," she said after a long while. "What you must be thinking: 'What's the matter with this woman? Doesn't she have a mind of her own?' " She looked up at me. "And the answer, Pat, is no. She didn't—not back then. She had spent a lifetime being taken care of by someone else. You're a man; you don't know what it's like. You don't know how hard it is to break out of that. Because you get so used to it, you don't even realize there's anything that you should break out of. I'm different now—better, I think; more complete. I won't pretend I don't need help sometimes. . . ."

"Everybody does, at one time or another. They call it being human."

"Well, these days I don't go crying to Josh every time a fuse blows. And I don't blindly put everything in his hands the way I did three years ago. I'm not like Ingrid Bergman in the movie—I know how to do my own thinking."

"I noticed you hissing at that part."

"I thought I was being discreet. Usually I boo and throw popcorn boxes at the screen." She sipped her drink. "Anyhow, back then it was completely natural for me to have big brother take care of everything for me. But when I found out he hadn't made a report about Fahy, I was furious. I wanted to call the police right away—in fact, I had the phone in my hand. But Josh stopped me. He stopped me by asking what I wanted him back for. And I realized he was right. What was the point? With his boozing and skirt-chasing and all, Fahy was no kind of husband. I may have been crazy about him, but I had to admit I didn't love him—not the way love should be, you know? In some ways, I think it was more like an addiction than love. And it wasn't two-way—as Fahy proved by deserting me. So I tried to let it go, pulled myself together, and got on with my life. With a lot of t.l.c. from Josh."

Josh, I thought. Always Josh. Good old johnny-on-the-spot Josh, there when you need him. Sometimes there *before* you need him, in fact, since Bob Glass had told me Feinman was at NorLan at six or six-thirty A.M. January fifteenth to say that Fahy wouldn't be coming in anymore. But Sharon Fahy had told me her husband didn't even get out of bed that morning until an hour or more later.

33

I called Joe Delgado the next morning, even though I knew what he had to tell me. It's bad form to ask the cops for a favor and then not follow through and see what they found for you. Cops tend to remember things like that the next time you ask for a favor.

"No missing person report on your Fahy," Delgado said, and I didn't let on that it was old news. "I got a little curious, so I cross-checked on the computer. He has a sheet—mostly alcohol-related: DWI, drunk-and-disorderly, a couple of assaults—and there's a notation that he may have moved on to greener pastures."

"But that's just based on his not being picked up and thrown into the tank for a long time," I said.

"That's about the strength of it," Delgado said. "Looks to me like maybe Fahy shuffled along and nobody was interested in finding out where to."

"You're probably right," I said. But he wasn't. One person had been interested: Sharon. One person hadn't been interested, because he already knew: Feinman. I was certain of it.

Fat lot of good it did me, my certainty.

I thanked Joe for his trouble, assured him I would someday tell him what it was all about, and put down the phone. I had made the call from a gas station that had been converted into a little grocery with self-service gas pumps. It was off of West Seventh, on Homer at Shepard Road, in another St. Paul neighborhood where lawlessness reigned, at least as regards municipal zoning. Behind the grocery-and-gas, to the south, was an apartment complex. South of it, a couple of office buildings and a couple of condominiums. Across from them, along Stewart Avenue, were some tired-looking houses and some ugly warehousey buildings. Half a block west, just off

Fort Road, was the Pearson plant—they of Salted Nut Roll fame. Directly across from the grocery was a monstrously ugly turquoise building that housed a printing and publishing company. A long time ago I had done some freelance writing for a couple of magazines published there, but one by one they all seemed to sink into oblivion or get scooped up by other publishers, and most of the people I had known there were now gone, either as victims in one of several corporate Nights of the Long Knives or by virtue of being smart enough to decipher the writing on the wall.

I drove back to my place.

I had rolled out of the sack at a pretty decent hour, especially considering that Sharon and I had been out kind of late for a school night, then proceeded to shoot most of the morning running a variety of mundane, inane errands that could have waited, culminating in my call to Joe Delgado from yet another pay phone in yet another exotic locale. The errands were of the return-library-books, buy-windshield-washer-fluid, get-stamps variety, and they were designed to keep me out of the apartment. Now exhausted—both the errands and I—it was time to go back and face the music.

The tune in question was the one that would be played when I opened the metal attaché case cleverly concealed back at the apartment. The case was a little too big to hide in the groove down the center of the dining table, so I had wrapped it up in a pillowcase and shoved it in with my dirty laundry.

Now I fished it out, carried it over to the dining table, and set it down. I poured out a cup of coffee, put the Bolling-Rampal disc in the portable CD player, fiddled with the volume and graphic-equalizers slides, and finally quit fussing and sat down.

I opened the case and started counting the money.

I finished twenty thousand dollars later.

Twenty thousand dollars. Mostly in hundreds, fifties, and twenties. That's a lot of paper. That's a lot of money. Do you know how long it ordinarily took me to make twenty thousand? My gross—not my adjusted gross but my gross gross—the previous tax year had been just a shade over fifteen thousand. Because I receive no salary, my income varies wildly from month to month, but for simplicity's sake let's call it twelve-fifty a month. So I would have to work sixteen months to make twenty thousand dollars. Sixteen months.

I had made this twenty grand for less than sixteen *hours'* work.

That was why I hadn't wanted to open the attaché. No, let's be honest: I was afraid to open it. Afraid to count the contents. Afraid that a little voice in the back of my head would say, *Leapin' lizards, look at all that loot! And what did you have to do to get it? Nothing much different than the usual head-banging you do for a lot less money. Why fight success? Instead of trying to beat 'em, why not join 'em? Be smart for once in your life!*

In fact the voice did indeed pipe up, in much the fashion as I had expected—but rather than a little voice it was a big loud booming voice that screamed inside my skull and drove me back out of the apartment. I hiked along Edgecumbe Road, following it as it sliced through Highland Park, dodging cross-country skiers on the trails set up on the golf course. I paused on the footbridge over Montreal Avenue, which divides the park in the other direction. The day was sunny, cold and crisp; breezy up here on the bridge. I leaned against the icy rail and watched the traffic pass below me.

A diplomat is routinely rotated from a foreign posting to his home country, then to another, different foreign country. This is to keep him from "going native"—that is, beginning to identify more with his host country than his home country. I was beginning to feel how easy it must be to go native—how easy it would be to say, Well, Feinman *might* be a wrong guy, but you know, I don't really have any proof. Maybe I can't find any because there isn't any to find. After all, he seems like a nice enough sort. And he's done all right by me so far. And his sister is real nice. And. . . .

Twenty thousand dollars.

I used to joke that I couldn't be bought, only rented. Now it didn't seem very funny.

Another unfunny line was, "If you're so smart, how come you're not rich?" Having money doesn't have much to do with being smart. A lot of smart people don't have much money; a lot of stupid people do. It's less a matter of being smart than of what you're willing to do, how much you'll put up with in exchange for money. Will you practice a profession you dislike? Will you work for a company that treats you like a dog? Will you ignore your spouse and kids? Will you sell your body or your soul—or both?

Will you break the law?

Don't get me wrong. I have nothing against money—quite the opposite. And I don't get all dewy eyed about the law of the land, either; I leave that to those who can afford that luxury. But I have some definite ideas about right and wrong, and which side of that equation I want to be on as much of the time as possible, and how I want to respond to those who are on the other side of it.

At least, I had always *thought* my ideas were definite. Back at the apartment, though, there was suddenly so much money in the room that I couldn't breathe, couldn't focus, couldn't think straight. I had to get out.

A long time ago I concluded that, as nice as money was, there was a limit to what I would do to acquire it. I have no patience for office politicians, for pin-striped posturers and pretenders, for driving the right car and belonging to the right club and socializing with the right people, for the too-firm handshakes and the too-hearty laughs and the too-earnest smiles with their little hints of desperation and deception at the corners. Oh, I could play in that arena; I had done so, early on, for more years than I should have. I probably could have stuck with it, and by now I probably would be pulling in five times the contents of Feinman's attaché. But it was more than I was willing to do—more than I was willing to do to myself. I consoled myself, in my impoverished condition, that I could at least look my mirror image in the eye every morning.

Now, nearly twenty years later, older and maybe wiser but certainly no wealthier, with all those nice pictures of Ben Franklin and General Grant and Andy Jackson smiling up at me from my dining table. . . .

I turned around on the bridge, facing the goofy five-way intersection to the east, at the foot of the Montreal hill. The intersection of Montreal and Snelling, with Lexington Parkway exploding out of the middle of it and shooting off diagonally north-northwest. It was hard to tell which traffic light controlled what; every time I had ever driven through that intersection, on any of my junkets to the town, broken wind-shield or headlight glass crunched under my tires.

It was almost identical to the five-way intersection of Deca-tur Street, the Northwest Radial Highway, and Happy Hollow Boulevard, just outside my apartment window back in Omaha.

Almost identical—but not quite. The difference was, that was home and this was not; that was my city and this would never be; in the other I was myself, good or bad, while here I was a stranger. Even to me.

I turned northward and went back the way I had come. That's what I had been trying to do for weeks now, after all: go back the way I had come. That was the point. That was the goal. No more forgetting that.

When I got back I called Steve Dimand. He answered on the third ring.

"This is Kilpatrick," I said. "My friend is interested in your product, but he can't use more than seventy-five, and he can't do any better than a hundred."

"That's kind of low. . . ."

"It's all he's prepared to go for. But he's ambivalent. If you want to wait until after the fact and see if you can find an-other customer, that's okay with him. He's in no hurry."

"Good," Dimand said. "I'll see what Wa—"

"You mean your partner," I said quickly.

"Uh . . . yes. I'll see what my partner thinks. It looks like the, um, event will be tonight. I'll talk to you later, Pat. Thanks."

I put down the phone and began piling the money back into the attaché. I could afford seventy-five hundred if it came to that. It seemed like a cheap enough investment, if it paid off the way I hoped.

No more forgetting.

34

Dimand did see me later—the next afternoon, in fact, at the club. I had stopped by to work off some tension, but Dimand straight-armed me before I made it ten steps inside the building. He was heated up over something.

"Pat. I have to talk to you, man."

He didn't hang around waiting to see what my reply would be, but grabbed me by the left arm and half-tugged, half-guided me around the glass cabinet in the lobby of the club, past Brad's cluttered desk, and through a doorway at the back of the little workspace. There was another office back here—Dimand's, to judge by the fake-wood nameplate on the desk—definitely not designed with the claustrophobic in mind.

Dimand shut the door.

I threw my gym bag onto the desk, which was noticeably barren, and myself into a low-slung bucket seat against the far wall, which wasn't really very far from anything in the room. Dimand paced, fidgety and restless and wired. After watching this for a little while, I said, "For someone who had to talk, you're a little on the silent side, Steve."

He stopped and looked at me, gnawing at a hangnail on his left thumb. "I've got a problem, Pat."

"Really? Well, congratulations on hiding it so well. Remind me never to play poker with you."

Dimand snorted a laugh that turned into a kind of giggle and stopped abruptly. "I need your help," he said quickly.

The humor of the situation—the guy who started all my woes now needing my help—struck me, but I managed to keep from breaking up. "Are you planning to give me something to go on here, Steve, or should I start guessing?"

"I've got a problem," he repeated. Then suddenly he grabbed a black leather bombardier-style jacket from a hook on the office door. "Come on, let's get out of here."

I sighed, stood, grabbed my bag, and followed.

Dimand was on his way out the front door by the time I caught up to him.

"Maybe just a clue," I said, "to give me a sporting chance."

He tossed something at me and I caught it by virtue of instinct rather than skill. "You drive," he said.

We got into the Jaguar. I had never so much as sat in one, let alone driven one. The interior was all leather and gloss, the scent was subtly erotic, and the overall effect was to make you feel that you should speak in a whisper. Though the day was sunny, it was far too cold to have the top down, or even to remove the roof panels, so I suppose I didn't get the full open-motorcar experience touted in the magazine ads, but there's no use crying about it. I slid the key into the switch but Dimand stopped me.

"Hang on a second," he said, and popped open the glove compartment. He took out a slender ebony box and removed the lid. The inside of the lid was mirrored. He set it mirror-side-up on the shelf formed by the glovebox door, then produced an amber medicine vial, a chemist's measure, and a single-edged razor blade.

I was surprised, and I was not surprised. Surprised once again that someone who had gone to the effort to build the body beautiful would subject it to that kind of abuse. And not surprised that coke would be his drug of choice. Despite the news magazines having declared it *outré,* a lot of snow still drifted around in a lot of the "right" circles. It fit Dimand's life-style. And it helped explain some of his behavior—not the least today's oddball antics.

He made a couple of lines disappear through a thin glass tube, then looked at me sidelong, questioningly.

"Can I start the car now?" I said.

He shrugged and began packing up his first-aid kit. "Let's roll, Kato," he said, and giggled.

The Jag surged to life with an almost alarming readiness, and purred contentedly.

"Where are we rolling to, Green Hornet?"

"Left out of the lot," Dimand said. "I'll give you directions."

The car slid out into traffic, with little assistance from me. I have never ridden in a Rolls-Royce, but someone who had once told me it was the perfect ride, like floating above the pavement rather than rolling across it. It was hard to imagine anything smoother than the Jaguar's ride, though. I wondered how much the car cost. It seemed déclassé to ask, even though the type of guys who drop big bundles on cars also seem to be the type of guys who love to tell you how much they dropped. Anyhow, I wasn't in the market. The money Josh Feinman gave me probably was enough for a good down payment, but unfortunately most of that money was already spent. My expenses had been high on this case, and there was no client to foot the bill. It seemed only fitting that Feinman's money be applied to that account.

A few blocks away from the club, Dimand said, "It was a put-on from the start."

I looked at him, then back at the street. "The heist."

He nodded. "Warren set me up."

"Well, what are friends for?"

"I never said he was my friend. He's a friend of a friend. A guy in my building. . . . Anyhow, the point is, the job was supposed to happen last night, but it didn't. I tried to find Warren for hours—and then it finally began to sink in that the idea was not and had never been to steal a load of wristwatches. The idea had been to fleece Steven Dimand twelve thousand dollars' worth." He pounded the dashboard in frustration. I winced for the car's sake.

"Calm down a minute. Maybe something went haywire. Tell it from the beginning."

He took in a deep breath and blew it out hard, and threw his head back against the leather headrest behind him. "Fine. I called Warren yesterday after I talked to you. He said the give-up was going to be that night—last night. Downtown. The driver is making his second-to-last delivery at about six—second-to-last so the truck won't be empty. We're to meet him out back of the store. He hands us the cartons, we take off, and he calls the police and says he's been held up at gunpoint by a gang of black kids." Dimand sighed again. "It was so perfect. The neighborhood's not too great, especially after dark, there's not a lot of traffic at that hour . . . just perfect."

"Now you know why they say there's no such thing as the perfect crime," I said. "Go on."

"Can't you guess? I showed up at the appointed place and hour. No truck. No Warren. I sat there like a schmuck for over an hour. I was afraid that the minute I left, everything would happen. Then I was afraid something had gone wrong. So I finally went to a phone and called Warren. Or tried to. There was no answer at his number, so I tried half a dozen places I thought he might be, places where we had met when we were planning the job. And then, like I said, the light started to go on. Nothing had gone wrong. Everything had gone exactly the way Warren had planned it from the start." He looked at me. "Want to tell me what a class-A fuck-up I am?"

"Is that what you wanted me for? Want I should give you absolution now?"

Dimand laughed humorlessly. "What I want is twelve grand. Preferably before I see Josh again."

I looked at him sidelong. "If I wanted to be in banking, Steve, I would be in banking."

"I'm not asking for a loan." He sniffed and cleared his throat. "I already sort of borrowed the twelve I gave to Warren."

I flashed back to what Feinman had told me, about putting Dimand in at the club because it gave him fewer opportunities to give the store away. Wishful thinking on Feinman's part, it looked like. "From the racquet club?" I said. "How? There can't be much cash money going through the place. . . ."

"No . . . but all that top-of-the-line exercise equipment costs money, lots of it. I turned back part of a shipment and arranged to have the refund check made out to me, not the club."

"In return for a small consideration."

"In return for a small consideration. The way I had it figured, the hijack would pull in at least seventy-five thousand. At least. My twelve was to come back right off the top, and Warren and I would split the remainder. I couldn't see how I could come out of it with less than forty thousand. Then I would reinstate the order for the equipment I had turned back, and no one would be the wiser."

"Meaning Josh. But your friend Warren threw a wrench into the works."

"Acquaintance."

"Now when Josh gets to looking through the paperwork,

he's going to discover that the club is short on the equipment order and the bank account is short the money. What I don't understand is what you want me for, if you don't want to hit me for a loan. You want me to talk to Josh for you?"

"Thanks, but I usually have Sharon handle that for me; she's got the knack. But I don't think Josh has to find out. I started thinking this morning, Pat, that you could help me get the money back. I'll still be out the five hundred I had to slip the equipment salesman, but I can cover that myself. What do you say?"

By now, with Dimand's directions, we were near W.A. Frost in St. Paul. Supposedly one of F. Scott Fitzgerald's hangouts when he was a kid in St. Paul, the restaurant was a bustling, noisy place with a vaguely English atmosphere. There was a terrace out back where round tables sat under Cinzano umbrellas during warmer weather than a Minnesota winter has to offer. Nevertheless, the place was doing a good business. I ended up putting the Jag in a lot a block down Selby Avenue.

Dimand looked at his watch, a slender gold number that probably cost a year's rent. Either Feinman gave his cousin a big allowance, or this escapade with Warren was not Dimand's first entrepreneurial gig—with at least some of the others having paid off as advertised. "When I was calling around last night," Dimand said, "trying to track down Warren, I found out he's a member of an investment club that meets here every Wednesday at noon. It's almost two—they should be wrapping up soon. The way I see it, Warren has money to invest today—he'll surely be on hand for this meeting." Dimand turned in the car seat and looked at me. He had that funny glint again, a half-glassy, half-bright look in his eye and a silly grin that couldn't decide if it really wanted to show up or not. "You carrying?"

"Just American Express," I said.

"That's okay. I am." He patted one zippered pocket of his jacket. The jacket was bulky, oversized, and you couldn't tell at a glance whether he had anything in his pocket, but something there thumped dully when he patted it.

I wasn't sure exactly how to read the situation—whatever it may have been—but any way I looked at it I couldn't see that it needed a coked-up hothead with a gun to complete the picture. I said, "Why don't you let me hold that?"

"It's all right," Dimand said soothingly. "I'm just going to let him see it—you know, just to scare him a little."

It would probably do the job: I hadn't even seen it yet and I was already scared.

"That's why I should hold it," I said, improvising. "The way to play it is like I'm some kind of muscle you've brought along to back you up."

The egg-sucking grin came out like the sun. "All right," Dimand said. "All *right.*" He unzipped the pocket and produced a silver .22, a silly little gun that can make a silly little hole in a guy. He handed it to me. "Let's go, Pat."

I waited out front while Dimand went in and reconnoitered the restaurant. It took him only a minute, maybe two. When he came out he was even more jazzed than before, which only made me doubly glad the .22 was in my pocket, not his.

"He's in there! With a group of people! They're standing up, getting their coats and things. I think they're getting ready to leave."

That seemed a safe assumption. "Okay," I said. "You point him out to me when he comes out. Then you stay right here and I'll bring him over to you. Then just follow my lead."

We were on the sidewalk in front of the place, about fifteen feet from the front door, which was at the corner. I moved so that my back was toward the door. Dimand was facing me. "My standing here will keep him from seeing you until we want him to. You make sure he's not looking this way, then point."

Dimand nodded. His pupils were large and he was breathing through his mouth.

A bit more time passed, then suddenly a noisy group came bustling out the door behind me. I didn't look. Dimand did, though, craning his neck this way and that, trying to see without being seen. "That's him," he finally said in a shrill whisper. "That's him—the one with the beard in the navy-blue coat."

I turned. Warren was a slender, dark-blond man in his mid-forties. He wore a full but closely trimmed beard and longish hair swept away from his face in that way that makes the wearer look like he's always heading into a strong wind. He was tugging on black kid gloves while chatting with one of his luncheon companions. I nodded to Diamond and moved away from him, stepping up behind and slightly to one side of the bearded man. "Excuse me," I said politely. "Warren, you and I have an urgent need to talk."

Warren half-turned to look at me. "I don't think I know you."

"You're right. But you know my friend." I took a couple steps to my left, revealing Dimand to him. That move also put Warren between me and his companion, so there was no one to notice my nudging the barrel of the .22 into Warren's side. No one except Warren, that is, who acknowledged it with a slight widening of the eyes and an even slighter parting of the lips. "He's been trying to reach you since last night," I added conversationally, just to fill time while Warren decided whether or not to say anything to his friend.

He glanced at me, made up his mind, and swallowed hard. Then he turned to the other man. "Excuse me, Dan, I need to talk to this man. I'll see you next week."

"Optimist, huh?" I said when the other man had moved off. I guided Warren over toward Dimand. He went readily enough. "Look what I found, Mr. Dimand. Weren't you just telling me how it's such a nice day, you'd like to take this man for a ride?"

"I'm glad to see you, Steve," Warren began enthusiastically, his half of a hearty handshake already in the air. "I've been trying to call y—"

I jabbed him in the side with the gun. "I didn't hear Mr. Dimand ask you any question, friend."

Dimand looked at me with that wild gleam in place. "Take it easy, Patrick," he said reasonably, picking up his cue. "This is a public sidewalk, after all." He looked at the bearded man. "Come on, Warren, let's take the Jag for a spin."

We did—Dimand at the wheel, me in the back with Warren and the .22. Just like they used to do on *The Untouchables*. As he climbed in ahead of me, I gave Warren a quick pat-down. Little chance that he was carrying, but it pays to be certain. And anyway, it added authenticity to the drama.

Warren tried again as soon as the car pulled out into the street. "Steve, listen, I can exp—"

I reached over and flicked the top of his ear with my middle finger, the way kids do. It stings, but no one's ever been hospitalized for it. "This is listening time, fur-face. So listen good, because we're not going to go into reruns here. You owe Mr. Dimand, right?"

"There was a mix-up," Warren said, quickly but not frantically. He was used to thinking on his feet. "Last night. The schedule got changed—the driver's schedule. Everything's pushed back to tonight."

"That's the wrong answer," I said, and moved the .22 from Warren's ribs to his temple. "You owe Mr. Dimand, right?"

Warren nodded rapidly. "Yes. Yes." Now he was frantic. That was good—I wanted him in unfamiliar waters, not someplace he thought he could dog-paddle out of like always.

"That's the right answer. You're pretty smart . . . for a dumbass. Next question: you're going to pay Mr. Dimand what you owe him, right?"

"Yes—yes." The head kept going. It was like watching one of those punching-bag clowns. "Absolutely. Every dime. I haven't touched it, Steve. It's even in the same envelope you gave it to me in. Twelve thousand. You can have it back. Sorry for the screw-up."

"Give me directions, Warren," Dimand said cheerfully.

"Right onto Lex. I'm up by Hamline University."

Dimand turned onto Lexington Parkway. Traffic was heavy with Twin Citians enjoying the pleasant weather.

"Excuse me, Mr. Dimand," I said, "but I think maybe you forgot about the nuisance fee."

"Nuisance fee?" Warren's voice was thin and a little strained. He had begun thinking that maybe he was going to walk away from this one unscathed after all. "What nuisance fee? What are you talking about?"

"That's the fee you have to pay for being such a nuisance to Mr. Dimand," I explained. "The current rate is ten percent."

"Twelve hundred bucks?" he squeaked. "I don't have twelve hundred bucks. Sure as hell not lying around my apartment! Where am I supposed to get twelve hundred bucks?"

"I don't know, Warren. Let's think on that the rest of the way to your place."

We drove on in silence, but it was only a few more blocks.

He lived in a standard three-story apartment building, dark shake-shingle siding and pink trim, three or four blocks from Hamline University. Warren's apartment was on the top floor, front. As soon as we entered the living room, I shut and locked the door. "All right, Warren, the way we play this scavenger hunt is you tell Mr. Dimand where his money is and he goes and gets it. You and me, we keep each other company the whole time."

"It—it's in the kitchen. In the fridge."

Dimand and I exchanged glances. "Cold cash," he said, sniggering.

We moved the party to that room, Dimand, Warren, and me, in that order. "Milk carton, in the back there," Warren said. Dimand pulled it out. It looked like an ordinary waxed-paper milk carton. Mainly because that's what it was. Warren must have opened it, poured the milk into a bowl or a pitcher, and carefully opened the top of the carton all the way. Then he put the manila envelope with Dimand's money—a hundred and twenty one-hundred-dollar bills—inside a plastic bag, crammed the works inside the carton, and poured back as much of the milk as would fit. Then he reglued the top of the carton so it looked like it had never been opened. It had about the right weight, and it sloshed convincingly when you lifted it.

Dimand was a lot less meticulous in handling it than Warren had been, though. He ripped it open in the sink and pulled out the plastic bag, patting it dry with a dish towel that had been hanging from the refrigerator-door handle.

"You get an A-plus for inventiveness, Warren," I said. "Now, what have you come up with regarding that nuisance fee?"

"I don't have that kind of money here." His voice was no longer frantic or fast-paced, but dull and almost resigned. He was telling the truth. He had lost the twelve thousand and now he figured he was standing at the edge of the abyss, and he was telling the truth.

"Maybe we should check the breadbox," Dimand chortled.

"Tear the place apart," Warren said. "I don't have any money here. But I've got a safe-deposit box at the bank. . . ." His voice gained some energy. "They're still open, it's just a few blocks from here. . . ."

"What do you say, Mr. Dimand?" I was slightly wagging my head even as I asked it. Warren had his back toward me, he didn't see the signal.

"Well..." Dimand said, milking it. "I don't think so, Pat. We don't want to drive around all day with this loser."

Which was the honest truth, whether he knew it or not. The longer we played out this farce, the higher went the odds that something would blow up in our faces. I sure as heck didn't want to walk into a bankful of people and take my chances.

"You're in luck, Warren," I said. "Mr. Dimand's going to let you owe him the twelve hundred. Isn't that great?"

"Great," Warren agreed, albeit halfheartedly.

"Now the thing is, Warren, that's ten percent per week. That means it's twelve hundred now, but if Mr. Dimand doesn't see his money this week, it goes up to thirteen-twenty—ten percent of twelve grand plus twelve hundred. The week after that it's fourteen fifty-two. That's ten percen—"

"I get it, I get it. I'll get the money to you tomorrow."

"Tomorrow's Thanksgiving," Dimand said.

"Friday, then. Okay?"

"Fine. You can messenger it over to the club," Dimand said cavalierly. Nice touch, I thought. Then I got us the hell out of there.

If Dimand had been high before, he was in orbit now. He let out a whoop and did a Gene Krupa number on the dashboard as I steered the Jaguar out of Warren's neighborhood. I doubted he would make trouble—I was pretty sure I had scared most of the starch out of him—but the last thing I wanted was to have him sic the cops on us, us and our coke-filled car.

"You were perfect," Dimand gushed. "Even *I* thought you might actually shoot the poor bastard! Warren must have been shitting down both legs!"

"Next time out—if there is a next time—do yourself a favor and don't part with any money until you see the goods."

I guess I was talking to the steering wheel. "And I *never* would have thought about turning his own game back on him and shaking him down for more money! Nuisance fee! Priceless, just priceless! Hang on a sec—"

I stopped for a stop sign. Dimand ducked down, opened the glove compartment, and got out his little black box. "Man, I feel like celebrating!"

"Looks to me like you've been 'celebrating' since about eight this morning."

He giggled and sucked some more money up his nose. "Hey, Pat, you want a toot? I'll drive."

"No to both offers, thanks. Don't you know that cocaine has gone the way of the three-piece suit and red silk tie, at least for this fashion season?" Dimand gave me a smirky, wiseass look and packed up the medicine chest. "Does Feinman know how much coke you do?"

"Where do you think I score it? Cousin Josh has it flown in special delivery. Tons of it. I think he thinks I sell it all. And I do, some of it, but it's always a good idea to know your product—"

"Flown in, huh?" I said casually. "From where?"

"From where do you think? From the source. Direct from the warehouse to you." Dimand started laughing. Coke, adrenaline, relief, and that sweet taste of victory—quite a heady combination. "Hey, Pat, what commercial did they used to say that in?"

"All of them, I think. Geez, if Josh is flying the stuff in direct, he must be able to move an awful lot of it. I know some people. . . ." I let it dangle.

"Oh, yeah, Josh is big," Dimand boasted. "And he's got all of the bases covered. He bought a crop-dusting service or something out in Farmland, U.S.A., somewhere out in the middle of the state. It's a completely legitimate business. Mostly." He laughed some more. "And he built a little airstrip down in Oklahoma, Missouri, some Godawful place. The plane flies up—it's a little thing, no bigger than Josh's plane, and it flies in below radar or above the clouds or however they do it—and it refuels in Collard Greens, Mississippi, or wherever the hell the place is. Maybe it sits on the ground there for a day or two, if they think things are warm. Then it flies on up to Farmland, and no one's the wiser."

Dimand was running like a faucet—it was the chemicals, both artificial and naturally produced. But cocaine induces paranoia, too, so I had to be careful not to say anything that would make Dimand suspicious of me. At the moment Di-

mand thought I was the greatest thing ever to come down the
road, but I still didn't want him to get the idea I was pumping
him for information. So I said, "This is a great car. If I stick
with your cousin, I might be able to swing one of these before
too long."

"Oh, yeah, I've driven them all—Audis, Mercedes, BMWs.
The Jag's the tops, no question. Even though they sent me on
a wild-goose chase last month—something about the brakes
going out without any warning, but the dealer didn't know
anything about it and the district office didn't know anything
and the national headq—"

"Computer screw-up," I said sympathetically. "What I want
to know is, if all these places have all this money invested in
computers, and they know everything about you including
whether you use waxed or unwaxed dental floss, then how
come they want you to write a thirty-digit account number on
your check and the envelope when you send them a payment?
Why can't they keep track of it on their end? They have computers; I don't."

Dimand laughed. "What are you, a consumer advocate?"

"Me and David Horowitz. Listen, speaking of consumers, do
you think your cousin needs any new outlets? Like I said, I
know some people, and if Josh's setup is half as good as you
say . . ."

"It's perfect," Dimand boasted. "Look. Where is all the attention focused? South Florida, the Mexican border, New
York pizza parlors, places like that. Those places are hot. Out
here, though—we have miles and miles of miles and miles, as
Josh says. Not too many people to get too curious. And even
if someone did get curious, well, there's an awful lot of geography to cover in these parts."

"Still, you have to get the junk into the Cities from . . .
wherever you said."

"Yeah, one of those places where they paint the name of the
town on the water tower. St. Somebody-or-other probably—
every third town in this state is St. Somebody-or-other."

Which narrowed it right down.

"Anyhow," Dimand went on, "there are trucks waiting for
the planes. Small trucks, not semis—Josh says semis are more
likely to be stopped for routine checks. Small trucks, delivery
trucks, trucks like the kind every farmer has. They hide the

shit in with a regular load and cart it into the Cities. I don't know where exactly—Josh thinks I'm better off not knowing." He laughed again, and when he was through with that he reiterated his desire to celebrate. "Let's stop somewhere for a drink, eh?"

"Don't you want to get back to the club and take care of that little 'loan' you took out?"

"There's plenty of time for that. Josh doesn't keep all that close tabs on what's going on. But he would miss that twelve thousand." Dimand shook his head, as if contemplating his fate if Feinman had found out about the money. "I owe you, Pat."

It was a day for ironies. "Forget it," I said.

"Not a chance. You saved my hide."

I laughed. "Yeah, like there was a real danger your cousin would have put you out of commission."

Dimand laughed too. "No, if he was going to do that, he'd have done it long ago. Some of the idiot stunts I've pulled . . . including this latest one." The thought of it brought back the laughter. "But no kidding, if Josh had caught wind of this fiasco, he'd have skinned me alive and then he'd have had Warren's head on a platter."

"Right," I said sarcastically.

"Hey, I'm not kidding."

"Come on. Josh? I *know* the man."

"You think so, huh?" He was a little stung. I had nicked his pride by insinuating that I didn't believe his cousin was the toughest kid on the block. "Well, lot of guys have made that mistake, Pat. But I'm telling you, if I had gone to Josh for help instead of you, Warren would be somewhere below the Wabasha Street bridge right now, wearing a concrete swimming cap. And I know that for a fact."

"Oh, come *on*, Steve." I hoped there was more to come. Details. Would Warren have had company down at the bottom of the Mississippi? Others who had had run-ins with Feinman—or a member of his family, which I knew from firsthand experience was the same thing. Dimand was flying pretty high, and I had no way of knowing how much of his talk was the truth and how much was the chemicals. I had no way of knowing what he knew or what he suspected. Was he exaggerating his cousin's exploits? Or was he telling me that

Warren would not have been the first pest Feinman had squashed?

These were not questions I felt inclined to come out and ask, and I could think of no good nonchalant way of bringing up the subject of murder.

Dimand, however, was at no loss for words. "But, man, I wish Josh could have seen the way you handled Warren. . . ." He shook his head admiringly. "Josh ought to send you to Omaha."

I worked to keep my voice level and my interest only polite. "Omaha?" I cleared my throat, which suddenly had become a little dry and tight. "Why would Josh want me to go to Omaha, of all places?"

"Oh, I had some trouble with this asshole from there a month or so ago. Josh sent some guys down there to teach him a lesson, but so far the stupid jerks haven't been able to find him. I told Josh, obviously the guy smelled something in the wind and went to ground, and we need to beat the bushes a little to flush him out. Now I think we should just pull the guys out of there and send you down. You know how to handle yourself."

That would be cute. Send me down to lay a trap for myself. The idea had some appeal. It would get Feinman's bully contingent out of my way, and my friends'—but for how long? When I—Pat Kilpatrick—didn't come up with any results (and how could he?), Feinman might simply send the bullies back in. Net gain: zero. Was there any way for Kilpatrick to convince Feinman that he had taken care of me—this was getting very schizo for me—and then simply vanish? No. Feinman would want more than Kilpatrick's word alone, and manufacturing acceptable "proof" would be damn tricky. Plus, that tack would not lead to the kind of conclusion I wanted the story to have, a solid The End in twelve-point type; instead, I'd get something like the "end" of a bad horror flick, with the door wide open for the supposedly dispatched villain to reappear if the box-office receipts warrant it. I had spent the last month or so looking back over my shoulder; I had no intention of living the rest of my life that way. I had come too far at too great a cost to be content with anything less than a grand finale.

"That would be a bad idea," I told Dimand casually. "I ran

into a little trouble down there. A few years ago. I don't think I'll be venturing back that way for a long time to come."

"Too bad," Dimand said. "Well, what's in Omaha, anyway?"

"Right," I said, trying to pump some enthusiasm into it. "What's in Omaha?"

Besides home.

35

Thursday came up windy and bright and cold—gnawingly, numbingly cold, the kind where your nose feels like it might snap off at any moment. Undaunted, though, Joshua Feinman insisted on cooking the Thanksgiving turkey on his backyard grill, a black Weber kettle somewhat smaller than a Gemini space capsule, in which Feinman had ignited approximately one U.S. ton of charcoal briquettes by the dawn's early light, letting them burn down to a nice orange bed of embers before the bird in question went to its fate. Feinman wheeled the barbecue up to the French doors at the back of his house, and every twenty minutes or so went out onto the patio and listened to the sizzling inside the Weber. He never cracked the lid for a peek inside; he just listened.

Feinman owned a big brick house along Minnehaha Parkway—"the Parkway," as it was universally known—in Minneapolis, near Lake Nokomis Park. Minnehaha, you of course recall, was the Indian maiden whom Hiawatha hauled through floodwaters to safety in Longfellow's poem. Not far from Feinman's house was Minnehaha Falls, an impressive sight when the spring runoff was heavy, and one which is said to have inspired Longfellow to write *The Song of Hiawatha.* Not that Longfellow ever came near the place: someone sent him a picture of it. So much for romance.

The house, at any rate, was a big two-and-a-half-story affair, narrow but deep, with a steeply pitched roof and rough, rustic brickwork outside, high ceilings and dark hardwood floors inside. Feinman had a kind of den or family room at the back of the house, and this is where he and Steve Dimand made base camp, monitoring several football games on the projection TV while Feinman made his periodic forays into the great outdoors. Sharon had established herself in the kitchen—while the master chef handled the poultry; everything else seemed to fall under Sharon's job description—where she put together the rest of the traditional menu to the accompaniment of something fruity on Minnesota Public Radio. I floated between the two rooms, spending most of my time getting in Sharon's way in the kitchen.

The plan was to sit down midafternoon, since Feinman had plans to hit the sack early in order to rise before the sun and meet some people to go hunting "up north." In the Twin Cities, everything else in the state is "up north"—regardless of where it may actually lie on the map. During a commercial break and a lull in the activity in the kitchen, Feinman invited me along. I politely declined.

Dimand jumped on it. "You see? I'm *not* the only man in Minnesota who thinks that getting up in the middle of the night so you can stand around in a freezing field or marsh or meadow waiting to kill or be killed by one of your companions *doesn't* sound like endless shits and giggles."

"Not this again," Sharon murmured under her breath. She was perched on the arm of the big leather chair I was submerged in, sipping a glass of zinfandel.

Feinman grinned, glanced at her, and let his gaze rest on me. "What do you say, Pat? Would you call that an accurate summation of your views?"

I had figured out the other evening at the club that this was part of some ritual between the two men, an endless mock-arguing of some difference between them. Unlike a true argument, though, these ersatz confrontations seemed to emphasize the cousins' closeness rather than point up or exacerbate their differences. Thus clued in to the ground rules, and estimating that the game would continue along preordained lines regardless of my input, I simply shrugged and took a sip of from my coffee mug, and said, "Safety orange isn't my color."

"Who's playing this afternoon?" Sharon said brightly.

The gambit didn't work; the conversation, if that's the word for it, stayed unchanged.

"Admit it, Josh," said Dimand. "There *are* some 'real men' who don't think they have to prove it by protecting the rest of us from ferocious deers and ducks. You *are* are 'real man,' aren't you, Pat?"

"Stop talking that way, Steve," said Sharon.

"I'm just not that big on hunting, that's all," I said.

"That's *all?*" Feinman was clearly enjoying this. He glanced at Dimand, his way of letting his cousin know he was about to bait him, albeit indirectly—through me. "Come on, Pat, you must have some kind of deep, heartfelt philosophical objection to it. I know Steve does. Do you think we're all a bunch of latent homosexuals who get off on shooting big guns? Little boys who never grew up? Or just bloodthirsty throwbacks to the Neanderthal era?"

"Joshua . . ." Sharon began.

"I imagine that of all the hunters in the world, there must be some of each of those types. Not all of them, of course; that defies statistical probability. I'm sure each one of them is a distinct and unique individual with a distinct and unique personality." I glanced up at Sharon, who was finding the exchange not the least bit entertaining, and mentally apologized for what I was about to do, which was prolong her agony. Then I looked back at Feinman and smiled equanimitously and said, "And I'm just as sure there's not a single sportsman in the whole bunch."

Feinman chuckled. "Oh, really."

"Oh, really. Look, you go out in camouflage, heavily armed, find a good hiding place, pull out your trusty, never-fail duck-, moose-, or wombat-call, give it a few toots, and wait for the victim to sail into view. Then you blast it to smithereens. Loads of fun I'm sure, but the sporty part eludes me."

Feinman was shaking his head sadly, like a teacher with a pupil who simply can't get the lesson. "Pat, Pat . . . like all the bleeding-hearts, you miss the point. I'll grant you there are some jokers who get their jollies from blasting the living daylights out of an animal, but for the rest of us the killing isn't the thing. It's being out in nature, it's using skills we don't usually use, it's being with some good friends, it's the stalking, it's the marksmanship . . ."

"It's being able to lash a bleeding corpse across the hood of your car," Dimand observed dryly.

"Well, at least this year we're getting it out of the way before we eat," Sharon said philosophically.

"Sorry, Josh," I said. "None of it holds water. There isn't a single thing you've mentioned that cannot be done without spilling blood. You want nature, go camping. Fellowship, take some friends along. Stalking, take a camera. Marksmanship, bring clay pigeons. The only thing you get from hunting that you absolutely can't get any other way is the killing. And that's fine. I'm not one of these people who gets all misty about your going out and knocking off Bambi while conveniently forgetting that my shoes and belt and supper are all courtesy of something that used to have big brown eyes. What I object to is calling it sport. The day a mallard can shoot back, it'll be a sport. Not until then."

"Hear, hear," said Dimand. The game was back on the tube and he turned his attention to it. This game, our game, was over as far as he was concerned.

Not so Feinman. His gaze remained on me even when the television set started displaying a string of meaningless statistics. His smile had never moved, although now it had taken on a hardness, like plaster when it's set. Quietly, he said, "So what is it you're saying here, Pat? That the only real sport is one man hunting another?"

"Maybe it is," I said. "But the same rules apply. When you hide in the bushes and come at someone from his blind side, that isn't sport."

"What is it, then?"

"I don't know . . . something else."

"Something we call 'survival,' maybe?" Feinman said. Then he turned back to the football game.

◇◇◇

Awhile later, during half-time, Feinman stepped out back to listen to the turkey. I went too, for a breath of fresh air. A breath's worth was about the maximum duration I cared to stay out for, given the temperature, but Feinman, with a glance through the French doors at his cousin said, "By the way, Pat, I want to thank you for helping Steve with his little 'situation.'"

I shrugged it off. "The man wanted to move some watches, I knew a guy who was willing to take a couple as a favor to me. He was probably just as glad the heist didn't come off."

"That's not what I mean. I know Steve got burned on the deal. I hear things. One of the things I hear is that you and him spent a lot of yesterday together. I look at Steve now, he's a happy guy. I put two and two together, I gotta figure you helped him get unburned, right?"

I said nothing.

"That deal smelled from the minute Steve told me about it,"
Feinman went on. "But I figured, you know, what the hell,
maybe Pat's right—maybe Steve needs to get his nose bloodied for once." He grinned. "Ironic, huh, that you're the one
who saved his butt this time?"

"What are you telling me, Josh, you would have let him
hang out there by himself?"

Feinman laughed. "Probably not. Tell me how good a
guesser I am. My guess is, I get to poking around, I'll find out
Steve's 'advance money' was my money all along. So Steve
gets burned, but it's my twelve grand that goes up in smoke.
So I would have had to save Steve's neck whether I wanted to
or not, just to save my own neck." He sighed. "There's no
winning. He gets in a jam, I yank him out. Only now he's got
two nursemaids watching him. You handle the situation
good?"

"You tell me, you're the one who hears things."

"What about this Warren jackoff? Did you take care of
him?"

"I don't think he'll consider your cousin any kind of a mark
in the future. But he isn't swimming under the Wabasha
Street bridge wearing a concrete bathing-cap, if that's what
you mean."

Feinman laughed. "What the hell does that mean?"

"It's what your cousin said would have happened if you had
got your mitts on Warren. Was he right?"

Feinman finished the drink in his hand and flung the ice
cubes out into the backyard, where they skittered across the
crusted snow. "I told you before, Pat: someone hurts my family, I hurt him."

"There's two kinds of hurt, Josh: the kind you get over and
the kind you don't."

"I suppose that's true."

"Which kind do you dole out?"

He was still looking out across the yard, where a row of tall
old evergreen trees guaranteed the yard's privacy. "I'm trying
to think what that is to you, Pat. Why should you be interested?"

I had been mulling that one over, off and on, for some time
now. Because, barring outstanding good fortune of a variety
that had not yet put in an appearance, I knew that sooner or

later I would have to quit flitting around the perimeter, playing it safe, and start zeroing in on the heart of the matter. There was good reason to believe Feinman was deeply involved in the drug trade. His cousin had told me as much. There was somewhat hazier reason to believe he was involved in murder. Either one could be my tool for prying him off me permanently. Mainly, it boiled down to which one came to hand first. At the moment it looked like the capital crimes, if any, were most promising. The conversation seemed to float that direction.

"Oh, I dunno," I said indifferently. "Maybe it's because your cousin indicated that you would have had his con-artist friend whacked, and that it wouldn't have been your maiden voyage. Maybe it's because David Nordquist was honestly terrified when he saw you last week, to the point of trying to bribe me—a complete stranger—to take you out. Maybe it's because of the load of soda we brought up from the bottom of that lake. Maybe it's because I'm sort of seeing your sister, and sort of doing the odd job for you, and sort of sitting around your house drinking your liquor and waiting for you to feed me Thanksgiving turkey, and sort of thinking that if I'm going to be that close to you I had better know what the hell you're involved in, just so's I know to duck when it's time to duck. Other than that, Josh, I can't think of a single reason why I should care one way or the other."

Feinman turned back toward me and nodded slowly, his lips pursed and his brow knit, taking it all in. He took it all in for so long that I had about begun to think he'd just blown me off. And then he said, "I never said I was a Boy Scout, right, Pat?"

I opened my mouth, but just then the door behind me opened and Sharon poked her head out. "There you are," she informed us. "Your timer's going to go off in about five minutes, Joshua, so I think we should open the wine. And unless you two like yours laced with cork, one of you guys had better do the honors."

I volunteered. I don't know what I had hoped to get out of Feinman—something closer to a confession, I suppose—but what I had been getting didn't come very close to it, and there seemed no point to standing out there in the arctic any longer. I moved to follow Sharon into the house, but Feinman stopped me. "Pat."

I turned back and looked at him.

"Remember what killed the cat, right?"

I followed Sharon into the kitchen. She handed me the corkscrew, and then she was in my arms. Her mouth was cool and tasted of zinfandel. After a bit I said, "If that's what I get for just volunteering, I can't wait to see what happens if I get the wine opened okay."

She waggled her eyebrows at me Groucho-style. "Haven't you ever hoid the expression 'Kiss the Cook'?"

"From where I stood, it was the cook doing most of the kissing."

"Only to start with—I was there too, you know. Anyhow, from where *I* stood it looked like you and my brother were plotting the overthrow of the Western world."

"Only selected portions of it. We were just armchair quarterbacking." The truth was, I couldn't have said what teams were playing if the sun, the moon, and six stars of my choice were riding on it. At least one of them was named after an animal, I think. The Cornhuskers weren't playing, which was the only thing I took much note of. In my home state, it's a foolhardy man who doesn't have at least a vague idea what Big Red is up to at any given moment.

A windup timer on the counter dinged, and Sharon disengaged herself from me to tend to something in the oven. I opened the fridge and freed the wine that was earmarked for the dinner table. Sharon said, "I'm glad you and Josh have hit it off so well. I don't think he has anybody to really *talk* to anymore . . . you know, eye-to-eye."

I got the foil peeled away from the top of the bottle and started the screw on its way. "He has you and Steve. I don't know many families that are as close as you three are." It was the truth.

She pulled out a couple of simmering casserole dishes and set them on the stovetop. "Yes, but that's different. It's what we were talking about before—like Josh is the father and we're the kids. They're roles we've all three played for so long, I don't suppose we could change now. We look up to Josh and Josh looks out for us." She came and stood by me. I had wormed the screw down into the cork; now I lowered the wings on either side of the corkscrew and the cork slid up smoothly and came away with a satisfying *pop!* "Then there are his business associates and his employees and so on,"

Sharon continued, "but I don't get the feeling that any of them are really his *friends,* you know? He seems to be able to let his hair down with you. I think it's good for him. I'm glad he has a friend. I'm glad that friend is you."

It was hard to meet her eyes. "Should I open a second bottle while I'm at it?"

"I suppose so—with four of us, the first bottle won't last long. Of course, every other book you read disagrees with the last one as far as whether you need to let wine 'breathe' and, if so, for how long." She opened the icebox and pulled out another bottle.

I said, "What do you mean, Joshua doesn't have anyone to talk to *anymore?"*

"I mean since Lisa and Amanda . . . since he lost them. Lisa and Josh had known each other since forever. Well, we all had: Lisa's family and our family lived on the same block. Lisa and Josh were always together, since the time we were in school. Everyone knew they would get married. They were just so *right* together. They were best friends. They shared everything. And when Lisa and Amanda died, Josh didn't have anyone to share with anymore, or anyone to share with him. I tried, but it's not the same. I'm the kid sister, and I always will be. That's why I'm glad you happened along. Of course, that's not the *only* reason. . . ."

Her lips were as soft as they had been a few minutes earlier, but all I felt was revulsion—at myself. I was a guest in her brother's home, preparing to share Thanksgiving dinner with him. At the same time I was romantically involved with—maybe even in love with—his sister. How could I turn around and destroy him?

The bigger question was, How could I destroy him without simultaneously destroying her?

36

The following afternoon I called my answering machine from a pay phone in the entrance to the Bakers Square restaurant in Highland. As the days had piled up on each other, Pat Costello's nonsense messages had gotten increasingly stranger and ever more surreal. The previous day's had been some inspired lunacy about wanting to sell me genuine India-rubber garden hoses, a spiel Pat delivered in a hilarious Eastern dialect: "Garding hoses I am wanting sell you of finest robber from Jubbulpore, very nize. . . ." I could hardly wait to see how he topped it today.

Apparently he couldn't figure out how: the answering machine's hollow robot-voice assured me there were no messages.

I checked my wristwatch against the clock on the wall over the front counter. Almost three. The arrangement was for Pat to leave his signal around noon or so, and me to retrieve it later in the afternoon. All the criteria were met, then—except for the signal part.

I dialed Decatur Street again, and the damn machine there delivered the same message: no message.

The message left–message erased arrangement was how we kept tabs on each other without the risk of direct contact. If Pat called and I hadn't wiped the previous day's messages, up to and including his at least, then he knew I was in a jam, or worse. If I called and Pat hadn't left today's message, then I knew he was in a jam. Or worse.

I made myself go back to my booth and stare out the window at the Ford plant across the street and drink decaffeinated coffee and wait. Bakers Square made the best key lime pie in the lower forty-eight, but they didn't make a lot of it in November, so I stuck with the ersatz coffee. In its own sweet time, the big hand on the wall clock crawled around to the twelve. I went back to the phone and called Decatur Street again and got the same results. During the past twelve minutes I had gone from concern to worry to panic. In that frame of mind, then, I broke security and dialed the drugstore.

No answer.

Now I was frantic. Nothing this side of divine intervention could convince Pat Costello to close the drugstore on the day after Thanksgiving. It's all his family can do to get him to close up on Thanksgiving day itself, not to mention Christmas day, Easter, and so on. Something was wrong.

Always look for the quick fix first: I tried again, with the same effect, then checked with the operator to make sure the line was okay. I have no idea how a telephone operator should be able to tell, but he assured me there was no fault in the line; it just wasn't being answered, that's all.

That's all.

I threw caution to the wind and dialed the Costello house. It rang four times, and with each ring my heart climbed higher up into my throat. Finally the line was picked up on the other end. A woman's voice—tentative and unfamiliar to me. Not Angela or any of the daughters. I asked for Pat.

"He's . . . um, he's not available right now. Could I take a message?"

"This is rather urgent. I wonder if you know where I can reach him?"

Except for a little cross-talk and some static, the line was silent.

"Look," I said impatiently. "I'm a friend of the family, I've known Pat since we were kids, and I would very much like to know what the hell's going on there. . . ."

"Nebraska?" A different voice on the wire, another woman, her voice weary and strained. "Is that you? Where are you?"

"Lucia?" The Costellos' oldest daughter. "Who was that other woman? What's going on there, honey? What's wrong?"

She took a deep breath. "That was my cousin Tina. . . . There's been an accident, Nebraska. Mom and Dad . . . last night. . . . I didn't know how to reach you. . . ."

Obviously the guy smelled something in the wind and went to ground, Dimand had said, *and we need to beat the bushes a little to flush him out.* "What kind of accident? Are they all right?"

"Car accident. They're both in the hospital. Mom can probably come home tomorrow, but Dad . . ." Lucia broke off raggedly. "I'm sorry," she said after a long while.

"Don't be silly. Tell me what happened." I realized that the fist I held the phone in had gone white. I switched to the other hand before I found myself owing the phone company for a crushed handset.

"They . . . drove Nana home after dinner last night. The accident happened on the way back. Witnesses said someone, another car, forced them off the road and into a stone wall. The other car . . . oh, God, the other car just kept going."

She broke down again. I held the line, and thought about Robert Olson in his hospital bed. Too many similarities for this to be an unrelated coincidence. True, Feinman's bullies hadn't pulled the Costellos from their car and beaten them into comas, but when they had done that to Robert, it was under the mistaken impression that my brains were the ones being scrambled. They were under no such misapprehension with Pat and Angela. Harming them hadn't even been the point of the exercise; they just wanted to get my attention.

They had it.

"I'm sorry," Lucia said again. She was twenty-two, in her last year in the pharmacy program at Creighton University. She had inherited dark features from both sides of her family, and was strikingly pretty in an exotic, almost offbeat way. Of course, in my mind she was forever a skinny, mouthy, slightly batty twelve-year-old. "Mom is pretty good. She has a couple of cracked ribs and a mild concussion. They want to keep an eye on her one more night, but it's just a precaution. Thank God she was wearing her seat belt. . . ."

"What about your dad?"

"Seat belt? What's a seat belt?" She laughed wetly. "He slammed into the steering wheel . . . he broke three ribs and his left leg, and he smashed his head against the windshield. They did surgery last night to relieve pressure on his brain. He . . . he hasn't woken up yet. . . ."

Christ. "All right, look, honey, everything's going to be okay.

You got that? I've known your old man thirty years or better, and he's just too damn stubborn to die, so let's forget that idea right now, okay? I'm not in town right now, but I will get there as soon as I possibly can. Tomorrow at the latest, all right? I'll talk to you then. In the meantime, if anything changes or there's anything you need, call my place and leave a message on the machine. I'll be checking it. Is there anything I can do in the meantime?" It was a stupid thing to say—I was over three hundred miles away, and the sum total of the Costellos' relatives was only slightly less than the number of scientific and technological breakthroughs the Soviets achieved first but never got around to mentioning—but you have to say it. It's the law.

I hung up and staggered back to my booth. The hinges at my knees needed oiling; my lips and fingers were numb and rubbery. I sat down and put my hands around the coffee mug. I assume it was hot, but my fingers neglected to forward the message to my brain. My brain was too busy, anyhow. It was replaying the little film clip of Steven Dimand sucking cocaine up his nose and saying, *I had some trouble with this asshole from there a month or so ago. . . . Josh sent some guys down there to teach him a lesson. . . . We need to beat the bushes a little to flush him out. . . .*

Overlapping the clip in a nifty special effect was another piece of film, this one depicting Josh Feinman in high dudgeon. *The only family I have in the whole world is my sister and my cousin,* he said over and over. *I'd sooner die than see them hurt. I'd sooner kill than let someone hurt them.*

There hadn't been much to say to that at the time; there wasn't much to say to that now. It was a sentiment I shared, in fact. My family consisted of a wife whose whereabouts were at the moment unknown to me, a scattering of distant relatives keeping their distance in distant places, and probably a handful of cousins and whatnot I didn't even know I had. So for all practical purposes, then, Pat and Angela and their eleven thousand kids were my family. I had known Pat longer than anyone else alive. Thirty years or so. In a transient society, that's quite a feat. He used to throw me out of his dad's drugstore back in the days when I had its comic-book rack confused with the public library. We had been through thick and thin, and whatever was in between.

I never had a brother. Pat Costello was the closest I ever came to that. By extension, his family had always been my family. Now someone had hurt them. I knew who. And I knew what had to be done now.

37

If you want to kill a snake, the place to start is not at the tail.

In a truly perfect world, I would get in the car now, drive over the Ford Parkway bridge into Minneapolis, park in front of Feinman's big house on Minnehaha Parkway, go up and ring the bell and, when Feinman opened the door, blow his fucking head off.

But in case you never noticed, the world is not perfect; right now the head of my particular snake was "up north" somewhere, hunting, and wasn't due back until Sunday.

I had options. I could sit around my one-room apartment and watch computer-colored versions of ancient holiday movies on my black-and-white portable TV all weekend. I could go pound Steven Dimand into pemmican. I could set fire to Feinman's house. But I was pretty sure I remembered how *It's a Wonderful Life* ends; and assaulting Dimand, though fun, would accomplish nothing; and arson, though likewise amusing, would accomplish even less.

I went back to the phone and looked in the Yellow Pages under "Airlines."

◇◇◇

Northwest—which owns the Twin Cities—had a direct flight leaving Minneapolis at 7:15 P.M. and arriving in Omaha at 8:17 P.M. Translated into the reality of modern commercial aviation, I was into the terminal at Eppley Airfield and heading for the Avis counter well before nine-thirty.

I had planned to head straight for Decatur Street—you know, give your audience what it wants, and all that. But I was unarmed, excluding boyish charm, and while I may at times be foolhardy, I try not to be *completely* foolhardy. For that reason I didn't waste much time thinking of landing on Koosje's doorstep either. Feinman's unsavories had done their homework to the extent of reading up on my friendship with Pat Costello; my relationship with Koosje was in the very next paragraph. I had to assume they'd be keeping an eye on her place, too.

I thought seriously about bothering Kim Banner; in fact, I was still thinking about it as I steered the rented Pontiac Sunbird out of the airport complex. If they knew about me and Banner, then they'd know she was a cop. That might give them pause. If not, Banner knew how to take care of herself. Also, I needed two pieces of equipment, both made of iron. One of them had four wheels; the other spit bullets, as the pulp-magazine writers used to say. Avis lacked the foresight to provide both kinds of hardware.

Having Banner in my corner could be very helpful, but it was too sticky. She would want me to take what little I had to the cops. If I refused, she would take it herself; she had sworn an oath. Conning her probably wouldn't work, and even if it did I wouldn't want to put her in a dicey position.

So in the end, I scrapped the idea. Banner would have too many questions, and would expect answers to them. I didn't have that many answers. My case against Feinman was mushy. Mushy, hell—it was practically nonexistent. It sure as heck wasn't a case. It was a shapeless mass of suspicions and speculations. What did I have? A briefcase full of coke, whereabouts currently unknown, that I could not prove was ever even in Feinman's possession. Dimand's account—probably exaggerated, and so far unsupported—of Feinman's drug dealings. Dimand's claim—similarly exaggerated, in all likelihood, and similarly unsupported—that Feinman had loaned lead swimwear to people who never came back with it. David Nordquist's terrified face, which led me to believe he had heard rumors about Feinman that caused him to fear for his very life.

Which all added up to not nearly enough to bargain with— my keeping silent in exchange for him keeping his distance. More than enough to get the cops interested, though, and that was to be avoided. An investigation could drag on interminably, and all the while my friends and I would still be at risk. Even if Feinman ultimately wound up behind bars, that was not a permanent solution to my problem. In fact, he would have double the reason to be gunning for me.

I needed to get mine first; then the law could have him.

Likewise, visiting the hospital was a lousy idea. Even though I had talked with Lucia twice more and knew there had been no change in Pat's condition, even though visiting hours were long ended, I was dying to stop by the hospital and see for myself. But, again, I had to assume that Feinman's unsavories would have the hospital covered—after all, they had put my friends there for the sole purpose of luring me out of hiding. The unsavories had the twin advantage of knowing what I looked like and, presumably, being armed. My clever disguise might help negate the former, but it didn't do much toward making me bulletproof.

I did have one small advantage, though. Since it was my one and only, I figured I had better use it.

They hadn't moved the Sky-Liner Inn during the past few weeks, nor had they condemned it. The Sky-Liner was a rambling, slightly down-at-heels compound of three one-story stucco buildings surrounded by a moat of asphalt. An old-fashioned pink neon sign at the driveway said SKY . . . LINER . . . SKY-LINER over and over, while a green neon airplane flew above the words in three stops, disappeared, and reappeared on the left end to repeat the trip. The three buildings were laid out parallel to one another, with the office on the end of the center building, nearest the entrance. I parked the Pontiac and went in.

The same clerk was on duty as last time, and she recalled me as soon as I showed my ID. I had no idea whether the paper was still valid—I assumed not—but I guessed that if I didn't know, she wouldn't either. If she did, she didn't let on. She was a large woman, tall and heavy with a round, beaming, apple-cheeked face—the sort of face that probably started the business about fat people being jolly. She was jolly, or at least friendly. One of those talkative types that cruel fate puts into solitary jobs.

The ID stuff out of the way, I said, "You remember when I was in here a few weeks ago, I asked about some guys staying in rooms thirty-seven and thirty-eight? I wonder if they're still around."

"Well, you know, it's funny." She leaned her meaty arms against the cheaply paneled counter. "One of those guys has been here all this time. Now that's real unusual, you know, because what with the airport and all, most of our people are here on business and they stay with us just a night or two. But this guy, he's been here almost a month now. Now, these five other men who were with him—and I know you only asked about the two that other time you were in here, but after that I sort of kept an eye on them, you know, and it was obvious that these six guys were together—anyhow, these five other men, they checked out back a couple weeks ago."

Six men. That made sense: three overlapping shifts, four men on Decatur Street, two men off. That's why the occupants of the Buick never showed up the last time I cased the Sky-Liner Inn: they weren't off duty yet. When I failed to show up after a week or two, Feinman recalled all but one man, to keep an eye on things. A cost-cutting measure. If they had set up taps on various telephones, one man would be sufficient to monitor the situation.

"But now those five other guys," the night clerk went on, "they showed up here again Thursday afternoon—Thanksgiving day, if you can believe it!—and checked in again. I wasn't here on account of I get Thanksgiving off, but I saw them when I came on tonight, and I recognized them. I'm pretty good with faces and names, you know, and that's important because we get a lot of repeat business here what with the airport and all."

"Thursday? Yesterday?"

She nodded. "I went and checked the cards. Yesterday afternoon they checked in."

Pat and Angela had been run off the road last night, Thursday night. Someone—Feinman or Dimand, although the final say must have been Feinman's—got tired of waiting and dispatched the bush-beaters, who went straight to work.

I said, "Are they in the same rooms as before?"

"Well, the one's still in thirty-eight, of course, on account of he never checked out, but we've been kind of full, what with the holiday and all, so the girl kind of had to split up the rest of them. . . ." She had brought a blue plastic recipe file from behind the counter and now was going through it. "Let's see . . . thirty-eight, right. Then forty and forty-one. And the others in the south building, four, five, seven, ten, and eleven."

"Others?"

"Oh, didn't I say?" A good Flatlander, she dropped the middle "d" out of "didn't": *dint.* "Yeah, those five fellows come back and brung two more with them." She smiled even more broadly than before, which I wouldn't have thought possible. "You know, word-of-mouth's the best advertising there is."

"Somebody told me that once," I said distractedly. Feinman had hired extra hands; obviously he believed that this latest move would bring me out of the woodwork. Obviously he was right. Eight men . . . figure four at Decatur Street, as before. One at the hospital? Two, maybe. One at Koosje's place? Or two. . . . But they'd have to sleep sometime—they guessed correctly that attacking the Costellos would bring me running, but they would have no way of knowing when. They'd have to set up shifts, as before, with at least a couple of guys scheduled for sack-time at any given moment.

I said, "Do you have any way of knowing whether any of them are in right now?"

"Not really," she admitted. "I can ring their rooms. . . ." She reached for the grimy beige phone on the counter.

"No, thanks," I said quickly. I leaned forward conspiratorially and lowered my voice a notch. "This is kind of a hush-hush thing, you understand. . . ."

"Yes, I see," she said solemnly. Her eyes were bright. "Will there be, you know, trouble?" She sounded hopeful.

"I hope not," I said fervently. "The best thing you can do is stay right here, and if you hear or see anything alarming—"

"Like shots or something, you mean?"

"Good example. You notice anything like that, get on the horn and call nine-eleven."

"Gotcha," she said, and I went back out into the night.

I climbed into my rental and drove slowly through the parking lot. The barracks-style buildings had units on either side, north and south, and likewise parking on either side. There was a fair number of cars—what with the holiday and all—but parking was conveniently set up so you could put your car right outside your room, perpendicular to the building. That meant license plates were easy to scan as I cruised past. So was the busted font that turned Buick into BLICK on the back end of a car that I recognized from Decatur Street.

It was parked in front of room thirty-nine. I consulted my notepad. Feinman's unsavories were using rooms thirty-eight, forty, and forty-one, which were in this, the northern-most building in the complex. The other rooms they had—four, five, seven, ten, and eleven—were in the southernmost building, with the building that contained the office set between them. That was good. What was better was that the three rooms in this building were around back, completely out of the view of anyone who might idly part a curtain in rooms four, five, seven, ten, or eleven.

The trunk of the Pontiac contained one of those ridiculous pint-sized spares that Detroit's whiz kids think make the trunks look bigger. At least the jack handle was full-sized, and good drop-forged steel. I took it with me for good luck, holding it along my right leg where it wouldn't be so noticeable.

I had to assume that at least two guys were off each shift; the Buick said they were here now, with at least one of them in one of these three rooms. If my stars were aligned properly, one of the unsavories would be in this building, the other—or others—clear the hell over on the other side of the compound in the south building.

It would be nice to be certain. I moved quietly past the rooms in question. The units must have all been mirror-images of each other; from the outside they went door, door, window, window, and so on. No light showed behind the curtains in the windows of thirty-eight, forty, or forty-one. No sound came through the windowless doors.

Ringing the rooms, as the night clerk had suggested, would have told me who was in and where they were. But it would have awakened them, and if I could catch them napping, so much the better. Worse, since the rooms were clustered together, with several of them being next-door to each other, and since motel walls are not noted for soundproofness, ringing these rooms in succession might tip off the personnel who were in.

Life's full of risks.

I tossed an imaginary coin and moved back to room thirty-eight.

"Hey, get up man," I said in a loud whisper while pounding the door with the heel of my hand. "Get up. The guy's here."

I quit pounding long enough to put my ear to the door. Dead silence from within.

But I heard the lock-chain rattling two doors down, room forty. Naturally. I bolted away from thirty-eight and was two steps from the door to forty when it opened to reveal a groggy man in blue boxer shorts and an undershirt that fought to cover his bulging gut.

"Hey, what the hell—"

"The guy's here," I repeated excitedly, "he just showed up. We got to get going—"

"Shit," the man in underwear said, turning back into the room. "Where's Tony?"

"Getting dressed," I said, and closed the gap between us. I took the curved end of the jack handle, the lug-wrench end, and jabbed him hard in the back, just above the roll of fat on his right hip. He bellowed and staggered into the room. I moved in after him and kicked the door shut behind me, hoping it had a self-locking lock on it—just in case the occupant of room forty-one was in and decided to come help his pal.

The room was dark, but enough light crept in between the curtains for me to see the man stumble toward a chair and table in front of the single window. There was something in the chair—his clothes, I guessed, and probably some accessories that the well-dressed thug was wearing this season. I held the jack handle like a baseball bat and cracked him hard across the lower back while he fumbled over the chair. He groaned loudly and stumbled away from the chair. I hit him hard again, on the side of his leg, and he went down, crashing into the bed.

I reached into the chair with my left hand and felt a hard leather shoulder holster on top of a pile of clothing.

I dropped the jack handle, grabbed the holster, and yanked out a flat, heavy Colt .45 semiautomatic. Not my favorite, but you know what they say about beggars being choosers. I found a light switch near the door; it worked a swag lamp over the table.

My dancing partner was half-slumped, half-crouched on the floor against his rumpled bed, one hand on his leg, the other on his back. He was groaning into the mattress.

I said, "Where are the others?"

He looked at me hatefully with watery eyes. "Fuck you."

I sighed, put the gun in my left hand, and reached down to

pick up the jack handle with my right hand. "Guns are noisy," I said. "Tire irons are nice and quiet. I wanted you in talking condition, but if you're not going to talk, then I don't care what condition you're in. You guys have put three of my friends in the hospital. The first of them had a busted skull. So if we mete out a little Old Testament-style justice. . . ." I stepped toward him, raising the jack handle high.

He brought up one hand to shield his head. "All right, all right. Christ. I think you broke my back. . . ."

"That's what I was trying to do. Where are your playmates?"

He made some comments about my ancestors, my family, my dog, and my sexual practices, but with a little more prodding got around to the information I was interested in. Of the eight badguys, four were watching my apartment, two were at the hospital, and two were standing down. The other off-duty bully, Tony, was in room four, in the other building.

"My stars are in alignment," I said.

"What the fuck does that mean?" my friend said irritably.

"It means I'm in a good mood, so I won't bash your brains in unless you give me a reason. On your feet, Egmont, we're off to the bathroom."

"What the fuck for?"

"To wash your mouth out with soap. On your feet."

He got up with some difficulty and no help from me. I motioned him toward the lavatory in the back of the little room, but as soon as we got to the door I popped him in the back of the head with the side of his gun. He went down.

He wasn't unconscious, but I didn't need him to be. I just needed him dazed long enough for me to grab a thin towel from the rack in the bathroom, tear it in half lengthwise, and get it wet in the toilet. Then I tied his wrists together behind his back and hauled him to his feet.

"Most accidents happen in the bathroom," I told him.

He cursed colorfully, so I knew he wasn't hurt too badly.

I got him lying down in the tub, facedown. Then I bent his left leg so the foot was pointing toward the ceiling, put his right ankle in the angle behind his left knee, and tied one end of the second strip of sopping towel around his left ankle and the other around the towel binding his wrists.

"That should keep you from walking in your sleep."

"You're a dead man, you fucker, you know that? Dead."

"You're right, Egmont, a gag would be helpful." I put one together with a washcloth and another strip of toweling, also soaked. Wet terrycloth is easier to knot tightly than dry, and as it dries the knots get hard and tough to worm open.

"I'll try to remember to have someone stop by for you later on," I said as I turned out the bathroom light. "But I expect to have a busy night, so I hope I don't forget."

I went out into the main room, heading for the door. As an afterthought, I stopped and took the Buick's keys from the table before I snapped out the light and let the door click locked behind me.

Then I went over to south building, room four, and repeated my stunning performance, reducing the odds against me by twenty-five percent.

38

There was no cellular phone in the Buick, nor did I come across walkie-talkie or other portable radio equipment in either motel room or the car. That was encouraging. If the unsavories were not in direct contact with each other, my job was easier.

I left the rented Pontiac where it was, stole the unsavories' little Buick, and drove into town. I had Egmont's Colt .45 in its holster under my left arm, plus a Smith & Wesson .38 revolver and a S&W .22 semiautomatic that I had swiped from Tony, the occupant of room number four. These guns were in my right- and left-hand overcoat pockets, respectively. I had no extra cartridges, but all three weapons were fully loaded. If that wasn't enough ammunition, then I was in so far over my head that I probably deserved whatever I got.

I stopped at a 7-Eleven on Farnam Street and picked up some additional supplies.

By eleven forty-five I was in good old Happy Hollow again, looking down on the old homestead. The lamp in my apartment was still burning. I would have to be sure to buy that brand of light bulb from now on.

They did not have the same rental cars as before, of course; they would have turned them in when Feinman reduced the payroll a couple of weeks ago, and got new cars when they came to town yesterday. But Tony had been more cooperative—which is to say more scared—than Egmont, and when I asked he readily blabbed that the Decatur Street contingent were using a burgundy Oldsmobile Cutlass Cierra and a red Honda Civic. He also told me that he and Egmont were supposed to relieve the team in the Olds at twelve forty-five. That made me an hour early. But the sight of the familiar Buick, I reckoned, should allay any suspicions they might otherwise have had.

From my somewhat elevated vantage point on Happy Hollow Boulevard, west of my apartment building, I could see both of the surveillance cars. The Olds was parked near where the Tempo had been on my last visit, on the little dead-end strip parallel to the Radial. The Civic was on the other side of the building, in the little parking lot off of the alley. As near as I could judge, the two cars did not have an unobstructed view of each other, between the apartment building and the tall trees in the yard in front of it.

I put the Buick into gear and backed up the hill until I was out of sight around the curve; then I straightened out the car and threaded through the neighborhood, finally emerging onto the Radial at Cuming Street, south of my place. I turned left onto the Radial, heading north toward Decatur. It was the direction from which the unsavories would expect the Buick to come.

I turned right at the light, onto Decatur, and then immediately left onto the dead-end, drawing up even with the Olds.

My car door was unlatched but unopened, and when I came up alongside the other car I took the Buick out of gear and waited.

After a little bit, the driver's door on the Olds opened and a stout, heavyset man lumbered out into the street. The passenger door started to open.

The stocky man covered the two or three feet between the cars. He had a half-puzzled, half-sleepy look on his saggy, jowly face. I opened my door a couple of inches.

"Hey, guys, what's going on?" the heavyset man began.

I opened the door all the way, fast and hard. It caught the heavyset man solidly, dead-center, and he went down in a way that suggested he wasn't getting up again soon. I flung myself out of the car and over him and across the distance to the Olds, slamming into it, my arms straight out across the windshield, the S&W .38 in my fist, pointed at the top button of the other man's overcoat.

"Don't," I said.

He didn't.

◇◇◇

I put them in the backseat of the Olds and tape-tied their wrists securely to the posts of the headrests on the front seat, using a roll of duct tape I bought at 7-Eleven. I also taped their

ankles together and gagged them with strips of tape. Then I
locked the car doors and tossed the keys off into a snowbank
somewhere in the night.

I had collected two more guns.

Successful as it had been, the routine wasn't going to work
on the guys in the Honda. It was parked between two other
cars, giving me virtually no maneuvering room. I fiddled with
the idea of simply calling the cops on them and letting the
unsavories explain what they were doing sitting there at midnight, but that didn't strike me as very satisfying. I liked the
idea of knowing they were out of commission more than I
liked the idea of wondering whether they had wormed their
way out from under the cops' questions.

I got back into the Buick and drove it up Decatur and down
Forty-fifth, parking it at the top of the alley that ran from
Forty-fifth to the Radial, passing by the south end of my building. I went down the alley on foot. Untended, overgrown
bushes and scrubby trees on either side of the alley kept me
safely hidden from the Honda's occupants until I was almost
down to the little parking lot. Then I crouched down and
ducked behind the dumpster.

There was room for about six cars back here; seven occupied the space. Counting from my end, the east end, the
Honda was the fifth car down.

Still crouched, I moved from the dumpster to the side of the
nearest car, Jim Marineaux's Celica. I paused, waiting for
something to happen, something that would indicate I had
given myself away. Nothing did.

I duck-walked around to the rear of the Celica, then to the
Escort next to it. The going was a little tough, not only because of my uncomfortable stance but also because the snow
removal left a lot to be desired and the packed-down snow
was treacherous. Eventually, though, I came up behind the
Civic. Someday I will write a learned paper on the evolution
of automobile models. When the Civic first came on the scene,
it was a ridiculous little sardine-can hatchback; now it was a
small and dignified sedan. And as it got bigger, the Thunder-
bird—to name one—kept getting smaller. Where would it
end?

I got down on the icy ground, on my back, and wriggled
feetfirst under the Honda.

Besides duct tape, I had bought a so-called hunting knife. It had a five-inch blade, pointed, with a serrated inch or so near the tip. I didn't know what you were expected to hunt with it, but it was sufficient for my immediate purpose, which was to deflate the right rear tire.

That side of the car dropped significantly, but there was still enough room for me nearer the left side. I waited, shivering, but not for long. The passenger door opened and a pair of feet attached to some ankles got out and walked around the back of the car, stopping near the ex-tire.

"Son of a bitch," a voice from above said.

The feet moved up toward the driver's door. "Goddamn tire's flat," the voice said. "Lemme have the trunk key."

The feet moved around to the back of the car. I heard the scrape of the key in the trunk lock, then banging and rummaging and swearing as the feet's owner struggled with the spare and the jack.

The spare came into view, plopped down onto the pavement, leaning against the back bumper.

When I judged by sounds and elapsed time that the feet's owner would be straightening up, encumbered by the jack assembly, I reached up and grabbed both his ankles and yanked them toward me. The ice underfoot did most of the work. He managed a gasp of surprise, then he went down like a Third World government.

I scooted out from under the car, staying below the level of rear- and side-view mirrors, and pounced on the guy. He was a husky man, red-haired, lantern-jawed. We recognized each other in the same instant. He was Terry Thoreson, Feinman's "security" man.

"Kilpatrick—" Thoreson said hoarsely.

I swore under my breath, and made sure Thoreson didn't get up again right away. Then I duck-walked around to the passenger side of the car.

The driver wasted only a few seconds before he got out of the car. "Hey, Terry, where'd you go?" he said jovially.

As he moved toward the rear of the car, I circled around to the front, around the front, and up behind him. I had the .38 out again, and when I was about a foot away from him, as he crouched over his friend, I said, "Hold it."

He froze.

"Very slowly now, on account of I'm afraid this thing might go boom. Straighten up, your hands where I can see them, and turn around. Slowly . . . slowly. . . ."

He did as instructed. He was a baby-faced man with a mop of incongruously gray hair and a straggly, Charles Bronson–type mustache.

I was pulling the roll of tape out of my left-hand coat pocket. "Take this and wrap the end around your right wrist five or six times, nice and tight—I'll be watching closely. Then I'll have you turn around and we'll take care of your left wrist. While you work, you can tell me where your other playmates are at."

I tossed him the tape.

"Two of them are back at this dive we're staying at," Mustache said, picking at the end of the tape. "Then there's two over on the other side of the building." I already knew that, but I didn't tell him so. I was only interested in checking out what Tony had told me. "Then there's two at whatever hospital they took this guy's friend to." He peeled a length of tape away from the roll, paused, and looked at me. "You're the guy, ain't you?"

"I'm the guy."

He half-nodded, and started to wrap the tape around his wrist.

Started, but didn't finish. Suddenly his arm shot out and the roll was flying at my head like a Frisbee.

I ducked, skidding on the ice. He was reaching toward his hip, groping for a gun.

I went down on one knee—it was the fastest way to steady myself—and brought up my arms, cradling my shooting hand in my left hand.

"Forget about it!" I yelled.

But he yanked his gun out of his hip holster and was bringing it into position.

On TV it happens in slow motion, but in real life it's exactly the opposite—too damn fast.

He brought the gun around and I squeezed the trigger of the S&W in my fist. I had never fired it. Every gun is different, and until you've fired one you don't know what it will do or even *if* it will do.

This one put a hole in the middle of the man's chest.

He sort of caved in on himself while simultaneously flying backward, away from me, tripping over Thoreson's unconscious form and ending up in a heap on the cold ground. The sound of the shot echoed through the sleeping neighborhood. A dog started barking somewhere, and two or three other dogs thought that sounded like a good idea.

I got to my feet and, my gun still extended, went over to the heap. There was enough light from the building and the street to tell at a glance that he was extremely dead.

"You stupid son of a bitch!" I yelled, and kicked his lifeless right leg.

39

I had good reason to be mad at the corpse in the parking lot. Its late tenant's macho stupidity had forced me to kill him, and within twenty minutes I was up to my uvula in cops—something neither I nor my uvula had wanted.

But there it was.

And there I was, stuck, for hours on end. Two patrol cars had responded to the original call—for which I supposed I had one of my civic-minded neighbors to thank—and I filled them in on what had gone down. They called for a sergeant, who in turn called in a lieutenant from Homicide. I had to fill the sergeant in, of course, while we waited for the lieutenant, and then I had to fill him in when he arrived.

Then we all went down to the station so we could go through it again.

On the plus side, the sergeant who had responded to the patrol officers' call was an acquaintance of mine. He was distinctly cool toward me, which I took to mean that life had gone on in my absence and my PI permit was now a thing for the history books. But at my urging he did call in and have a couple of officers sent over to Bergan-Mercy Hospital, where they bagged the last two of Josh Feinman's unsavories. Cops have no use for a defrocked PI, but none of them is willing to let citizens suffer on account of that.

Me, I was no citizen. As far as cops are concerned, a disgraced private investigator is considerably less desirable than a bathtub full of pond scum, and worthy of almost the same regard. They were disinclined to cut me any slack. They were dismayed by my insistence on sticking to one and only one story. They were vexed by my refusal to trip over it no matter how many times and from how many different directions they made me run through it again. They were peeved and generally put out by their inability to convince me to slip the noose around my neck, just for size. . . .

"Let's go through it one more time, Nebraska. Just to make sure we have it straight." Lieutenant Des Vickery was a light-skinned black man, early fifties, wiry except for a potbelly that strained against the lower buttons on his shirt. I didn't know him, and I had the feeling that getting to know me better was not high on his list. Thad Novak was the cop I knew slightly, the sergeant. We had always gotten along well enough, but that was in the past. When I had had the bad sense to get my license revoked, I had offended them in a way that could never be made right again. That's how it is with cops and private cops. There's a bond, not as strong as the one between cops, but a bond nevertheless. And like the bond between cops, once it's broken, it's broken. It can't be fixed. You may have all the greatest reasons in the world, and your former friends may understand that and even agree with you in principle, but it doesn't matter. You're out.

So there was no point my being ingratiating, or angry, or insulting, or smartass. No point telling Vickery that I had gone through the story "one more time" half a dozen times already, so if he hadn't got it straight by now he never would. No point clamming up or demanding they either charge me or kick me, or doing much of anything except go into robot mode and lay it all out "one more time."

I said, "About a month ago, a friend of mine was attacked, badly beaten, and put into the hospital. Robert Olson, two o's. It occurred to me at the time that the beating might have been intended for me. We're roughly the same build and coloring, we live in the same building, and he was driving my car when he was assaulted."

"What was he driving your car for?" It was Novak's question, every time.

"His was in the shop. He was working a night shift, so it didn't inconvenience me any."

"Go on," said Vickery. He sounded as bored, as robotlike, as tired as I must have.

"When I got back to my place later that morning, back from

the hospital, it looked like someone had started to tamper with the lock on my door. There was no indication they had gotten in, but it made me suspicious. That night—or, rather, early the next morning, about two o'clock—as I was returning home from a date, I noticed some men in a Ford Tempo parked on Decatur Street near my building, where they'd be in a perfect position to monitor anyone's comings and goings."

"How many men?"

"I misspoke. I shouldn't have said 'men,' because I don't know for a fact if there was more than one or, if so, whether they all were males. All I know for a fact is that the car was there and someone was in it. I saw the flare of a cigarette lighter inside the car."

"Didn't you investigate?" He made the last word a sneer.

"I tried to, unobtrusively. I drove up Decatur, past the Tempo, but its windows were too darkly tinted to let me see anything. Then I drove down the alley on the other side of the building. There was a Buick parked back there, the same one I borrowed tonight."

"Borrowed," Novak coughed sarcastically.

I ignored it. "There's a floodlight on that side of the building, as you probably noticed when you were out there tonight, and by that light I could see there were two people in the Buick. I took them to be men."

"And what did you do then?" Vickery asked.

"I got the hell out of there. I had an emergency stash of money elsewhere, just in case something like this ever came up and I couldn't get home. I went for the stash, then I checked into a hotel. The next day I got in touch with my friend, Pat Costello. I told him what was happening—what little I knew of it—and that until I knew who had sent these guys and why, I was going to disappear. We set up a kind of 'lifeline,' using the answering machine at my place, to let each other know we were okay. That's how I found out today—yesterday—that Pat wasn't okay. That's when I decided to come back, shake up the pot, and see what happened."

"Good job of shaking," Novak said dryly.

"And where have you been all this time? What have you been doing?"

This was where the story stopped being the whole truth and nothing but, and became sort of a distant cousin to it. I didn't want Joshua Feinman's name to come into this. What I knew about him was far from sufficient to make a case, but more than enough to get the law interested in trying to make a case. I didn't have any objection to that, except for the fact that it could take forever and a weekend, during which time my Feinman problem would not go away. If anything, in fact, it would be worse—because now, thanks to the jerk who had forced me to boot him off the mortal coil, my head was up out of the hole. As soon as Terry Thoreson was out of the arms of the law and back in touch with Josh Feinman, Pat Kilpatrick was out of a job. That didn't give me much time to figure out what to do about it.

"I spent part of the time here, in Omaha, nosing around, seeing if anyone knew anything, had heard anything. . . ."

"Who's 'anyone'?"

"People I know. People I've met knocking around over the years."

"They got names?"

"Probably. But none's coming to mind."

"Uh-huh." Vickery sounded infinitely tired. He looked into the bottom of a big coffee mug, decided the contents didn't appear too deadly, and drank. No one had offered me a cup.

"You said you spent part of the time here. What about the rest of it?"

"Minneapolis."

"Why there?"

"The last case I had done had a Minneapolis angle to it. When I came up dry on this end, I figured the thing to do was to start with the last job I had done and work backward from there, see if I had torqued off someone I should have left untorqued."

"What," said Novak, "a swell guy like you?"

"And that case was about . . ." Vickery prompted.

"About a month ago."

He looked up from his coffee and grinned humorlessly. "This is thin ice you're on, Nebraska. You seem to think you've got some sort of client-privilege thing going for you, when what you've got is squat. The courts have never recognized PIs as having the same rights as doctors and lawyers, and you aren't even a PI anymore. My advice to you is to start talking."

"I've been doing nothing but talking for four hours now," I said calmly. "The case in question happened before my license was revoked, and since I was employed by a lawyer, his 'client-privilege thing' extends to me."

"Yeah, yeah." Vickery waved it off. "So tell us about Minneapolis."

"Nothing to tell. I went, I knocked around, I came up empty, I came back, and you know the rest."

"Empty, huh?" said Novak. "It always take you that long to come up empty?"

"Sometimes," I said. "Plus, you have to remember I was trying to be discreet. That slows you down. Take my word for it."

Novak's face colored but he said nothing.

Vickery stared into his coffee without much interest. He was not thrilled with my account. It put me in hot water, what with my leaving trussed-up unsavories, let alone the dead one, all over the landscape, but it wasn't enough to bring the water to the nice rolling boil he would have liked. In the end, he had nothing worthwhile to hang on me. We both knew that the badguys were badguys, and as such weren't going to press charges against me. We both knew I had shot in self-defense. We both knew that the noises Vickery had made about my carrying concealed weapons without a valid permit, my swiping the Buick from the motel, and so on, were just that—noise. By the time the cops were on the scene, the various guns I had collected were no longer concealed on my person but neatly arranged on the hood of the Honda; there was no one to say they had ever been concealed in the first place, let alone on me. Likewise, there was no one to say that the Buick had come into the picture courtesy of me—which is to say that the guys who could have said weren't exactly rushing forward to do so.

In any event they were the sort of lame, pointless, asinine charges that any self-respecting police officer is embarrassed to be associated with.

Finally, then, Vickery put down his mug, looked at Novak,

and said, "Get a machine in here, will you?" Then he looked at me.

"We'll go through it just once more," he said. "For the record this time."

Steven Dimand did not strike me as an early-riser, especially not a Sunday-morning early-riser. He did not exceed my expectations. At 8:14 I jabbed my thumb against the round button next to Dimand's name in the foyer of his building; almost two minutes later his groggy voice *Yeah*ed into the intercom mike.

"Pat Kilpatrick, Steve. We have to talk."

"Jeez," he sighed. "Come on up, then." The lock on the inner door brattled.

Dimand looked like he had been pulled through a knothole. His sparse hair couldn't decide which direction to go, so it tried them all. His face was drawn and gray, his eyes were bloodshot and runny, and his movements were slow and sluggish. He wore a long flannel robe with wide powder-blue and royal-blue stripes, and maybe or maybe not anything underneath. He let me in and closed the door after me and shuffled toward the kitchen. I glanced toward the glass doors at the far end of the living room, the scene of our row nearly a month ago. The bloodstained chair had been removed; otherwise everything else looked the same. I followed Dimand into the L-shaped kitchen.

"Coffeen a minnit," he mumbled. A white Braun coffeemaker gurgled softly on the counter.

A teenage boy, thin and pale with long, straight hair down into his eyes, wandered sleepily into the room. His robe was identical to Dimand's. "What's going on, Steve?" he asked foggily. To me he said hi and smiled shyly.

"Hi," I said.

"Just a little business, Jamie," Dimand said, fiddling with the coffee. "This is a friend of mine. Pat." He looked at the boy. "Why don't you go back to bed? It's still early."

"Let me have a cup of coffee," Jamie said. He took it and left the room, tossing a "Nice to meet you" over his shoulder as he went back down the hall.

"Same here," I said. When I heard a door close I said, "Nice kid."

Dimand nodded and handed me a coffee cup. "I've only known him a couple of weeks." He poured a cup for himself. "Come on, let's get comfortable."

I followed him diagonally across the hall to a fair-sized room crammed full of wide-screen stereo TV, hi-fi equipment, a Nintendo deck, a couple of VCRs, and some other electronic gewgaws. The "media room," as the magazines have it. There also was a low, black-leather-and-chrome sofa and a matching lounge chair that looked like it would have been more at home in a dentist's office. Dimand shuffled over to the wall unit that housed most of the video stuff as well as several shelves of black videotape boxes. He scanned the boxes' spines, then selected one. "Little pick-me-up?" he said with a glance at me.

I wasn't sure what he meant, so I hoisted my coffee an inch and said, "This will do me."

He shrugged, set down his cup, and popped open the plastic box. Inside was a plastic bag stuffed with small pills. He fished out a handful and downed them like they were Red Hots, without a chaser. Then he replaced the videotape box and picked up his cup, turning to face me with a grin that he thought was sly but, given his condition and appearance, merely looked sick. "Have a seat, Pat." He gestured toward the sofa and chair. "What's on your mind?"

I drank. The coffee was good, hot and strong and smooth. "I saw Eric Sperry yesterday."

He froze, the edge of his cup a hairsbreadth from his lip. He thawed quickly, though, and completed the move, sipping deeply from the steaming cup. He took his time. When he was ready, he repeated the name ruminatively. "Eric Sperry. . . ."

"Yeah, you remember." I set my cup on a black-surfaced end table near the sofa and removed my do-nothing glasses, folding them into the breast pocket of my sport coat. "About a month ago? He was staying with you, I came and got him and took him home to his parents in Omaha."

He was looking at me hard now, and when I mentioned the

Big O his red eyes narrowed and and muscles below his cheekbones twitched involuntarily. "Son of a bitch," he breathed.

It hit him in two stages. First the realization of who I was. Then the realization of what that meant. He staggered to the sofa and dropped into it, sloshing coffee on his robe and his bare foot. If it was hot, he didn't let on. "Oh Christ," he mumbled thickly. "Oh Christ, Oh Christ . . ."

I had expected a rematch, a repeat of our first meeting. That's why I had set down my coffee, to be ready for the assault. Clearly, though, there was to be none. Dimand merely sat, bleary-eyed and rumpled, shaking his head in disbelief and muttering; there was no fight in him. Probably the product of some heavy-duty Saturday-nighting followed by self-prescribed medication to come down off it far enough to get some unrestful sleep.

In a way, I was disappointed. It would be easier to do what I had to do to him if he tried to split open my head first.

I retrieved my coffee and drank some, giving Dimand time to play things through in his head. Eventually he remembered I was there, looked up at me with glassy eyes and a slack jaw and said, "I don't get it. I don't understand. What are you doing here, what do you want, why are you bothering me. . . ."

That was a laugh, me bothering him. Which one of us hadn't slept in his own bed for a month?

"I had a nice long talk with Eric," I said. "He's doing pretty well. Things aren't a hundred percent yet between him and his parents, but they're talking, at least, and seeing a family counselor and—"

"What is it you want?" Dimand yelped, spilling some more coffee. His voice was high and thready; his words collided with each other in their haste to get out of his mouth. "You want me to tell Josh to lay off you? Okay, all right, you got it. Just leave me alone."

"Thanks for the gesture, Steve, but it's not quite enough. Three friends of mine have wound up in hospital beds because you picked a fight you couldn't finish and were too petty to leave alone. Yeah, you're going to tell Josh to lay off me . . ." I moved to the wall unit, and took down a small metal case from a high shelf.

". . . But you're going to tell him *my* way."

I popped the case and lifted out the Sony Handycam eight-millimeter videocamera.

"And what do you say we remember the day in pictures?"

41

Feinman got in slightly before six P.M. that evening. Someone dropped him off in front of the house and he came tramping in, hauling a duffel and a couple of canvas gun bags, via the side door into his kitchen. I was waiting for him behind a small desk in the den at the back of his house. After a certain amount of noisemaking elsewhere, Feinman came into the den. He switched on a table lamp near the door and moved straight to the bookcase on the wall opposite me. He had a small collection of bottles and glasses there. He poured himself a short neat Scotch, then turned toward the television set and caught sight of me.

If he was surprised, he didn't show it. Maybe he knew what I had noticed—without really meaning to notice—on Thursday, namely that the patio doors would offer little resistance to someone who really wanted to get into the house, and the semisecluded backyard would only help. In any event, Feinman merely stopped, frowned a little, and said, "Patrick." He sipped his drink.

I turned on a green-glass-shaded lamp on the desk. Feinman's eyes fell toward the .38 on the desktop near my right hand.

"How was the hunting?" I said.

He shrugged. "Sometimes you come home empty-handed, right? But like I said the other day, the killing isn't the main thing anyhow." He took another sip and nodded toward my right hand. "What's with the hardware, Pat? You sticking me up?"

"On the contrary, Josh; I'm making you a gift. There, on the TV set." I cocked my head that direction.

He went over and picked up the videotape, slid it out of its cardboard sleeve, looked at it, looked at me. "Gee, and I didn't get anything for you."

"We'll have to see if we can't come up with a suitable return gift," I said. "Go ahead, Josh—play the tape."

Feinman shrugged again, fired up the big television set, and shoved the videotape into the VCR's gaping mouth. After a moment Harry Reasoner's face was replaced by Steven Dimand's.

Feinman looked at me. I looked at him. "Make yourself comfortable, Josh," I said amiably.

◇◇◇

The camera did not do much of a job of smoothing out Dimand's rough edges; he still looked like yesterday's breakfast warmed over, and his voice was a rough, slightly slurred monotone. But what he had to say came across clearly enough.

The first thing you heard was my voice. It had that hollow, foggy sound of a voice that isn't on-mike.

"Tell me about Brian Fahy," I said.

Dimand's eyes flickered up toward the camera, toward me, for an instant. In that same instant Josh Feinman inhaled sharply and reached for the Benson & Hedges pack in the pocket of his flannel shirt.

On the TV screen, Dimand cleared his throat and said, "What do you want to know?" Despite mumbling, he came through fine on the camcorder's built-in condenser microphone. I had taken full advantage of Dimand's electronic toys, lashing the camcorder to a standard VHS machine and simultaneously making two copies of Dimand's statement, one on an eight-millimeter cassette about the size of an audiocassette, the other on the ordinary half-inch tape now in Feinman's deck.

My disembodied voice again: "I want to know what really happened to him."

Dimand sniffed loudly and cleared his throat again. "Shit. He . . . Josh killed him."

"Your cousin, Joshua Feinman, killed his brother-in-law, Brian Fahy?"

"That's what I said," Dimand said irritably.

My eyes were on Feinman, but his were glued to the set.

"Why?" my voice said on the TV.

" 'Cause he didn't like him." Dimand giggled semihysterically. It buzzed on the TV speakers.

"Jesus Christ," Feinman grumbled.

"Feel free to fast-scan through any of this that you already know," I said. He barely glanced at me.

On the set, Dimand said, "Fahy was a creep—a real bastard. He treated Sharon like dirt." A little life crept into Dimand's voice. "She couldn't see it. Or wouldn't. I suppose she was in love with him, though God knows why. He ran around on her, drank or gambled away every dime he ever saw, and disappeared for days at a time without a word, leaving Sharon to worry herself sick. A real prince."

Feinman's fingers were white around his Scotch glass.

"They used to fight a lot, too," Dimand went on. "Sharon and Fahy. And one day things got out of hand and he hit her. Hard. I saw her the next day and that side of her face was swollen up . . . it looked like an eggplant. . . . When Josh found out, he wanted to skin Fahy alive. Sharon begged Josh to leave Fahy alone—she said it was all her fault, Fahy didn't mean to hit her, all that garbage. That only made Josh more livid, but Josh is kind of funny—the angrier he gets, the calmer he seems. I guess Sharon must have thought she had him all cooled down, but the minute he left Sharon's place he called me and said we were going out."

Feinman got up and came over to the desk, where he crushed out his cigarette in a big metal ashtray. His eyes were locked on my face, and a small muscle under his left cheek quivered. "He sounds like a fucking zombie," Feinman growled. "What did you do to him?"

"Your cousin's good at messing himself up all by his lonesome. He's got a pharmacy that would be the envy of Mr. Rexall himself."

Feinman glared at me, but he didn't argue. In all likelihood he knew the truth about his cousin—he probably knew several truths about his cousin—even if he liked to pretend otherwise.

Dimand's videotaped image was saying, "We bounced around for two or three hours until we caught up with Fahy. He was coming out of this dive he hung out at over in St. Paul. He was pretty drunk. We followed him a few blocks, to a lot where he had parked his car. Then we grabbed him and pounded the shit out him him." Dimand grinned raggedly at the memory. "He didn't even try to fight, he just laid there like a slug with his arms up around his head." He giggled nervously. "Joshua told him the next time he laid a hand on Sharon, he'd kill him."

"Then what?" my voice asked.

"Then nothing," Dimand said. "We left him there and went home. Only Fahy. . . ." He shook his head. "The man was so stupid. Josh set him up with a job and everything, all he had to do was keep his mouth shut and his nose clean, but he couldn't even manage that much. Stupid. The next day he called Josh and said he would clear out, disappear and never see Sharon again, in return for twenty thousand dollars, cash."

Feinman stood near the desk, a second cigarette between his lips, his eyes on the television, taking it all in. I had picked up the gun and was holding it in my right hand, in my lap.

"What did Josh say?"

"He told Fahy he would call him as soon as he got the cash together. Then he called me. He was incensed—insulted. It wasn't so much the idea of it. I think Josh would have suggested something like that himself if he had thought Fahy would go for it. But only twenty thousand . . . it was like Fahy was saying that's all he thought Sharon was worth, a crummy twenty thousand. He would have been better off to ask for fifty, a hundred thousand. But like I said, he was stupid."

"Fucking mick bastard," Feinman said in agreement.

I had no quarrel with that.

"Anyhow," Dimand continued, "I asked Josh what he was going to do. He said he was going to pull the money together, and that he wanted me standing by. He said he didn't want Fahy to get the idea that he could come around again anytime he needed money. This was going to be 'the last dance,' he called it. That night he called me again and said we were set up for seven-thirty the next morning."

"January fifteenth?" I prompted.

"Yeah, I don't know—that sounds right. It was damn cold, anyhow, and the sun wasn't even up yet. Joshua picked me up in a drafty old Blazer he had borrowed somewhere. We drove downtown. Josh's company ParkCo was building a parking ramp down by Orchestra Hall. It was almost finished, but not open yet. The lights weren't hooked up or anything, and it was like pitch black on the lower level, where we met Fahy. He was late."

Feinman went back over to the bookcase on the other end of the room and refilled his glass.

"I stayed in the car. Josh got out, Fahy got out. Josh handed him a briefcase and Fahy opened it. It must have had money in it, 'cause he closed it again and started back toward his car. Then Joshua socked him square in the back of the head." Dimand put a hand to the back of his own skull; I don't know if he even realized it. "Fahy dropped like a rock. Josh stooped over him a minute, then came back and opened the back of the Blazer.

" 'Give me a hand,' he told me.

"Fahy was still alive, still breathing, but he didn't look so hot. I asked Josh what he was going to do, but he just handed me a flashlight and told me to hold it steady."

Dimand took a deep breath and let it out. The exhalation quivered on the tape's soundtrack. "I need a drink," he said.

"At nine o'clock in the morning?" my voice-over said. *"Sunday* morning, no less?"

"You fucker."

"Great," I said, "now we have to bleep that out before we can go on the air."

Dimand gave the camera a dirty look, then raked a hand through his uncombed hair, what there was of it, sniffed, and went on:

"Hell. . . . Well, anyhow, I held the flashlight. Josh got a fast-food sack—Burger King, McDonald's, whatever it was—out of the car. He took a pair of handcuffs out of the bag and put them on Fahy. Then he took out a plastic bag, one of those heavy, filmy kind, and put it over Fahy's head. Then he took a roll of duct tape and wrapped the tape around Fahy's neck, you know, sealing the bag."

Dimand was silent for a long time. The only noise on the tape was the almost subliminal hissing sound of an open microphone. He didn't look up into the camera.

Finally he said, "Josh put the stuff in the hamburger sack and took it back to the Blazer.

"There was a big cardboard box in the back of the car; a washer or a dryer or something had come in it, but it was empty now. Joshua told me to help him, and we got it out of the car and put Fahy in it. Josh had one of those guns, you know, that you use to put metal strapping around a carton, and we used that to seal up the box. Then we got the box back into the Blazer."

I had the remote-control with me at the desk; now I hit the pause button and Dimand's spiritless face froze on the screen.

"Should we play the rest of the tape, Josh, or do you have the gist of it?"

He said nothing, but only sat there smoking, staring at his cousin's image on the television screen.

I said, "I assume you know how it ends. You drove Fahy's car to a public lot and parked it. It was winter, so naturally you had gloves on. Dimand followed. Then you took over the wheel of the Blazer and headed out of town, west, on Highway 212. Then 169 down through Shakopee. South and west, down state highways and county highways, and finally unpaved country roads. After a couple of hours, you came to an abandoned farmstead—'out in the middle of nowhere,' Dimand said, but I suspect he thinks anyplace is nowhere if it isn't in sight of a skyscraper.

"Obviously you had done some checking, found out about this place. You knew right where the old cistern was, around behind the house, where you would be invisible to anyone who happened by on the road out front. You and your cousin got Fahy out of the car, out of the carton, out of the handcuffs and plastic bag. He was dead by now, of course. You dumped him into the cistern and replaced the ancient iron lid. Then you drove back to the Twin Cities, disposing of the items in your fast-food bag one by one, at several different gas stations and convenience stores along the way. The last thing you did was stop by your appliance dealership and see to it that the carton went into the incinerator. Hope I didn't spoil the ending for you."

Feinman remained as motionless as his cousin's picture on the tube.

"You're very thorough, Josh, I have to give you that. No doubt you withdrew the cash from your friendly neighborhood bank, so there would be a trail in case anyone ever came looking for Fahy. 'Look, I withdrew the money on January fourteenth, gave it to the man, and that's the last I saw of him.' "

He looked at me expressionlessly.

"Then you took care of the remains, told your sister you'd handle the missing-person report, didn't, and convinced her that she was better off without Fahy. Which I can't argue with. Unfortunately, you told your warehouse manager, Glass, that Fahy wasn't going to be in anymore first thing that morning—when you went to get the big carton, I suppose. If Fahy had skipped without warning, how did you know he was going to vanish an hour or so before he even left his place? There were other . . . incongruities, too, between your version and Sharon's. Nothing I could hang my hat on, but plenty to make me curious."

"What if I told you what happened is, Fahy said he wanted twenty grand to go away and leave my sister alone, I gave it to him, he went away, and that's the last we've seen of him?"

"Then I would say, Why would your cousin lie about it?"

Feinman barked a laugh and moved back to the bottles in the bookcase. "Are you kidding? Anyone could see he was loaded to the eyeballs. What'd you do, Pat, dope him up to where he'd parrot back anything you told him?"

"You saw him as I found him when I turned up on his doorstep. And his statement is his own. You can hear my voice clearly enough on the tape when I spoke—I wasn't feeding him his lines." All I had done was point out the morals and drug charges he was looking at if he didn't cooperate with me; all I had done was tell him that Eric Sperry was prepared to tell his story if need be; all I had done was remind him that Eric was underage, and so was Jamie, the boy in the other room. . . .

The VCR's freeze-frame time limit was up. The machine kicked itself out of the playback mode and an after-shave commercial flickered up onto the screen. Feinman walked over to it, snapped off the TV, and ejected the videotape.

"You can keep that," I said. "It's a dub."

Feinman faced me, a sneer on his face. "Ah, so that's your game, right, Pat? Blackmail?"

"As a matter of fact . . . yes."

He sighed. "How much?"

"Put away your wallet, Josh—I'm actually going to save you money. The deal is, my original copy of your cousin's TV debut stays safely stashed away somewhere . . . as long as you stay the hell away from me and mine. Peaceful coexistence, as they used to say. Do we understand each other?"

"I don't understand you at all, Kilpatrick," Feinman said. "What do you mean, stay away from you and yours? What in hell are you talking about?"

"This is where I should whip off my mask and reveal my true identity to the stunned onlookers. Instead, I just do this"—I took off the phony eyeglasses and put them on the desk—"which isn't nearly as dramatic, and tell you that my real name isn't Patrick Kilpatrick. Nebraska is real enough, I guess, for our purposes."

Feinman frowned, and then his eyes widened a fraction.

"Yes," I said, "the same Nebraska. How many others could there be?"

"Jesus Christ," Feinman said. He emptied his glass at a gulp and sat down heavily, groping distractedly for his cigarettes. "I don't believe it. I do not fucking believe it." He lighted up.

"Go on," I said, "make the effort."

He seemed to remember I was in the room. A little of the color that had bled out of his face came back. He took the cigarette out of his face and, with a sideways nod toward the mute television, said, "You got goose eggs, my friend. That tape's all you got, and that tape's nothing. Hell, you cleaned Steve's clock once, who's to say you didn't threaten to do it again if he didn't give you want you wanted? Who's to say you didn't shoot him full of something so he didn't know what he was saying? Who's to say you didn't phony up the tape somehow?" He laughed sourly. "Who the hell's gonna believe a word of this . . . this junk?"

"I dunno, Josh . . . I sort of thought maybe I'd run it for your sister and see what she thought."

His face lost its expression again and his eyes fixed on me in a frozen, unblinking stare. I remembered what Dimand had said, how Feinman appeared calmest when he was the most agitated.

"You goddamn son of a bitch," he said quietly after a long silence.

"The feeling's mutual. I've had to send flowers to three friends in the hospital thanks to you. I've been in hiding for a month, taking all kinds of elaborate precautions which I subsequently discovered were completely justified. I've learned that you're a big enough frog in your own pond, but you're not connected. There's no one going to put a contract out on me if I take you down right now." I still had the gun in my hand; I lifted it now, testing its weight, eyeing it speculatively. "And believe me, if you had been within arm's length on Friday, when I found out about my friends, I would have ended this drama then. As it is, I've already bagged my limit for the weekend. I'd just as soon we handle this in a halfway civilized fashion. You stay off of me, and Sharon never receives a package from my own private video club."

"You son of a bitch," Feinman repeated. "You wouldn't do that. You wouldn't do that to her."

"I wouldn't want to, because I know it would hurt her—but I would do it. It's up to you."

"Dammit, Pat. I trusted you."

"Bad idea, wasn't it? You know what the kicker is, Josh? In a lot of ways, you're a pretty good guy. I like you. We have things in common; your sister says we're a lot alike. But the difference between us is, you can't let people be. I mean the people around you, the people you say you love—your sister, your cousin, even your brother-in-law."

"I never loved that son of a bitch."

"You have to run their lives. In the case of Brian Fahy, you couldn't control him—and you couldn't risk his weakening your control over Sharon—so you killed him. Which is the ultimate control."

"Christ, do I need a psychology lecture from you?"

"You control by being the Great Protector, the father figure, the one everyone turns to for help. That makes them dependent on you. But it makes you dependent too, Josh, because once you establish yourself like that, you have to keep playing the part. The first time your cousin comes to you and says, 'I picked a fight with this guy and I lost, so now I want you to go beat him up,' and you say no . . . then that's it. You've lost your following. You come down here to the same level with everybody else. You couldn't stand that, Josh, and frankly, I'm not sure your family could either. Anyhow, I don't much care. I just want to know what to do with my copy of that videotape. Keep it under wraps or pop it in the mail? What do you say?"

"Goddamn it." He pounded the arm of the chair. Ash from

his cigarette fell onto his shirtfront but he ignored it. He looked at me with the same expression a hard-boiled egg has just before you eat it.

"You son of a bitch," he reminded me. "What the hell *can* I say?"

"Where I sit, only one thing."

"Get the fuck out of my house."

"I'll take that as a yes."

42

A heavy whistling sound, a soft, short *whoomf* in the darkness, and then an explosion of pain across my shoulders. I went down, as graceful as a brick. The snow must have been cold; I didn't notice. My only concern, my only conscious thought, was to move as quickly as possible away from the source of the pain.

The *whoomf* whistled through the night again. I was trying to get to my feet, but ditched it midway through and dived into the thick fitzers that ran from Joshua Feinman's front stoop eastward across the front of the house and around the corner. The pain across my back had dulled enough that I could feel the evergreen branches and needles, stiff with cold, dig into my face and any bit of exposed skin they could find.

Something smashed into the bushes just west of my head. It was dark and squarish and obviously heavy, and it threw up a cloud of snow when it hit.

I half-rolled, half-trampolined out of the vegetation, trying to get at my gun. It was in its holster, under my sport coat, under my overcoat. Which was buttoned.

"You son of a *bitch!*" a voice roared—wailed, rather; there was a kind of frenzied anguish in the voice, heavier than any anger or hatred it may have contained.

The bright light over Feinman's front door went on, providing a welcome supplement to the pale, nearly useless illumination from the Parkway. The light was behind my assailant; all I got was a silhouette of him and something he brandished like a baseball bat.

Whoomf!

I ducked, clumsily, still off-balance and ailing. Whatever he was swinging connected, slamming into my left upper arm. I heard myself groan loudly, and grabbed at the weapon. I caught hold of it somehow—part of it, at any rate. The part

I had was a slim, hard rod. I got as good a grip on it as its smooth surface and my gloved fingers would allow, and yanked it toward me, kicking out at whoever was on the other end.

I was rewarded with a satisfying grunt, and then we both tumbled into the snowy yard, pummeling each other as best we could manage under the circumstances.

"What the hell is going on?" I hadn't noticed Feinman coming outside, but now he jumped down from the stoop and waded through the snow. It was a little more than ankle-deep here. Feinman was coatless, and carried something in his right hand.

My assailant sort of levitated off of me, and I heard Feinman's voice say, "Jesus Christ, Steve, what the fuck do you think you're doing?"

I rolled away from the melee. My breath was coming in ragged sobs and my face burned coldly where the fitzers had skinned it and my eyes were tearing from the cold and the pain, and my right hand was still wrapped around Steven Dimand's weapon. You have to be an idiot to get behind the wheel of a car in this part of the world at this time of the year unless you have a good shovel in the back end, and this was a good shovel. A short, heavy, no-nonsense example of the species, with a wide, bucketlike scoop, a short hardwood handle, and a steel grip on the far end.

Dimand tore himself away from his cousin's grip. The stoop light hit his face fully for the first time; it was twisted into a grotesque parody of its usual self.

"I'm gonna tear this little bastard's head off," Dimand bellowed. The anguish was still there—a frantic, almost hysterical quality that suited the odd dull-bright look in his eyes. My guess was he had spent most of the seven or eight hours since I left him medicating himself into a rage bordering on the insane. His movements were jerky, almost spasmodic, and his voice was on the verge of cracking.

"Forget about it," Feinman said loudly, trying to cut through his cousin's hyperactive fog. "It's over."

"The hell—"

Dimand lunged at me. I brought up the shovel, crosswise, my hands on either end of the handle. Think of Little John meeting Robin Hood in the Errol Flynn flick. I slammed my

makeshift quarterstaff into Dimand's chest. He staggered
back a few inches, but he didn't fall down like a good sport.
I had underestimated the extent to which pharmaceuticals
were calling the shots for him. He grabbed at the shovel, and
we strained against each other for a long moment, fighting
over ownership. He was very strong, and I suppose he was
assisted by the extra oomph that crazy people are reputed to
have. He managed to yank the handle out of my left hand, and
tried to twist it around out of my right. In the process, the steel
grip came around and clipped me on the side of my head, just
below my left ear. The inside of my skull turned into a plane-
tarium for a few seconds, and I lost my grip on the other end
of the shovel handle.

Feinman tackled him.

"You stupid jerk!" he yelled into Dimand's ear. "He has us
over a barrel. He has you on tape—"

"He made me, the fucker." Dimand was facedown in the
snow, struggling to be let up, but Feinman had the advantage
now. "He was gonna—" He let out a baleful shriek and tried
to grab me. I was more than two feet beyond his reach, but he
grabbed nevertheless, coming up with nothing more than
handfuls of snow, which he flung at me impotently.

"You bastard," he wailed. "You fucking bastard. . . ."

"Cut it out, Steve." Feinman was speaking softly into Dimand's ear, soothingly, as you might talk to a frightened animal. "Forget about it. He won, that's all. It's over. . . ."

"You bastard . . . you bastard. . . ." He was quieting down
now, his physical and emotional efforts finally depleting his
artificially induced reserves of energy. Tears glinted on his
face, and his voice was a ragged sob. "You bastard. . . . He
made me, Josh. I didn't want to, you have to believe me . . . he
made me tell. . . ."

"I know, Steve . . . it's all right. Everything's all right. Nothing bad's gonna happen."

"He made me tell. . . ."

"Forget it, okay? Okay? Huh? You all right now, Steve?"

"I'm cold," Dimand said.

I was too. I climbed slowly and painfully to my feet.

"Okay," Feinman said. "Let's get up now, huh? We'll go
inside and warm up, right? Everything's fine now, Steve. Let's
get up. . . ."

Feinman climbed off his cousin and struggled to his feet. The yard sloped here, which didn't make it easier.

The object in Feinman's right hand had been a gun. It still was a gun, in fact, but it was no longer in Feinman's hand. I suppose he dropped it during one of his tussles with Dimand. In any event, when Feinman crawled off of Dimand and Dimand rolled over onto his back, there it was—a little 9-millimeter pistol, maybe a Browning; at the moment, my interest in it didn't extend beyond the fact that it was pointing at me.

Dimand got to his feet, grinning a stiff, unnatural, grin that in that light made his face look like the image on a Jolly Roger. A funny, high-pitched noise came out of him—not a giggle, exactly; not a snigger or a keening. Just a funny noise that slid an ice cube down my spine and made my scalp prickle.

My own gun was still securely buttoned away. The shovel was a good four or five feet from me, nearer to Dimand than to me.

"Hell," a voice said. It sounded a lot like mine.

When someone is aiming a gun at you, that in turn is pretty much where your attention is aimed. Peripherally, though, I was aware of Feinman looking up at the sound of that single word from me, looking at me, then looking at the focus of my attention.

"Dammit, Steve," he said hoarsely.

Feinman was a lot closer to Dimand than I was. He jumped at him. I jumped at him. The gun went off.

A not-quite-instant replay of two nights ago. The cops, the ambulance, the questions. The confusion. The curious on-lookers, safe behind their windowpanes—more of them than the other night, since this was much earlier in the evening. The sorting out and the laying of blame. That's always the bottom line: who's to blame?

Well, who was? Joshua Feinman for siccing his bullies on me? Steven Dimand for urging Feinman to get back at me for him? Me for bloodying Dimand's nose in the first place? Eric Sperry for running away? Eric's parents for not being more understanding of him? *Their* parents for not raising them to be more understanding? And on and on. In the end, we should each take the credit or the blame for our own little piece of the whole and go on from there.

The great American legal system is somewhat less philo-sophically inclined, unfortunately, and its uniformed repre-sentatives can chew up an enormous lot of your time trying to pinpoint *the* person to hang the rap on.

So it was hours before I got to the hospital.

It was a Xerox copy of every other hospital or hospital addi-tion built since the Eisenhower administration. Hard lino-leum floors, hard fluorescent lights, hard plastic furni-ture—as inviting as a beehive, as soothing as Vesuvius. Like the hospital Robert Olson had been in. Like the hospital Pat Costello still was in.

I found Sharon Fahy drinking vending-machine coffee from a paper cup. "How is he?"

I might have been transparent, the way she looked at me. Her eyes were wide and unfocused, bloodshot from the tears that had come and gone long ago, long before I could be there with her. Her skin was stretched too tightly across her skull and bleached to a ghostly shade by the brutal light from over-head. Her mouth was a grim gash across her face.

I repeated the question.

"Not . . . not good. He's still in surgery. He lost a lot of blood. The bullet nicked a vein or an artery or something. . . ." She focused on me for a moment. "But it missed his heart," she said. There was a plaintive, pleading quality to her voice, as if she had to make me understand something, something that would make everything all right once I understood it. "It missed his heart," she repeated carefully. "Completely. How can it be so bad if it missed his heart completely?"

Her face was eager and expectant. My answer was impor-tant. The right answer was, If it misses the heart you're okay. But the true answer was, The human body is a closed system and it's meant to stay closed. Any time you open it up, whether with a bullet or a scalpel, it is to a greater or lesser extent a crapshoot.

I kept my mouth shut and moved to take her in my arms. She pulled away from me, pretending it was because she didn't want to spill her coffee. Her expression was no longer eager. It had tightened up again, reverted back to the ugly mask it had been before, and her eyes refused to meet mine. When she spoke again, it was to the cup between her hands. "What happened, Pat? What really happened?"

Even after spending most of the evening with the police asking that very question, nothing sprang to mind. There was always that old standby, the truth, but to resort to that as my answer would only lead to a great many more questions, the answers to which were hard indeed.

Hard. Easy, but hard.

Besides, I had made a pact with Josh Feinman. I had in-tended to keep my end of the bargain, and I believed he in-tended to keep his. As far as I was concerned, the pact was still in force; as far as I was concerned, it would stay in force even if Feinman didn't come through his long surgery.

I said, "What about your cousin?"

"They admitted him. He finally went to sleep. The police . . . Steve wasn't making very much sense. I guess he took a lot of all kinds of drugs. I didn't think . . . you know, he always takes such good care of himself and everything, he hardly even drinks. They said, the police said Steve tried to kill you."

I didn't say anything.

"I don't understand, Pat. Steve liked you. Why would he try to kill you? It doesn't make sense. None of it makes any sense."

"No," I agreed. "The drugs, I guess. . . ."

"The drugs. Poor Steve."

Poor Steve.

"His shooting Josh was an accident—anyone can see that. As for me, I've got nothing against him; I already told the police I have no intention of pressing any charges against him. He wasn't in his right mind. He wasn't responsible." As near as I could tell, he had never been responsible for any damn thing, and now my name was added to the list of people covering for him, making allowances for him, making it smooth for him. I choked down the emotion I felt rising in me and went on. "This episode is going to make him see how badly messed up he really is, and how badly he needs help. You'll see to it that he gets that help. And Josh, he's strong; he's determined, and that counts for a lot in situations like this. He'll come through. You'll all come through—that's what you have to hold on to."

"I can't imagine Joshua . . . not being there."

"Then don't. Imagine him, being there, and don't let go of that picture. 'Act as if you had faith, and faith will follow'—I heard a priest say that once." I reached over to her and grasped one of her hands. It was warm from the coffee cup, but only on the surface; beneath the skin it was as cold as the snow on the ground outside.

Sharon let me hold her hand for a moment, neither resisting nor returning my grip. But then she slowly, with gentle determination, pulled it away from me.

"You don't have to stay here, Pat."

"I want to. There's nothing I can do, but I sti—"

"No. You've done enough already, haven't you?" she snapped. Her eyes flashed toward me now, and there was no affection in them. But just as quickly as it had erupted, the emotion receded and her gaze returned to her lap. She seemed to make several attempts to talk, but didn't follow through. I was silent too; stunned. She found words first:

"I don't know how," she said with great deliberation, "I don't understand exactly how, but this is your fault. Everything is your fault. I can't say how or why, but it's something I know."

"Sharon, I—"

She silenced me with a look. No anger or hatred there this time; this time there was absolutely nothing. She looked at me the way you look at a stranger, and when I looked back a stranger is what I saw. Whatever we had was gone. Steven Dimand had killed it with a single shot.

"You made me feel good, Pat," Sharon said. "You made me feel special. You made me feel things I hadn't felt for a long time—not since Fahy left—and even some things I hadn't ever felt. But there is something very, very wrong. With you, or with me, or with us . . . I don't know. All I know is . . . I don't want to see you again."

I had wondered, worried, about how I would handle my departure, how I would break the news to her, how I would soften the blow, how I would come up with a plausible reason for not promising to stay in touch or come back someday or any of the other things you always promise when you separate from someone. In my conceit, it never occurred to me that love can die as quickly as it blooms, and that my leaving might not cause Sharon as much pain as I had thought.

There were things to be said . . . and nothing to be said. Nothing that could be said. Sharon was right: something was wrong between us. I couldn't tell her what it was. I had made a bargain.

I stood up and looked at Sharon a long moment. "I hope Josh gets better," I finally said. Oddly enough, I meant it.

Then I turned and walked away.

MY m.ys
REY